PAUL CLEAVE

JOE VICTIM

First published in Great Britain in 2017 by Mulholland Books
An imprint of Hodder & Stoughton
An Hachette UK company

1

Originally published in New Zealand in 2013

A CIP catalogue record for this title is available from the British Library

Paperback ISBN 978 1 473 66472 2
eBook ISBN 978 1 473 66473 9

Typeset in Goudy Oldstyle Std

Printed and bound in Great Britain by Clays Ltd, St Ives plc

Hodder & Stoughton policy is to use papers that are natural, renewable and recyclable products and made from wood grown in sustainable forests. The logging and manufacturing processes are expected to conform to the environmental regulations of the country of origin.

Hodder & Stoughton Ltd
Carmelite House
50 Victoria Embankment
London EC4Y 0DZ

www.hodder.co.uk

Praise for Paul Cleave

‘Riveting and all too realistic. Cleave is a writer to watch.’

Tess Gerritsen

‘Cleave leads us on a tantalizing, mouth-watering spectre of horror, never knowing what will be revealed around the next corner, or turning of a page.’

Suspense Magazine

‘Dark, bloody, and gripping, *Blood Men* is classic noir fiction. In Paul Cleave, Jim Thompson has another worthy heir to his throne.’

John Connolly

‘An intense and bloody noir thriller, one often descending into a violent abyss reminiscent of Thomas Harris, creator of Hannibal Lecter.’

Kirkus Reviews

‘Anyone who likes their crime fiction on the black and bloody side should move Paul Cleave straight to the top of their must-read list.’

Mark Billingham

‘A pulse-pounding serial killer thriller . . . The city of Christchurch becomes a modern equivalent of James Ellroy’s Los Angeles of the 1950s.’

Publishers Weekly (starred)

‘Paul Cleave writes the kind of dark, intense thrillers that I never want to end. Do yourself a favour and check him out.’

Simon Kernick

‘Gripping and darkly funny.’

Globe and Mail

‘An intense adrenalin rush from start to finish, I read *The Laughter-house* [illegible] tic!’

S.J. Watson

ALSO BY PAUL CLEAVE

The Cleaner
The Killing Hour
Cemetery Lake
Blood Men
Collecting Cooper
The Laughterhouse
Joe Victim
Five Minutes Alone
Trust No One
A Killer Harvest

To Stephanie (BB) Glencross and Leo (BBB) Glencross.
We'll always have Turkey . . .

PROLOGUE

SUNDAY MORNING

Well, live and learn.

I suck in a deep breath, close my eyes, and squeeze all the way on the trigger.

The world explodes.

It explodes with light and sound and pain, and it's not right, because it should be exploding with darkness. There should be a shroud of black enveloping me, taking me away from all of this. I'm in control—Slow Joe is a winner—and proof of this comes when my life starts flashing in front of me. The darkness is mere moments away, but first I must go through images of my mother, my father, my childhood, time spent with my auntie. Hours and hours of footage from my life is broken up into snapshots then condensed into a two-second movie, one scene flicking into the next like watching an old film projector. The images speed up. They flash through my mind.

But that is not all.

Sally is flashing across my mind. No, not my mind, but my field of vision. She is right in front of me, against me, her clumpy body pressing me all over in the way she has always wanted to. There are a dozen voices.

I hit the pavement and my arm flies out to the side. Sally's flesh is pushed aside by my body. It rolls over my limbs, trying to swallow me like a soft couch. I'm not dying yet, but I'm already in Hell. I pull the trigger without any target, and it turns out without any success because the gun is no longer in my hand. Sally is crushing the air out of me and I'm still not real sure what's going on. The world is topsy-turvy and there is a packet of cat food pressed up against my shoulder. My face is burning and is wet with blood. There is high-pitched screaming in my ear, a monotonous tone that won't end. Sally is pulled off me, she disappears only to be replaced by Detective Schroder, and I have never been so relieved in my life. Schroder will save me, Schroder will take Sally and hopefully lock her away in the kind of place fat girls like Sally ought to be locked away.

"I'm . . ." I say, but I can't even hear my voice over my ringing ears. I can't figure out what's going on. I'm so confused. The world is shifting off its axis.

"Shut up," Schroder yells, but I can hardly hear him. "You hear me? Shut up before I put a Goddamn bullet in your head!"

I have never heard Schroder talk that way, and I guess for him to talk that way to Sally means he's really, really pissed off at her for jumping on me. I suddenly feel closer to him than I ever have. But the pain I'm in, the fact that Fat Sally just folded her flesh around me, now I'm thinking I want the bullet he's offering her. I want that sweet, sweet darkness and the silence that will come along with it. But I stay quiet. Mostly.

"I'm Joe," I shout, in case they can all hear the ringing tone too. "Slow Joe."

Somebody hits me. I don't know who, and I don't know if it's a punch or a kick, but it comes out of nowhere and my head snaps to the side and Schroder disappears for a moment and the side of my apartment building appears. I can see the top floor and the guttering, I can see dirty windows and cracked windows and somewhere up there is my apartment, and all I want to do is make my way inside and lie down and try to figure out what's going on. It all goes blurry and seems to run into the ground, like the colors of a watercolor painting all leaking away, leaving only reds, and it stays that way as I'm dragged up onto my feet. My clothes are wet because the sidewalk is wet because it rained all night.

"I forgot my briefcase," I say, and it's true. In fact I have no idea where it is.

"Shut. The fuck. Up, Joe," somebody says.

Joe? I don't understand—is it me these people are being mean to, and not Sally?

I can't feel my hands. My arms are behind me and they're locked so tight they won't move. My wrists hurt. I'm pulled along, my feet stumbling, and I try to focus on the ground and I try to focus on what is happening and can do neither, not until I look over at Sally and the men restraining her, Sally with tears on her face and suddenly the last sixty seconds all come flooding back to me. I was walking home. I was happy. I had spent the weekend with Melissa. Then Sally had pulled onto my street and accused me of lying to her, accused me of being the Christchurch Carver, then the police had shown up, then I'd . . . I'd tried to shoot myself.

And failed, because Sally had jumped on me.

The ringing in my ears fades a little, but everything stays red. There's a police car ahead of me that wasn't there a few minutes ago when Sally pulled onto the street. One of the men dressed in black opens the rear door. There are lots of men in black, all of them with guns. Somebody mentions an ambulance and somebody says "No way" and somebody else says "Just bloody shoot him."

"Jesus, he's getting blood all over the seat," somebody says.

I look down, and sure enough, there's enough of my blood all over the seat and floor to keep some cleaner just like me disgruntled for a few hours. There's a trail of it leading back to my gun. Sally is standing over there no longer being restrained. Her face and clothes splattered with blood. My blood. She has this wet look on her face that makes me feel sick in ways I can't identify. She's staring at me, probably trying to figure a way to climb into the backseat of the car and crush herself all over me again. Her blond hair that was in a ponytail a few minutes ago is now hanging loosely, and she takes a few strands of it and starts chewing on the ends—a nervous tic, I guess, or a seductive gesture for the two police officers standing next to her who, if they see her doing it, might just try to blow their own brains out like I did.

I blink the redness away and a few seconds later it starts flowing back into my field of vision.

Two guys enter the car up front. One of them is Schroder. He gets behind the wheel. He doesn't even look around at me. The second guy is dressed in black. Like Death. Like the rest of them. He's carrying a gun that looks like it could do a lot of damage, and the guy gives me the kind of look that suggests he wants to see just how much damage it can do. Schroder starts the car and turns the siren on. It seems louder than any other siren I've heard before, as if it has more of a point to make. I don't get to put on a seat belt. Schroder pulls away from the side of the road, jumping forward so fast I nearly fly out of the seat. I twist around to see another car pulling in behind us, and behind that is a dark van. I watch my apartment building get smaller and I wonder what kind of mess it's going to be in when I get home tonight.

"I'm innocent," I say, but it's like I'm talking to myself. Blood enters my mouth when I speak and I like the taste of it, and I know that if we were to drive back home we'd see Sally licking her fingers, liking the taste of it too. Poor Sally. She has brought these men to me in a storm of confusion, and what was becoming the best weekend of my life seems to be heading down a path of the worst. How long will it take me to explain my actions, to convince them of my innocence? How long until I can get back to Melissa?

I spit the blood out.

"Jesus, don't fucking do that," the man in the front seat says.

I close my eyes, but my left one doesn't close properly. It's hot, but not painful. Not yet anyway. I straighten up and get a look at myself in the rearview mirror. My face and neck are covered in blood. My eyelid is flopping about. I shake my head and it slips over my eye like a leaf. It's not hanging on by much. I try to blink the eyelid back into place, but it doesn't work. Hell, I've had worse. A lot worse. And again I think of Melissa.

"What the hell you smiling at?" Man in Black asks.

"What?"

"I said what the hell—"

"Shut up, Jack," Schroder says. "Don't talk to him."

"The son of a bitch is—"

"Is a lot of things," Schroder says. "Just don't talk to him."

"I still think we should pull over and make it look like he tried to escape. Come on, Carl, nobody would care."

"My name is Joe," I say. "Joe is a good person."

"Cut the bullshit," Schroder says. "Both of you. Just shut up."

My neighborhood races by. The sirens on the police cars are flashing and I guess they're in a hurry to let me prove what they already know about me—that I'm their Slow Joe, I'm their buddy, I'm their friendly, warm-feeling retard, a trolley-pusher of the world who only ever tries to please. People in other cars are pulling over for the traffic train, and people on the street are turning to look. I'm in a parade. I feel like waving. The Christchurch Carver is in handcuffs, but nobody knows it's really him. They can't do. How can they?

We hit town. We drive past the police station with no slowing down. Ten stories of boredom that show no signs of getting less boring anytime soon. I will be out tomorrow to begin my new life with Melissa. We keep driving. Nobody talks. Nobody hums anything. I start to get the feeling that Schroder has changed his mind, and they are going to make it look like I escaped, only it'll be me escaping from somewhere outside of the city limits where nobody can watch me gunned down. My clothes are soaked in blood and nobody seems to care. I'm not so sure they can be cleaned up. We stop at a set of red lights. Jack is staring in the rearview mirror as though trying to unlock a puzzle. I stare back at him for a few moments before looking down. My legs are covered in red drops and smears. My eyelid is hurting now. It feels like it's been rubbed in stinging nettle.

We come to a stop at the hospital. A bunch of patrol cars form a semicircle around us. It's starting to rain. We're a month away from winter and I'm getting a bad feeling I'm not going to get to see it. Jack does the gentlemanly thing and opens the door for me. The other men in black do the less gentlemanly thing and point their guns at me. Doctors and patients and visitors are staring at us from the main doors. They're all motionless. I figure we're putting on quite the show. I'm helped out of the car. Things are fine, I think, except they're not. Sitting down they were fine, but not standing up. Standing up the world is full of handcuffs and guns and blood loss. I start swaying. I drop to my knees. Blood flicks off my face onto the pavement. At first Jack seems about to try and stop me from falling any further, but then he thinks better of it. I topple forward. I can't bring my hands around to break my fall, and the best I can do is turn my head away from the ground so the damaged eyelid points to the sky, but for some reason I get confused—probably because I'd been staring at it in the rearview mirror for the last few minutes—so I end up turning that part of my face toward the ground. I can see lots of boots and the bottom half of a car. I can see two hungry-looking police dogs being restrained on leashes. Somebody puts a hand on me and rolls me. My eyelid is left behind on the wet parking lot pavement, surrounded by blood. It looks like a slug has been murdered down there, an invertebrate crime scene, where soon other slimy little fuckers will try and figure out what happened.

Only that slimy wad of flesh belongs to me. "That's mine," I say, feeling the heat from the wound worm its way through the rest of my body. My eye is watering and blinking doesn't work.

I do what I can, a ragged line of skin hangs like a way-too-short curtain over my eye.

"This?" Jack says, and he steps on it distastefully as if grinding a cigarette butt into the ground. "This was yours?"

Before I can complain they pick me up and I'm moving again. Even though it's an overcast day, the world is bright and I can't blink any darkness into it, not on my left side anyway. I can't blink the sweat or the blood or the pain away either. A team of men surround me and I can hear them talking among themselves. I can hear them hating the laws that require them to bring me here when their ethics suggest otherwise. They think I'm a bad person, but they have it all wrong.

A doctor approaches. He looks scared. I'd look scared too if I saw a dozen armed men coming toward me. Which I saw for the first time about ten minutes ago. Everybody else near the main doors are either standing with hands over their mouths, or standing with cell phones in their hands and filming the action. News networks all over the country will be showing some of this footage today. I try to imagine what effect that will have on Mom, but my imagination doesn't stretch that far because I become distracted by the doctor.

"What's going on here?" the doctor asks, and it's a good question, except it's coming from a guy who's in his fifties wearing a bow tie, and that makes him somebody worth staying away from.

"This . . ." Schroder starts, and he seems to struggle for the next word. "Man," he spits out, "needs medical treatment. He needs it now."

"What happened?"

"He walked into a door," somebody says, and a group of men start to laugh.

"Yeah, he was clumsy," another man says, and more men laugh. They're bonding. They're using humor to start coming down from whatever high they're on. A high I gave them. Except for Schroder and Jack and the doctor. They look deadly serious.

"What happened?" the doctor asks again.

“Self-inflicted gunshot,” Schroder says. “Grazed him deep.”

“Looks worse than a graze,” the doctor says. “You really need this many men around?”

Schroder turns back and seems to do a mental count. He looks like he’s about to nod and say they could do with a few more, but instead he signals to about half the team and tells them to stay put. I’m pushed in a wheelchair and my hands are uncuffed only to be recuffed to the arms of it. They wheel me down a corridor and lots of people keep looking at me as if I’ve just won a Mr. Popularity contest, but the truth is nobody knows who I am. They never have. We pass some pretty nurses that on any other day I’d try to follow home. I’m put on a bed and cuffed to the railing. They strap my legs down and I can’t move. They strap and cuff everything so tight it feels like I’m encased in concrete. They must think I have the strength of a werewolf.

“Detective Schroder,” I say, “I don’t understand what’s going on.”

Schroder doesn’t answer. The doctor comes back over. “This is going to be a little painful,” he says, and he’s half right, getting the *little* wrong, but nailing the *painful*. He prods the wound and examines it and shines a torch into it, and without the ability to blink it’s like staring at the sun.

“This is going to be more than a few hours’ work,” he says, almost talking to himself, but loud enough for the others to hear. “Going to need some real detailing here to give him any kind of functionality, and also to minimize scarring,” he says, and it sounds like he’s about to give an estimate then tell us how much it’s going to be for the parts. I just hope he has them in stock since mine is still out in the parking lot.

“We don’t care about scarring,” Schroder says.

“I care,” I say.

“And I care too,” the doctor says. “Damn it, the eyelid is completely gone.”

“Not completely,” I say.

“What do you mean?”

"It's back at the car. On the ground."

The doctor turns to Schroder. "His eyelid is out there?"

"What's left of it," I say, answering for Schroder, who then answers for himself by shrugging.

"You want this guy out of here quicker, we're going to need that eyelid," the doctor says.

"We'll get it," Schroder says.

"Then get it," the doctor says. "Otherwise we have to graft something else that will work. And that'll take longer. Can't have him not blinking."

"I don't care if he can't blink," Schroder says. "Just cauterize the damn thing and glue a patch on his face."

Instead of arguing or telling Schroder he's out of line, the doctor finally seems to realize that all these cops, all the tension, all the anger, that must mean something special. I can see it occurring to him, I watch through one good eye and one bloody eye and he starts to frown, then slowly shake his head, a curious look on his face. I know the question is coming.

"Just who is this man?"

"This is the Christchurch Carver," Schroder answers.

"No way," the doctor says. "This guy?"

I'm not sure what that's supposed to mean. "I'm innocent," I say. "I'm Joe," I say, and the doctor jams a needle into the side of my face, the world shifts further off its axis, and things go numb.

TWELVE MONTHS LATER

CHAPTER ONE

Melissa pulls into the driveway. Sits back. Tries to relax.

The day is fifty degrees maximum. Christchurch rain. Christchurch cold. Yesterday was warm. Now it's raining. Schizophrenic weather. She's shivering. She leans forward and twists the keys in the ignition, grabs her briefcase, and climbs from the car. The rain soaks her hair. She reaches the front door and fumbles with the lock.

She strolls through to the kitchen. Derek is upstairs. She can hear the shower going and she can hear him singing. She'll disturb him later. For now she needs a drink. The fridge is covered in magnets from bullshit places around the country, places with high pregnancy rates, high drinking rates, high suicide rates. Places like Christchurch. She opens the door and there are half a dozen bottles of beer and she puts her hand on one, pauses, then goes for the orange juice instead. She breaks the seal and drinks straight from the container. Derek won't mind. Her feet are sore and her back is sore so she sits at the table for a minute listening to the shower as she sips at the juice as her muscles slowly relax.

It's been a long day in what is becoming a very long week. She's not a big fan of orange juice—she prefers tropical juices, but orange was her only option. For some reason drink makers think people want their juices full of pulp that sticks in your teeth and feels like an oyster pissing on your tongue, and for some reason that's what Derek wants too.

She puts the lid back on the juice and puts it into the fridge and looks at the slices of pizza in there and decides against them. There are some chocolate bars in a side compartment. She peels one open and takes a bite, and stuffs the remaining bars—four of them—into her pocket. Thanks, Derek. She finishes off the open one while carrying the briefcase upstairs. The stereo in the bedroom is pumping out a song she recognizes. She used to have the album back when she was a different person, more of a carefree, CD-listening kind of person. It's *The Rolling Stones*. A greatest-hits package, she can tell by the way one song follows another. Right now Mick is screaming out about blotting out the sun. He wants the world to be black. She wants that too. He sounds like he's singing about the middle of winter at five o'clock in New Zealand. She hums along with it. Derek is still singing, masking every sound she is making.

She sits down on the bed. There's an oil heater running and the room is warm. The furniture is a good match for the house, and the house looks like somebody ought to take a match to it. The bed is soft and tempts her to put her feet up and prop a pillow behind her and take a nap, but that would also be tempting the bacteria in the pillowcase to make friends with her. She pops open the briefcase and takes out a newspaper and reads over the front page while she waits. It's an article about some guy who's been terrorizing the city. Killing women. Torture. Rape. Homicide. The Christchurch Carver. Joe Middleton. He was arrested twelve months ago. His trial begins on Monday. She is also mentioned in the article. Melissa X. Though the article also mentions her real name, Natalie Flowers, Melissa only thinks of herself as Melissa these days. Has done for the last couple of years.

A couple of minutes go by and she's still sitting on the bed when Derek, wiping a towel at his hair, steps out of the bathroom surrounded by white steam and the smell of shaving balm. He has a towel wrapped around his waist. A tattoo of a snake winds its way from the towel up his side and over his shoulder, with its tongue forking across his neck. Some of the snake is finely detailed, parts of it really just sketched outlines with more to follow. There are various scars that go hand in hand with a guy like Derek, no doubt an even mixture of good times and bad times—good times for him and bad times for others.

She lowers the newspaper and smiles.

"What the hell are you doing here?" he asks.

Melissa turns the briefcase toward him and reaches out and presses pause on the stereo. The briefcase actually belongs to Joe Middleton. He left it with her the same day he never came back. "I'm here with the other half of your payment," she says.

"You know where I live?"

It's a stupid question. Melissa doesn't point it out to him. "I like to know who I'm doing business with."

He unwraps the towel from his waist, the entire time keeping his eyes on the cash in the briefcase. His dick sways left and right as he starts drying his hair.

"It's all there?" he asks, still drying his hair, his face at the moment behind the towel and his voice muffled.

"Every dollar. Where's the stuff?"

"It's here," he says.

She knows it's here. She's been following him ever since their initial meeting two days ago, where she gave him the first half of the payment. She knows he picked up the stuff only an hour ago. He went from there to here with no stops in between with a bag full of items his parole officer wouldn't be too pleased about.

"Where?" she asks.

He wraps the towel back around his waist. She figures she could have just come in here and shot him and searched the house anyway, but she needs him. The stuff probably won't be hard to find. She figures a guy who would ask *You know where I live?* to somebody standing in their bedroom is the kind of guy who hides things in the roof space or under the floor.

"Show me," he says, nodding toward the money.

She slides the briefcase toward him on the bed. He steps forward. The twenty grand is made up in fifty- and twenty-dollar bills. They're stacked neatly into piles with rubber bands around them. Over the last few years most of her income has been through blackmailing people or burglaries, some from the men she's killed, but a few months ago she came into some pretty good money. Forty thousand dollars, to be precise. He thumbs through some of it and decides it must all be there.

He moves over to the wardrobe. He drags a box of clothes out then lifts the patch of carpet and digs a screwdriver into the edge of the floor and Melissa finds herself rolling her eyes, thinking how lucky guys like Derek are that they can't be charged for stupidity along with other crimes. He pries up the boards. He pulls out an aluminum case the length of his arm. Melissa stands up so he can lay it on the bed. He pops the lid open. There is a rifle broken into separate pieces, all of it slotting into foam cutouts.

"AR-fifteen," he says. "Lightweight, uses a high-velocity, small-caliber round, extremely accurate. Scope too, as requested."

She nods. She's impressed. Derek may be stupid, but being stupid doesn't mean you can't be useful. "That's half of it," she says.

He goes back to the manhole. Reaches in and pulls out a small rucksack. It's mostly black with plenty of red trim. He sits it on the bed and opens it. "C-four," he says. "Two blocks, two detonators, two triggers, two receivers. Enough to blow up a house. Not enough to do much more. You know how to use it?"

"Show me."

He picks up one of the blocks. It's the size of a bar of soap. "It's safe," he says. "You can shoot it. Drop it. Burn it. Hell, you can even microwave it. You can do this," he says, and starts to squeeze it. "You can mold it into any shape. You take one of these," he says, and picks up what looks like a metal pencil, only with wires coming from the end of it, "and stab it in. Attach the other end to these receivers," he says, "then it's just a matter of firing the trigger. You've got a range of a thousand feet, further if it's line of sight."

"How long does the battery in the receiver last?"

"A week. Tops."

"Anything else I need to know?"

"Yeah. Don't mix them up," he says, and holds up one of the remotes. "See this piece of yellow tape I've put across it? It lines up with the piece of tape I've put on this detonator. So this," he says, holding up the detonator with the tape, "goes with this," he says, holding both the remote and detonator together.

"Okay."

"That's it," he says, and starts packing them into the bag.

"I need your help doing something else," she says.

He keeps putting things away. "What kind of something?"

"I want you to shoot somebody," she says.

He looks up at her and shakes his head, but the question doesn't faze him and doesn't slow down his packing. "That's not my thing."

"You sure?" She holds up the newspaper and shows him a picture of Joe Middleton, the Christchurch Carver. "Him," she says. "You shoot him, and I'll pay you what you want."

"Huh," he says, then shakes his head again. "He's in custody," he says. "It's impossible."

"His trial starts next week. That means transport every day, twice a day, back and forth from jail to the courthouse. Five days a week. That's five times a week he's going to step out of a police car and make his way into the courts, and five times a week he's going to step back out of the courts and into a police car. I already have a spot where he can be shot from, and an escape route."

Derek shakes his head again. "Things like that aren't always as they seem."

"What do you mean?"

"You think they're just going to drive him the same way every day, and just drop him off outside the front door? That's where your spot looks over, right?"

She hadn't thought of that. "Then what?"

"They're going to mix up the route. They're going to try and get him there in secret. They might put him in a normal car. Or a van."

"You think so?"

"A trial this big? Yeah. I'd put money on it," he says. "So whatever plan you think you might be hatching, it isn't going to work. Too many variables. You think you can just hide in the building somewhere and take a shot? Which building? Which direction is he coming from?"

"The courthouse doesn't move," she says. "That's not a variable."

"Uh huh. And which entrance will he be using? They're going to mix that up too. That's why whatever spot you think you're going to shoot him from is probably not going to work."

"What if I can find out the route? And the way he'll be going into the courthouse?"

"How you going to do that?"

"I have my ways."

He shakes his head. She's getting sick of all the negativity. "Doesn't matter," he says. "It's just too hard a job. Shooting somebody like Joe, nobody's going to get away."

"Who can help me?"

He puts a hand to his face and strokes the bottom of his chin. He gives it some serious thought. Then comes up with an answer. "I don't know anyone."

"I'll pay you a finder's fee," she says, trying not to sound desperate, but the fact is she is desperate. She'd already had a shooter lined up for this, but it fell through. Now she's running out of time.

"There is nobody," he says. "Sourcing weapons is one thing," he says, "but it's not like I have a Rolodex full of people we can call if we want somebody dead. It's the sort of thing you have to do yourself."

"Please," she says.

He sighs, as if the idea of letting down a pretty lady is just too painful for him. "Look, there may be somebody I can call, okay? But it'll take a while."

"I need a name in the next few days," she says.

He laughs, his mouth opening so wide she can see a few missing teeth near the back. She hates seeing that kind of thing. Hates people with missing teeth about as much as she hates being laughed at. "Lady," Derek says, and she hates being called lady too—it's impressive Derek has just gone three for three. "It's just not going to happen. Even if my guy could do that, he would never accept to do it so quickly. Killing somebody is about homework," he says. "It's about the money too, but not this late in the game."

"So you won't call him?" she asks.

"There's just no point. I'm sorry."

"Okay," she says. "Then show me how to put the rifle together."

"It's simple," he says, and he picks it up piece by piece and attaches it, metal locking into metal, each piece making a satisfying click, him telling her along the way what each piece is called. It takes him less than a minute.

"Again, but slower," she says. "Pretend I've never used a gun before," she says, but of course she's used a gun before, and she'll be using one again soon too. Real soon. As soon as he's finished showing her how.

He takes it apart. Puts it back together. This time it takes three minutes. He shows her how to load it. Then he takes it apart and puts it back into the case and shuts the lid and latches it closed.

"Anything else?"

"Ammunition," she says.

He unzips the front of the rucksack with the C-four buried inside. Reaches in and pulls out one box of ammunition. "There's two more just like it in the bag," he says. "Point two two three Remington," he says. "All armor-piercing rounds."

"Thank you," she says.

She shoots him twice in the chest through the newspaper, the silencer allowing the neighbors to keep on being neighborly without fighting the need to call the police. She knows shooting the guy who gave you the guns is somewhat of a cliché, but it's a cliché for a reason. She figures that arms dealers, just like taxi drivers and helicopter pilots, always know they'll never make it to retirement. He drops where he stands. The look on his face is one she's seen before, a look of disbelief mixed with anger and fear. She puts the pistol back into the briefcase along with the newspaper. She goes over to the manhole and reaches in and finds another bag. It's most of the original money she gave him. Which means he probably used some of it to buy the gun and explosives. This is his profit.

"I believe you," she says, looking down at him, and he would thank her for agreeing with him, but all he can do is slowly open and close his mouth, a spit bubble of blood growing and shrinking. "If I can't find somebody to shoot Joe for money, maybe I can find them to shoot him for another reason. Thanks for everything," she says, "and I'm going to keep the bag too," she says, holding it up. "I like the color."

She guesses he has another minute to live, two at the most. She takes one of his chocolate bars out of her pocket and starts working away at it. She enjoys the sugar rush about the same amount as she enjoys watching Derek die. Which is a lot. She starts the stereo back up while he's doing it and the world for Derek, just like *The Stones* warned him earlier, becomes as black as night.

CHAPTER TWO

"You passed the test," he says, and it's just more bullshit that I've heard for the last twelve months, and to be honest I've stopped listening to it. It seems people have made up their minds. Somehow this topsy-turvy world has taken upon itself to convict me without even getting to know me.

I look up from the table I was staring at to the guy doing all the talking. He's got more hair on his face than on his head, and I start wondering how flammable it is, starting with the comb-over. He seems to be waiting for an answer, but I'm not sure what he's going on about. My short-term memory since being in jail has packed its bags and left—but my long-term goals are still the same.

"What test?" I ask, and I ask not because it interests me, but because at the very least it relieves the boredom. If only for a moment. "Joe isn't not remembering test," I add, just for fun, and the words sound a little over the top, even to me, and I regret them.

The man's name, Benson Barlow, sounds pretentious, and in case you weren't quite sure he even has leather elbow patches on his jacket to drive home the point. His thin smile looks obnoxious. In other times, better times, I'd cut that smile off his face and show him how it looked hanging all bloody in his fingers. Unfortunately these aren't the best of times. They're the worst.

"The test," he repeats. He looks smug. He has that annoying look people get when there's something they know that you don't, and they're dying to tell you and trying to stretch it out for as long as they can because they like being the only one to know. I hate people like that almost as much as I hate people who say *Open mouth, insert foot*. But, to be fair, I hate other people too. I'm an equal-rights kind of guy. "The test you took. Half an hour ago."

"Joe took a test?" I ask, but of course I remember the test. It's like he said—it was only half an hour ago. My short-term memory may not be that great these days when every day is the same as the last, but I'm not an idiot.

The psychiatrist leans forward an interlocks his fingers. He must have seen other psychiatrists doing that on TV or maybe they taught it in psych 101 just before they taught him how to sew on the leather patches. Wherever he learned it, he doesn't look as good doing it as he must think. This whole thing is a big deal for him. It's a big deal for everybody. He's interviewing the Christchurch Carver for the people who want to lock me away, and he's trying to find out just how insane the Carver really is, and he's learning that I'm a big bowl of retard.

"You took a test," he says. "It was thirty minutes ago. In this very room."

This very room is an interview room that is an awful room by anybody's standards, particularly by Benson Barlow's, I imagine, yet is nicer than the cell I currently live in. It has cinder block walls and a concrete floor and a concrete ceiling. It's like a bomb shelter, only one that would collapse in on you if a bomb actually hit it, which, to be honest, would actually be a relief. It has a table and three chairs and nothing else, and right now one of those chairs is empty. My chair is bolted to the floor and I have one hand cuffed to it. I don't know why. They think I'm a threat, but I'm not. I'm a nice guy. I keep telling everybody. Nobody believes me.

"Here?" I ask, looking around at the different concrete views. "I don't remember."

His smile widens, he's trying to give me the look that suggests he knew what my response would be, and I get the idea that maybe he did. "See, Joe, the problem is this. You want the world to think you're mentally challenged, but you're not. You're a sick, twisted man, nobody will ever question that, but this test?" he says, holding up a five-sheet questionnaire that I filled out earlier, "this test proves you're not insane."

I don't answer him. I get the bad feeling he's leading somewhere with this. And the smirk on his face tells me it's not somewhere I want to go.

"This question here," he says, and his voice rises and makes it sound like a question. He points to one that was pretty easy for me to answer. Some of the questions were multi-choice, some of them I had to fill in. He reads it out. "It says *What color is this dog?* And what did you tick? You ticked yellow. The dog is red, Joe, yet you ticked yellow."

"It's yellowish," I tell him.

"This one here? *If Bob is taller than Greg, and Greg is taller than Alice, who is the tallest?* You wrote *Steve*, and then you said that Steve is a fag," he says, and the way he says it is enough to make me laugh, but the prospect of where he's going is enough to keep me worried, so everything balances out and I stare impassively at him.

"Steve is tallish," I tell him.

"There is no Steve," he says.

"What have you got against Steve?" I ask.

"This test has sixty questions in it. You got every single one of them wrong. Now that takes some real effort, Joe. Forty of them are multiple choice. Statistically you should have gotten a quarter of those right. At the least, a couple. But you got none. Only way you could get none right would be if you knew the right answers and chose the wrong ones."

I don't answer him.

"That actually proves you're not dumb at all, Joe," he says, carrying on, and he's really warming up now, really hitting his stride. He even unlocks his fingers. "Actually proves the opposite. That you're smart. That's what this test was designed to do. That's why it's full of stupid questions." His smirk turns into a full-blown smile. "You're smart, Joe, not brilliant, but smart enough to stand trial."

He opens his briefcase and puts the questionnaire inside. I wonder what else is in there. It's a nicer briefcase than the one I used to own.

"Joe is smart," I say, and I put my big goofy smile on, where all my teeth show and my face lights up. Only these days it doesn't light up as much. The scar running down the side of it tightens and my eye droops a little.

"You can cut that bullshit now, Joe. The test proves you're not as smart as you like to think you are."

My smile drops away. "What?"

The shrink's smile widens and I think that's because he thinks I'm not getting his point, and I'm not, and that's because he's not making it. "It was a time test. It helps weed out the guys not smart enough to pretend they really are that dumb."

I shake my head. "I don't understand."

"That's the only genuine thing you have told me," he says. He stands up and walks to the door.

I turn in my seat, but don't stand up. I can't, because of the cuff.

He reaches out to knock on the door, but holds back. Instead he turns toward me. I must look pretty confused, because he goes ahead and explains it. "It was a time test, Joe. Sixty questions. It took you fifteen minutes. That's four questions a minute. Each one of them you got wrong."

"I still don't follow," I tell him. Surely it's a good thing that I can be that dumb that quickly.

"You got them wrong too quickly, Joe. If you were as dumb as you wanted us to think, you'd still be doing the test now. You'd be drooling over it or licking the pages. You'd be thinking really hard searching for the answers. You didn't search at all. You just answered each one in quick fire succession and that's where you went wrong. You're no idiot, Joe, but you were too dumb to figure out what was going on. I'll see you in court."

"Fuck you."

He smiles again. His thousand-dollar smile that he'll practice before being called up to speak in front of a jury, the thousand-dollar smile that won't be worth a cent after I get out of here and learn where he lives and take that nice-looking briefcase off him. "That's the Joe everybody is going to see," he says, and then he knocks on the door and is escorted outside.

CHAPTER THREE

It's almost been a year since I was arrested. It's felt longer. Every day for about a month I was the headline news. There were photos of me on every front page across the country. I even made some front pages around the world. Some were my ID photo from work; some were pictures of me younger, provided by schools I had gone to; and many were of me being arrested and many more were of me coming out of the hospital. Those of me being arrested were all snapped on cell phones. Those at the hospital were taken by reporters who arrived while I was still in surgery. Of course I was on TV a lot too. Footage from the same two events.

There were requests for interviews that I wasn't given the chance to accept or turn down. One week after the surgery I stood up in court and pled not guilty and was denied bail and was told a trial date would be set. Photos and footage were taken of me there too. My face was red and puffy, the eyelid purple, there were stitches and patches of ointment and I could hardly recognize myself.

Then I started making the news only once a week. Other killers came and other killers went, taking up the headlines as more blood was spilled in the city. Then I was yesterday's news, a mention of me perhaps once a month—if that.

Now the trial is less than a week away, and I'm the headlining act once again.

My arrest set a chain of events into motion. Actually, those events started two days before my arrest when the police figured out who they were looking for. Of course you could even say that chain of events was put into motion the night I met Melissa. I met her in a bar. We got on well. I was walking her home thinking how nice it'd be to see her naked and perhaps with a few twisted limbs and definitely some blood too, only she was thinking how nice it'd be to tie me up and rip apart my testicle with a pair of pliers. She was the one who got her wish because in the bar she had figured out who I was. She tied me up to a tree in a park and while she clamped the pliers on my testicle and squeezed, I could do nothing but wish for death. Her death, at first, and then my death.

Only it didn't work out that way. Instead she tried to blackmail me for money, then I filmed her killing Detective Calhoun, and then we fell in love. Opposites attract—but so do people who enjoy hurting others.

I made my way home, and that week Melissa kept showing up at my apartment to help me. At least I thought it was her who had come to help me. I was out of it most of that week, delirious. Half the time my head was full of bad dreams and the other half even worse dreams. It turned out I was wrong about who was helping me. It was Sally that had come to my apartment, not Melissa. Fat Sally. Simple Sally. And in the process of helping me, Simply Fat Sally, or, The Sally as I now think of her, had seen some things she shouldn't have. The Sally had touched a parking ticket I had hidden away, a parking ticket I had hoped to use to frame Detective Calhoun for murder. Only the card had her prints on it too, so the police came to her house, and the rest, as they say, is one fucking annoying history.

So the chain of events was started. The police went to my apartment on a Friday night, only I wasn't there. I was with Melissa. They searched it and found a whole bunch of stuff that wasn't too helpful for my cause. Then they waited for me, and I didn't show up, and then they decided that I had run. Only I hadn't. I came home on the Sunday morning and there was one police unit waiting for me. They radioed in, a minute or two later there were a dozen. I pulled a gun. I tried to shoot myself. The Sally stopped that from happening. She jumped on me and pulled the gun away.

From there I was taken to the hospital. I started making the news. Then I began to experience loss. I lost my freedom. I lost my job. I lost my cat. It was a cat I had found weeks earlier that had been hit by a car. When I made the news, the vet who had taken care of that cat recognized me, and they came and picked it up. I lost my apartment. My mom started getting interview requests, and my mom would say all sorts of weird shit. Life moves on for everybody on the outside, but inside these walls life feels like it's come to a standstill. If anybody ever wants to know how twelve months can feel like twelve years, all they have to do is get arrested for murder.

My prison cell makes my apartment look like a hotel. Makes my mom's house look like a palace. Makes the interrogation room look like an interrogation room. It makes me miss all of those places. It's one room that's about twice as wide as the bed and not much longer, and the bed I have isn't that big to begin with. A real estate agent would call it cozy. A funeral director would call it roomy. I got four concrete block walls, one of them with a metal door stamped into the middle of it. No real view to talk of, just a small slot in the door that looks out to more concrete and metal and other cell doors if you can get the angle right. It's a neighborly kind of place because there are people in cells to my left and right, people that won't shut up, people who have been in here a lot longer than I have and who will continue to be in here long after I've been found not guilty.

On one side of me is Kenny Jefferies. Kenny Jefferies is a man of three lives. In one life he is, or was, the guitarist for a heavy metal band. They called themselves Tampon of Lamb. They released two albums and built up an audience of people who like their music on the raw and bloody side, and went on tour. Then they released a greatest-hits album, and then people found out about Jefferies's second life, which meant no more tours and no more albums. It was his second life that made him a household name—the media began to call him Santa Suit Kenny. In his second life he was a child rapist who would dress up as Santa to draw his victims away from their parents. As one of the prison guards here said a while ago, only the children can know which of those two professions Jefferies was better at. The guard summed it up by saying *I sure as hell hope he was a better rapist than he was a singer, because he was a fucking awful singer.*

Jefferies's third life is as a convict. Sometimes he sings or hums music I can't understand. Sometimes he'll play a guitar that isn't there, he'll strum the air and sing about torture and pain, which must hurt his throat. When I think about heavy metal music, I think the evolution of mankind has peaked and we're surfing the downslope to becoming monkeys again.

On the other side of me is Roger Harwick—though more commonly known as Small Dick. And it's not like when people call the big guy Tiny to be ironic. Harwick struggled with his victims. It's not that he didn't have the desire to perform, he just didn't have the "tools." My guess is he was attracted to children because he thought they'd be a better fit. Only he was wrong. It made him famous in the media because his failed attempts made him a joke. He was the comical child molester—or at least as comical as a child molester can be—and compared to some of them in here, it makes him hilarious. So right now I'm surrounded by celebrity pedophiles—and it's the safest place to be. That's why I'm here. Away from general population, where my neck won't get snapped by any one of a thousand inmates up to the task. My entire cellblock is full of guys like Jefferies and Harwick. In the mornings we're all kept in our cells, but when twelve o'clock comes around we're all let out into a common area, thirty of us in total, not too many inmates to control. Some of us stick to ourselves, some try sticking filed-down toothbrushes into each other, some try sticking body parts into each other. We share a kitchenette and a bathroom, and we can go outside into a caged area big enough to swing a dead puppy, but too small to swing a dead hooker by her ankles. If small is cozy in real estate terms, then a real estate agent would list this entire cellblock as being super fucking cozy.

There isn't a lot I can do in my cell, but I do have options. I can sit on the edge of my bed and stare at the wall, or I can stare at the toilet, or I can sit on the toilet and stare at the bed. It's been a painful twelve months. There's the occasional interview from the psychiatrist, but after this morning's performance I think those might be over. My mom has come to see me twice a week every week. Monday and Thursdays. For the most part it looks like prison is all about boredom. If I was in general population I'd be less bored, but I'd also be dead. All I have is a couple of books in the corner of my floor and people in cells next to me who can't go three hours without masturbating loudly. Next door, Santa Suit Kenny is humming "Muff Punching the Queen." It's the title track of their first album and the song that made them famous. He's tapping his foot against the floor. I pick up one of the romance paperbacks and open the covers, and the words blend into one and hold no attraction for me whatsoever. I keep thinking I ought to write my own book. Teach some people the truth about romance. But that's a stupid idea. Nobody would read it. But maybe they would read anything written by the Christchurch Carver. Maybe I should write a book on how I would have done the things they are saying I did, if I could remember doing them. Of course, if that were true, and I really couldn't remember any of it, it would really just make it a book full of blank pages. I remember every detail, every woman, every word spoken. I think about them a lot. It's the memories you have that stop you wrapping a sheet around your throat and hanging from the end of the bed.

I throw the romance paperback back down in the corner. It makes no sense I'm still in here. I am better than this. Smarter. It makes no sense I couldn't talk my way out of this when Schroder and his henchmen came for me. I can't imagine spending twenty years in here. I'm only weeks away from becoming the same amount of crazy I've been pretending to be over the last few years.

Most of all, I can't stop thinking about the stupid test.

It should have been so obvious. I missed the point completely. Is it possible I'm not as smart as Barlow told me I wasn't?

Santa Kenny goes quiet, and I'm pretty sure I know what he's doing. Small Dick—or Little D as he's called around here—has struck up a conversation with the guy in the cell next to him. It's a shit conversation because they're talking about the weather. They have no idea what it's like outside because there's no view. But they talk about the weather a lot, those two. I'd have thought they'd talk more about what they had in common—the reasons they are in here—but it turns out they don't talk about that much at all. It's like the memories are too exciting for them. They are pure adrenaline. It's like if they touch on those experiences they're going to start climbing the walls.

The sound of a door opening further up the corridor makes everybody in the block go quiet. There are footsteps down the corridor and voices outside, then the footsteps stop a few cells down from mine. I peek out the slot in the door, sure others in here are doing the same. There are three people standing out there. I recognize two of them.

"Ladies and gentlemen," one of the two guards says, a guy by the name of Adam. "Let's have a warm round of applause for the return of one of your favorite cellmates," Adam says. "He's come back to us after fifteen years in jail, six weeks on the outside, and the last three weeks in suicide watch. You know him, you love him, the one, the only, Mr. Caleb Cole."

Nobody claps. Nobody makes a sound. None of us know him personally. None of us care. Caleb Cole wasn't in our cellblock. We've seen him on the news, but really, who gives a fuck?

"Come on, ladies, that's no way to treat a friend. Caleb will be joining your group because he's no longer fit to be placed into general population. He has . . . what's the word we keep hearing? That's right—he has *issues*. So what do you say, Caleb, don't be shy, you have a word for your new roommates? Want to share some of your *issues* with them?"

If Caleb does have a word for us, he keeps it to himself. I remember twelve months ago being given the same treatment. Two guards escorting me down here and introducing me to what, they said, was my new family. I remember the absolute fear as few people clapped, and I got a few wolf whistles too, which, thank God, never led anywhere, and when asked to say a word I had the same response as Caleb. I've seen this a few times now, and nobody ever says anything. Back when I was first brought in, I didn't know how I was going to make it through that night, let alone the months before the trial began. I mentally committed suicide about a hundred times, my mind drifting down those paths and visualizing the outcome, every time realizing nobody would really care. Maybe Melissa.

Deciding there's no more fun to be had at Caleb's expense, they carry on, a cell door is opened further down from me and out of my line of sight. Thirty seconds later it's closed, this time no doubt with Caleb on the inside. Caleb Cole is a killer. He was in jail for killing, he was released, and then he killed some more. Some people just have it in them. Some people say a serial killer can't change their spots.

The same guards who escorted Caleb to his cell now come to my cell and the door opens up. It means they're going to take me somewhere, and I figure somewhere has to be a lot more interesting than here. They come into my cell.

Adam looks like one of those guys who spends two hours a day in the gym and two hours in the evening in front of a mirror watching his hard work pay off. The other guard, Glen, looks like he's probably right there alongside Adam the entire time. I bet they get together once or twice a week to fuck each other senseless and talk about how much they hate gay guys. Adam stands in front of me, muscles bulging at his uniform, the kind of muscles that a blunt screwdriver could bounce off. Some of the guys in here have found religion since being locked behind bars. They say Jesus will provide. I look around, but Jesus doesn't provide me with a sharp screwdriver. All He's giving me are the same two assholes who have used those muscles He provided them to push me around almost every day since being here. Into walls. Into the floor. Into doors.

"Let's go," Adam says.

"Where am I going?"

He shakes his head. He looks angry. Maybe the bench press is broken. "Un-fucking believable," he says, "but you're going home, Joe."

My heart skips a couple of beats and I develop some kind of tunnel vision, where the walls disappear and all I can see is Adam as he's talking to me. But that's not all I can see—I can see myself walk through the door of my apartment and lie down on my own bed. I see women in my future. I see other dead people too—like Adam, like Barlow, like Glen. I can't talk. My mouth hangs open and my eyes stretch wide and I can feel a goofy smile forming and I just. Can't. Talk.

"The charges have all been dropped," Glen says, and his face is scrunched up like he's been sucking on a bad piece of fruit. Or on a good piece of Adam.

"Some stupid fucking technicality," Adam adds.

I still can't talk. All I can do is smile.

"Let's go," Adam says, and he almost spits the words at me and, just like that, my prison experience is over.

CHAPTER FOUR

The days are getting shorter. Colder. Most days the forecast says tomorrow is going to snow yet it doesn't get there, and Schroder is never sure whether to blame the weatherman or Mother Nature. Last year had a summer that felt like it wasn't going to end, with warm days late into May. This summer was on the same track until a few weeks ago. Earlier in the year a heat wave scorched the city and took lives. In this weather it's hard to remember those times. The good thing about the cold is that it keeps the loonies inside because it's too miserable to be outside mugging people. Crime always has a way of being scaled back in the winter. People at work are leaving houses that feel like refrigerators and nobody really wants to break into those. So it's a good time of the year to be a cop. Only Carl Schroder isn't a cop anymore. Hasn't been for over three weeks, since the night he killed that woman and his rank—along with his gun and badge and all the shitty benefits that came along with it, including the shitty pay—was taken away.

Every day since losing his job he's still felt like a cop. It's annoying. Every day for the first two weeks he woke up and wanted to put on the badge and ended up putting on sweatpants and a jacket and hung around the house all day helping his wife and being a better dad to his kids. Every night he went to sleep seeing the woman he shot and hating that he had to make that decision and knowing he'd make the same one again. The third week he worked. His new job doesn't require him to shoot people.

This is now his second week on the job. The drive out to the prison is miserable. It was raining when he woke up, raining when he ate breakfast, raining when he got the phone call to come out here, and even though the forecast for tomorrow is supposed to be fine, he's sure it'll be raining then too. The window wipers make it all clear before the rain turns it back into a blur. There are paddocks full of cows standing in mud, sheep wearing drenched woolen jerseys, and still there are farmers out there making the circle of life happen, making food, making milk, making money, driving around in their tractors as the rain keeps on coming. The grass shoulders off the side of the road are flooded. Small shrubs are under water. Birds are flapping around in it. The window wipers are struggling to cope. Every few miles there are warning billboards about not driving tired, or speeding, or driving drunk. One says *The faster you go the bigger the mess*. Superman would disagree. The faster he went the more people he saved. He once went so fast he went back in time and fixed a lot of messes before they began. Christchurch needs somebody like him.

A truck coming toward him hits a flooded section of road, splashing water up over Schroder's windshield—more than the wipers can immediately handle—so for two seconds he can't see a thing, a scary two seconds when you're driving blindly on a motorway. He puts his foot on the brake and slowly presses it down until the windscreen clears. When it does, the view doesn't change. Just more rain, more gray sky.

He has the radio on as he drives. He's listening to a national talk radio station. People are phoning in and the DJ is making conversation. It's current events, and the current event people want to talk about is the death penalty. It's been ongoing for the last few months. It's the national debate. People are for it. Other people are against it. Emotions are strong. Those for it hate those against it. Same goes for the other side. There is no middle ground. No sitting on the fence. People can't understand other people's point of view. It's dividing the country, dividing neighbors, dividing family and friends. Schroder, personally, he's for it. He sees no problem dishing out a little of the same pain that killers have inflicted on this city. Half the people phoning in to the radio station share his opinion. Half don't. Either way they want to be heard.

"It's not about justice," somebody says, a guy by the name of Stewart who is phoning in from Auckland, where, according to Stewart, the rain is of biblical proportions. "It's about punishment," he says, which is pretty biblical too, come to think of it.

It's a twenty-minute drive to the prison that takes thirty-five in this weather. He hears a dozen different viewpoints. The DJ is trying to be impartial. Schroder could flick the dial and hear the same debate on about six other stations. The good news is that there is going to be a referendum. A vote is taking place. For the first time that Schroder can remember, the government is going to listen to the people. At least they are saying they will—after all, it's an election year. The leading question to the prime minster and to those running against him is: Will the next government follow the will of the people? And the answer is yes. That means, technically, by the end of the year the death penalty could be back in place, if that's what the people want. He wonders what direction that will take the country. Back into the dark ages? Or into a future where people aren't killing each other as often?

Hard to know.

But depending on the vote, he may just get a chance to find out.

Schroder turns the radio off. Next week, when Joe Middleton's trial begins, will be a nightmare. He's heard a rumor that the prosecution is going to ask for the death penalty if indeed the death penalty becomes law. There are going to be people outside the courthouse. They're going to be carrying signs. Pro-death. Anti-death. Victim rights. Human rights.

The prison comes up on the left. He slows down and takes the turnoff, a speeding van almost rear-ending him, and a minute later he comes to a guard post. He shows his identification to a guard with the same amount of humor as a tumor. Up ahead is the entrance. Beyond that construction workers are assembling another wing of the prison. Even in the rain they're working, eager to get the job done, eager to make more room for more criminals. Whoever said crime doesn't pay also should have added that crime is a billion-dollar industry with all that it touches—new prisons, lawyers, funerals, insurances. It's the only thing booming. Another car pulls in behind him into the parking lot. He parks and sits still for a few moments, wishing he had an umbrella, but knowing he probably wouldn't use it even if he did. He looks over at the car parking next to him. A woman, all alone. She kills the engine and he can't see her clearly enough to know what she's doing, but he's been around enough women to know she's probably putting something into her handbag or getting something out, a simple job that can take his wife five minutes to do since her handbag is like a time capsule dating back to before they met. She opens the car door. She's pregnant. From the looks of the way she's trying to squeeze herself out of the car, she got pregnant sometime about a year ago.

"You need a hand there?" he asks, getting out of his car, and he has to almost shout to be heard over the rain. Before he's even finished the sentence he's soaking wet, and so is she, only just her face and belly at this stage.

"Thank you," she says, and she reaches up and takes his hand. Rather than him pulling her up, she almost pulls him back into the car, and he almost lets her since it's drier in there. He strengthens his back, switches on the stomach muscles he's slowly losing, and pulls. She stumbles forward and has to wrap her arms around him, and he almost topples, grabbing at the car door to stay balanced.

"Oh my God, I'm so sorry about that," she says, pulling away from him.

"You picked a hell of a day to visit somebody," he says.

She laughs, a very sweet laugh that her husband or boyfriend must love hearing. "You think today is going to be any better than tomorrow?"

"Supposed to be sunny," he says, "but maybe the snow they picked for last week might finally arrive." He's curious as to who she's visiting. Maybe her boyfriend or husband is locked up out here. He doesn't ask.

"Can you . . . I hate to ask, but would you please grab my handbag for me?"

"Sure," he says. She steps aside and he reaches into the car and grabs her handbag off the passenger seat. "No umbrella?"

She shakes her head. "It's only rain," she says.

He closes the door for her. "Torrential rain," he says, and there's no point in hurrying now, he can't get any wetter.

She smiles. "I like it. The rain is . . . I don't know, romantic, I guess." She breathes in deeply. "And that smell," she says. "I love that smell."

Schroder breathes in deeply. All he can smell is wet grass.

They walk up to the main doors together, the woman has her hand on her stomach the entire way, and he figures she should be keeping that hand much lower, ready to catch what is surely going to fall out of her at any second. He opens the door for her.

"You look familiar," he says, but he can't place her. It's more he gets the feeling she looks like somebody he used to know. He looks at her red hair—it's full and wavy and comes down to her shoulders and he imagines she spends a long time looking after it with hair moisturizers and shampoos. She's wearing a light brown shade of eye shadow to match, and red lipstick too. "Do I know you from somewhere?"

"Ha, I get that a lot," she says, and they're inside now, out of the rain. "I used to be an actress," she says, "before this happened," she adds, patting her stomach.

"Oh really? I've just gotten into the TV industry myself."

"You're an actor?"

He shakes his head. "A consultant. What would I have seen you in?"

"Well, this is kind of embarrassing," she says, "but nothing much. Just shampoo ads, mostly. And some hotel ads. Often you'll see me behind the desk, or sitting by a pool, or in the shower. My career is really taking off," she says, giving a grin. "Though with the baby you won't see me again for a few years, unless it's a diaper ad. Well, I hate to be rude, but nature calls," she says, and she pauses next to a small corridor with a sign indicating that the toilets are only a few feet away. "You have children?" she asks.

"Two," he says. Water is starting to puddle around his feet.

"This is my first," she says. "I think he's going to be a practical joker. I mean, at the moment he finds it funny to have me running off to the bathroom every ten minutes. Thanks for . . . for the lift," she says, smiling.

"Anytime."

He walks up to the counter, on the other side of which is a very large woman. There's a piece of Plexiglas between them. It feels like being in a bank. Last time he came out to the prison was back in summer when Theodore Tate was being released, and then all he did was wait out in the parking lot. Tate was a buddy of his who used to be a cop, but who became a criminal. Then he became a private investigator. Then a criminal again. Then a cop. Then a victim. Tate has been a lot of things, and Schroder makes a mental note to go and visit him. It's been a few days.

"I'm here for Joe Middleton," he says, and he hands over his ID.

Her face tightens a little at the mention of Joe's name, and so does his. Joe Middleton. For years that slimy bastard worked among them, cleaning their floors, empting their rubbish bins, the entire time using police resources to stay ahead of the investigation. Joe Middleton. Schroder got the credit for arresting him, but the entire thing was a fuck up. They should have gotten him sooner. Too many people died. He felt responsible. A lot of them did. And so they should—they let a killer walk among them.

"He's five minutes away," the woman says, and Schroder knows that no matter what this woman says, that's the way it is. She doesn't look like somebody you'd want to mess with. She looks like she could singlehandedly run the entire complex out here. "Take a seat," she says, and points behind him. He knows the drill. He's waited out here before—just never as a civilian. It's different. He doesn't like not having a badge.

He moves over to the seats. He's the only one here. The pregnant woman is still in the bathroom, and he remembers what it was like with his own wife, and how in the end she refused to be more than thirty seconds away from a bathroom.

He sits down, his wet clothes pushing against him. The chair is a solid plastic one-piece with metal legs. There's a table with magazines on it. Add some coughing people and a screaming baby and it would be just like a doctor's office. He can hear drips of water coming off him and hitting the floor. The guard looks over at him and he feels guilty about the mess he's making. He expects that any second now the *Take a seat* woman is going to throw him some paper towels, or throw him a mop, or throw him out.

Five minutes. And then he has to face the man he arrested a year ago.

The Christchurch Carver.

The man who made a fool of them all.

CHAPTER FIVE

This must be what it's like to win the lottery. Or what it's like to win the lottery and not even have bought a ticket. Both guards look sick. Adam looks like he wants to punch me. Glen looks like he could do with a hug. The news sinks in and I feel my Slow Joe game face taking shape. The world that shifted off its axis twelve months ago is righting itself. What was out of whack is now in whack. Nature correcting itself. The laws of physics correcting themselves. My Slow Joe smile feels great and seems to fit a lot better than it did earlier when I was with Barlow. It's the big smile that shows all the teeth, and if I can't get it under control it's going to break my mouth in half. My scar hurts as it shifts around the smile, looking for a comfortable position and not finding one, but I don't care about the pain. Not now. I'm going to be home again. I'm going to have the chance to carry on doing the thing I love to do. Get some new pet goldfish. Buy some nice sharp knives. Get a really cool briefcase.

Adam looks at Glen, and then he starts to laugh, the muscles in his neck straining out from his shirt, and when he starts to laugh then Glen laughs too. They stare at each other for two seconds, then both look at me. "That was fucking great," Adam says, and he's looking at me, but talking to his boyfriend. "You see his face?"

"I didn't think it'd work," Glen says. "I really didn't. Oh man, you totally picked it."

"I told you," Adam says. "I told you he was dumber than anybody really knew."

"What?" I ask, but of course I know what. It's a practical joke. In an ideal world, I'd stab these guys to death for making me look like a fool. But this isn't an ideal world—proven by my surroundings and lack of knife. I play along with them—because to do otherwise would be to show them who I really am.

"He still doesn't get it," Glen says, his voice rising, trying to hold back a laugh. He sounds eager, as if excited to be making his point. Whatever that point is. "You think they're ever going to let you out of here?" he asks, directing his question at me. "Come on, asshole, there's somebody here who wants to see you."

I take a step toward them. "Should I . . . should I bring my books?" I ask, and boy I'm good. Very, very good.

"Oh my God," Adam says, and starts laughing all over. "Oh my God, he still doesn't get it!"

"Stop being such a fucktard. Let's go," Glen says, and he grabs hold of my arm. There's a dark tone in his voice, the eagerness and excitement gone. He's on edge. He sounds like he's ready for me to try something, or more likely he's wanting me to try something that will give them permission to find out if a man's skull can be crushed between a forearm and a bicep.

"I'm . . . I'm not going home?"

"You crack me up," Adam says, and Glen agrees.

They lead me back to an identical room to the one I was in earlier with the shrink. I sit behind the desk and they don't handcuff me and I know what that means. That means I'm going to be talking to somebody who has the ability to beat the shit out of me. The guards leave the room. I stand up and start pacing it. I'm faced with the two fundamental decisions of prison—sit down and do nothing, or pace the room you're in. I study the concrete walls. Great architecture. A real timeless quality. I reach out and touch them. Prisons all over the world from last century to the next century are going to have these same walls. In a thousand years I doubt they will have improved on the design. The door opens up. Carl Schroder walks in. He's soaking wet. I'll update the weather conversationalists when I get back to my cell.

"Take a seat, Joe," Schroder says.

I take a seat. He takes his jacket off and hangs it over the back of the chair. The front of his shirt is wet, so is the collar, but the sleeves look mostly dry. He rolls them up. He brushes a hand through his hair and flicks the water off his fingers. His hair is longer than the last time I saw him, the fringe has grown out and is plastered over his forehead. He wipes a drop of rainwater off his nose. Then he sits down. He doesn't have anything with him. Just his jacket. His wallet and keys and phone are probably out in a tray somewhere. He stares at me and I stare at him, and then I give him the big Slow Joe grin, the one with all the teeth.

"I hear you're having a hard time," Schroder says.

My grin disappears. Some people it's just wasted on. "I hear you're the one having a hard time," I say. "Joe hears you were fired," I tell him, and he was fired for showing up drunk to a crime scene. I wonder if it's people like me that were the reason for people like him to start drinking. The thing is, showing up to work drunk as a cop isn't a fireable offense. It's something you would be suspended over, and perhaps demoted, but getting fired? No, not when the police force is struggling to recruit enough people. Schroder was fired for something else, but I can't imagine him sighing, leaning back, and going *Well, Joe, here's what really happened.*

"Joe must hear a lot of things," he says. "And Joe must know there's a real shitty future ahead of him. You're not getting away with any of this, so at least drop the fucking act."

"Joe likes actors. Joe likes TV shows," I tell him.

His eyes give a half roll, then he pinches the bridge of his nose.

"Look, Joe, cut the bullshit, okay? I know you have a lot of time up your sleeve these days, but I'm not here to waste mine. I'm here to make you an offer. Your trial starts in four days. You—"

"You're no longer a cop," I tell him. "Why are you here? How many times have you come to see me over the last year, asking about Melissa? I keep telling you—"

"That's not why I'm here," Schroder says, putting out his hand.

Since my arrest they've been offering incentives for me to talk, but at the same time they've been telling me I'll never see the light of day again. "Then why are you here?" I ask.

"I want to know where Detective Calhoun is buried."

During my time back before I was arrested, one of the victims attributed to me was a woman by the name of Daniela Walker. Only I didn't kill her. The person who did staged the scene so it would look like she was another victim of the Christchurch Carver. It annoyed me. In fact, it annoyed me so much that I investigated her death, and found she had been killed by Detective Inspector Robert Calhoun. Calhoun had gone to talk to her at her house to try and convince her to press charges against her husband who used to beat her, and somehow Calhoun ended up beating her himself. My plan was to pin all of my killings onto him. It didn't work out that way. It wasn't me who killed Calhoun. I abducted him. I tied him up. But it was Melissa who drove the knife into him.

I shrug. "Is he an actor?"

"He's a policeman. The man you filmed being killed."

"So he is an actor then."

His fists tighten, but only marginally. "I don't know how it's felt for you, but time's been flying for me. It's like the crime rate in Christchurch took a break. People are still partying in the streets. Since you've been arrested the murder rate has plummeted. I'm no longer a cop, but the city doesn't need as many cops anymore."

"That's bullshit," I tell him. I watch the news. Bad shit is still happening out there. I'm just not part of it. "What do you want?" I ask.

"Truthfully? I want to pick this chair up and crack it through your skull. But I'm here because we need each other's help."

"Help? You have to be kidding."

"I didn't come here to kid with you, Joe."

"Why isn't my lawyer here?"

"Because lawyers get in the way, Joe. And the help I need from you doesn't require a lawyer."

"I'm an innocent man," I say. "When the trial begins, people will learn that I was sick. I'm a victim in all of this. The things they say I did—that wasn't me. That's not the real me. The courts don't punish victims."

Schroder starts to laugh. In the years I worked around him it's the first time I have ever seen it happen. He leans back in his chair, and suddenly he starts wheezing. He seems to get caught in a cycle where the laughter makes the situation even funnier, and he starts to cry along with it. His face turns red, and when he looks up at me he starts to laugh some more. I get the feeling if I were to laugh along with him he'd put me on the floor with his knee in my back and my arm twisted and broken behind me.

His laughing slows. It stops. He wipes his face with the palm of his hands. I can't tell what's tears and what is rainwater.

"Oh, Jesus, Joe, that was good. That was really good. And it was really what I needed because it's been a shitty few weeks." He sucks in a deep breath and fires it out fast, slowly shaking his head. "*I'm innocent*," he says, and his smile returns and for a moment I'm worried he's going to start laughing again, but he keeps control. "I can't believe you said that with such . . ." he seems to search for a word, and settles on "conviction. Please, you have to say that when you get up on the stand. Deliver it just like that. You'll make a lot of people happy."

"Why are you here, Carl?"

"Well, well, that's a surprise. That was good, always acting like you were forgetting my first name over the years. I gotta hand it to you, you were very convincing."

"If I wasn't convincing, that would make you a moron," I say, just pissed off at him now, the same way I'm getting pissed off with everybody. "Just tell me what you want."

His smile disappears and he leans forward. He puts his arms on the table and folds them. "You think you're pretty smart, don't you."

"If I'm the man you think I am, then I've already proven I'm smarter than you. But no, I'm not that man. Which proves I can't be that smart."

"Yeah, well, you were too smart this morning for that psych test. That zero percent rating of yours. You know what that was, don't you? That was your ego. That was you proving to the rest of the world just how smart you thought you really were, but the results are back, Joe, and that ego of yours fucked you over."

"Whatever," I say, annoyed that he knows about the test. I guess word gets around, even if you've been fired from the force.

"Truth is, I kind of like the way you sounded when you were mentally challenged. Kind of went with your look. That's why you pulled off that routine so well. I mean, of course you fooled us, Joe, because you played the perfect fool."

"Yeah, yeah, I get it, okay, Carl? You're trying to make fun of me, trying to put me down, what is it you want that doesn't need my lawyer present?"

He leans back. He doesn't interlock his fingers like the psychiatrist. Maybe he's come to the same conclusions about psychiatrists that I have.

"You said you needed my help," I say, prompting him, and his face twists up a little as though the words have cut him somehow. "Hell, Carl, you look pretty pale. You feeling okay?"

"Twenty thousand dollars," he says.

I must have missed part of the conversation. "What?"

"That's what I'm here to offer you."

I start to laugh as hard as he did earlier, only mine is forced, not real at all, and the act doesn't work. I end up coughing, and a few wet strands of something warm fall out of my nose and hit the desk. My eyelid locks up, and I have to reach up and close it manually to get it working again. Schroder sits there silently the whole time, just watching me, shifting occasionally to adjust his wet clothes.

"We got your DNA," he says. "You drank and ate at your victims' houses. You were found with Detective Calhoun's gun. We've got audio tapes you made from our conference room so you knew where our investigation was at. We got a parking ticket that was once in your possession that led to a body at the top of a car parking building."

"We? You're a cop again now are you?"

"We've got your DNA everywhere, Joe. We have so much on you that—"

"You're still saying *we*," I point out.

"That you're embarrassing yourself with this insanity plea," he says, carrying on. "A guy can't kill as many people as you did and get away with it as long as you did unless he was in complete control of himself."

"Or unless the police force is made up of monkeys and morons," I say. "So is this meeting over, Carl, or are you going to tell me what it is that you want that involves twenty thousand dollars?"

"Like you know, I no longer work for the police force anymore," he tells me. "In any capacity."

"No shit. I'm surprised you're working at all. I saw the footage of you showing up drunk to a crime scene. It made good TV viewing. You deserved to be fired."

"I work for a TV show now."

"What?"

"It's a show about psychics."

I slowly shake my head, hoping to shake something loose in there that will help any of this make sense, but I'm missing the bits and pieces to make that happen. A psychic? Money? What the fuck? "What the hell are you on about, Carl?"

"It's a show about psychics who help solve unsolved cases."

"What's that got to do with me?"

"They want to look at your case."

"My case? I don't have a case, Carl. I haven't hurt anybody."

Schroder nods. No doubt he expected this answer. "Okay, let me speak hypothetically here," he says. "Let's say you know where Detective Calhoun is."

"I don't. All I know is that he's dead."

"But we're being hypothetical here, Joe."

"I don't know what that means," I tell him. "Hyper what? Hyper pathetic? I'm not good with big words."

He closes his eyes and pinches the top of his nose again for a few moments. "Look, Joe, this show," he says, talking into his hand, "they're willing to pay you twenty thousand dollars on the chance that you may know where the body is." He pulls his hand away from his nose and interlocks his fingers with his other hand. "Giving us a location would in no way suggest your guilt. In fact both you and the show would sign waivers to say you could never discuss with anybody that you gave this information. Now, hypothetically, if we found the body, what would your guess be that there is anything the police could use to find Melissa?"

I think about it. I set fire to Detective Calhoun's dead body, and I buried it. There's nothing there for the cops to find, just ashes and bone and dirt, maybe a few fragments of clothing.

"Look, Joe, we know Melissa killed him. We know you hid the body. You have nothing to lose by telling us where he is, and a lot to gain."

"What does the show need with the body?" I ask, but the words are barely out of my mouth before I know the answer. They want to find it. They want to put on some stage show with the dead, probably with the late Detective Calhoun, probably some psychic surrounded by candles and going into some kind of fuck-knuckle trance. Then he'll lead them to his remains. The TV viewing public will love it. The show will gain ratings, it'll gain attention, the psychic on the case will gain a fan base for more shows, maybe even write a book. "Wait," I tell him. "I've figured it out. The psychic wants to eat him."

"Yeah, Joe, that's right."

"What the hell am I going to do with twenty thousand dollars?" I ask.

"You can use it to make yourself more comfortable," he tells me. "Money is as good in here as it is anywhere else. Hell, maybe you can use it to get yourself a better lawyer."

"First of all, Carl, no, money is much better out there than in here. Secondly, I don't know where this dead guy is," I say, and before Schroder can react I raise a hand in a stopping gesture. "But maybe I'll think about it overnight. Twenty grand isn't going to help the thinking, though. In fact I'm having a psychic vision of my own. I'm sensing . . . I'm sensing that if it were fifty grand I might be more helpful."

"No way," Schroder says.

"Yes way. The way I see it, Carl, Sally got paid fifty grand after you arrested me, right?" I ask, and it's true. Last year there was a fifty-thousand-dollar reward for my capture, and somehow The Sally—the overweight, Jesus-loving maintenance worker at the police station—was given that reward. Somehow through a series of fuckups, The Sally figured out what the police couldn't, and that led them to my door. "So if you're going to hand money out like candy, then I want my share."

He doesn't say anything.

"Hyper pathetically you should get me those contracts you're talking about. Hyper pathetically for fifty thousand dollars I might take a guess as to where Detective Calhoun is."

"So you'll do it?"

I shrug. Hypothetically I just might.

"Clock is ticking, Joe. You have till tomorrow to decide."

"I'll think about it," I tell him. "Come back tomorrow and bring the contracts."

Schroder stands back up. He grabs his wet jacket and doesn't put it on, just drapes it over one of his dry arms. He moves to the door and bangs on it. It's opened and we don't hug, he just walks out the door without even a good-bye. I wait in the room to be escorted back to my cell, my world is about waiting, and now I have something new to think about while I'm doing it—and that's trying to figure out what kind of power fifty thousand dollars could buy in a place like this.

CHAPTER SIX

The fact is she had a plan. A good plan. A two-person plan. There was her, and then there was him—the second person of the two-part plan. A guy by the name of Sam Winston. Sam let her down. Maybe it was something that men with girls' names do. Sam used to be in the army. She met him over the summer when he tried to break into her house.

She almost killed him, but she saw something in Sam, the same something others see in sick kittens and dogs with three legs, a kind something that makes you want to help. And he hadn't been trying to break into her house, not really—it'd turned out he used to live there a few years earlier before drugs had taken away his money and chunks of his memory and sent his wife packing. He'd come back. He'd been drunk and furiously unwilling to accept that his key wasn't fitting into the door.

That was the thing about Christchurch—it was a small world, a world full of coincidences, and people bumped into people like that every day.

Sam had been discharged from the army five years earlier. He hadn't seen any action, unless you included getting so high that he crashed a fuel truck into the mess hall and injured half a dozen men, *but nobody died* as he told her proudly. Sam was angry at the world, angry at life, though he never told her exactly what it was he was angry about. He was happy to follow her around and do what she asked. He really was like a three-legged dog. A pet, really. Until he started to figure out who she was. By then they'd been planning on how to shoot Joe for a good two months. Then he got dollar signs in his eyes. She saw it happen. The news was on and the police had figured out her real name. There were pictures of her coming up on the screen and he kept looking at them and then at her, and his eyes widened as if big cash-register dollar signs were ringing off behind them.

So things didn't work out with Sam after that. That was a week ago. She had to leave him and move on. And, just like any good-hearted pet owner would do, she put him down gently.

The trial starts Monday. Today is Thursday. She doesn't want Joe deciding to start talking all about her because the prosecution makes him an offer he can't refuse. She doesn't want to shoot him on Tuesday, or Wednesday, or a month into the trial. The plan was for Monday, the plan has fallen though, but the new plan can be for Monday too.

At the moment people don't look at her and see Melissa. They see a pregnant woman on the cusp of bursting, they see a mom-to-be. What they don't do is take a good look and wonder if she could be a killer. People are easy to fool. She's been fooling them for years now. She's learned that wigs and hair dye and fake eyelashes and being nine months pregnant can make you anybody you want to be. Even Schroder, good old ex–detective inspector Schroder, didn't recognize her. She could see him trying to place her, but there was no chance. They see fat pregnant chick and don't see beyond that. He bought the acting story hook, line, and sinker, because she gave him no reason at all to doubt her. She can be a different person from who she was yesterday, and she can be a different person tomorrow. It's how she's been free to do what she wants all these years. It's how she survives.

Right now the person she wants to be is dry. This rain is soaking through her clothes. She's shivering. She waited five minutes on the chance Schroder noticed his keys were missing, but the detective is a former detective for a reason, and that's probably one of them. Schroder's car is about as messy as she'd expected it to be. Fast-food wrappers covering the mats in the backseat, children's clothes, a car seat for a baby. Nobody is watching her. The weather is way too bad for anybody to think much beyond getting from point A to point B in a way that stops them from drowning. She said earlier to Schroder that she likes the rain, but the truth is she hates it. It surprises her that she still lives in this city. She was born here. Raised here. Raped here. Her sister was born here. Raised here. Raped here. And murdered here. There's a lot of memories in Christchurch, not many of them any good. There are other cars in the parking lot, but she's not concerned about anybody coming out at the wrong time and spotting her. She's almost done here anyway. And if Schroder were to come outside now and catch her, well, she'll just have to stab him and drive away with him in the backseat. It'd be a shame because over the last few minutes she's come up with a very specific plan for Schroder's future.

Schroder is still well informed for a guy who is no longer a cop. Which is what she was hoping for after *I don't want to shoot anybody* Derek pointed out Joe's route to the courthouse might not be the route she had imagined. She had to get the information from somewhere, and she figured Schroder would have it—after all, he was the lead on the Carver case. He was easy to follow too. She knows where he lives and where he works. She doesn't know why he was fired. Something to do with drinking on the job is the official story—a whole bunch of cops showed up drunk at a crime scene a month ago—but she thinks there's more to it than that. She doesn't know what, exactly. And she doesn't really care. All that matters is Joe, and what matters here is what Schroder knows about Joe, and about how Joe is getting to court.

There's a box in the backseat containing files from Joe's case. There are copies of crime scene reports, lots of photographs, evidence detailed down to the specifics. There's a photograph of her, back when she was another person. She holds it up and runs her thumb over the smooth edge of it. It was taken a few weeks before she started university. God, that was ages ago. She wasn't just a different person back then, but a completely different person. New look, new personality—staring into the photograph is like looking at a stranger. The person staring out at her had hopes and dreams. She was going to be somebody. That girl had no idea—she was innocent, she had no idea of her potential. Despite everything, she smiles at the memory of the picture being taken. The picture is as different as the day was different. Lots of sun. Blue skies. It was summer. Good times. Her best friend, Cindy, took the photograph. She's leaning against a car and has a big smile and an easygoing nature. Cindy and her were heading to the beach. Cindy ended up fucking two guys in the sand dunes at the same time then crying all the way home, disgusted at herself. She hasn't seen Cindy since leaving university, and she wonders what ever became of her, but she doesn't wonder enough to ever look her up.

She folds the photograph into her jacket pocket.

She finds what she's after a few pages down into the box. The route the police will be taking to the court. She scans through it. She sees Derek was right. She absorbs the facts. Then uses her cell phone to snap a photo. She puts it back, then carries on looking. There's a second thing she wants too. The cell phone number and address of the man that is going to help her. That's another idea Derek gave her. Obviously Derek was an ideas man. She finds what she's looking for and photographs that too.

She's glad she came out here. She almost turned around and left him to it once she realized where they were going, but turning around isn't in her nature. Plus, who knew when there'd be another opportunity to go into his car? And time is short. And, of course, Schroder is now part of her escape plan. She takes out the C-four. She reaches up and under the steering column, right around toward the back of the car stereo. The square block changes shape slightly as she jams it to a stop back there. Then she reaches back under and jams the detonator into the not-so-perfectly-square lump of clay, the receiver attached to the end of it.

She gets back to her own car. She yawns heavily for a few seconds—she was up half of last night and more than anything right now she wants to take a nap, but can't. She drives past the guard booth who asks her to pop the trunk to make sure nobody is hiding in there. When she gets out to the motorway she pulls over and takes off the baby bump, and suddenly she's no longer nine months pregnant, no longer overweight and needing to use a bathroom every fifteen minutes. She tosses it into the backseat. She tosses the red wig back there too.

She programs the new address into the GPS function of her cell phone. Like always, it takes her and her GPS application a few minutes to come to an understanding, but they get there in the end, and then she has the directions of the man who is going to help her shoot Joe Middleton. But first she needs to go into town. She needs to find a new place where Joe can be shot from. And she already has a pretty good idea where that will be.

CHAPTER SEVEN

The prison officer has bloodshot eyes, as if every night while he sleeps the unibrow above them extends downward and scratches at them. He hands over the tray of Schroder's belongings. Car keys, wallet, phone, coins—actually, that's a negative on the car keys. He looks into the empty tray, then pats down his pockets.

"My keys aren't here," he says.

The prison officer doesn't look impressed. He looks like he's being accused of something. "You didn't give me any car keys."

"I must have."

"Then they'd be here," the prison officer says, his unibrow turning into a uni-V.

"That's my point. I gave them to you and they should be here."

"And my point is that if you did give them to me then I'd have just given them back. Maybe you dropped them. Maybe they're hanging out of your car door. Maybe they're in the ignition. Maybe you left them at home and walked here."

Schroder shakes his head. "Unlikely," he says. "To any of those."

"No. What's unlikely is that I'd hide them from you, or steal them. What's unlikely is that I gave them to some guy locked up inside and told him to take a joyride. Tell you what, you go take a look outside. If they're not there, then you come back in and we watch the security footage," he says, and points to a camera above the desk. "I can bet you a hundred bucks right now that you didn't hand any keys to me."

Schroder looks up at the camera, then pats down his pockets again. Did he lock his car? Of course he did. He always does. Only this time he was distracted by the pregnant woman. Distracted enough to leave them in the ignition? Maybe. Certainly distracted enough not to notice he didn't put them into the tray when emptying his pocket. But does he ever? When he comes here it's just like going through security at an airport—he doesn't really notice what he's taking out of his pockets, all he's focused on is making them empty.

"Okay," he says. "I'll check outside."

"You do that."

Schroder follows the corridor back the way he came, past the waiting area, past the corridor to the bathrooms, past more puddles of water that have formed from other visitors. He stands at the door and puts on his jacket then heads into the rain. There's a similar number of cars in the lot as before—some gone, some new ones. The pregnant woman's car is gone. Probably whoever she was visiting she couldn't visit for long, her future baby pushing against her bladder would have put an end to that. He tightens his collar.

His car is locked. His keys are lying on the ground next to where the pregnant woman's car was. He must have been carrying them in his hand. He must have dropped them when he caught her. He feels like an idiot. Part of him thinks he ought to go back inside and apologize to the prison officer, but it's a small part, nowhere near big enough to make him actually do it. The guy was too big a dick for that.

He gets into the car and peels the wet jacket off him and

tosses it into the back next to a box full of files from the Carver case. One of the sleeves lands on top of it, so he leans back and flicks it aside, not wanting water from his jacket to soak onto the files—files he shouldn't have. The Carver case has lived with him for the last few years—it would come home with him, it would invade the room of his house that he had turned into an office, an office he made his wife promise never to go into because the content inside would give her nightmares. In a way the file invaded his marriage too. He would work at work and he would work at home when there was spare time, of which there wasn't much because of the kids. Then that all changed and he lost his job, and all the copies of documents and photos he'd brought home had to be returned. Only he made copies of those copies first, and it's some of those copies that occupy the cardboard box in his car. It wasn't his case anymore, but with the trial coming up he wanted to be prepared for whatever came his way.

What he really wanted to come his way was a chance to strangle Joe. Hell, he's imagined his hands around his neck a thousand times. He's imagined shooting him, stabbing him. He's imagined setting him on fire. He's imagined a lot of things, all of which end very badly for Joe Middleton. He's confident many people across the city have imagined all those same things.

Honesty being the policy and all that, not a day has gone by when Schroder hasn't hated himself too. A serial killer was in their midst. They saw him five days a week. The bastard even made him coffee. Schroder doesn't deserve to be a cop. None of them do. How many hours does that add up to? How many minutes did Joe make fools of them all?

The drive back into town isn't any different from the drive out here. Same view. Same animals. Same guys in tractors making more money than he'll ever earn, but they're getting up far earlier every morning than he'd ever want to. The rain is still persistent. It's beating down on the car and he isn't sure he can make it through winter. If things don't work out well with the new job, maybe it's time to leave the city. He could pack the family in the car and drive up to Nelson, the sunshine capital of New Zealand. He has a sister who lives up there. Nelson is the kind of place where everybody has a relative who lives there because it's so damn nice. He could work at a vineyard. Pick grapes and make wine. Or become a tour bus driver—take people on wine-tasting tours and watch them get trashed.

Joe. Fucking Joe. Thoughts of Nelson disappear and, like always, Joe replaces them. When the trial is over maybe then he can get some closure.

There aren't too many cars on the roads, but what traffic is there is much slower because of the weather, giving the appearance of a slight traffic jam. It worsens as he gets toward town. He has a lunch date with Detective Wilson Hutton, which he's going to be late for. He pulls over and uses his cell phone to call his ex-colleague to give him an extra fifteen minutes, but before he can the phone rings anyway. It's Hutton.

"I was just about to call you," he says.

"Listen, Carl, sorry, but I'm going to have to cancel lunch," Hutton says.

"Let me guess," Schroder says, "another homicide?" It's meant to be a joke, and Hutton is supposed to say no, but as soon as Schroder says it he knows it doesn't sound like a joke at all—it's just his bad mood coming through by suggesting the worst-case scenario, and anyway, there's nothing funny about people dying. He already regrets saying it.

"Yeah, body was found this morning," Hutton says.

"Ah, shit," Schroder says.

"Well at least this time the victim was a bad guy, Carl, so don't start feeling too bad."

In that case Schroder doesn't feel bad at all. The world with one less bad guy in it? Why would he?

"Details?" Schroder asks, and he stares out the window at a campaign billboard looking down over the intersection. The billboard is for the already prime minister who is hoping to do what Schroder wasn't able to do this year—keep his job. A vote for him is a vote for the future of New Zealand, according to the poster, but doesn't specify if that's a better or worse future. The prime minister has the look of a confident man, even though the polls suggest he doesn't have the right to be. The election is only a few months away. Schroder isn't sure who he's going to vote for—probably for the candidate who doesn't put up as many distracting billboards at intersections.

"Sorry, Carl, you know I can't do that."

"Come on, Hutton . . ."

"All I can tell you is that it's bad."

"What kind of bad?"

"Not the kind of bad you're thinking of. Listen, I'll tell you when I can."

"A drink tonight?" Schroder asks.

"Why? So you can pump me for information for that TV show of yours?"

"Weren't you the one who said they believed in psychics?"

"I'll give you a call if I can make it," he says. "Later, Carl," he adds, and hangs up.

Schroder tosses his phone onto the passenger seat next to the folder with *Finding the Dead* sketched across the cover. He wonders what Hutton means, and how bad it can get in a city where bad things happen a lot.

Now that he's missing lunch he heads straight in to the TV station. He swallows his pride while still maintaining the sensation of selling his soul, and steps out into the rain and heads into the building to talk with Jonas Jones.

CHAPTER EIGHT

I'm left sitting in the interview room by myself for a few minutes until Adam and Glen come back in.

"Your choice," Adam says. "Your lawyer is due here soon. You can either wait here for half an hour or we can take you back to your cell."

It's all the same to me. Almost. The difference is that here is a little bigger and I don't have to listen to other prisoners. "I'll wait here."

Adam shakes his head. "You don't get it, do you," he says.

"Get what?"

"You don't get to make choices. I heard you've already fucked up one test today, and now you just fucked up another. Come on, let's go."

They lead me back to my cell. We go through more doorways and pass other prison guards, more concrete walls and concrete floors and no daylight, no escape, no future. They make fun of me along the way, innocent kind of fun, really, especially compared to the fun I'll have with them when my lawyer gets me out of here. When I was unfairly arrested, I was inundated by offers from lawyers all wanting to become my best friend. They wanted to defend me and they wanted the fame and business that came along with it. My trial is going to be the biggest the country has ever seen, and whoever defends me will become a household name. I couldn't afford a lawyer, but that didn't matter. My first lawyer's name was Gabriel Gabel, a forty-six-year-old partner of Gabel, Wiley, and Dench. Apart from having somewhat of an unfortunate name, Gabel was my lawyer for six days when news of the death threats against him were made public. He was my lawyer for six more days after that before he disappeared off the face of the earth.

After that, a second lawyer jumped at the chance to defend me, the case somehow having become more famous since Gabel's disappearance. Again it was six days before the death threats started flooding in, and this time my lawyer didn't simply disappear, but was found in a car parking building with his head caved in by a hammer. I'm not sure how hard the police looked for his killer. I can't imagine task forces hanging out in the conference room at the police station coming up with big ideas, I can't imagine much overtime was put in. I doubt any of them lost any sleep.

No more lawyers wanted to be my best friend anymore. I was assigned a lawyer by the courts, and the death threats stopped. My lawyer was a man who didn't want to defend me, but who had no choice, and that was made clear to the public. If the public kept killing my lawyers there would be no trial, and ultimately the public wanted a trial more than they wanted another dead lawyer.

Since then I've seen my lawyer less than half a dozen times. He doesn't like me. I just think he needs to get to know me better. The trial starts in a matter of days, and I've been in jail twelve months and the wheels of justice seemed to have ground to a halt, only now they're slowly moving forward again. Or wheels of injustice, really.

I think about what Schroder offered and I wonder if this is it for me, this cell, this part of the jail, if this is the best I can hope for. I wonder if fifty thousand dollars can make my life any better and decide that it can't make it worse. The two prison guards send me through a final door to my cellblock and leave me to it. The cell doors are open, and the thirty of us who share this cellblock are free to roam around as far as the room allows, which isn't far. We can chat, we can sit around a communal area and play cards or share stories, or sneak into one another's cells for some fucking or some fighting. I sit in my cell and stare at the ceiling and suddenly I'm no longer alone.

"What makes you so popular?" Santa Kenny asks, and he's standing in the doorway leaning against the wall. I haven't been in the mood any other time to make conversation, and now is no different. I ignore the question, and a few moments later he fires off another one. "What do they want? Are they still trying to make you look guilty?"

I pick up one of the romance novels. I've read them all a couple of times, but there isn't much else to do. This one I'm reading backward, trying to kill some time, enjoying the happily-ever-after becoming corrupted as the man with the abs and chiseled jaw and the woman with the beautiful hair and fantastic boobs drift apart to a time before they ever met.

"They just don't get it," Santa Kenny says. "They see us, the city is in a state of paranoia, and they see us and they target us for their blame. They can't find the real guys, but they hate us because somebody always has to pay."

I put the book down and look up at him. "It's crazy the shit that makes us look guilty," I tell him. "Hell, just because you were caught in a stolen car wearing a Santa suit with an eight-year-old boy locked in the trunk," I say, "that doesn't mean anything."

"Exactly," Santa Kenny says.

"And the fact it was in April didn't help. It made you stand out."

"Exactly. So what, it's a crime now to wear a Santa suit around Easter?"

"Shouldn't be," I tell him. "You think it's a crime to wear an Easter Bunny outfit during Christmas?"

"And how the fuck was I to know that kid was even in the back?"

"No way you could have."

"And I wasn't stealing the car, I thought it was mine. Looked like mine. And it was dark. People make mistakes."

"Things look different in the dark," I tell him.

"That's my point. That kid, he thinks I'm the one who took him, but how could he know that when I put a blindfold over his eyes?"

"Right," I tell him, and we've had this conversation before, quite a few times actually. I guess I could use some of the fifty thousand dollars to pay somebody to shut him up permanently.

"Play some cards?" he asks.

"Maybe soon," I tell him.

He shrugs, like *soon* is an insult to him. "Lunch in twenty minutes," he says, and then he disappears. I pick the romance book back up. I stare at the pages and read some of the same words over and over. If I ever write a book where men and women fall in love, it'd be real, it'd be the kind of thing I had with Melissa. I miss her. A lot.

The two prison guards come and get me again. They really seem to have taken a shine to me today.

"Good news," Adam says.

"I'm going home?"

"See? Sometimes you do catch on quick," he says.

They lead me back out of the cellblock. Weirdly I'm thankful for the break in the routine. These next few days are going to be like that because of the trial. A month ago, and a month before that, and a few more before that were all the same. I wake up. I stare at stuff. I eat. I stare at more stuff. Then it's lights out. Next week I'll be put in front of a jury, and there's no way they'll convict me. I'm Joe. People like Joe.

I'm taken back to the same interview room. My lawyer is waiting in there already. He props his briefcase up on the table and for a moment I wonder if it's full of knives. He's in his late fifties. He has just the right amount of not looking so young that he's cocky, and not looking so old that all the experience and wisdom he has gained will be spilling into a coffin along with the rest of him before Christmas. His name is Kevin, and Kevin is wearing a nice suit that I would never wear, cologne that makes me feel sick, and has an overweight wife that I would never touch. The photo of her clipped inside the lid of his briefcase must weigh as much as the briefcase itself.

The guards handcuff me to my chair. Then they leave.

"I got some news for you," Kevin says.

"Good news I assume?"

He shakes his head and frowns. "Bad news."

"I'll have the good news first."

"Err . . . you're missing the point, Joe," he says. "It's bad news, worse news really."

"Then the bad news first."

"The prosecution is making you an offer."

"That's good news," I tell him. "They're letting me go?"

"No, Joe, they're not. But they do think in the interest of expediting things, of saving taxpayer money, and of avoiding the risk of turning this whole thing into a circus, they are offering you life in jail without the option of parole. They're trying to avoid what is looking to be a streetful of people protesting for or against the death penalty."

"Death penalty? I don't get it," I say, but I'm afraid that I do.

"That's the worse news, and I'll get to that in a second."

"No, no, you'll get to it now," I say, wanting to wave my hands in the air, but unable to. What are you talking about?"

"I said I'll get to it, Joe. First there's more bad news. There's been a hiccup with the insanity defense."

"What kind of hiccup?" I ask.

"Benson Barlow."

"Who's that?"

"He's the psychiatrist the prosecution sent to speak to you. He hasn't submitted a formal report yet, but I've been given a heads-up, and it's very damning of you. Basically he's going to say you're faking everything."

"It'll be his word against mine."

"Well, Joe, we can argue that at a trial, but I don't see much hope in this. Barlow is an extremely respected psychiatrist, whereas you're an extremely reviled serial killer. Whose word do you think will carry more weight?"

"Mine," I say. "Nobody likes psychiatrists. Nobody."

"I know the plan is to plead an insanity defense," he says, "but here's the thing, Joe, and this is what I've been telling you since I've been your lawyer—it's not a great defense. You got away with murdering these women for so long that you had to be sane to do that."

Schroder said a similar thing. "Then why can't I remember any of it?" I ask, remembering each woman in turn, the horror in their faces, the blood, the sex. Mostly I remember the sex. Good times. "You're talking like you think I'm guilty," I say. "And I still want my trial. Now, what the hell is this death penalty you're talking about?"

He adjusts his tie, making me think that out of all the ways to kill somebody I've never strangled anybody with a tie. I'll put it on my bucket list. "Here's the thing, Joe. Since you've been in here things have changed out there. In a way you've made that happen. People don't like the way Christchurch has gone, and you've become, well, you've become the poster boy for that. People try to figure out how it all started, and you're the guy they point to. There's a referendum taking place. The government is spending nine million of the tax payers' dollars to get their opinion on whether or not to bring back the death penalty."

I exhale hard through my nose, almost scoffing. I've seen that on the news, but it's not going to lead anywhere. It's all bullshit.

"They're sending out voting forms to everybody on the electoral roll. The country wants to be heard, Joe, and everybody over eighteen years old is going to get that chance. I have to be honest with you. Judging by the climate that isn't good news for you. So the prosecution is offering you a deal. Plead guilty now, accept you're never going to get out of prison—"

"But I'm innocent!"

"Again, or they're going to push for the death penalty."

"But the referendum . . ."

"You ever read the Bible, Joe?"

"Only for the recipes in the back."

"An eye for an eye," he says, ignoring my answer. "That's what this referendum comes down to. And it will pass. Trust me on that. And if it passes, you're going to swing."

"Swing?"

"That's how they used to do it here, Joe. They used to hang people. Hasn't happened since nineteen fifty-seven, but if you don't take this deal you're not only going to go down in history as being the Christchurch Carver, you're going to go down as the man who brought back the death penalty."

"But—"

"Listen to me, Joe," he says, and his tone is the same as the one I grew up with, and I don't like it any more now than I did then. "Listen to me. They want to start hanging people. Okay? They think it's the only path back to a civil civilization. It's an election year. And the politicians are listening to the voters. They're being asked if they'll pass the law if the public votes for it, and they're saying they will because they want the votes. It's a minefield. You need to take this deal. You have to listen to me when I tell you it's the only way of saving your life."

"You can save my life by getting me out of here," I tell him. "I can't help what I did. It wasn't my fault. With drugs and counseling I can . . ."

He starts tapping his fingers on the table, starting with his pinkie and rolling on down to his thumb, over and over. "I tell you to listen to me, but you're not listening."

"What?" I ask.

"Let me put this to you more simply, Joe. You," he says, and he stops rolling his fingers so he can point one of them at me so I know exactly who he means. "Are. Completely. Fucked," he says, pointing hard with each word. "So take the deal and tell the police everything they need to know about Melissa, about where Detective Calhoun is buried. Let the city avoid an unpleasant trial. There are going to be masses of people protesting. Half want to kill you, the other half only want you in jail forever—but all of them hate you. It will get ugly. You have no supporters here, Joe. Nobody on the jury is going to be on your side."

"I can't do life in here. I can't do twenty years," I say, and I begin to imagine it. I imagine being in my fifties, my hairline sliding back the same way my father's did. I imagine trying to steal a car. I imagine the mechanics of stuffing somebody who I wasn't getting on well with into the trunk with bad hips and perhaps a dash of arthritis too. I try to imagine sneaking up somebody's set of stairs with a knife in my hand and a bad back, having to use a cane. The world comes out with brand-new, twenty-five-year-old women every year that I'd like to visit, and I imagine spending some quality time with one of them in her bathroom then leaving my hairs in her sink. I'm used to these women looking at me with fear in their eyes. What will they look at me with in twenty years? Humor?

"No deal," I say. "I want the trial. At least I have a chance. There's no difference between twenty years and the death penalty. What if I die in jail in eighteen years? It all would have been for nothing. I want another option."

The whole time Kevin is slowly shaking his head, scratching the side of it at the same time. Small pieces of dandruff land on his spotless suit jacket. "No, Joe, you're missing the point. *Life* is life in this case. It's not twenty years. It's not thirty years. *Life* is you never stepping beyond these walls again. Take it, or in a year's time you'll be getting fitted for a noose."

"If the law passes," I say.

"In theory it *could* go either way. But it won't. It will pass. The decision is yours. You've been given twenty-four hours to decide."

"How can they do this to an innocent man?" I ask.

My lawyer sighs and leans back, not an ounce of belief anywhere in his features. He looks like he's frustrated, like he's been trying to tune into a TV station he can't quite land on.

"I don't need twenty-four hours," I tell him. "I'm innocent. The jury will see that."

"Joe—"

"They can't convict a man for being sick, and that's what I was. I was sick. It's not right. There must be human violations against it. We must have other options."

"You're out of options, Joe. You didn't leave yourself many options when you got caught with that gun, or that videotape in your apartment. The trial is only a show, Joe. The jury hasn't been picked yet, but it's already made up its mind. The whole world has. And you pass up this deal and you could be swinging from a rope in a year."

"I'd rather that than life in here. Send our shrinks in. Let them evaluate me. They can go up on the stand and contradict everything Benson Barlow will say about me."

"Listen, Joe, for the last time, I'm telling you it's not going to work."

"I'm not taking the deal."

"Fine," he says.

"Anything else?" I ask him.

"Like what?"

"I don't know. Something encouraging, maybe. Seems all you ever do is bring me bad news. Seems like you're just trying to bring me down."

"I'll let the prosecution know you're rejecting the deal," he says. He glances at his watch. "You're talking to our psychiatrist at nine o'clock in the morning," he says, as if I'd forgotten the time. "Don't fuck it up."

"I won't."

"We'll see about that," he says, and he stands up, knocks on the door, and leaves.

CHAPTER NINE

Melissa parks outside the house and stares at the front door for two minutes, getting her thoughts in order. It's a typical house in a typical middle-class street. Twenty or thirty years old. Brick. Garden slightly overrun compared to the neighbors'. Tidy, warm, livable, boring. She has the window wipers off, so the view becomes distorted as more rain gathers on the windshield. She planned what she wanted to say on the way, now it's just a matter of seeing if it will work.

She looks at the fat suit and wonders if it's worth putting on, and decides that it is. And instead of the red wig, she goes with a blonde one. She climbs out of the car and holds a newspaper over her head and dashes for the front door. She isn't sure if he'll answer, if there's going to be anybody home—after all, it's only one in the afternoon. After twenty seconds she knocks again, and then there are footsteps and the rattle of a chain.

The door opens. A man in his late thirties opens it. He has black hair that is slowly receding. His stubble is black on his cheeks, but gray around his chin. She can smell coffee. His skin is pale white—as if he spent summer, last summer, and the summer before that all indoors. He's wearing a red shirt that's hanging over blue jeans, and cheap shoes. She hates it when people wear cheap shoes. It's poor form. Already she's starting to think this is a bad idea.

"Can I help you?" he asks.

"Mr. Walker," she says, and it's not a question but a statement because she saw Walker's photograph in Schroder's file.

"Are you a reporter?" he asks. "Because if you are, you can fuck off."

"Do I smell like I just went through your garbage looking for tidbits of information?"

"No . . ."

"Then I'm not a reporter," she says.

"So who are you?"

"I'm a woman who has a job proposal for you."

He looks confused, as well he should. "What kind of proposal?"

"Can I come in?" she asks. "Please, it's important, and it will only be a few minutes and I'm sick of standing in the rain and my feet are tired."

He looks her up and down and seems to finally notice that she's pregnant. "Are you selling something?"

"I'm selling you the chance to sleep like a baby," she says.

"Huh. You must be selling some kind of miracle pill," he tells her.

"It almost is."

"A miracle pill disguised as a job proposal?" he asks.

"Please, just a few minutes of your time, then it will all make sense."

Walker sighs, then steps aside. "Fine."

"Are the kids at school?"

"Yeah."

She puts the wet newspaper down by the door. "Then lead the way," she says.

He leads her down a hallway where there are photographs of the kids, of his dead wife. There's even a photograph of the house he used to live in. Melissa has been to that house. A year ago she killed Detective Calhoun in that house. Joe was there. It turned out there was a video camera there too. Joe really could be a tricky little bastard when he wanted to be.

"Have a seat," he says, pointing to a couch beneath the window in the lounge, "and make it quick. I don't want you going into labor and messing up the carpets."

She isn't sure if he's joking, then decides he isn't. She sits down. The fat suit has a hollow in the side of it, and inside that hollow is the pistol. She rubs at her stomach the way pregnant woman do, feeling the end of the silencer pushing against her hand. Walker sits down in the couch opposite. The furniture is new. All of it. The couches, the coffee table, the TV—none of it older than a year. Walker is creating a new life for himself. Only that life is a little disorganized. She has an angle to the hallway they came in and she can see the calendar is displaying last month's month. The carpet needs vacuuming—there are chip crumbs resting in the top gap between the cushions of the couch. There are empty coffee cups on the table and about fifty times as many rings on it, as if no drink was ever put into the same place twice. Everything may be new looking, but it's also tired looking. The same way Walker is tired looking.

"So," he says. "What is this job you're selling?"

"Your wife was murdered," she says.

"Listen—"

"By Joe Middleton," she says.

He starts to stand up. "If this is about—"

"He killed my sister," she says.

He pauses halfway between sitting and standing. He looks like a man about to grab his back before having to lie on the floor for three days. She isn't sure whether he'll keep rising or if he'll sit back down. Then he slowly lowers himself.

"I'm . . . I'm sorry," he says.

"My sister never hurt anybody," she says. "She lived her life in a wheelchair."

"I read about her," he says. "It was . . . I mean, all of it was horrible, but what he did to her was, well, was something . . . extra bad," he says, his voice becoming sympathetic.

"It was," she says, and she read about the woman in the wheelchair too. She never met her, but her own sister was murdered so she can imagine how it feels. Right now she is being relatable. It's going well.

"Listen, I know you're hurting," Walker says, "but I'm not in the right space to come along to your group-counseling session, I've already told you that. I appreciate the offer, just like I appreciated it last time, but—"

"I'm going to kill him," she says.

He stares at her and says nothing. The couch is uncomfortable. There are kids' toys around the room, helping to mess up the floor and the rest of the furniture, and this is why she never wanted kids. They take up space and they take up time. They might be good for reaching under the couch for loose change, but beyond that all they do is give a room really bad feng shui. She holds back a yawn and rubs her stomach and carries on.

"You're not here from the group?" he asks.

"I want you to help."

"Help?"

"I want you to shoot him."

He cocks his head slightly. "Why don't you shoot him?"

"Because I'm in no condition to shoot anybody. Look at me," she says. "And because it's a two-person plan."

He looks at her. "Just how are you planning on shooting Joe? Walking into the prison and asking if you can see him in his cell?"

"No."

"Then what? Shooting him in the courtroom next week?"

"It's not that either. It's simpler than that. I already have a gun."

"Listen—"

"Wait," she says, and she holds up her hand. "You want him dead for what he did, don't you?"

There is no delay in his answer. "Of course I do."

"And don't you want to be the one to make that happen?"

"Yes."

"Then I can give you that. I can help you make him suffer," she says, "and I can give you this." She opens up the briefcase and turns it toward him.

"How much is in there?" he asks.

"Ten thousand dollars."

"Is that what it's worth? To kill somebody?"

"This, this is just money," she says. "The payoff is in the satisfaction. He murdered your wife," she tells him. "He broke into her house and he ripped off her clothes and he—"

"Stop," he says, and he lifts up his hand. "Stop. I know what he did."

"Don't you feel it?" she asks. "It's like a heat. It races around your body—this heat, this need, this desire for revenge. It burns inside you. Keeps you awake at night with bad thoughts. It runs your life and ruins your life and it doesn't get better."

"I feel it," he says. "Of course I feel it."

"I wake up at night sweating and shaking, and all I can think about is wanting to kill him. And we can do it," she says. "Together we can do it and nobody will know it was us."

He shakes his head. "I hate him, I really do, but I don't want to throw my life away because of him. If anything goes wrong then we're both going to jail."

"Nothing will go wrong," she says, but it's already too late—she's trying too hard to sell him and she didn't want to try at all. She had wanted him to want to do it. She wanted to show up and say *I want to shoot Joe Middleton* and she had wanted him to say *I'm on board—show me how—no matter what the plan is I'll make it happen*. Perhaps her first idea was the best, to pay somebody to do it. She thought there would be an advantage in getting somebody grieving to do the job. This way she can supply the gun, the plan, and she can supply the outcome too. She's starting to worry that what is a two-person plan will have to be changed into a one-person plan—only she doesn't have a one-person plan.

"Don't you want revenge?" she asks.

"Of course I do. But not enough to risk going to jail. I'm sorry. I still have a family."

"So you won't help."

He shakes his head.

She closes the briefcase and stands up and rubs her belly. "Before I go, tell me, you mentioned group-counseling sessions."

"You think you can find somebody there to help you?"

"It's worth a shot."

"There's a group that meets every Thursday night."

"Thursday?"

"Yeah. Today. They're family members and friends of homicide victims. I haven't been, but from what I've heard there's quite a big showing of people who have been hurt by the Carver. You're going to have plenty of people to choose from. You'll get so many volunteers you're going to have to start turning people away."

"Where and when?"

"Seven thirty," he says. "They meet at a community hall."

"Which one?"

"I don't know. Somewhere in town."

"You'll go to the police?"

"Hell no. I wish you the best of luck. I really do. I want nothing more than for somebody to nail that sick bastard. It just can't be me. I'm sorry."

She makes her way to the front door. He follows her. She thinks about what Joe told her about this guy, how he used to beat up his wife. It was Detective Calhoun who figured out Tristan Walker was always around when his wife and door occupied the same moment in space in time.

There's nothing worse than a wife beater.

"You're sure you won't help me?" she asks, picking up the wet newspaper.

"All I want is to be left alone," he tells her.

She keeps rubbing her belly when she steps out into the street, leaving Tristan Walker alone just like he asked.

CHAPTER TEN

The air-conditioning in the TV station is a season behind, or so he's been told, and Schroder believes it too since it's still blasting cold air. No doubt it'll get around to pumping out warm air just when spring starts turning into summer. The station belongs to one of the major networks, coming into existence around the same time Joe Middleton started making the news. Until then there was only a local TV station in the city, the major ones were up in Auckland. But then suddenly Christchurch became the capital for crime, it became the place where journalists wanted to be. It also became the place where producers wanted to shoot crime shows. He once had a guy theorize that flights into Christchurch take longer every year the further the city slips into Hell—though the current temperature makes it an arguable point.

He catches the lift. There is elevator music, classical stuff he can't imagine anybody ever liking. Especially him. Or maybe it's just that he doesn't like it because he doesn't like being here. Another person gets on the lift next to him, and the two of them stare straight ahead, each of them making a big effort not to speak to the other. His stomach is rumbling, reminding him he skipped out on breakfast and he could end up skipping out on lunch too. On the fourth floor he steps into a corridor and makes his way past a makeup room, a cafeteria, offices, and down to Jonas Jones's office. The studio itself where they broadcast from is on the floor below, and Schroder wonders if Jones has a certain satisfaction being above it all.

He doesn't knock on the door. He figures there's no need when you're going to see a psychic. He opens the door and walks inside. Jones is sitting behind his desk with his shoes off, polishing them.

"Ah, I'm glad you're back," Jonas says.

Schroder isn't glad. There are a few reasons he lost his job being a cop, and Jones is one of them. Schroder had never killed anybody before this year, and the nightmares he has about that probably wouldn't get any worse if he were to put a few bullets into Jonas.

"I spoke to him," Schroder says, sitting down opposite the desk. He's tempted to put his feet up. The office has framed pictures of Jonas on the walls meeting other celebrities—a bunch of actors, some writers, some popular local figures. There are photos of him at book signings, even one of him signing a book for the prime minister that helps Schroder decide who he's going to vote for.

"And?" Jonas asks. "Or are you just going to keep me hanging?"

"And he's thinking about it."

"Thinking about it? Come on, Carl, I'm sure you could have done better than that. You offer him the twenty grand?"

"Of course."

"How much more did he want?"

"Fifty."

"Fifty is good," he says, and Schroder thinks about what Joe said earlier, about Sally being paid out that fifty-thousand-dollar reward. It was police work that got them there last year, and Sally was part of that. Was she a big enough part to have earned a reward? No. Not in his opinion. But the money wasn't coming out of his pocket, and he was happy to see it go to her. It was as much a publicity stunt at that stage as anything else. There will be more rewards in the future, and if the public see that kind of money being paid out, then they'll be more willing to offer up the names of people doing bad stuff. It's all part of their new *Crime doesn't pay, but helping the police does* campaign.

"Yeah, fifty is good," Schroder says back to him.

Jones pauses to look at him for a few seconds, then goes back to work on his shoes. "We had budgeted for a hundred," he says, scrubbing at them even though they already look clean. "Can you imagine it?" he asks. "Imagine how it will be, with us finding Detective Inspector Robert Calhoun?"

Schroder has been imagining it, and it makes him feel sick. "I just don't get why you don't use the psychic powers you keep reminding us that you have," he says, and he's said it before and he'll say it again, just as Jonas has explained it before. It's his way of reminding Jonas every day that he knows the psychic is full of shit.

Jonas turns the shoe in his hand examining it, or perhaps examining his reflection in the shiny leather. "It doesn't work that way," he says. "If it worked that way every psychic in the world would be winning the lotto. It comes and goes, and it doesn't work with everybody. I've been trying with Robert, but just haven't gotten anything. It's another realm we're tapping into—there are no hard and fast rules, you have to feel your way—"

"I get it," Schroder says, and holds up his hand. He wonders if hating himself will reach a peak and subside, or whether it's going to follow the current curve until he reaches the point he has to take up drinking and then smash every mirror in his house.

"No, you don't get it," Jones says, "and you never will. Not everybody in the spirit world wants to be spoken to, Carl. You don't get it because you don't want to get it."

"Well, whether I get it or not, Joe has the offer. He'll let us know tomorrow. Hardest part is giving him a reason to need the money."

"Surely he can use it to buy protection inside," Jonas says.

"He already has protection. He's in a cellblock with a bunch of people who all need protection."

"Well, then he can put the money toward a better defense."

Schroder smiles at him. "Maybe. But after the last few lawyers wanting to defend him, I'm not sure there'll be any takers."

Jonas stops scrubbing the shoe and stares at Schroder. "So what else do you suggest we offer him?" he asks, sounding annoyed.

Schroder shrugs. He isn't sure. "He'll either accept it or he won't. I guess with the timing and everything he doesn't really need the body found right now."

"Well, let's hope he sees the merit in telling us."

"It's still not right," Schroder says. "Doing it this way."

"He's getting prosecuted for so much as it is," Jones says, "and we all know he didn't actually kill Calhoun. He may have staged it and set Melissa up, but he's not the one who killed her and tied him up. When are you heading back to see him?"

"Same time tomorrow."

"Okay. Okay, good." He puts the shoe down and leans back in his chair. "What are you going to do with your signing bonus?"

Schroder isn't sure, and wishes Jonas hadn't asked. The signing bonus is ten thousand dollars. That's what he gets if Joe takes the deal. Joe gets fifty and Schroder gets ten and they're both making money off a dead detective and Schroder's curve of hating himself keeps reaching for the sky. "I don't know," he says, but he thinks he does know. As much as his family could do with it, it feels like blood money. He already has a few charities in mind—only when that check arrives he's not so sure how willing he'll be to part with it.

"You must have some ideas," Jonas says. "Why don't you treat your family to something? A holiday, perhaps? Or a new car?"

"Maybe," Schroder says. "Or maybe I'll treat my mortgage to an injection of cash."

Jonas laughs. "It's a good bonus," he says. "If it all works out as planned, there may be other bonuses in the future."

Schroder doesn't answer him. He hates thinking of his future these days.

"Tell me, Carl, what do you make of this referendum?" Jonas asks, changing the direction of the conversation.

"I think it's a good thing," Schroder answers, happy to move away from the bonus that puts him deeper into Jonas's pocket.

"You agree with the death penalty?"

"That's not what I mean," he says, even though he will be voting for it. "I mean it's a good thing that the people are going to be listened to."

"I agree. You know what I heard?"

"What?"

"I heard the prosecution will be asking for it if Joe is found guilty."

"I heard the same thing," Schroder says. It's not exactly a secret. "It makes it difficult to suggest to a man that fifty grand is useful when he's going to be put down anyway."

"But we don't know that. Even if the public votes for it, it may be years before it comes into play, and even more years before Joe is executed. Could be ten years away. Longer. Surely the money can be useful to him for that amount of time."

Schroder nods. He hates agreeing with Jonas, but he's right.

"Do you think there's an angle here?" Jonas asks.

"What kind of angle?"

"I don't know, not yet. But if Joe is executed, maybe that's good for the show. Do you think that, if the referendum is voted in and the death penalty is reinstated, and let's say the government makes an example out of Joe and executes him within the next year or two, do you think we can use that? Somehow, for the show? I'm thinking that if there are other victims of Joe's, other bodies, we could get him to talk. Somehow. And then—"

"And then after he's dead you'll be in touch with him and he'll tell you where these people are?"

"Something like that, yes. I don't know. Not exactly. I can see the pieces there, I can feel the potential, I'm just trying to piece it all together. I don't know what we could offer Joe that he would accept. But if we can figure something out, well, there could be a much bigger bonus in it for you. What do you think?"

He decides not to tell Jones what he really thinks. Instead he goes with, "I'm sure you'll work it out."

"I'm sure I will," Jones says, his mouth stretching into a smile. He goes back to scrubbing at his shoe. "Tell me, have you heard anything about this morning's homicide?"

"Probably less than you."

"I've heard the victim was shot twice in the chest," Jonas says. "Could be a professional killing."

"So I do know less than you."

"At the moment, yes, but you have the ability to find out more. Maybe there's something in this for us. How about you look into it? Give some of those detective friends of yours a call."

The problem is the detective friends haven't been great friends since Schroder started working for the TV station. "I'll do my best. I'm due on set in an hour."

"You want some lunch first?" Jonas asks, putting his shoes back on. "I'm starving."

"I've already eaten," Schroder says, and gets up and heads back to the elevator.

CHAPTER ELEVEN

Same view. Same voices. Every day like the last, only this week things are more exciting with all the visitors coming to see me. Once the trial is over I'll be back home and never having to worry about jail again—or visitors, for that matter—unless I get sent to a psychiatric hospital for a year or two first. Then I just have to worry about being gnawed on by other inmates and getting used to pastel-colored rooms.

I wait in my cell alone, which is the best kind of company in a place like this and really sums up the jail experience I've had so far thanks to the fact that nobody has tried to rape/stab me. After a while I need to stretch my legs a bit so I head out into the communal area where, if you were to take a poll, you'd learn I'm one of thirty innocent men. I'm Slow Joe. I'm a victim to my needs. I'm Joe Victim. I kill time chatting with a prisoner who was arrested and convicted after setting fire to a pet store. There were cats and dogs and birds, and there were fish. Lots of fish. I keep thinking of a way I could kill him. Fucking fish killer. There's nothing worse.

The pedophiles and other high-risk prisoners are chatting to each other, some playing cards, the damn weather a hot topic of conversation again. Others have retreated to their cells, and not all of them alone—laughing coming from some of them, grunts and whispers and the sounds of pillows being bitten coming from others.

The day drags on. Every day does. I wasn't kidding when I said I'd rather be hanged than endure this for the rest of my life. This isn't exactly living the dream.

After a while we're escorted into the lunch hall. Different cell-blocks all eat at different times, and our slot is one thirty. Lunch is made up of food that has to encompass at least forty different elements on the periodic table. It's a colorless and flavorless exercise that lasts fifteen minutes, but, surprisingly, always leaves me feeling full. The trays are made from thin metal that can't be broken into sharp useful pieces. The tables are all bolted to the ground, as are the long seats we share. Half a dozen guards all stand around the perimeter of the room watching us. The food is wet enough so you can hear everybody else chewing. Another inmate, a guy by the name of Edward Hunter, stares at me as he eats, gripping his knife quite hard, while I stare at the man who burned down the fish store, gripping my knife hard. But even though I'm staring at him I'm thinking of Melissa and how much I miss her. We could have been great together.

Or will be.

Once the jury lets me go.

I take my tray over to the table where Caleb Cole is and sit down next to him. There are scars on his arms and hands. He has the face of a man who has experienced a lot of physical pain. He has the kind of thinness and skin about him that suggests he's lost a lot of weight in a short time. Prison food isn't going to reverse that. He looks up at me then back at his food.

"My name's Joe," I tell him.

He doesn't say anything.

"It's Caleb, right?"

Still nothing.

"So, Caleb, I was thinking, maybe you and me could be friends."

"I don't want to make friends," he says, talking into his food.

"Everybody needs friends in here," I tell him. "You were in here for fifteen years, so you know that, right?"

"Fuck off," he says, which isn't a great way to start a friendship.

"We have a mutual friend," I tell him. "A guy by the name of Carl Schroder. He arrested you, right?"

"I can't talk about Schroder," he says, still looking at his food.

"Why not? He's the one who arrested you, right? Just before he was fired. I just want to know what happened that night. Something happened, I'm sure of it."

"Like I said earlier, fuck off, okay?"

"You feel like you owe him something to stay quiet?"

"Schroder is the reason I'm in here with you, and not in general population."

"Yeah? So why are you acting like his best friend?"

He stops eating. He puts his knife and fork down and twists toward me because I haven't fucked off like he originally asked. He puts his hand onto the side of my tray and slides it off the edge of the table. It crashes onto the floor with a loud bang and the food goes everywhere. Everybody in the room is staring at me. They've all gone quiet.

If he were a woman, I'd know what to do. I'd stab her right where she was. But he's not a woman. And he's not a man that I've already clubbed with a frying pan or shot or stabbed in the back. I suddenly feel very much out of my depth.

"I'm glad you came over to see me," he says, and suddenly I feel nervous. "I was in the hospital for a bit after being arrested, then they had me on suicide watch. They thought I wanted to die, and back then that was true. Not now. See, I have more to do before I want to die. Things to take care of. That's why I can't talk about Schroder. See, I just need to be left the fuck alone for the next twenty years so I can get out and carry on with my life."

"I heard you carried on with it a few months ago," I tell him. "Carrying on with your life doesn't bode well for others. That's why you're back in here."

"You think you're funny, don't you."

Yes. "No."

Sound starts back up in the room. More conversation. We stop being the center of attention.

"See, the thing is," he says, "even if I do make it another twenty years, the people I want to see on the outside may not even be around. So I'd have put up with twenty years of bullshit for nothing. That's a depressing thought. It's been with me since getting arrested. It gets me down. It's why I was on suicide watch. What got me through that was figuring I needed to focus on other things. And in a place like this, a man doesn't have too many options."

"One option is to tell me about Schroder," I remind him.

He shakes his head. "I already told you I'm not telling you about Schroder. Never. I tell you about him, and I'm back in general population."

"Come on, what did he do?"

"I think I'm going to start focusing on you."

"What? Why?"

"Because you're talking to me right now. Because I've been thinking about you over the last few weeks. Everybody in the city has been thinking about you. Tell me about your trial. I've heard things. I've heard you're running with an insanity defense."

"What of it?" I ask.

"My daughter was murdered," he says. "Fifteen years ago. You heard about that?"

I shake my head. Other people and the things that happen to them don't bother me unless it relates to me somehow.

"She was murdered by a guy who should have been in jail, but you want to know why he wasn't?"

I shake my head. I don't really want to know, or care. He takes the headshake as an indication to carry on.

"Because he'd escaped conviction two years earlier of hurting another little girl because he used an insanity defense."

I slowly nod. This is good. Very good. "So what you're saying is it works."

He stares hard at me. Then he slides his food tray away from himself and steps out from behind the table. He's thinner than me, a little taller, but there's something in his face that is frightening. I think if he were put into general population he'd get by just fine.

"I don't want you using an insanity defense," he says, and maybe he should be my lawyer. "People need to be responsible for what they did. It's not right that doctors can come along and make it otherwise."

"It truly isn't my fault I did the things they say I did," I tell him. "I don't even remember any of it."

"Uh huh. So you're using it," he says, pointing at me. "The defense. You're using the defense. The same defense that allowed my daughter to be killed."

"How old was your daughter?" I ask.

He's not ready for the question, but he's been studying because he knows the answer. "She was ten."

"Then there's no reason we can't be friends. No reason you can't help me out and tell me what Detective Schroder did to lose his job."

"I don't follow."

"Well your daughter was too young to be my type."

He stares at me angrily and I'm not sure why. All I can put it down to is his jealousy. I'll be getting out of here in a matter of weeks, and he's stuck here for twenty more years, and that's the kind of thing people in here don't like.

"Three days," he says.

"Three days for what?"

"Your trial starts in three days, so that gives me three days to decide whether or not I want to kill you," he says. "I'm in here for twenty years no matter what. Killing you won't add to that. Killing you may even get my sentenced reduced. I'll think about it," he says. "I'll let you know soon," he says, and he walks away.

I watch him go. Nobody else does. Nobody is watching me either—they've all gone back to their meals. My meal is all over the floor and Caleb's is mostly still there, so I start in on his. I think about his three days and wonder if it's possible he can do what he just said. Three days to kill me. But I see it as three days to win him over. Show him some of the Joe charm and get him talking. I see it like that because I generally have a positive outlook on life—it's why people like me so much. Even so, my hands are shaking a little as I eat.

Thursday afternoon carries on and, like all other Thursdays and Mondays, I have a visitor. It seems as if today people just can't get enough of me. From Monday the country won't be able to get enough of me. They're all going to be glued to their TV sets watching the news.

The same two asshole guards lead me down to the visitors' area. It's a much bigger room than the rooms my last two visitors spoke to me in. It's the size of a large conference room that can accommodate perhaps a dozen prison members at a time, along with those coming to see them, and along with some guards. Today the room is mostly empty. A couple of prisoners talking with their wives. With their kids. There are hugs and tears and there are guards watching everything with eagle eyes. There's a baby in a pram that keeps staring at me, and for a moment I wonder what life would be like having children. If I had a son I could teach him to fish, to throw a ball, to use a hooker and not pay. Then I think about nappy changes and sleepless nights, and I allow myself a few seconds to think about that life, then I turn toward the person who has come here to see me.

My mother.

She is sitting in the corner with a handbag clutched in her lap and an old man by her side. She doesn't look like she has aged.

If anything, she seems to look younger. She is certainly dressing better. And she looks happier. I hope that's because of Walt, and not because her only and favorite son is in jail.

She starts smiling the moment I sit down opposite her. It's unusual. If my mom can smile it means I can win the lottery.

"Hello, Joe," she says, and she leans forward as though to hug me, and manages to restrain herself by simply touching my arm. "You look well," she says, and there must be something wrong with her if she can smile and give me a compliment at the same time. I'm going with brain tumor. Or she's had a stroke. I don't ask her how she is.

"Hello, son," Walt says, even though I'm not his son—it's just an old-person thing to do, like forgetting to put their dentures back in or drying the poodle in the microwave. I don't answer him and he looks away, finding something interesting in the texture of the brick wall over my shoulder, perhaps thinking the same thing I was earlier about them being timeless.

"Mom," I say, "I've missed you," which isn't exactly true.

"I wanted to bring you some meat loaf," she says, "but I wasn't allowed."

"I think it is allowed," I say.

Walt says nothing. In fact nobody does for about ten seconds. Until my mom carries on, her beaming smile beginning to really annoy me now because it's making me want to smile too.

"We've got great news," she says, and her use of the word *we've* suggests the news isn't going to be about me, or about me getting out of here, but about her and Walt, and unless that great news has something to do with her kicking him in the balls and setting him on fire it isn't something I want to hear.

"I hate it in here," I say. "I didn't do any of the things they say I did, or at least I don't remember doing them. I'm sick. I don't even know how they could think—"

"We're getting married!" she says.

"Plus there are some people here that want to kill me. They have to keep me in a separate—"

"Can you believe that? Married! Could life be any better?" she asks.

"It could be, if there weren't people in here who want me dead."

"We're in love," she says, "and we see no reason to wait. We're going to marry next week. It's all so sudden, but exciting! We want you to be there."

"I was hoping you could be my best man," Walt says.

"Oh, what a wonderful idea," Mom says, and squeezes Walt's arm while giving him a look she has never given me—a look that I imagine can only be described as *loving*.

Walt looks happy to have gotten the squeeze. That better be all he's getting.

"You're getting married," I say, finally letting her words settle. "Married."

"Yes, married, Joe. On Monday. I'm over the moon!" Mom says.

"I might not be able to make it." I say.

"Because of the jail thing?" Mom asks. "I'm sure they can arrange for you to be released for the wedding. I'll talk to somebody about it."

"It won't happen," I say. "There is no chance at all. My trial starts the same day."

"Then it's perfect," she says. "You'll already be out of jail. We only need you for an hour."

"I don't think the police are going to agree to that."

"Don't be so negative," she says.

"Why don't you wait until I'm released?"

"Why do you have to always be difficult?"

"I'm not trying to be difficult," I tell her.

"You are trying, and well done, Joe, because you're succeeding. Already you're ruining our day!"

"Perhaps leave the boy alone, dear," Walt says. "He'll come around in his own time. It can't be easy on him getting a new father."

Mom seems to think about what Walt says, which is a new trick because I don't think she's ever thought about anything I ever said. "No, I guess it can't be," she says, still giving me a sour look.

"I'm not trying to be difficult," I say again. "It's just that, well, the people on TV seem to think I'm guilty, but you can never trust those guys," I say, and I know the news is all about sales, all about selling fear, and isn't an accurate representation of how the country is feeling. "What about the newspapers? What do they say?"

"I don't know," Mom answers.

"You don't know?"

"We haven't been reading them," Walt says.

"We just haven't been keeping up on the news," Mom offers. "We don't watch it and we don't read it."

"But I am the news. Surely you'd keep up on me."

"The news is depressing," Mom says.

"And depressing," Walt adds.

"We haven't been following the news at all. Why would we?" Mom says.

"Because I'm in the news," I say.

"Well, how am I supposed to know that?" Mom asks, sounding short.

"You'd know if you cared enough to turn on a TV and watch anything other than one of those damn English dramas."

"God, we have to tell you," Walt says, and he leans forward. "Last night, you wouldn't believe who turned out to be Karen's real father."

"It was exciting," Mom says.

I listen to them tell me about the program, and I store the information and I think about Pickle and Jehovah, my goldfish from another life, and how I'd tell them about the same program, and I wonder if they used to think the same thing I'm thinking now. I hope not. I miss them. My little pets with their five-second memories—they wouldn't even remember dying.

"Can you believe we're really getting married?" Mom asks, when a guard comes over and tells us our time is nearly up.

"I can't believe it," I tell them, and I don't want to believe it either.

"You don't have to call me *Dad*," Walt says, "at least not yet."

"He'll come around," Mom says.

"Of course he will," Walt says. "He is your son."

Mom stands up. She's carrying a plastic bag full of something. Walt follows her move. She moves toward me and gives me a hug. It's a tight bear hug in which I can smell old-lady perfume and old-lady soap and old lady.

"He's so much better than your father," she whispers. "And I'm glad you're not gay, Joe. The things the police told us that you did—no gay man would do that."

"He's definitely not gay," Walt says, because my mom's whispering is loud enough for him to hear. My mom has no idea how to whisper.

"And nor are you," my mom says, pulling back and looking at Walt. She giggles a little bit. "But after what we tried last night, you wouldn't know."

They both laugh. The floor falls away from me and I collapse into the chair. My mom turns to leave, but seems to remember the plastic bag she's carrying, and hands it to me. "These are for you."

"What?"

"These. Are for you," she says, louder and emphasizing each word as if trying to break a language barrier.

I take the bag from her. It's full of books. Which is great because I need more books—not as much as I need a gun—but it's still good.

"They're from your girlfriend," she says.

For a moment the prison fades away, and I remember myself cuffed to a tree with a pair of pliers hovering around my nuts. Then I remember lying in Melissa's bed, the way her body felt, the tight curves, the way her eyes would close when she was focusing on the way things felt between the sheets. My heart races and I feel the skin on the back of my neck start to tingle. "My what?"

"She was very lovely," Walt says, and mom gives him the kind of look she usually gives me—the one where she just bit the end of her tongue and her face scrunches up in pain.

"Who gave them to you?" I ask.

"We already told you," Mom says, and they start to walk to the exit. A guard moves toward the door to let them out. "We'll see you Monday," she says. "It'll be a small affair. Ten people at the most. You should ask the prison warden today so he'll have plenty of time to organize letting you out."

"I'll be—"

"Your cousin Gregory will be there," she says. "He has a new car."

"In court."

"Joe—"

"I'm sorry," I say, holding up my hand. "I'm being difficult."

"You are, but I love you anyway," she says, and she leans down and gives me a hug and then she is gone.

CHAPTER TWELVE

Lunch is a big breakfast. It consists of bacon and eggs and sausages and coffee—all of it very, very good. A breakfast like that can change the way a man will look at life—at least that's the blurb beneath it in the menu under the heading "Heart Stopper." Halfway through the meal Schroder sees no reason to doubt either the blurb or the name.

He is sitting alone at the counter filling the hole that's been growing inside of him since missing breakfast. There's blood on the floor and a chalk outline of a body six feet to his right. Two of the tables are overturned and there's some broken glass. There are fifteen people in the diner and he's the only one eating. Evidence markers are scattered around the room, photo evidence scales that measure the size of blood drops and handprints and footprints. Fingerprinting powder on various surfaces. Crime-scene tape by the door.

Just like a crime scene.

Well, almost like a crime scene.

Another phone call to Detective Hutton gave him little in the way of information about this morning's homicide, but enough to know that there's nothing of value in it to Jonas Jones, and enough to know what Hutton meant when he said it was a bad one. The victim was an ex-con who did time for smuggling weapons into the country. The smuggling was one thing, but what those weapons were used for was a whole different thing. He didn't care who the buyers were, just as the buyers didn't care about the people who would have died if they had managed to detonate the various explosives they were trying to stack around the parliament building in the country's capital city. Schroder wasn't so sure much of the public would have cared either if the country had woken up one morning a hundred politicians shorter than the day before. The guy who imported the explosives was Derek Rivers and Derek was treated to twelve years of cinder-block views. He was released from jail a year ago, and this morning was treated to two shots to the chest. According to Hutton, electronic explosive sniffers have confirmed that Rivers has recently been in touch with explosives.

"There was a manhole in the wardrobe," Hutton had told him. "He'd stored weapons and explosives under there. Our best guess is whoever he bought them for is who shot him. That means somebody is covering their tracks. That means—"

"The explosives are going to be used for something pretty bad," Schroder had finished for him before they'd hung up.

Schroder could remember Rivers from the case way back when. He was a real piece of work. Not the kind of guy anybody is going to miss. Nothing in it for the psychic. Not yet. Maybe if somebody manages to blow something up and take a lot of lives—then there's a whole lot of somethings in it for Jonas.

Jonas Jones.

He can barely stand the smug bastard. In the past Jonas has ruined cases, gotten in the way, he's released information to the public that has sprung police traps and gotten people hurt. There are no real psychics, but somehow Jones has a loyal fan base that seems to be growing by the day. And, if Jones is to find Detective Calhoun's body that fan base will grow stronger, it will grow in numbers, and no doubt Jones will churn out another bullshit book. At the very least it will make for great TV.

In some ways he hopes Joe keeps his mouth shut. Trumping that desire is Calhoun's family's right to have his body returned. In the background, of course, is the bonus. Despite everything, he needs the money. His family does. He's profiting on something bad, but hey, dentists profit on cavities, roofers profit from storms, car wreckers profit from accidents.

Sometimes Schroder likes to think that, honestly, he didn't have any real choice but to accept the job. After all, he was unemployed. He has a select set of job skills that were of no use because he couldn't be a cop again, and though he had applied for a PI license, he had been turned down with no explanation within a week of applying. He was sure it was something to do with the police department. Somebody somewhere had thrown a wrench in the works because they felt the last thing the city needed was another private investigator. He could flip burgers. He couldn't sell cars. He could go back to school. He couldn't work in retail. And when the TV studio approached him to be the police consultant on set for Jonas's show, plus for other TV shows, he took it. He gave it only a day's thought. It was better pay than being on the force. Fewer hours. Less bullshit. Only dealing with Jonas made him want to shower more. If it was all about Jonas, he'd rather have shot himself. But it's not. It's about his family, about paying the bills, about keeping the house, about forging ahead and finding a new career path.

And anyway—dealing with Jonas is only a small part of his job and, right now, not part of his job at all.

One of the producers of the TV show *The Cleaner* comes over and tells him he needs to finish up, that shooting is going to begin in fifteen minutes. The show is about a pair of crime-scene cleaners who struggle with the emotional impact of a rising crime rate, centering around a main character on the edge of a nervous breakdown who, scriptwriters have told him, keeps thinking about how he could get away with a murder of his own since he can make a crime scene "disappear." They're currently shooting the sixth episode, with the first going to air in two weeks' time. Already there are billboards up across the city, ads on TV, articles in newspapers to promote the show. If the reviews are good, it will continue to be shot. It doesn't bother Schroder either way. This show, or the next show, or another show—he gets paid the same either way. He guesses *The Cleaner* has an okay concept—he's not big on TV shows—but it's his job to help stage the scenes and to give authenticity to them. The diner they're shooting in today is a real diner, closed for the afternoon, but the owner, who is being paid for having his business shut for the day, offered to cook Schroder a quick lunch. Schroder isn't big into hugging people, but he definitely could have hugged that guy.

He finishes up his meal and hides the plate behind the counter. The story, so it goes, is that two men broke in during the night and tortured the owner for information, pounding bits of him into the floor with a hammer, getting blood and bone in places that require elbow grease and chemicals and witty banter and no doubt some mood music too when it goes through editing.

The actors get into their positions.

"Everything good?" one of the scriptwriters asks him, and the scriptwriter is wearing a T-shirt with the words *Climb on board Uncle Daddy's love bus* across it, and Schroder wonders if the scriptwriter scripted that himself. He hopes not—because that doesn't look good for the show.

Schroder takes one last look out over the scene. "For the most part it all looks fine."

"Most part?"

"Chalk outline," he says, and not for the first time.

"I know," the scriptwriter says.

"I know you know," he says. "But cops really don't use them."

"But movie and TV people do, and it's what people expect to see," the writer says, and not for the first time either. "People don't like not seeing things they're expecting to see. It messes with them."

"You don't give people enough credit."

"Really? You were on the force for what, fifteen years? Twenty? Do you think people really deserve a lot of credit?"

Schroder smiles. He concedes the point. "You're good to go," he says.

Schroder stands off to the side of the room and watches the action take place. Hopefully it'll look better when it's on TV, because at the moment it just looks like a badly performed play. Thirty minutes into it his cell phone starts to vibrate. He takes it out of his pocket and checks the caller ID. It's Hutton. The cameras aren't rolling so he steps outside, not having to worry about sound.

"Something's happened," Hutton tells him.

"Yeah?"

"May be related, may not be. But Tristan Walker was found dead about fifteen minutes ago. He was shot twice in the chest in his house."

Tristan Walker. Husband of Daniela Walker. Daniela Walker, victim of Joe Middleton. Shot twice in the chest just like Derek Rivers. "Shit," Schroder says.

"Yeah, that sums it up."

"So the theory is?" Schroder asks, and he's already working on one of his own.

He can almost hear Hutton shrugging. "We don't know," Hutton says. "I mean, this morning we thought it was about a potential bombing, but now we've got the husband of one of the Carver's victims. The same victim that we were never entirely sure that Joe actually killed," Hutton says.

There were always things about that particular homicide that didn't fit with Joe's pattern. Joe has been asked about it, but like all the homicides, he's sticking with the story of not remembering. It's a story that won't work well for him in court. It can't do. Then he thinks about what the scriptwriter said, about giving people too much credit. Nothing in the legal system is a sure thing. Schroder starts walking to his car.

"We want you to come here," Hutton says. "If it's related to the Carver case, you should be here. It was your case. You might see something that's relevant."

"I'm already on my way," he says, and hangs up.

CHAPTER THIRTEEN

Exercise hour is mandatory, unless you've just been shivved or raped by one or more of the other inmates, which, in general population, is mandatory too. All thirty of us are outside in the rain, with views of wire fences and guard posts that look like small air traffic control towers. There is nowhere to run, except back and forth across the yard, which I guess must be the point of exercise hour. I feel my own humanity the most when I'm around these people. If Schroder came and saw me right now, he'd see it. He'd see I'm just an innocent man.

I walk the perimeter of the yard feeling the rain on my face, letting it soak my clothes, because after exercise hour is shower hour, and our Thursday showers come with a change of jumpsuit. For an hour a day I get to stretch my legs and it's never long enough, and I never get to stretch them toward any of the nice women this city has to offer. Outside the walls the sounds of machinery fill the air—sparks of metal fly as grinders cut new pieces of steel and hammer drills dig holes into brick, construction taking place as a new wing of the jail is added, more room added for the increasing prison population. Some of the guys start kicking a soccer ball around. Only way football could be any gayer would be if they stripped off their shirts after scoring a goal and group hugged. My dad used to love football. Others are pushing weights, working on stretching the slabs of muscle where tattoos are flexing under the strain.

Melissa visited my mother.

That's what I keep thinking about as Caleb Cole stares at me from across the yard with the kind of look that tells me he still has a long way to go to warm to my insanity defense. I try not to look at him, but every minute or so I'm curious if he's still watching me so I glance in his direction, only to find that he is.

I look out the fence where there are other fences and other patches of field. Beyond the furthest of fences is freedom. Joe Victim needs that freedom. Joe Victim was never meant to be contained in a place like this. Joe Victim needs to spread his wings and fly.

I turn my thoughts to my mother and Walt, which is unfortunate because I end up thinking about what they're going to get up to on their honeymoon. It makes me feel ill. Walt, with his wrinkly hands on my mother, my mother's wrinkles sagging in all the places no man other than Walt would want to see, the way all those wrinkles lock into place like snapping pieces of a jigsaw together. I'm starting to think the only way to get rid of those thoughts would be to walk across the yard and hand Caleb Cole a sharpened toothbrush. Instead I focus on the books mom brought in for me.

From my girlfriend.

From Melissa.

The plastic bag was taken from me by the guards, but I was allowed to keep the books. The bag was considered a weapon. The books were considered a joke. Adam laughed at the titles. I'm sure he's still laughing about it. Melissa visited my mother and gave her a handful of romance paperbacks to give to me, but why?

There are only two reasons I can think of. The first is that she knows I really love romance novels. Spending two nights with Melissa and having her stalk me the week before, she learned that in my heart I am nothing but a true romantic. Her books are a gift to me to help me pass my days before we can be together again.

The second reason needs looking into, and when exercise hour finishes I walk back to my cell before shower hour and start looking for it. I pick the first book up. It's called *Bodies of Lust*, and at first I think it might be more than just a romance novel, that it might be more of a description of the nights I spent with Melissa before my world was thrown off course, but reading a few pages at random I quickly learn otherwise. I flick through the book, looking for bent pages, looking for highlighted passages, or any kind of pencil markings, but there is nothing.

I open book two. An envelope falls out and lands on my stomach. My heart skips a beat, but when I turn it over I see it's already been torn open, no doubt by the guards when they were checking for drugs. So whatever message Melissa has written for me, they've seen it. I open it up. It's a card. Only it's not from Melissa. It's from my mother. It's a wedding invitation. It has a picture on it. It's an illustration, not a photo, and in the illustration two cartoon hands are cutting the wedding cake with a big knife. It reminds me of a knife I used to have. I read the details and shake my head while doing so. I put the card back into the envelope and pick the book back up.

There are no hidden messages in it. The same goes for the other books. Books with bad titles and bad writing and bad characters that make me warm inside when I read them. No markings, no messages, no point, and the guards would have flicked through them for the same reason well before my mother ever handed them to me. But there has to be something, otherwise why would Melissa give them to me? And she would have known she couldn't write in them, or underline things—because she would have known the books would be searched. So what then? What am I missing?

I open *Show Love to Get Love*, which, I'm pretty sure, could be the worst title ever picked for a book. But these kinds of books all normally have bad names. It's part of the appeal. Bad names and ripped men on the covers, women wearing sheer clothing. Except in this case the title sounds like a self-help book. I get a few chapters into it, realizing that the way for Belinda, the main character, to find love is for her to give her love to as many men as she can in the hope that one of them will look past the fact that she's acting a little like a whore.

It's a short book and I'm a quick reader, but I still skim it because even though time is something I have plenty of, I feel an urgency to find Melissa's message. I figure skim the books now, and if I miss the message then read them in detail later. So I find out Belinda's fate, which is to marry a rich man who used to be a gigolo, but who was left ten million dollars by an old lady he used to service. It's a timeless classic.

I'm halfway through another when shower time arrives. The group of thirty somehow separates itself into different social classes. They do it by the crimes they committed. They see some crimes as better than others. Healthier, I suppose. Somehow that makes them better people. I don't know. It's a strange world, but here I am living in strange times, where a guy can burn down a retirement home with twelve people inside and be treated like a king compared to somebody like Santa Kenny, who raped three children and got caught with a fourth. Lines are being drawn all over the place in this world and none of them make sense. I don't know what lines to stand behind, which ones to cross. I'm in the serial-killer gang all by myself even though I'm not the only serial killer in here. Edward Hunter, he's by himself too. He killed a bunch of people and people call him a hero because they were bad people, but that doesn't set him free. Caleb Cole is in a group of one too. We should be forming a club. We should get T-shirts made up.

There is nothing fun about showering with other naked men—though, for some reason, my father's voice pops into my head and tells me it doesn't have to be that way. I'm not sure what he's getting at—but his voice has popped into my head every other time I've stood naked in front of all these other men. It's humiliating.

The showers are like gym showers, a large communal area with plenty of different sprays and lots of taps and plenty of tiles everywhere. It's a concrete floor with a dozen different drains. The air is thick with steam and the water a little too hot and there are only a few cakes of soap to go around so we have to share, which is pretty awful when they get handed to you with the occasional pubic hair caked into the surface. A few minutes into the shower and suddenly the men immediately to my left and to my right move further to their left and right and I'm alone.

Then not so alone, as Caleb Cole comes up to me.

"I've made my decision," he says.

The water is pouring down on us. Steam is rising. The air is thick and I feel a little light-headed. "And?"

"And I'm going to kill you," he says, and his fist moves so quickly I don't even see it happening, not until it hits me solidly in the stomach, knocking the air out of me and dropping me to my knees. Caleb takes a step back and cradles his hand against his chest and covers it with his other one.

"Hey," one of the guards calls out, "what's going on there?" he asks, but the steam is too thick for him to see that well and he's too dry and lazy to really come and check.

"He slipped over," Cole shouts out. "People slip in showers."

I look up at him, but stay on my knees, which is not a great height to be at in a room full of naked men unless you're a football player.

"Is that right?" the guard shouts back.

"Yeah," I say. "I slipped."

The guard doesn't respond.

"As soon as I find something I can shape into a blade, I'm going to cut you open," Caleb says, and he starts washing himself down while staring at me, the scars across his body disappearing behind lathers of soap. "What do you think about that?"

I think I need to find something sharp too.

"I can pay you," I tell him. "Twenty thousand dollars."

He stops soaping himself. He twists his head and his eyes narrow. "What are you talking about?"

"To leave me alone," I say. "I'll pay you twenty thousand dollars and you can use that money to pay somebody to finish the job on the outside that you're going to have to wait twenty years to do yourself."

He slowly nods, the sides of his mouth turning down as he does. "Okay," he says.

"Okay, you'll take it?"

He shakes his head. "Okay, I'll think about it," he says. "Something like that is going to require a lot of thought." He rinses off the soap. "I'll let you know tomorrow," he says, and then he disappears back into the steam and I'm left alone on my knees, wondering now what my chances are of even making it to trial.

CHAPTER FOURTEEN

Fate is on her side. Melissa didn't think so, not when she had to put two bullets into Sam Winston and not when she had to open fire a couple of more times today, but it's led her to the support meeting and if fate wasn't on her side then the meeting would have been on any other day of the week and not today. Statistically she had a one-in-seven chance. Or, the other way of looking at it is she had a six-out-of-seven chance the meeting wouldn't be today. That's not luck, it's fate. Good fate. Her life has been full of bad fate. Her sister, herself, bad shit happening. Now it's good shit. Like finding the building earlier opposite the back of the courthouse, unfinished, the construction company gone broke the way construction companies are apt to do in this day and age. Seven stories of half-completed offices, a whole bunch of them with perfect views out over the back of the courthouse. She decides to wait and see what else fate can take care of tonight before embracing it.

Finding the support group wasn't hard. Three minutes online is all it took. And it's not just a support group for victims of Joe

Middleton, but for other victims too—or, more accurately, family of victims who, so it seems, have labeled themselves as victims. It's a community hall in Belfast, a suburb to the north of the city that on bad days smells like the dump only a few miles away and on other bad days is just Belfast. There are twenty cars in the parking lot out front, and hers makes it twenty-one. It's still raining and still cold, but the forecast suggests an improvement over the next few days.

She takes her umbrella—actually, it used to belong to Walker up until earlier today—and makes her way into the hall, keeping a close eye on the ground to avoid the puddles forming where bits of pavement have broken away. She walks alongside a pair of elderly people who have their arms around each other as they share an umbrella. They nod at her and offer a kind smile. She wonders if they're here because she killed their son. She has changed wigs again—this time she's gone black.

The older man holds the door open for his wife, and keeps the door open for Melissa and she smiles at him and thanks him and can't think of anybody she's hurt who looks like them. She steps into a hall big enough to hold a wedding reception and ugly enough to hold a twenty-first birthday party. Every wall is covered in wooden paneling. The floor inside the doorway is wet with footprints and she steps around them carefully, not wanting to fall over in front of these people and have to fake an early labor. She can see and hear the heaters in the hall blasting out hot air, but it's still cold in here. She closes her new umbrella and leans it up against the wall where there are a dozen similar ones. She takes off her jacket and carries it over her arm. There are thirty people in here, maybe thirty-five. Some are standing around in groups of two or three and chatting with some kind of familiarity. Others are by themselves. A set of chairs form a circle at the far end of the room, and beyond the chairs is a stage where in the past she guesses bands have sung and fathers have given speeches. At the moment there are more chairs than there are people. A long table has been set up with coffee and sandwiches. She wonders if in a few years all these people will begin to socialize, if meetings in summer will be held in parks and people will bring along picnics. Happy little social groups and lifelong friends brought about by death and misery, perhaps some intermarrying and interbreeding to go along with it. Both she and Joe have contributed to that. They should be proud.

"How far along are you?"

The voice comes a couple of feet from her left and almost makes her jump. Melissa turns toward the woman and smiles. She doesn't know what the hell it is with women and why they keep asking her this when they see the bump. They think it's their Goddamn business. Women who have shared the experience of giving birth seem to think that gives them the right to talk to any pregnant stranger they want to.

"Baby's due next week," she says, rubbing her stomach.

The woman smiles. She can only be four or five years older than Melissa. She's wearing a wedding ring and Melissa wonders if she has been pregnant or wants to be, and wonders if the man she wanted to make her pregnant is no longer in this world.

"Boy or a girl?" she asks.

"A surprise," Melissa says, smiling, because it really would be a surprise. She's wearing a wedding ring of her own and she begins to twirl it around on her finger. She's seen married people do that too. "It's what we both wanted."

"I saw you come in alone," the woman says, and her smile disappears. "Your husband, he's not . . . not why you're here, is he?"

"No, no, thank God," Melissa answers.

The woman nods slowly, a sad look on her face, then holds out her hand. "My name is Fiona Hayward," she says.

"Stella," Melissa says, simply because it's the name she decided to use on the way over here. She takes the woman's hand. It's warm. "Your husband—is he why you're here?"

"He was murdered nearly a month ago," Fiona says, and her voice catches a little and her tears well up a little. "At home. Some madman followed him home and stabbed him."

"I'm sorry," Melissa says.

"Everybody is," Fiona says. "At least they got the guy. And you?"

"My sister," she says. "She was murdered."

"I'm sorry," Fiona says.

"Everybody is," Melissa says, then smiles at the woman who smiles back and nods. "It was a long time ago," Melissa adds, remembering her sister, the funeral, the toll it took on her family.

"This is my first time here," Fiona says. "I don't know anybody, and I feel somewhat nervous about being here. I had plenty of friends and family offer to come with me, but, well, I wanted to come alone. I can't explain why that is, really. Truth is I didn't even think I would come along, but, well," she says, then gives a small nervous laugh, "here I am."

"My first time too," Melissa says, trying to think of a way to free herself from this conversation. She thinks about the gun in her pregnancy suit. She draws comfort from it.

"Do you mind if . . . if I sit with you?"

Yep. She thinks about taking that gun out. "That would be nice," she says.

People are starting to fill the seats. Some are carrying coffee. Some drag their seats a little closer together. When everybody is seated a man in his mid to late fifties goes around picking up the empty chairs and moving them beyond the circle, others dragging their seats forward to close the gaps. He has a few days' worth of stubble and a pair of designer glasses and expensive shoes. Attractive, with good taste, gray hair—but only in the temples, the rest of it dark brown. Everybody keeps chatting among themselves until Designer Glasses takes a seat then everybody goes quiet. Melissa can't take her eyes off him.

"Thank you again for coming along," he says, his voice is deep and, in other circumstances, probably seductive. Melissa likes him. "I see there are a few new faces in the crowd," he says, "and I hope the rest of us can offer you some support and companionship, and some hope too. We're all here out of tragedy. We're all here because we faced an incredible ugliness. For those who don't know me, my name is Raphael." He smiles. "My mother was an art scholar," he adds, "hence the name," as if Melissa should care, "and my daughter was a murder victim," he says, "hence why I'm here."

He delivers the line with the casualness of somebody who's said it a hundred times.

"This support group," he says, "was created from loss. My daughter's name was Angela, and she was killed last year by Joe Middleton," he says. "He took away a daughter, he took away a wife, and he took away a mother. A few of you are here because of him, and others are here because of similar men to Joe, or similar women," he says, and there's a moment where Melissa thinks everybody in the room is going to turn toward her, but of course that doesn't happen. "I'm a full-time grief counselor," he adds. "I've been helping people for nearly thirty years, and yet when I lost my daughter I could do nothing to help myself until I realized I needed to be with others like me. So we're all here to help each other," he says, smiling as he looks from face to face, spending an extra second on Melissa because there's more of her to take in. "We're not here to make the pain go away, because nothing can do that. We're here to share it, to understand it. We're here because we need to be."

Melissa has to suppress a yawn as she looks around the room at the faces. She didn't have time for a nap and the best she can hope for is that this won't take long. She's so tired she could sleep for the next twenty-four hours. Out of all these people, though, somebody will help her. She just has to invest an hour. Or however long it is these meetings go. Talking about your pain doesn't make it go away. When her sister was killed she had to talk to a shrink every week for a year and it didn't help an iota. All the shrink kept doing was looking at her legs.

Everybody is staring at Raphael. Lots of warm bodies for her to choose from, and she doesn't doubt one of them has to be angry enough at Joe to shoot him.

The trick is to figure out who.

CHAPTER FIFTEEN

The first thing Schroder has to get past is the ring of media vans that have shown up. They're blocking the end of the street, along with the local sightseers. With all the murders in Christchurch he's surprised people still come out to watch the show, especially in this weather. There really is, he supposes, nothing quite like a good homicide. It makes for great reality and it makes for great TV. The reporters are holding up umbrellas and the camera operators are wrapped in wet weather gear and the cameras are protected by plastic linings. What the city needs—no, strike that—what humanity needs right now is a bolt of lightning, something strong and biblical to come down from the heavens and land in the middle of them all. He wonders if that's something Jonas Jones might think he can arrange.

He can't get the car past them. There's no way through, and the only way he could give it a good go would be to hit them at a pace somewhere near the speed limit and scatter them all like bowling pins. He has no siren and therefore has to park on the wrong side of the crowd, with them and a lot of rain between him and the scene.

The exhaustion he was feeling in his last few months of being a cop wasn't turned in with his gun and badge. Instead it's been dogging him like a head cold that won't go away. He reaches into his pocket and pulls out the packet of Wake-E tablets that he always keeps within reach these days and swallows one of them, then decides to chase it with another. In five minutes the exhaustion won't be gone, but it will be bottled inside him with all that other exhaustion he's built up over the years.

He climbs out of the car into the rain and shoulders his way through the onlookers. The officers guarding the cordon have to take a double take as he approaches them—they know he's no longer a cop, but they're thinking perhaps that's no longer the case. Before he can start explaining himself, Kent comes toward him, an umbrella keeping the rain off her. She has a quick word to the officers and then Schroder lifts the crime-scene tape and ducks under it. The house is in a quiet neighborhood, not the same house the Walker family used to live in. That place was burned down the same night Detective Calhoun went missing. Burned down, no doubt, by Joe. Since then the land was sold. This one is half the size, a single-story place that's perhaps five years old at the most, the same color scheme from one house to the next, pale browns and grays that look washed out by the rain.

Kent holds the umbrella higher so it covers them both, just not that well. He has to take his shoes off at the door and put on a pair of nylon booties. The body is in the hallway, just inside from the front door. Hutton comes and joins them.

Schroder feels like he's back on the job. The smells and sights and sounds all confirm he's in an authentic crime scene and nobody is going to draw a chalk outline around anything and ask him if he thinks the dialogue could be tightened. He's cold and wet and miserable, which completes the sense of realism. He can see down the end of the hall into the lounge. Dark brown carpet and plush sofas and warm color walls. All very homey, except for Tristan Walker himself, who is lying on his side with one hand on his chest and the other hand pinned beneath him. It's been twelve months since he last saw Tristan Walker. Walker was staying with his parents at the time. Schroder went there to tell him they'd made an arrest.

Kent and Hutton couldn't be more opposite. Hutton is overweight. He wasn't that way when he joined the force, couldn't have been because he never would have been accepted, but now the guy consumes so much sugar he has to stay out of the rain for fear of dissolving. Hutton remains on the force because he's so large it would almost be like firing two detectives—though, ironically, it was simple for the department to fire Schroder. Back when Caleb Cole made him kill somebody.

Kent is attractive. Stunning, even. The kind of woman you look at and would give up a week of your life just to see her smile. No doubt half the guys here are in love with her.

"This is the third victim," Kent says.

"Huh?"

"The third victim," she repeats.

He lets the information settle for a few seconds. "You're telling me you've got two others like this?" he asks.

Kent smiles at him. "I'm glad your mind has stayed sharp since leaving the force, Carl. That's some quick addition."

"You should see me with crayons," he says. "I always stay within the lines."

"Sounds like you're living on the edge." She steps around the body so they can talk to each other, the three of them forming a triangle with a dead guy in the middle.

"Victim one was last week," Kent says. "Guy by the name of Sam Winston."

"I read about him in the papers. He was found in an abandoned building in town. From what I read it looked like he was killed by a drug dealer."

"That's what we thought too. Name mean anything to you?"

Schroder shakes his head. "Should it?"

"Probably not. He used to be in the army until he was discharged five years ago. He had a pretty big drug problem, hence why we believed that was related to the way he died. He wasn't even in the army for long. Two years. After that he spent his days being unemployed and earning unemployment checks."

"And now you think there's a connection."

"It looks the same. As soon as the bullets are pulled from Walker we'll send them to ballistics and check for a match."

"So you only have a theory?" Schroder asks.

Hutton shakes his head. "We have a time line," he says. "People get killed in all sorts of strange ways in this city," he says, "but not often by guns, and here we've got three victims within a week all with the same gunshot pattern."

Schroder nods. It's too much to ignore. "No connection between Walker and Rivers?"

Kent answers the question. "We've got a guy who sells guns and explosives, and another guy who's trained in using them. But no connection between them."

"Not yet anyway," Hutton says.

"And nothing between either of those two and Walker," Schroder says.

"Just the way they died," Kent says.

"Walker didn't have a drug habit?"

"If he did, he kept it well hidden. There's nothing here to suggest he was using."

"So what do you want from me?" Schroder asks.

"We want you to help us with Walker," Kent says. "You knew him. You spent time with him and his family. What would a guy like Walker have in common with Rivers and Winston?"

"I didn't know him, I just interviewed him. Several times," Schroder says, and that was because there were indications that Walker used to beat his wife, and indications that perhaps the wife hadn't been killed by Joe Middleton. For a while there Walker was a suspect. But ultimately Walker had an unshakable alibi for her murder, and they came up with no other suspects.

"Come on, Carl," Kent says, "you were the lead on the Carver investigation. You know why we've asked you down here."

Schroder nods. He knows this is why he's here. Like Hutton

said, it's all about the time line. Three killings all within a week, all within days of Joe's trial starting. Hutton and Kent think it's related to the Carver.

"Okay," he says. "Tell me where you're at."

"We have a theory," Hutton says.

"An ex-con, an army dropout, and Walker," Kent says. "They were planning something together, or working with somebody who is planning something, and it involves explosives."

"We have forensics," Kent says. "Shell casings. We have hairs. Long hairs. Same blonde hairs at each location. No DNA, because they're synthetic."

"So the killer was wearing a wig," Schroder asks.

"Seems like it," Kent says. "And most likely a woman. Men don't tend to wear wigs that are shoulder length. Plus the hairs were found in the lounge too. Which means if they belong to the person who shot him, then she didn't just knock on the front door and shoot him when he answered. It means she was inside. Of course it could be two different things. They could belong to somebody who he talked with inside, and it could be somebody else who came to his door and shot him."

"Fingerprints?"

"All over the place," Hutton says, "and most of them we've ruled out. Nothing so far with any matches."

"And you want to know if I think Melissa is involved," Schroder says. "That's why I'm really here. Because Joe's trial starts next week."

"None of the prints we've found so far match hers," Kent says. "But do you think it's possible? She's staying hidden somehow. It only makes sense she's using some techniques to change her appearance. Of course she's probably wearing a wig."

"It's a completely different MO if it is her," he says. "Different signature. None of these people were in uniform. None were tortured. If it's her, why is she targeting these people?"

"Because of the time line," Hutton says. "We're less than a week out from Joe's trial."

"We're running background checks on all of them," Kent says. "We're seeing what they have in common. Where their lives intersected. The problem is they may not intersect. It's possible they don't know each other, but they know a common denominator."

"Okay," Schroder says. "Okay. Let's think about it. Think it through," he says. "Let's play with the idea that it's Melissa. What reason has she got? Let's break it down one victim at a time. Let's start with Sam Winston," he says. "Why work with him?" he asks, and he wonders what the scriptwriter for *The Cleaner* would make of this. Not realistic enough? Not fast-paced enough? Too much standing around and thinking?

"We're still piecing it together," Kent says.

"Okay," Schroder says, knowing the scriptwriter would be disappointed. "Let's focus on the timing of it all. Melissa or not, we could be dealing with somebody who's going to make some kind of a statement. We could be looking at a courthouse bombing, or a police station bombing. We know Melissa likes killing people, but she's more into the personal touch. I don't see a mass bombing being her style. Her style is torturing people."

"But if she tortured these people, we'd immediately know it was her," Hutton says, "which would give her a good reason not to if she's trying to hide the fact it's her. And the only reason she'd hide that is if she has something planned that is much bigger than any of this, and explosives have a way of being used for bigger things."

Schroder nods. It's a good point. "What about Walker," he says. "What's the coroner say?"

"She says there's three hours between the two murders," Hutton says, "with Walker being the second one of the day."

The three of them go quiet as they all don't see it adding up together. There are other people walking around the scene—other cops, people looking for clues. Others are out in the street interviewing neighbors who all saw nothing. They can hear the rain on the roof, still hammering down, making a miserable night that much more miserable. Somewhere out there a dog starts barking and doesn't want to stop.

"Who found the body?" he asks, hoping the answer isn't going to be *the kids*.

"His kids," Kent says. "Normally, he'd pick them up from school. He was late. A teacher gave them a lift home after they couldn't get hold of him. So the teacher and the kids came by. I'm pretty sure you can figure out the rest."

Schroder is pretty sure he can too. He's spoken to other kids at other times who have found other murdered parents, just as other parents at other times have come home to missing or dead children. He imagines one of the children screaming, the other one shaking their father to wake him up, the teacher trying to pull them away from the body while phoning the police. He imagines those kids right now with relatives who can't find a way to comfort them. He can't afford to let his imagination continue down that path. It's something he's always had to block. Otherwise it would overwhelm him.

"So to sum up," he says, "we don't know if we're dealing with Melissa, or if we're even dealing with somebody relating to the trial or the case. Tristan Walker was going to be testifying for the prosecution, which maybe is a connection. And Rivers, well, he was in jail for twelve years and Joe is in jail now, so we need to see if there have been any cellmates in common."

"I'll look into the jail connection," Hutton says.

"If it's related to the case, it's possible other family members of victims could be targeted too," Schroder says, continuing to think it through. Kent and Hutton stare at him as this possibility sinks in, and the idea makes him feel sick. He glances at his watch. The day has been slipping away, most of it on the diner set for *The Cleaner*. He promised them that he'd be back. He has to remind himself that's his job, not chasing down leads for a police department that fired him and no longer pays him and who will throw him onto his sword if the truth of what he did ever comes out.

"There's a victim's support meeting," he says, then glances at his watch. "It's going on now. In one room you're going to have a whole lot of people involved with the case, people affected by Joe, some of them will also be testifying. It might be a good thing to go there. A way of speaking to most of the people involved in one sitting."

Kent thinks it over. Hutton is doing the same thing, but his attention is probably divided by a chocolate bar he has stashed in his car somewhere.

"Okay, let's go," Kent says.

"*Let's?*" Schroder asks.

"Yeah, you and me. I'll even let you drive."

CHAPTER SIXTEEN

"I have a question," Melissa says.

She's been here an hour now and all that's happened is she's gotten colder and older and bored. The new people to the group didn't have to talk, they didn't have to identify themselves or tell the others why they were there, didn't have to go *My name is Jed, it's been fifteen days since my last sibling was murdered—Hi Jed*. Some did, some didn't. Mostly those who spoke were regular members, regular people, the kind of people you stood behind in a coffee shop and never thought of again. They moaned and complained and Melissa just wondered why in the hell they just don't get on with life, like she did. Find a hobby, people! Fiona Hayward didn't talk. She just sat silently clutching her hands, no doubt the same way she did at her husband's funeral.

Everybody turns toward Melissa.

"Go ahead," Raphael says.

She clears her throat. "Well, this referendum . . ." she says, and a murmur goes through the crowd, a unifying sound that tells her she's touched a hot topic, one where everybody in this room is on the same side.

Raphael puts his hands up and waves his palms down slightly. The crowd goes silent. "Carry on," he says.

"Well, this referendum coming up, we all get the chance to vote on the death penalty," she says. "My sister, she was murdered," she says, and she was murdered by a policeman who raped her first, killed her second, and took his own life for thirds. Some would call that a hat trick. She would call it a piece of bad luck followed by a piece of even worse luck followed by a piece of great luck. She doesn't mention any of this. "And I'm thinking, if anybody deserves the death penalty, it's Joe Middleton," she says. "His trial starts next week, and trials can be tricky things. I mean, he deserves to die, that's what I—"

"He totally deserves to die," somebody calls out, a woman on the opposite side of the circle whose face is red and angry and hasn't seen makeup in a long time, her black hair long and messy.

"I second that," somebody else says, this time a guy a few seats away. Everybody pauses, waiting for more outbursts, and there's only one more, a *Kill the fucker* from a guy two seats down.

"Go ahead," Raphael says.

"Well, what happens if he gets away with it? What happens if he pleads that he's insane and the jury lets him go? What then? He goes free? That's not fair. Not fair to me, to my sister, not fair to many others in this room. What do we do then to make sure he gets justice?"

"It's a good question," Raphael says, and Melissa knows it is. It's why she asked it.

"With a simple answer," a man further along the circle says. "We kill him."

Another man stands up. "Yeah, we kill him. Hunt him down and shoot the bastard."

Raphael puts out his hand. "Sit down," he says. "Please, we're not here to condone violence."

"We should be," the woman who first spoke out says, and

Melissa studies the people speaking up, adding them to her list of possible partners. At this rate everybody in the room would probably be willing to help. She could have an army.

"That's not what this is about," Raphael says. "Miss . . . what's your name?"

"Stella," Melissa says. "I couldn't handle it if he got away."

"Well, Stella, he won't get away," Raphael says, his voice hardening, and in that moment Melissa forgets about the others in the room because she has a strong sense about Raphael. It's the same sense she got last year when she first met Joe Middleton. It's something she's developed over the years since her university professor raped her, a sense that was drummed into her as she lay pinned and bleeding beneath him. Raphael is her guy. She can sense it. Some people can see poets inside people, or a sense of peace; others have gaydar. Her thing is seeing the anger inside people, and there's definitely something dark inside Raphael, the exact something dark she was hoping to find tonight.

"But if he does? If he's found not guilty?" she asks.

"Then we get him," somebody from across the circle says, but Melissa doesn't look in that direction, doesn't see who the voice belongs to, because she only has eyes for Raphael now. Raphael with his blue eyes behind the designer glasses staring back at her, Raphael with the pulse in his forehead and a tightening jaw. Yes, there are bad thoughts behind those bright blue eyes. No doubt about it.

"He'll be in protective custody, or he'll be placed somewhere nobody knows. It hurts," she says, "it hurts missing her and if, if Joe were to get away I'd kill myself, I'd . . . I'd just kill myself."

Fiona puts an arm around her and Melissa fights the urge to shrug it off and shoot her. Most of the people in the room are leaning forward now.

"Stella," Raphael says, and Melissa holds a hand up to her face and Fiona grips her a little tighter.

"I need a bathroom," she says, and she slips out from beneath Fiona's arm and gets up and rubs her belly and heads toward the back of the hall. People try talking all at the same time. She can hear footsteps following her. She makes it to the bathroom and splashes water onto her face to streak her makeup so it looks like she's been crying. Then Fiona comes into the room.

"Are you okay, honey?"

"I'm fine," Melissa says, and wipes at her face.

"Are you sure?"

"Positive."

"Raphael said it was time for things to start wrapping up," she says. "Everybody seems worried about you, and I get the idea you're not the first person to have run in here crying. Can I get you a coffee? Oh," she says, then looks at Melissa's stomach, "perhaps some water instead?"

"I'm fine."

"The others are talking about a protest on Monday," her new best friend says. "They're going to the courthouse to support the death penalty. I want to go, but don't think I will. I should go, but . . . but I think it's all just too much for me. I'm not sure if that makes sense. Does it?" And, without waiting for an answer, she goes into her next question. "Can I walk you to your car?"

"I want to clean up first," Melissa says.

"I don't mind waiting."

"I'm fine," she says. "Really, please, don't worry about me. I think I just . . . just need to be alone for a little bit."

"Of course," Fiona says. "I know how you're feeling." She opens the door, pauses in it, and turns back. "I don't really know if I got anything from any of this," she says, "but I think I'll come back next week. Will I see you here too?"

Melissa nods.

"Maybe bring your husband," Fiona says.

"I will."

"Okay, well, I'll see you later," she says, as both women walk out of the bathroom.

Others are heading their way to use the bathroom, others are heading out of the hall, Raphael is stacking chairs. Some are drinking coffee. Everyone she passes stops to talk to her to ask if she's okay. She tells them she's fine. The others are talking about the protest on Monday. She has left her jacket over her chair, so she walks toward it and toward Raphael.

"Are you okay?" Raphael asks, and up close he smells of musky aftershave and reminds her a little of her father—only a much handsomer version. It makes her realize how much she misses her parents.

"I'm sorry about my outburst," she says.

"I'm sorry about your sister."

"I'm sorry about your daughter."

Raphael nods. No doubt he's sorry too. He carries on stacking chairs, but does it in a way that he doesn't put his back to her.

"Do you ever think about how it would feel to hurt the man that took her away?" Melissa asks.

The chair Raphael has in midair he returns back to the floor. He puts both hands on the back of it and faces her. "Let me ask you something," he says. "Why are you here?"

"Why is anybody here?" she asks. "To find some sense of understanding. Some closure."

"There is no closure," he says. "Often there's no understanding either." He stares at her and she stares back, and she's impressed at how well he's hiding the darkness behind his eyes, but it's there. No doubt about it. "But these are just things we say because we need to hear them. What I'm specifically asking is why are you here? Who was your sister? Was she a victim of Joe's?"

"Yes," she says, and immediately knows she has made a mistake. He's going to ask her who her sister was.

"Who?" he asks.

"Daniela Walker," she says, going with Daniela since she met and killed Daniela's husband earlier today, which means there's one less person to be able to call her a liar.

He doesn't pause, doesn't show any signs that he knows she's lying. "I'm sorry about Daniela," he says.

"Why did you really start this group?" she asks.

Now he does pause, just for a fraction, but long enough to

make her doubt whatever he's going to say. "To help people," he says. "Why do you think I started it?"

"To help people," she says. She wishes she could just come out and ask him to help her kill Joe. He's the perfect candidate. Would it be that simple? "I guess I came along because I wanted somebody to tell me that no matter what happens, Joe will be brought to justice."

His jaw tightens again as he slowly nods. "He will be."

"Are you voting for the death penalty?" she asks.

"Yes," he says. "We've been organizing a protest over the last month," he says. "We spoke about it while you were in the bathroom. You're welcome to come along."

"You're protesting against it? I thought you said—"

"We're protesting against the people who are protesting against it," he interrupts. "There's going to be a gathering outside the courthouse of people not wanting the death penalty reinstated. We're going to be there to be heard too. These people, these humanitarians, they have no idea what it's really like."

"Yeah, I know," she says. "And if the bill is passed and Joe is sentenced to death, it could take ten years."

"That's quite possible," he says. "Probably even likely."

"Can you live with that?" she asks.

He frowns and angles his head slightly. "Are you suggesting an alternative?"

"I'm just after closure," she says, treading carefully.

"And what does your husband think?"

"He left me," she says. "He says I haven't been the same since my sister died."

He looks her up and down, at the pregnant stomach, and no doubt he's thinking her husband is a bastard. "When Angela died," he says, "Janice left me too. A thing like that, well, marriages often don't survive."

"If you could be the person to do it," she says, "if you were the one to pull the lever or push the button or do whatever it is to finish Joe, would you do it?"

"No," he says, and he picks the chair back up and puts it into the stack. "I wish I could, but it's not who I am."

She rubs at her belly again. This has been a huge waste of time. Three days left and fate led her to the wrong place. It's her own fault for believing in fate. And she feels stupid for seeing something in Raphael that obviously isn't there.

"I should be going," she says.

"It was nice meeting you," he says.

She grabs her jacket and heads to the back of the hall. Her stolen umbrella has been stolen. She wonders if that's the universe finding balance. Others are leaving the parking lot—some are standing under the edge of the building chatting, and some of them are smoking. Others are still inside using the bathroom and sipping coffee. It's still pouring with rain, and the wind has picked up and tugs at the umbrellas of the others out here. She walks carefully to her car and unlocks it and gets in, the jacket protecting her upper body, but her pants are soaking wet. She hates driving in the pregnancy suit, so she takes it off, an awkward procedure that takes about half a minute because she didn't take her jacket off first. Nobody can see her through all the rain inside her dark car, and even if they could nobody would know what she was doing.

She gets the bump off and tosses it into the backseat, and she's getting ready to remove the wig when the passenger door swings open and Raphael climbs in.

"So, Stella," he says, "looking at her stomach and then at the bump in the backseat, the bump that still has her gun inside it, "how about you tell me why you're really here?"

CHAPTER SEVENTEEN

The fresh jumpsuit is a little stiff, washed with too much starch and not enough care and certainly without any love. It scratches at my neck. I keep trying to adjust it. Shower time is over and we're an hour away from being put back into our cells, but I've come back to mine anyway to be away from Caleb Cole and his thoughts, and to spend some time alone with my own.

I pick up one of the books Melissa gave me, not the same one I started reading earlier. There are six books in total. The people on the covers with flawless skin and defined muscles all look happy because none of them are facing a possible hanging. I scan through the book looking for Melissa's message. There are no pencil marks. No marked pages. I flick through the third one, no longer reading, just looking for signs, but still no dog-eared pages, no slips of paper coming out, no underlined passages. Same with the fourth book. Same with the fifth. There is no message here. Same with the sixth. The books have all been read before. The spines are broken and the pages a little dirty.

I head out into the common area. The only privileges we have right now are TV privileges. One TV for thirty people doesn't seem like much of a privilege, but it certainly helps with the boredom. The buttons have been removed from the set and the remote control lives somewhere beyond our cell walls, which means there are no arguments between us as to what we want to watch. The remote will occasionally make an appearance in the hand of a prison guard if there's something on that he thinks we may want to watch. Which there never is.

Tonight is the news, but me, my cellmates, we are the news, so we don't bother watching it since it's nothing more than a window into our lives, or the lives of people just like us. It's on, just footage blurring into more footage the same way the tedium of jail blends into more tedium. Colors and shapes of people doing shit, getting shot, going to war, and stealing from the economy. Ads come and go—pills for diabetes, pills for blood pressure, pills for getting an erection, pills that I'd need too if I were to try touching the women in those ads. All those guys need to do to wake up a flagging erection is to corner somebody half their age.

A current-events show comes on after the news. There's a stage with gray carpet and blue walls, and in the middle stands a man behind a podium. He's talking to the camera. After a minute he's joined by two more men who have podiums of their own, one to the left of the stage and one to the right. They walk out to what can only be described as unenthusiastic applause, as if the people in the audience were dragged in from jury duty.

The guy on the right is the prime minister. He's a bald guy in his late forties and the thing about bald guys is I don't like them. I didn't vote for him. I didn't vote for anybody. The other guy I have no idea who he is, but must be the guy wanting to be prime minister, but if I did vote I'd vote for him on account of him having hair. And this is where the world doesn't make sense. A bald guy running the country, and yet I'm the one in jail?

Santa Suit Kenny is playing cards with Roger Small Dick. They're a few yards down from me sitting opposite each other at a table. They're playing *memories*, where all the cards are shuffled and laid facedown and they have to try to pick them up in pairs. I'm pretty sure it's a metaphor for their future if both men get out of here. Picking up children in pairs. Lying them facedown. Making memories. But who am I to judge what goes on in the privacy of somebody else's basement? Caleb Cole is watching me while I try to make out it's no big deal that I'm being watched. Others are reading books, which makes no sense because they could just as easily read them in their cells.

Edward Hunter is off being medicated somewhere, probably preparing for his own trial coming up later this year. There are benches along the side of the room where people are sitting and smoking.

The volume of the TV is low and the subject matter dull, until I hear the moderator, a good-looking guy with thick, brown hair that must be dyed, say "People are angry at crime. The homicide rate is bloody appalling," he says, and over the years I've seen this guy on TV it's become apparent he likes to hear himself swear, it's obvious he feels the word *bloody* adds a gravitas to his words and labels him as a *Go get 'em* kind of guy. Sometimes he'll use the word *bastard* too. He's working his way up to saying *fuck-knuckle*.

"Is the next government prepared to spend more money on law enforcement, more money on prisons, and more importantly, is the government elected this year prepared to follow the will of the people if that will turns out to be a want for capital punishment? Why don't you answer first, sir," he says, looking at the leader of the opposition.

"Well, first of all," the leader of the opposition says, "I think the current government has done an extremely poor job on crime," he says, frowning at the moderator and then at the camera. "As prime minister, first thing I'll do is divert more funding to the current police force, and we'll start recruiting drives because we need more officers," he says, "because at the moment our men and women in the police are overworked, underpaid, exhausted, and leaving."

"Yes, yes," the moderator says, "but your party has made those promises before and when given the chance, never followed through. Just as the current party made those promises before the last election."

"The current party has let us all down," the man answers, ignoring the first part of the moderator's statement. "And that's why we need a change."

"But it was your party," the prime minister says, and he points at the guy running against him, "who cut funding to the police department five years ago."

"That's completely untrue!" his opponent says, as if he's just been accused of stealing candy from a baby and groping its mother.

The moderator nods and holds up his hands. "Gentlemen," he says, "please, all in good time. Now, the same day people are voting for a new prime minister they're also voting on—"

"That's not a great choice of words," the prime minister says, smiling. "It won't be a new prime minister they'll be voting for, but the same one."

The moderator nods. "Yes, yes, I apologize for that, however we'll know more later this year, won't we? But the point is, the same day the people are voting for a *government*, they're also voting on capital punishment. If you're prime minister," he says, looking at the leader of the opposition again, "will you allow that law to pass? Are you for capital punishment?"

The leader of the opposition's face has reset back to its factory default, the look of a man who is happy and determined and knows how to run a country, a man who knows he'll probably win just for not being bald. "Well, Jim, it doesn't matter what I'm for, it's what the people are for."

"So you're saying you'll go with the will of the people. Is that right?" Jim asks.

"If there is an overwhelming demand to bring back the death penalty, then my government would certainly explore that option."

"Explore?"

"Yes, exactly. We have to be careful," he says. "If there was a referendum and the people decided they wanted never to pay taxes again, are you saying we should follow their will?"

Moderator Jim is nodding. "Yes, yes, I see your point. And you, Mr. Prime Minister?"

"If that's what the people want," the prime minister says, the studio lights gleaming off his head, "then we'll make it happen. I promise. Because unlike my colleague's example of a referendum on taxes, the death penalty is a reality. Nobody wants to pay taxes, but we all know we have to do it. Nobody wants killers out on the street, and that's something we can do something about. We won't be messing around with exploring options. It's time we take a firm stand on crime. If the country votes to bring the death penalty in, then my government will make it a priority and have it introduced by the end of year. That's a promise," he says, and my skin goes cold as I stare at the TV set. This man wants to kill me. He's giving me nothing to make me change my opinion about bald people. "Don't make the assumption that we're going to hang every criminal who goes through the court system. It will only be used in extreme cases."

"Cases like Joe Middleton?" Jim asks.

Some of the guys around me whoop at the mention of my name and somebody slaps me on the shoulder and gives me a *Way to go, Joe*. But at this rate the way Joe is going to go is by hanging. My skin gets colder.

"Yes, I imagine so," the prime minister says.

"And what about those already in the system?"

"They've been sentenced already," the prime minister says, "and we can't retroactively alter their sentences. What we can do, though, for future criminals, is make their sentences tougher."

"So in the case of Middleton," Jim says, "who I think you'd agree has become a catalyst for this entire pro- and anti-death movement, his trial starts next week. It may last two months, so it will be over around the same time as the election. Will his sentencing be held off until the bill is passed?"

The prime minister gives a small grin. "Jim, you're getting ahead of yourself and also off topic." Then he wags his finger at him, like a teacher telling off a child. "It's a good try, but I won't be drawn into a matter that shall be decided by the courts. I think you'll find both myself and my opponent are here to debate the issues, not to debate how Joe Middleton's trial should be run."

"Go Joe," somebody yells out from across the room, and I look up to see one of the smokers up on the bench giving me the thumbs-up. A couple of others start clapping. Caleb Cole is still staring at me as if the referendum is a pointless exercise because he's going to kill me anyway.

The topic goes from me to the economy. They lose me about six words into it. Good economy or bad economy, prison life isn't going to change. It's not like we're all going to declare bankruptcy and get evicted if things are bad, and it's not like we're getting champagne breakfasts if things are good.

I get up and move back into my cell. We're only fifteen minutes away from being put into them anyway. I lie down on my cot and stare up at the ceiling and wonder just how it is I've come to be in here—the bad luck, the out-of-whack world that would have done this to me. I think back to times in the real world not so much more than a year ago, where things were good, where The Sally would bring me sandwiches at work and at night I would either visit my mom or somebody I had taken a fancy to. Then I think to that Sunday morning when The Sally showed up outside my apartment, where The Sally jumped on me when I tried to shoot myself, and then, like other times I've thought about this, I wonder whether or not she did the right thing.

Everybody hates me.

Everybody except Melissa.

I pick up the books and try to find her message.

CHAPTER EIGHTEEN

The gun is still inside the fat suit. Right now Melissa has no weapon. Her keys are in the ignition. She can grab them. Stab Raphael with them a few times. Messy but effective, but loud too because he'll scream, and people will see it, and suddenly she's not driving out here with a partner in crime like she wanted, but driving out of here in the back of a police car. She'll go for it and hope for the best, if that's her only option. But right now she'll play it out—see where things go. She has a good instinct for things, and right now it's telling her this could be a good thing.

"You can start by explaining the outfit," he says, pointing his thumb into the backseat. "Are you a reporter? You writing a book? Who are you really?"

"It's none of that," she says.

"I know a lot of the victims' families," he says. "Daniela Walker, we asked her husband along, him and the kids. He said no. But her parents came. They were even there tonight. You'd have known that if she really was your sister," he says, and Melissa knew it at the time—she knew giving a name was a mistake, but he was good, way too good at not letting her know he knew it at the time. She'll have to be careful about that. "So, let me ask you again, who are you really?"

"My name really is Stella," she says.

"Bullshit."

She shakes her head. "It's true," she says with enough conviction to convince him—or maybe he's doing that thing again where he knows she's lying, but is hiding it.

"But Joe Middleton didn't kill your sister."

"No," she says. "He didn't. But . . ." she says, and she wipes at her face, smudges some of the raindrops across it and hopes it looks like tears, "but he did kill, kill my baby," she says.

"Bullshit," he says.

"It's true," she says. "He . . . he raped me. Last year. I was pregnant. Three and a half months pregnant and I lost, I lost the baby," she says. "It's why I wear the . . . wear the baby suit," she says, "because I wanted nothing more than to be nine months pregnant, to be at that stage of giving life, but I never got there, I never got there because he killed my baby and my husband left me, he didn't want to touch me after that because somehow he blamed me, and he hated me for not going to the police. So I'm sorry I lied, I'm sorry I wore a pregnancy suit, but I wear it because it makes me feel better, it makes me feel like things are the way they're supposed to be, that my life stayed on the track I'd worked so hard to put it on. Only it isn't, things aren't the way they should be because that bastard hurt me, he took away my baby and he hurt me and I want him dead. I want him dead and I thought that if I came along here tonight maybe it would help me forgive him, or forgive myself, but all I want now more than ever is to put a bullet in him. A lot of bullets. I want him dead and I guess . . . I guess I wanted to find somebody who felt the same way. I have a plan," she says, "a plan to kill Joe, and I wanted . . . I want somebody to help me do it."

He says nothing. Five seconds go by. Ten. She's sure he believes her. He's just thinking it through. There are a few options, but not many.

"I'm . . . I'm sorry," he finally says.

"He killed my baby," she says.

"You should have just told us."

"Told you? What? Go in there and tell everybody I wear a pregnancy suit because I can't face the fact my baby died, and how I sometimes pretend I'm still pregnant because it brings me comfort?"

He doesn't answer. How can he?

She lets the silence build. The rain keeps hammering on the roof. The passenger door is still open and occasional gusts of wind bring water into the car. Raphael is playing out several scenarios in his head. She's playing out different ones. His involve whether he should help her or walk away. Hers involve whether she should stab her keys into his eyes first or into his throat.

"And if you found somebody to help you, what then?"

"I don't want there to be a trial. I want Joe dead, and I want to be the one to make it happen. I don't want his lawyer getting him off on some technicality. I don't want him being a free man and going into hiding. I want to kill him."

"And you have a plan," he says.

"A good plan."

He's slowly nodding the whole time she tells him this, nodding and rubbing a hand over his chin. And thinking. There's a lot of thinking going on behind those designer glasses. "Twenty minutes," he says. "I need twenty minutes to finish putting everything away and lock up. Wait here for me. I think we might have a few things to talk about. I think we have a few things . . . in common."

"Twenty minutes," she says. "For you to call the police?"

"No," he says, and she believes him. "Will you wait for me?"

She nods. She'll wait. He gets out of the car. He closes the door and walks back toward the hall, head down and collar turned up as the rain hammers him. He reaches the step when another car pulls into the parking lot. He turns toward the lights that sweep across him, and holds his hand up to his face to shield his eyes.

The car comes to a stop. The engine dies. Carl Schroder steps out into the rain.

CHAPTER NINETEEN

Raphael is tired.

He can't remember the last time he had a good night's sleep. He has had them since his daughter was murdered, but only when his body has become so exhausted all its core systems have shut down and it was either sleep or die. Often he'd hope it was the latter, only to wake up to find it was the former. Often he thinks of ways to change that. Life isn't great when you wake up in the morning and think about what your friends will say about you at your funeral. It's not great thinking about the way you'll die, the best way to not make a mess for everybody, and there are a lot of ways—a lot of clever ways and a lot of simple ways. He has planned his suicide how many times? A hundred? A thousand? Once a day, sometimes five times a day, sometimes more. Sometimes he can't figure out why he hasn't done it already. It's just a matter of time. He knows that. Whenever he hears about somebody who has killed himself, he thinks *Seems like a good idea to me*.

Of course he wants to be strong. Wants to be strong for his dead daughter, for his son-in-law, and of course for his grandchildren. Not that he ever sees any of them. Three months after Angela died, his son-in-law moved away. He took the kids with him and traveled to the other side of the world. He had family in England. In a small village somewhere. A village, he said, that didn't harbor crazy people like Joe.

Raphael is more alone than he has ever been in his life.

He stands in the doorway and watches the car pulling into the parking lot. Probably some other poor bastard who's lost somebody in this city. The car comes to a stop. One person climbs out. Then a second. Both of them flick their collars up against the rain and walk quickly toward him. Schroder and somebody else. His heart races a little. Police don't come visiting unless they have bad news. His wife? Oh God, has his wife followed through on his fantasy? Has she upended a bottle of sleeping pills?

"Detective," Raphael says, his voice a little shaky. He offers his hand.

"It's no longer detective," Schroder says, shaking it, "just Carl now. This is Detective Inspector Rebecca Kent," he adds, and then says to Kent, "and this is Raphael Moore."

He looks at Kent. Her hair is wet and strands are stuck to the side of her face. He has the urge to reach forward and stroke some of them away, and thinks he has that urge because Detective Kent is an extremely attractive woman.

"It's an awful night," he says, and he figures if he can just keep them talking about the inane, then he won't have to hear about the real.

"You've just wrapped up a session?" Kent asks, and all three of them glance through the open doorway into the hall where there are six stragglers sipping coffee and talking. He wonders if the two detectives—no, wait, one detective and one no-longer-detective—recognize them. At some point over the last few years these people were all given bad news. It's a bad-news kind of country, a worse-case-scenario kind of city.

"About ten minutes ago," Raphael says, looking back at them now. "Has something happened? Is it my wife?"

Schroder shakes his head. "No, no, it's not that kind of visit," Schroder says.

Raphael breathes a sigh of relief. Thank God. He glances back inside. Hopefully the others will leave soon. Hopefully he can get rid of these two quickly. He wants to get back to Stella. Stella with her fake baby and her plan to kill Joe Middleton, and really, has there been a day that has gone by where he has not thought about murdering Middleton just as often as he's thought about killing himself? "We haven't seen you in a while, Carl."

"I know. I'm sorry, I've been busy," Schroder says.

Raphael doubts that's it. In the beginning both he and Schroder thought it was good to have a police presence at the group, but it turned out they were wrong—it turned out a police presence gave the group somebody to blame.

"You should come back," Raphael says. "It was helpful. It made the people here feel like they had a voice. So why are you here then? Something to do with Middleton? This about his trial?"

"In a way," Schroder says, and he steps closer to the doorway, but the rain is still getting him. Raphael doesn't make any more room. He wants to keep this meeting outside. Wants to keep it short.

"Was Tristan Walker one of your group?" Kent asks.

"Tristan Walker?" he asks. "To be honest," he says, "I'm not so sure I'm comfortable telling you who comes along here. I mean, all of these people have the right to privacy," he says, and the moment the words are out of his mouth he knows it makes no sense—half a minute ago he was asking Schroder to start coming back.

"Please, Raphael," Schroder says, "don't make this difficult for us. We wouldn't be here if it weren't important."

Raphael nods. "Why? Has he done something?"

"Did he come to the group?" Kent asks, and she flashes her smile at him and for a brief moment Raphael wants to tell her everything about his secret fantasy to wrap himself in plastic and hide himself beneath the house and take a bunch of pills so that nobody will ever find him, nobody will ever know what happened, so that he will have just disappeared from this life and this world. He imagines a lot of men would give in to that smile, and on other nights he would too. But not tonight. Not with Stella waiting for him, not with thoughts of killing Joe Middleton running around in his head.

"I contacted him a few times, but he always said no, then I stopped trying."

"Why'd you stop trying?" Schroder asks.

Raphael shrugs. "Well, he wasn't thrilled with me contacting him," he says. "But then I heard a rumor and realized he wasn't really the kind of person I wanted in this support group."

"What kind of rumor?" Kent asks.

"I heard he used to beat his wife," Raphael says, rubbing his hands to keep them warm. He heard it from another person in the group who heard it from a cousin or a neighbor or some such thing. "Is it true?"

"He's never been charged," Schroder says, rubbing his hands too.

"That isn't the same as you telling me it wasn't true. So why are you here asking about him? Has he beaten somebody else up?"

"He was murdered this afternoon," Kent says, burying her hands into her pockets.

"Oh," Raphael says, and he takes a small step back. "Oh," he repeats, and isn't sure what else to add. He can't say *Good, he probably deserved it,* because he doesn't know for a fact that the guy was a wife beater, and even if he was, does that merit the death penalty? The appropriate sentiment comes to him in the end. "Shit."

"Walker was due to testify at Middleton's trial," Schroder says. "Just like you are. And other family members of victims. You probably had a dozen people in your group tonight who are all testifying."

Walker slowly nods. The rain every ten seconds or so washes over them as the wind pushes it sideways. He thinks about what it's going to be like testifying. He's thought about it a lot. He's thought about how far he could make it from the witness box to Joe before somebody stopped him. He thought about how difficult it would be to smuggle a weapon into the building. About carving a knife out of wood or bone. He thought about how many men it would take to stop him. All those thoughts were only a fantasy—the best he knew he could do was form this group, help others, and starting next week they would protest.

"What are you saying?" Raphael asks. "You think some of us are targets too?"

"We can't rule it out," Kent says.

"Who would want to target us?"

"We don't know," Schroder says, but Raphael doesn't believe him. Something in his voice makes Raphael think Schroder may have an idea.

"So what can I do?" Raphael asks.

"We were actually hoping to get here before the meeting was over," Schroder says, "so we could talk to you all as a group."

"Well, I know who some of them are," Raphael says. "I can make a list. And we're all meeting again on Monday."

"Another session?" Kent asks.

"Actually, no," Raphael says. "We're meeting outside the courthouse. We're going to protest against those who are going to protest against the death-penalty referendum. There'll be around thirty of us from the group going, and all of us will probably bring somebody, and no doubt there'll already be others going anyway. Could be hundreds," he says, but really he's hoping for thousands and doesn't see any reason why it won't be. Like he thought earlier, it's a bad-news kind of country. All that bad news has left a bad taste in a lot of people's mouths—plenty of anger to go around, plenty of people willing to show up.

"And you're leading it?" Kent asks.

"No," Raphael says. "Just taking part. There is no leader."

"But you're helping organize it," Kent says.

"I'm just doing my part as a concerned citizen."

"You do know a protest like that has every possibility of getting out of hand," Kent says, her voice hardening. "For both sides."

Raphael frowns. "We need to be heard," he says. "And we have every right to peacefully protest. We have every *legal* right. Joe Middleton is exactly the reason we need this law brought in," he adds, keeping his voice level, but inside he's yelling at her. "I intend to offer my complete support. We're all planning on it."

"And if somebody gets hurt?" she asks. "Then what?"

"We're all victims," Raphael says. "We've already been hurt. All we're doing is peacefully protesting against the anti–capital punishment movement, and against the current system. I'm sure there will be enough police on the scene to keep everybody in check," he says, but truth be told he isn't so sure. Not having enough police hasn't done well for the city over the last few years—and perhaps Monday's protest won't be any different. But it's not his job to keep the city safe. It's Kent's job. And people like Kent. And people like Schroder too.

"Was Tristan Walker part of the movement?" Kent asks. "Was he going to be there?"

Raphael hadn't heard anybody use *movement* to describe what he's doing. It doesn't quite fit right in some way. "We are a group of people trying to change the country," he says, "and if that makes us a movement, then so be it."

"And Walker?" Kent repeats.

"I don't know. I hadn't told him about it, but maybe he was coming. I'd have hoped he would be."

"Were there any new faces tonight, anybody suspicious?" Schroder asks.

Raphael puts his hand to his chin and crosses his forefinger over his lips, then slowly taps the finger up and down. All he can think about is the woman in the car. "Suspicious? In what way?"

"Somebody who didn't belong," Schroder says.

He shakes his head, the finger remaining in place. "No, nobody," he says. "I mean, there were new people here, there often is and always will be as long as people keep getting murdered. As for somebody suspicious, no, nothing. Nobody who didn't belong."

"You sure?" Schroder asks.

"It's not like somebody came in here covered in blood and

waving a knife," he says. "Most people when they come, they don't speak. It's almost like an AA meeting. People are nervous. They don't know what to expect. They want to hear other people's pain before sharing their own. It takes them a few weeks to open up. We're doing good work here. We're helping people."

"What about a woman?" Kent asks. "Were there any women tonight who stood out?"

"A woman?" he asks, and he has to make a conscious effort not to look back at the car. "Why? Was it a woman who killed Tristan Walker?"

"Nobody is saying that," Kent says, "but there's a woman we're hoping to question. A blond woman," she adds.

A blond woman. The woman in the car has black hair. Even so, the woman in the car wants to kill Joe. Why would a woman who wants to kill Joe also want to kill Tristan Walker? He thinks about the others who came along. There were blond women there, there always are, but there are . . . what? Fifty thousand blond women in the city?

"You have a name? Or any other features?"

"Just blond," Kent says, glancing at Schroder first. "A woman wearing a blond wig."

"That's not a lot to go on," Raphael says. "There were new faces here tonight, there always are, and we don't have any kind of sign-in sheet. There were blond women here tonight, but nobody stood out."

"How about you make us that list," Kent says, "of the people you do know who came along."

"It'll take me about five minutes," he says.

"We can wait."

Raphael nods once, then moves back inside. The final few people are leaving. They say their good-byes and offer sad smiles. He starts working on the list, but doesn't put Stella on it, not wanting to draw attention to a woman who had no reason to hurt Walker, and who has the potential to bring him so much happiness.

CHAPTER TWENTY

I'm getting hungry again even though dinner was only an hour ago. The easiest way to kill an appetite in a place like this is to think about what it is they're serving. I do that now and the hunger pains fade a little. Then I make the mistake of thinking of a tender steak, some fries, some barbecue sauce. The harder I try not to think about it, the more I can taste it. It's a last-meal kind of meal, and perhaps that's what I'll chose if it turns out I have an appointment with the hangman's noose.

Of course the way to make sure that never happens is to find Melissa's message. I flick through the books again, knowing there's nothing in them, sure there's nothing in them, and finding just that everywhere I look. It's almost time for lights out. Our cell doors have all been locked so it's just me, my cot, my toilet, and books that aren't telling me what it is I want to hear. I can hear my neighbors in the cells next door. They're talking to themselves. Or talking to their imaginations.

Six books.

One message.

Or perhaps no message.

Frustrated, I begin throwing them into the corner of my cell, creating a game in seeing how close I can get them to land to each other. The other game, the one that Melissa is playing, is lost on me.

I pick the books back up. And throw them again. It's the most fun I've had in my cell. I kill ten minutes, wondering if it'll be this easy to kill the next thirty years, or if I'll be killed instead. The six books land in the corner. I pick them up. Line up the spines. Tap them so all the edges are level. Then throw them again. Tomorrow Caleb Cole is going to come and find me. Tomorrow may be my last day in this world.

I pick the books back up. Line up the spines.

I look at the titles.

Twilight Angel. Show Love to Get Love. Bodies of Lust. Love Comes to Town. The Prince of Princesses. Twilight Angel Returns.

Maybe that's where the message is. Somewhere in the titles. I take the first word from each one. Twilight. Show. Bodies. Love. The. Twilight. I mix them up. Twilight bodies. Show the bodies. That bit works. Show the bodies. Twilight twice doesn't work so much. Where does love fit in? Is Melissa telling me to show the police where the bodies are? The only one they're looking for, or at least know whose to look for, is Detective Calhoun's, the man Melissa murdered and the man I buried, the same man Schroder's psychic wants the location of.

I don't know. It's a stretch. But Melissa does know where Calhoun is buried. Roughly. Because it made sweet pillow talk. The message—if it is that—says to show them, not tell them.

I don't know. And the love?

So rather than being Negative Joe, a Joe nobody would like, I continue to be Positive Joe. Optimistic Joe. Likeable Joe. I imagine being outside. I imagine showing Schroder where Calhoun's body is. Not telling him. Not drawing him a map. But leading him along the dirt path to the dirt grave where Calhoun's body is shrouded in dirt. I imagine four or five other policemen with us.

Guys in uniforms with guns on their waists. Maybe even the men in black who arrested me. I imagine walking—a few men ahead, a few behind, all of them waiting for the first sign of trouble. The air cold. The ground damp. Birds in trees that have been stripped of leaves. Then, from out of nowhere, gunshots start shattering the calm silence of the day.

Only it's not daytime at all, it's evening, it's twilight, and Melissa is specific about that. Except she's not being specific about which twilight. She knows my mother would have visited me today. She knows I'll have gotten the books and would have figured out the message. She knows leading the police to the scene takes time, so she wouldn't be planning on it today. Trial starts Monday, so she must be planning on it for tomorrow. In two twilights' time, including today. Which makes perfect sense.

Tomorrow I have to show Schroder where Calhoun is buried.

Unless . . .

Unless what? Unless I'm seeing a message that isn't there?

Positive Joe steps back in to save the day. He takes me back into the scenario. Twilight. We're walking in a straight line. The gunshots. Birds take flight. The shots echo like thunder across the landscape. The policemen have no idea which direction they're being shot from, then it's over—their uniforms have red stains blossoming across them. Blood soaks into the dirt as Melissa steps into view. She wraps her arms around me and hugs me and kisses me and everything is okay now, everything is all right, and she leads me away from all the dirt and all the blood and into a life far from the jail cells with the pedophiles and the prison wardens, far away from Caleb Cole and his decision-making process, away from Glen and Adam and the hell they've been putting me through, away from it all and into bed and away from the darkness.

Negative Joe is coming around. He's thinking that Positive Joe just may be on to something here.

Six book titles. Show the bodies at twilight. Love.

Now I'm convinced. Now I feel like an idiot for not seeing it earlier. It's clever. Very clever, and Melissa is as clever as they get. That's why she's still out there. It's why the police can't find her.

And she's going to save me.

Because she still loves me. Love.

When I lie on my bed I feel something I haven't felt in some time—a sense of hope.

CHAPTER TWENTY-ONE

Raphael heads inside and Kent and Schroder stay in the doorway. They have to step aside twice as more people leave, an elderly man nodding and saying "Detectives" on the way out as a greeting. Schroder recognizes an elderly couple who look like they have aged twenty years since he came to see them five years ago with the news their son had been murdered for a pocketful of change and his sneakers. The guy who had done the murdering had spent the change on a hamburger and had made it about halfway through before he was put into cuffs.

"Maybe we should have mentioned Melissa," Schroder says.

"We agreed not to for a reason," Kent says. "I shouldn't have to remind you we don't know if she's involved, and if we start mentioning her then we risk people looking for facts that aren't there. We can't mention things we don't know. Next thing it's in the news, and false information like that might upset her. It might prompt her to make an example out of somebody. And if it is her, then we can't afford to give her a heads-up that we know it's her."

"I know," Schroder says, tightening his jaw. "I used to do this for a living."

She smiles and it breaks the tension. "I know. I'm sorry," she says.

The conversation reminds him of the kind of talks he used to have with his partner, with Theodore Tate, after Tate stopped being his partner and became a private investigator after his daughter was killed. Four weeks ago Tate started the process of becoming a cop again. He's still in that process—though it's on hold as he fights for his life in a coma. It's almost as if the two men have exchanged roles. Tate is becoming a cop, and Schroder is becoming whatever the hell it is that Tate was. Maybe even something worse. Tate and Tate's wife have swapped roles too—the same accident that cost Tate his daughter also put his wife into a vegetative state—she came out of it the same day Tate went into his.

The same day Schroder killed that woman.

It's a topsy-turvy world. Go figure.

"I'm still thinking it wouldn't hurt," he says. "We should tell him."

"You heard him," Kent says. "There were no women here acting suspiciously. And really, what reason would Melissa have for coming here? It was a good idea earlier," she says, "and it still is. We'll track down the list of names, and of course we'll get the prosecution witness list and work with that."

Only it won't be *we*, it will be *them*. He's not part of this. Now after a couple of years of dealing with Theodore Tate, he finally sees where Tate was coming from because he's now going through the same damn thing. Some things are just impossible to let go.

"Maybe we should show him the photograph of Melissa anyway," he says. "But not say it's her."

Kent sighs.

"We just say it's a person of interest," he adds.

"And maybe he'll say he's seen her in the news."

"And maybe he'll say he's seen her around."

She slowly nods. "Okay. You got one?"

He jogs back to the car, his footsteps splashing rain off the ground and soaking the bottom of his pants. He leans into the back of the car and opens the case file and the photograph of Melissa isn't where it should be. He flicks through the rest of the contents, flicks through them again, then looks on the floor and around the rest of the backseat while the rain soaks into his legs and lower back. The photograph is of Melissa back when her name was Natalie Flowers, before she named herself after her dead sister and started killing people. He searches under the seats. It's fallen out, but not in the car. Maybe it's back at the house. Or in a gutter somewhere, soaking up water the same way he's soaking it up.

He jogs back to Kent. "Can't find it," he says.

"I'm sure it doesn't matter."

"I'll show him one tomorrow."

"Carl—"

"I know, I know, it's not my case," he says, holding up his hand. "I'm just trying to be helpful." His cell phone starts ringing. He grabs it out of his pocket and checks the caller ID. It's the TV studio. He should have been back on set by now. He puts it on mute and lets it go through to the answering service. Tomorrow *The Cleaner* is shooting a scene in the casino, where the main characters are cleaning up after a weekend of high-roller suicides.

"Well, while you were looking for the photograph," Kent says, "I've been thinking. You heard what Raphael was saying about the protest? What if that's what's going on here? What if this has nothing to do with Melissa, but everything to do with the referendum? We were told in a briefing this morning that there could be as many as five thousand people showing up outside the courthouse against this damn thing, saying it sends the country back into the dark ages. And for all we know Raphael could end up with hundreds of people in support of the referendum, maybe more, all of them saying it's the way of the future. That's a lot of people all trying to be heard. That's a ripe breeding ground for somebody with explosives to make a point."

Schroder thinks about it. "You think Raphael knows something? You think the explosives are for somebody from his group?"

Kent shakes her head. "His group is antiviolence," she says. "By the very nature of their group they don't want people being hurt."

"That's one way of looking at it," Schroder says, "but the opposite is true too. The very nature of the group means they're pro-violence because they want revenge. People always think the ends justify the means."

"Revenge, yes, but not against innocent people."

Schroder nods. He's feeling tired, and confused statements like his previous one prove it. When he's done here he'll head home, and maybe he can get a few hours of uninterrupted sleep before the baby wakes up. "You're right," he says, rubbing at his eyes.

"But people are all kinds of crazy," she says. "Somebody in either camp may just think explosives will help make a point. Somebody might think hurting people will help the greater good." She stares at him for a few seconds. "Are you okay, Carl?"

Before he can tell her that he's fine, Raphael comes back to the doorway. He's aged a bit since he saw him last year, but he's still a good-looking guy, the kind of guy you'd see playing the prime minister on TV. If one of the shows Schroder is consulting on ends up tackling some political plot lines, he should offer Raphael the role.

Raphael hands them a list of names. "It's all I could remember," he says, and there has to be close to twenty names on it.

"Do the names Derek Rivers or Sam Winston mean anything to you?" Kent asks, revealing names that are going to be on the news soon anyway. By the end of the day the country will know somebody is out there shooting some of its citizens—albeit not very nice citizens.

Raphael scratches at the side of his head, his fingers disappearing into his hair. "No. Should they? Are they dead too?"

"And you're sure nobody stood out?" Schroder asks.

He gives it a few more seconds of thought. Then nods. "Positive," he says.

"Thanks for your time," Kent says, and they all shake hands and then she and Schroder are dashing back across the parking lot and into the shelter of his car.

CHAPTER TWENTY-TWO

It wasn't just Schroder who showed up in the car—there was a woman with him. Melissa has seen her around. She makes it part of her job to know who's manning the front lines of crime fighting. She doesn't know her name, but knows she's a recent addition. It doesn't take a lot of wondering to figure out why Schroder is with her. The Carver case. They've found Tristan Walker and now they think there may be a link, and the Carver case was Schroder's case, so now they're asking him for help. What she can't figure out is the connection they made to come here.

When Schroder pulls away with the woman, Melissa takes the safety off the gun and tucks it down by the seat. She puts the trigger for the C-four back into the glove compartment. She was ready for Raphael to point at her, then for Schroder to come over, and if that'd happened, then she would have provided some *ka-boom* for Schroder and the woman and some *bang-bang* for Raphael too.

Nobody else has come out of the hall for a few minutes now. Raphael finishes whatever it is he's doing and comes outside. He locks up the door behind him, though Melissa can't understand what there is inside that anybody would want to steal—the furniture wasn't any better than the stuff you sometimes see on the side of the road with cardboard signs that say *free*. Maybe he's locking the door so people won't dump stuff inside. Maybe that's what's been happening and that's where their current furniture has come from. Raphael tightens his jacket and runs over to her car.

"That was the police," he says.

"Really?" she says, doing her best to sound surprised. After tonight's performance she's thinking she should have been an actress.

"Somebody was murdered today," he says.

"Oh my God, that's awful," she says, and holds a hand up to her mouth. "Was it somebody you knew?"

"Well, not that awful," he says. "The guy was a wife beater."

Cue the frown and the confused look. "So why did the police come here?"

"Because his wife was one of Middleton's victims," he says. "And he was going to testify at the trial."

"I don't follow," Melissa says.

"The police think maybe somebody is targeting people involved with victims of the family. People who are testifying."

"That's . . . that's crazy," she says, quite pleased to be hearing it, forcing herself not to smile. If that's the connection, then she has nothing to be worried about because it really is crazy. "Is it? I mean, are we all in danger?"

The inside of the car is getting colder by the minute. She turns on the ignition and turns on the heater. There is only one other car left in the parking lot other than hers. It must belong to Raphael. It's a dark blue SUV with the spare wheel bolted into the back, and on that wheel is a cover that says *My other car was stolen*. It reminds her of a phrase she heard a while ago—*Welcome to Christchurch, your car is already here*.

"I doubt it," he says, "but they wanted a list of people who were here tonight."

She wants to ask if she was on that list, but doesn't bother. *Stella* isn't a name that will get them far. And if she asks, well, then that might make him suspect something.

"I want to hear about your plan," he says.

"Why? So you can go to the police?"

"No," he says, shaking his head. "So I can help you. If I wanted to go to the police, I'd have just done it."

She knows that, but she asked it because she's on an Oscar-winning performance here. "My plan is to shoot Joe before he even makes it to trial," she says.

"Is that it? Is that your plan?"

"There's more," she says.

"I would hope so," he says.

Then she says nothing. She stares at him, and after a few seconds he starts nodding. He's figured out the next step. "But you want to know if you can trust me."

"Can I?"

He stops nodding, the glow of the dashboard turning his face orange. The heater is slowly starting to warm up. "When Angela was killed," he says, "I wanted to die. I wanted to buy a gun and put the barrel in my mouth and kiss the world good-bye. Losing her was the hardest thing I've ever had to go through," he says, and for a moment Melissa thinks of her sister. "Soon after she died, me and my wife—well, often a marriage can't survive that kind of thing. And ours was one that couldn't. There wasn't much that kept me going. But I came to realize I wasn't the only one. Others were suffering too. I thought maybe somehow I could help them. But not a day goes by when I don't dream about killing the man who killed my daughter. And there are other Carvers out there too. Other men taking away our little girls. This group, it's at least something," he says, "but the truth is if I could form a group of vigilantes to watch over the city and clean up the trash, I'd do that too. I keep seeing it, like something out of a western, you know? A group of do-gooders riding into town, you know, gunslingers. John Wayne types. Clint Eastwood types. But I can't do that. Can't make that happen. But what I can do is help you. I'm on borrowed time. Just waiting for something to make a difference. Something to live for. And that something is to kill Joe. I don't care about my life. My life ended last year. This support group is like life support for me—it keeps me ticking, it keeps me breathing—but I'm not alive, not really, I'm just holding on. Killing Joe will bring me peace, and once I have peace, then I can let go of everything around me. I can . . . I can die happy. So please, Stella, tell me you have more than just a plan. Because if you don't, all I have are my dreams. I will do what it takes. Absolutely what it takes."

"Can you use a rifle?"

"I'm sure I can figure it out. Is that the plan?"

"When it comes down to it, are you going to be able to pull the trigger?"

Raphael grins, the grin turns into a smile, and then he holds out his hand to tick off his points. "I have two problems," he says. "The first problem is I want Joe to be able to see me. I want him to know who I am. So shooting him with a rifle from a distance doesn't sound like my kind of thing. I'll do it, if that's all there is, but I'd rather be up close. I want to see the life drain out of his eyes. I want my daughter to be the last thing he thinks of."

"And the second problem?" she asks, and she knows he's going to tell her it's about suffering and torture. Of course it is. Suffering, torture, and a good dose of payback.

"The second problem is I want him to suffer. A bullet in the chest means he won't suffer for long. So if that's your plan and there's no way to modify it, then that's your plan and I'm on board, but if we can—"

She reaches out and touches him on the forearm. "Let me stop you right there," she says, "because my plan will solve both of your problems," she says, and this couldn't have gone any better. It's fate. Gotta be. It's fate and her ability to see something in people that others can't see. It's come from experience. It was a steep learning curve that started the night her university professor tore her clothes off her.

"Trial starts Monday," he says. "Is that enough time?"

"We have three full days," she says. "That's just the right amount of time we need to make sure this happens."

CHAPTER TWENTY-THREE

I'm dripping with sweat and the ski mask is making my face itch. Ski masks are a strange invention. I've never seen people on TV, at the Olympics, or in movies wearing ski masks covering their faces when they ski. They have woolen hats and thick jackets and gogglelike sunglasses, but they don't look like bank robbers. Really they should be renamed robbery masks. Or rapists' masks. But I'm wearing one at the moment, and it's getting damper with sweat by the minute. It's a sunny day, a non–ski-mask-wearing kind of day for most people, with blue skies and, like all sunny days, it makes me feel good. There are shapes in the few clouds up there, I see a knife, I see a woman, I see bad things happening among those clouds. I don't need to pick the lock to the front door of the house because I have a key, and I use it to make my way inside. I make friends with the cold air spilling out of the fridge, and I make closer friends with an ice-cold beer. Not Coke, but beer, because Coke isn't on sale. I sit down at the table and I can hear sounds coming from the bedroom, snoring mostly, the occasional creak of bedsprings as weight is shifted. Then I realize it's no longer daytime, there are no blue skies, and it's midnight. Time has jumped forward and I'm not sure how, that's just the way time works when you're dreaming. I scratch at the mask and readjust it, then I open up my briefcase and touch the blades that are in there.

I stay in the kitchen, and after a while the snoring stops, there are footsteps, a light comes on from further up the hallway, then two minutes later a toilet is flushed. Then more footsteps and my mother comes into the kitchen where I'm still sitting.

"*Who are you?*" Mom asks.

"I'm not Joe," I tell her, because the last thing I need is my mother thinking I'm a bad person. From there on I let my knife do the talking. It speaks to her over and over until her and me and the kitchen are all on the same page. It's messy. It always is.

"And that's how it always goes?" she asks, and the *she* in question is sitting opposite me.

I'm back in the interview room and back to reality. It's Friday morning and the day started with high hopes when I looked at the books from Melissa and read her message again and again. Then there was breakfast and some eye contact with Caleb Cole before the guards came and got me. It's interview time with my psychiatrist. My psychiatrist leans forward and steeples her fingers. It must be something they all do. Must be something that on day one in psychiatry school, the teacher shows them some grainy, black-and-white footage from the forties and makes all the students practice how to sit in a way that makes them look smart. Kind of ironic for people in this particular field not to recognize how dumb they look. Good part about my psychiatrist is she looks a lot of other things too. She looks attractive. And as good as that is, it's also bad. It's distracting. It's making Joe think the kind of things that got Joe here in the first place. There's a small recorder in front of her, storing each word to memory.

"It doesn't always go like that," I tell her. "Mostly. I don't know. I didn't used to dream. But now I'm not so sure, because the dream feels so familiar. Like I've been having it my entire life. Sometimes I wake up from it certain that's what I've done, that my mother is dead and that's why I'm in here. Once I was so convinced of it I wanted to call her to make sure she was okay," I say, though that last bit about calling isn't true. "Sometimes I've poisoned her. Once I even snuck into her house dressed as a burglar and frightened her to death. The dreams always feel real."

I don't add anything more, though I could. I'm not really sure what the correct answer is. The psychiatrist's name is Alice and I've already forgotten her last name. Truth is I've kind of forgotten her first name too. It may not be Alice. It may be Ellen. Or Alison. Or even Ali-ellen. I try to keep my eyes on Ali's face, on those smooth cheek bones, that jawline, those big beautiful blue eyes of hers. I try to stop my eyes from roaming over her body, the curves like a treasure map to a whole lot of places I'd like to uncover and plunder and carve an X into. She's dressed in a pair of black trousers and a cream blouse that must be a bitch to get blood out of. It's not low-cut and the trousers aren't tight.

There's no need to ask her if the answer I gave her was the correct one, because she's already told me there are no correct answers, which we all know is bullshit. She told me it wasn't her job to say what was right or wrong, that it was her job to evaluate me and then share that information with the courts. Of course she was lying when she said that. If I told her I could remember every detail of every victim and that the reason I killed them was because I enjoyed it, that would be considered a wrong answer. There are a bunch of right answers, which will make her rubber-stamp my insanity case—I just have to figure out what they are.

She unsteeples her fingers. "Have you always had bad thoughts about your mother?" she asks, and she wouldn't be asking that question if she'd met my mother.

"It depends on what you mean by *bad thoughts*," I say. "We all have bad thoughts."

"But we all don't dream about killing our mothers."

"We don't?"

Her eyes widen a little, and something I said must have

shocked her, but I'm not sure what. "It's not common, Joe, to have those dreams. Not at all."

"Oh," I say, genuinely surprised, and it registers with her. I must act more genuinely surprised as the conversation goes on. "But they can't be considered bad thoughts if you're asleep, right? Nobody can control their dreams."

"This is true," she says. "The women you've killed," she says, and I put my hand up—the one that isn't cuffed to the chair—and interrupt her.

"I don't remember any of it," I say.

"Yes. I know. You've said already. But you didn't kill your mother and yet you dream that you did. You don't have dreams of other people?"

I shake my head. "No. Never."

She nods. And I know what she's thinking. She's forming a connection between my mother and these people. She's trying to figure out if each of these women I killed was a way for me to kill my mother without killing her, that these people were surrogate victims.

"Tell me about your mother," Abby-Ali says, and her voice is seductive, sultry, and I can't figure out why they'd have sent a woman into a place like this to interview a guy like me, then realize she must have a bad-boy complex. Then I realize that isn't it at all—a woman testifying in my defense is going to play well with the jury. They're going to see that she spent time with me and in that process the percentage of rape and murdering that went on between us was an absolute zero. My approval rating is going to go through the roof.

"She's getting married," I tell her.

"How does that make you feel?"

I bet asking that question was the next thing she mastered right after the hand steeple and before they learned how to sew leather elbow patches onto jackets. *Remember, students, if all else fails, fall back on "How does that make you feel?"* That's what psychiatry seems to be. An *if all else fails* routine. Psychiatrists not comfortable with their own opinions, and having to solicit answers from their patients first.

"Feel? It doesn't make me feel anything," I say.

"It doesn't make you feel angry?"

"Why the hell would it make me feel angry?" I say, feeling angry, not just at Ellen, but also at my mother.

"It might make you feel abandoned," she says. "It could make you think that your mother is forgetting about you and your situation and moving on to a new man in her life, whereas you've been the only man in her life since your father died. When's the wedding?"

"On Monday," I tell her.

She nods, as if that confirms it then. "The day the trial begins."

"I don't feel any of that stuff you just said," I say, more angry than ever about my mother. Already she has moved on. Already she has proven the only person she cares about other than herself is Walt. "I just don't understand why she chose now to get engaged, now, of all times, and if they are getting engaged now, why get married next week? Why not give it a few years first?"

"You want them to put their lives on hold?" she asks, and she asks it in a way that I can't tell whether she's judging me or not.

"On hold? Yeah, I want them to consider it. I mean, what harm could that do? Put it on hold at least until the trial is over."

"Maybe they think you're never getting out of here."

I shake my head. I don't think anybody can really be thinking that. "They're wrong."

"Because you didn't kill anybody?"

It's an important question, and one she no doubt rehearsed a few times on the drive out here.

"I know I killed them," I say. "That's what everybody keeps telling me. In the beginning it was hard to believe, but if you have a thousand people all telling you the sky is going to fall, then it's going to fall," I say. Then I look glum. My *Joe is sad* look. Tried and perfected on others. "I guess if that's true, then I don't deserve to be let out of here. I guess I do . . ." I say, then add the slight theatrical pause, count off one beat, off another, "I guess I do deserve to die. That's what . . ." pause, one beat, two beats, "that's what they're going to do. They're going to kill me, you know. They're going to pass this bill everybody on TV is talking about and I'm going to be number one on the hanging list."

She doesn't answer. I don't mean any of what I said, and I'm not sure whether she believes it either. The silence grows and I feel the need to fill it with something that makes me sound retarded, but not too retarded.

"I mean, the things they say I did—that just isn't me. I'm not that person. Ask anybody. Ask my mom, or the cops I used to work with," I say, and a series of events starts running through my mind—previous women, previous victims, eggs jammed in mouths and the groans of the dying. I shift a little in my chair, thankful the table is in the way of her seeing my growing erection. It's one of the few times I've hated something being between it and a woman like Ali.

"You don't remember any of it?"

"I know it sounds like a cliché. I know it's probably what you expected to hear, and the fact you're hearing it proves I'm making it up. Bad people always remember what they do. It's why they do it, so they can remember. I guess. All I want is to be better," I say, "and if I did do the things they say I did, then I want to be made to never do that kind of thing again. Maybe this is a waste of time. Maybe they should just keep me here and lock away the key."

"Throw away the key."

"Huh?"

"The expression is *throw away the key*."

"What key?"

Amanda goes back to interlocking her fingers. She touches her two forefingers to her lips. "Not many people would say what you just said," she says, "about deserving to be locked away. It sounds very honest."

"It is."

"The problem, Joe, is that it also sounds very manipulative, which is something the prosecution psychiatrist is claiming you to be."

I don't say anything. I know she's on the cusp of a very important decision. I know I could easily overdo it right now. Best to say nothing. Best to trust that I've already done an awesome job in convincing her.

"It's one of those two things," she says, "but I don't know which."

I don't know what the correct response is, either in words or in emotion. I don't know what to start faking next. Should I thank her, say something insightful, or should I start flopping around on the floor like a fish?

"The problem is you acted like you were mentally challenged," she says.

"I didn't act retarded," I say. "That's just how they saw me."

"The problem was with them?"

"I don't know. Maybe. Maybe it was with me. They all looked down on me, though. They pitied me for some reason. I always knew that, I just never knew why. Maybe they look down on all janitors the same way because we aren't as cool as them."

"Why didn't you ask?"

"How would that have gone? *Excuse me, Detective, but why do you think I'm a moron?* That wasn't going to happen. They always made me feel inferior around them all," I say, and Slow Joe is gone now, and Fast Joe is here, Smart Joe, and Smart Joe is on a roll. "Maybe that's why they saw me like that."

"That's another big insightful take on things," Ali says.

I don't answer. The problem with Smart Joe is that sometimes he can be too smart for his own good.

"I want to learn more about you," she says. "We have the weekend. Everything you say to me is confidential. I'm working for you and your lawyer, not for the prosecution."

"Okay."

"But if you say something that makes me believe you're lying, then the session ends and I don't come back, and I get up in court and I tell the jury exactly that. So basically, Joe, though I'm working for you, I'm also working for the truth. You have three days in which to be honest."

Three days in which to not get caught out lying. I can manage that. Or, if things go to plan with Melissa, I won't need it. "Okay," I tell her, knowing as far as honesty goes, we're not really off to a great start. "So where do we begin?"

"I want to talk about your past."

"My past? Why?"

"In this dream you have, do you ever take off the mask? Does your mother ever recognize you?"

I think about it. In the dream sometimes I'm drinking beer or sometimes Coke, sometimes I'm driving a blue car or a red car, other times the house is different too, my house or her house or one of many other houses I've been in. My mom can be wearing a nightgown or a dress. Sometimes my goldfish are there and I'm sprinkling crumbs of meat loaf into the water for them. The ways I kill her are different. Only thing that never changes is me. I always wear the mask. Even when I put rat poison into her coffee I'm still wearing the mask.

"No," I tell her.

"Are you sure?"

"Not really. I mean, I don't think so."

"And your mother? Does she know who you are?"

I think about it. Then half nod, then half shake my head. "She might do. She looks shocked. She's wearing her Christmas look."

"Her Christmas look?"

"Yeah. That's what I call it. Her look of surprise. It's a long story."

"Well, we need to start somewhere," Ali says. "How about we start with that?"

And that's what we do.

CHAPTER TWENTY-FOUR

I remember I used to believe in Santa Claus. My parents would always make a big deal about it. I'd wake up in the morning and the cookies and milk would be gone, there'd be soot around the base of the fireplace, and Dad would always tell me he'd heard Santa up on the roof and glimpsed a reindeer. I was always excited he'd been, but disappointed I'd missed him. Christmas Eve I'd always try my best to stay awake, and not know I'd failed until I woke up around seven in the morning with the sun breaking through my curtains. Santa had a way of sneaking into your house without anybody knowing he was there at the time. It's something we have in common.

The Christmas that really stands out for me was when I was eight years old. At that stage the belief in Santa was over—though years later I would come to believe in people like Santa Kenny. Back then my mother was a different person. My father was too. I'm not really sure what my father was. He was different in a way even now I wouldn't be able to identify. Whatever it was, I think my mother knew it too. It was a problem between them, and when there were problems Dad would always hang out with William—or Uncle Bill, as we called him. Uncle Billy wasn't really my uncle, but Dad's best friend, though a few years after that Christmas Uncle Billy didn't come around anymore, as him and Dad and Mom had some kind of falling out. I think a lot of the time the problem between Mom and Dad was Uncle Billy.

I gave my mother a kitten for Christmas. It was a black-and-white, seven-week-old kitten I'd gotten from a friend at school whose pet cat had dropped a litter of them. I swapped a magazine for the cat. The kid didn't tell his parents and I didn't tell my dad, and if we had then it all would have gone very differently. The look on Mom's face when she saw the little kitten is a look that has stayed with me forever. Her Christmas look. It's where her lips peel back in a violent sneer and her teeth come forward like a shark. Her eyes open so wide it seems there is nothing left to hold them in. It's the kind of expression where she has just looked deep into her worst nightmares only to find that every one of them is coming true. My mom never liked the kitten. At first I thought that made her a mean lady, a coldhearted lady, because everybody loved kittens. Everybody.

It turned out not to be so much that my mother wasn't a kitten person. It was more that she wasn't a dead-kitten person. She didn't like them after they'd been sealed inside a wrapped cardboard box with a ribbon around it for five days. At eight years old I wasn't a mind reader. All these years later and I'm still not.

I tell Ali and Ali takes notes. The prison chair is uncomfortable and I'm handcuffed to it, which is perhaps the only reason Ali is in here all alone with me. She either has trust issues or is well aware that the last twelve months have been lonely for me and that in ten minutes' time, when they'd be mopping her up off the floor, I'd be telling the guards I'd had another memory lapse.

"Did you know the cat was going to die?"

"I never thought about it," I say, and it's true. I didn't. I just thought it would be one nice thing I could do for my mother. It turned out it wasn't. Turns out I've never done any nice things for my mother. Except get arrested. Her life really seems to be running smoothly now for her and Walt.

"You didn't check on it? Or think it'd need food?"

"It had a name," I say, and the words are out of my mouth before even thinking about it. "His name was John."

"You named the cat John?"

"It was dead, like my Grandfather John, who'd died earlier that year."

"So you named the cat after it died? After your grandfather?"

"Who wouldn't name a cat?" I ask.

She scribbles more down on her pad. "How did you feel when she opened the package and you saw it was dead?"

"I don't know. Sad, I guess."

"You guess?"

"Wouldn't anybody feel sad?"

"Sad or angry. But you're only guessing, aren't you, Joe. You don't know what you felt."

I shrug like it doesn't matter. Maybe it does. I don't know. It feels like she is trying to trap me somehow, and I don't know in which way. Is this woman trying to help me? The answer comes to me a moment later. This isn't about me. It's about her. It's about her career and the next step she will take along it once all of this is over for her. Maybe I'll be the topic of a medical paper in her future.

"Joe? What are you thinking about?"

"The cat."

"Tell me, honestly, were you sad?"

"Of course," I tell her.

"Because the cat died? Or because your mom was angry at you?"

Because I'd swapped one of my favorite magazines for something that was now useless. That was the real truth. "Both. I guess."

"You have to stop guessing, Joe. What about your father? What happened?"

"What do you mean?"

"When he saw the cat. What did he do?"

"Well, Mom had dropped the box on the floor in front of her. It had tipped on its side and the cat had spilled out. It didn't look anywhere near the same as when I had put it in there, plus now that the box was open it stank. My dad used the lid to scoop it back into the box and carried it outside and he buried it."

"I mean what did he do to you, Joe?"

"Nothing."

"Did he hit you?"

"Yeah, he hit me. Is that what you wanted to hear? He slapped me across the face so hard it bruised. It was the only time he ever touched me. He came into my room later that day and he hugged me, and he told me he was sorry, and he never hit me again. It was all so sudden I didn't know what was going on. For a day I thought he was angry that I hadn't given him a dead cat too."

Amy doesn't answer. I smile a little. "That was a joke," I say. "The last part."

She smiles a little, and she's thinking that her PCJ—Prince Charming Joe—has just arrived. Only problem, as far as she can see, is I'm in prison for multiple rape/homicides. She knows, like we all do, that love does find a way. She's thrilled because PCJ has a sense of humor—and that's a plus. Women always bullshit about humor being the most important thing. They say it's more important than looks. Hopefully it's more important than history too. Women also dig scars, but my scar twists one side of my face into a Halloween mask, and sometimes I can still feel the heat of my skin burning from where the bullet tore the flesh open. I start to smile, but whatever moment is developing between us is suddenly lost when my eyelid becomes jammed when I blink and it looks like I'm winking. She frowns a little.

"It gets stuck," I say. "Since the accident." I reach up and tug it down and it stings a little bit and then starts working again.

"You call it an accident?"

I shrug. "What else would I call it? I didn't intend any of this."

"Then by that logic, people who get cancer could call that an accident."

"But I don't have cancer," I tell her.

"Okay, Joe," she says. "If you didn't intend it, and if you really can't remember what you did, why were you carrying Detective Calhoun's gun, and why did you try to turn it on yourself?"

It's a good question. An annoying question that has been put to me a few times now. Thankfully it's one that comes with an easy answer. "I don't remember that either," I tell her.

"Joe—"

"It's true," I tell her, and I touch my free hand back up to my eye. The doctor warned me it would catch occasionally for the rest of my life. I don't know why or on what, and he didn't seem in a real information-offering mood. He seemed more interested in who he was treating, and how he was going to tell the boys about it that night at the bar.

Her expression relaxes a little. "Does it hurt?"

"Only when I'm awake."

"Let's move on," she says. "Did you ever try giving your mother another pet?"

I scoff at the thought. "No. She wouldn't have appreciated it."

"I meant an alive pet, Joe."

"Oh. Well, no, the same thing applies."

"Did you ever kill any more animals?"

"You're implying I killed John," I tell her.

"You did kill John."

"No, the cardboard box and lack of air killed John. Me being eight years old is what killed John. It was an accident."

"Like your scar is an accident."

"Exactly," I say, pleased she's beginning to understand.

"You still haven't told me, Joe, whether you killed any other animals?"

"Why would I?" I ask, but yes, I have killed other animals—I've done it to get what I want from people.

"Okay. I think we're pretty much done for today," she says, and she starts to shuffle her pad back into her briefcase. It's a similar model to the one I used to carry my lunch and my knives and my gun around in, and for a moment—for a brief second—I wonder if it's actually mine.

"Why?"

"Because you're not being forthcoming, that's why."

"What?"

"The animals. I asked you twice and twice you avoided the question. That suggests you don't really want my help."

"Wait," I say, and I try to stand up, but the handcuffs keep me down.

"I'll think about coming back tomorrow," she says.

"What does that mean? That you might not come back?"

"I have to decide whether or not you're faking everything you're saying. Whether you're telling me what you think I want to hear. Not remembering what you did to these women, I don't know, it might be a little hard for me to buy. I've seen it before. I could be seeing it now. Problem with the insanity plea is you seem very aware of what you're saying."

I say nothing. It seems saying nothing works better for me.

She moves to the door and bangs on it.

"Wait," I tell her.

"What for?"

"Please. Please, this is my life we're talking about here. I'm scared. There are people in here who want to kill me. I have no idea what the fuck I've done over the last few years, I'm lost and I'm scared and please, please, don't go. Not yet. Even if you don't believe me, I just need somebody to talk to."

The guard opens the door. Ali stands there staring at me and the guard stands there staring at her.

"Ma'am?" he says.

She looks at the guard. "False alarm," she says, and she moves back to the table. The guard manages to multitask a shrug with an eye-roll while closing the door.

"Do you want to see more of me or not, Joe?"

Ideally, I'd like to see as much of her as I can. If it weren't for the handcuffs and the guard outside I would make the effort to see every inch of her.

"Of course."

"Then play it straight with me, okay?" She sits back down. She leans forward in her chair and to her credit she doesn't interlock her fingers—at least not immediately, not until after she asks "Are you going to stop playing games with me, Joe?"

"Yes."

"Let's go back to your childhood."

"There isn't much to tell. My mom and dad were normal."

"Your father killed himself," she says. "That's not normal, Joe."

"I know that. I meant, you know, the family dynamic was normal. Dad would go to work and mom would stay at home and I would go to school. The only thing that changed was we all got older."

"How'd you feel about him killing himself?"

I shake my head. This isn't a subject I really want to talk about. "Are you serious? How do you think I felt?"

"Are you checking for answers, Joe?"

"No. Of course not. I was angry. Upset. Confused. I mean, the guy was my dad. He was always supposed to be there. He was meant to protect me. And he just, you know, just thought *fuck it* and ended things. It was pretty selfish."

"Did you get any counseling at the time?"

"Why would I get counseling?"

"Did your father leave a note?"

"No."

"Do you know why he did it?"

"Not really," I say, but that's not entirely true. I have this dream sometimes, which, sometimes, I think might actually be a memory rather than a dream. It was the Uncle Billy factor. I came home to find Dad and Uncle Billy in the shower together nine years ago. I don't know if my father would have killed himself if I'd given him the time to really think about it. I think he would have. Better that than living with mom's anger. His suicide was less a suicide and more of his only son nudging him a little closer to heaven. I think that's where he wanted to go since I heard him saying *oh God, oh God* over and over before I opened the bathroom door. It was the less painful solution for everybody involved. And not painful for me at all. Of course, that might just be a dream. . . .

"You sure? You look like you're remembering something."

"I'm just remembering my dad. I miss him. I always miss him."

"Some professionals would call what your father did a *trigger*."

"What?"

"A *trigger*. It means an act that forces you to behave differently. A triggering event."

"Oh. I understand," I say, not so sure I do. I didn't shoot him. I tied him up and stuffed him into his car and put a hose running from the exhaust and through a gap in the window. At least that's what Dream Joe does sometimes.

"I want to talk more about your childhood."

"Because you think there are more triggers?"

"Possibly. Your story about the kitten—"

"John," I interrupt.

"John," she says. "Your story about John makes me think there are going to be other triggers. Tell me, Joe, do you like women?"

"Joe likes everybody," I say.

She looks at me for a few seconds, saying nothing, and I'm sure she's about to tell me off for referring to myself in the third person. I used to do that when I was a janitor and it worked well. Here, I'm not so sure.

"What's your earliest traumatic memory?" she asks.

"I don't have any."

"Something to do with women," she says. "Your mother, possibly. Or an aunt. A neighbor. Tell me something."

"Why? Because that's what the psychiatric textbooks say?" I say, a little too quickly, but I say it that way to stop my mind from traveling back to when I was a teenager.

"Yes, Joe. That's why. I know what I need to hear from you, and I get the strong impression you also know what you need to say. I'm going to give you sixty seconds to tell me something that happened to you when you were young. Trust me, I'll know if you're making it up. But something happened and I want to know what."

"There's nothing," I say, leaning back. I start drumming my fingers on the table.

"Then we're done here," she says, and she starts to put the tape recorder back into her bag.

"Fine," I tell her.

She finishes packing up. "I won't be back," she says.

"Whatever," I tell her.

She makes it to the door. Then she turns back. "I know it's hard, Joe, but if you want me to help you, you have to tell me."

"There's nothing."

"There's obviously something."

"Nope. Nothing," I tell her.

She knocks on the door. The guard opens it up. She doesn't look back. She takes one step, then another step, and then I call out to her. "Wait," I tell her.

She turns back. "What for?"

"Just wait." I close my eyes and tilt my head back and rub my hand over my face for a second, then put my hand in my lap and look at her. The guard looks more pissed off this time than the last time when Ali moves back to her chair. He closes the door again.

"It happened when I was sixteen," I say, and I start to tell her my story.

CHAPTER TWENTY-FIVE

Raphael wakes up feeling like a new man. He feels ten years younger. No, twenty. Hell, he feels like he *is* twenty, even if his muscles do ache like he's fifty-five. Which he is. He rubs at his shoulders as he climbs out of bed. He opens the curtains. He went to sleep in rain, but he's waking in sun. It still looks cold out there, but it's blue skies and no wind and that makes what they have to do this morning so much better. He showers and stares at himself in the mirror for a minute afterward, wondering what he always wonders these days—which is what happened to his body, his face, to the years that have gone by. He thinks about Stella, Stella who is broken on the inside, Stella who is going to help fix him.

He has time for a good breakfast. These days he doesn't tend to eat much. It's pretty obvious when he has his shirt off. Having no appetite combined with being too lazy is the reason. And work—not that he's really working much these days. But today he's going to make the effort. Today he's celebrating. He makes waffles. Mixes up the batter and pours it into the waffle maker, one after the other, more time-consuming than he thought it'd be, but waffles always catch you like that. He eats them with maple syrup and strips of bacon. He drinks a cup of coffee and a glass of orange juice. God he feels good. For the first time in over a year he doesn't feel numb inside, doesn't feel hollow. For the first time in over a year the anger is stomping around his body looking for an outlet. He even had a name for the anger back then. The Red Rage. The Red Rage would keep him awake at night, trying to figure out a way to get revenge for his daughter, only he never could. He didn't know who had killed her. He wasn't a cop. He couldn't figure it out. And then Joe was caught and the Red Rage had to deal with the fact there would be no revenge here because Joe was in jail, so the Red Rage went into hibernation.

Raphael never thought he'd see it again.

He reverses out of the garage. The morning isn't quite as cold as he thought it was going to be when looking out his bedroom window. The plan he has with Stella relies on good weather, and the forecast suggests that's what's on the menu. The roads are dry, but the lawns and gardens are still wet. It's forty-five degrees and might climb another one or two, but not much more. Traffic is thin. Raphael has the radio on. It's talk radio. Raphael is obsessed by it. Has been for the last few months. He keeps thinking he ought to make a call. Others are. They're sharing their opinion about the death penalty, those who are calling all having an extreme position on it.

His position is extreme too.

He drives to the same coffee shop he went to last night with Stella. It's an independent store that goes by the name Dregs, and has old movie posters stuck across every spare inch of wall, even one of the windows is blotted out by movie cards. He doesn't go in this time. Instead Stella is waiting in her car in the parking lot out back that services a dozen stores, including a few hairdressers and a novelty sex shop. He pulls over next to her and pops the trunk. He helps her load the stuff from her car into his car. She isn't wearing the pregnancy suit.

Then they're driving together. Talkback radio still on. People still ringing in.

"I honestly don't know what people are thinking," Raphael says to her. "How can anybody be against it? How can anybody look at a monster like Joe Middleton, and say he has rights? People are getting confused. They see putting criminals down as murder, but it's not murder. How can it be, when the people being executed aren't human?"

"I agree," she says, and of course she agrees—they wouldn't be doing this if they didn't see eye to eye on all of this.

They get stuck behind a truck on the motorway, a lorry two trailers long and full of sheep, the ones on the edges staring between the wooden slats of the walls out at the scenery racing by, not knowing their lives are flashing in front of their eyes just as quickly as the view, not knowing that trucks full of sheep tend to head to places where they take the *live* out of *livestock*. That would be murder too, according to the people against the death penalty.

But not Stella.

She was a good find. Eager. Angry. Capable. And, truth be told, a little scary. And since he's admitting things to himself—quite the stunner. Last night he was hollow inside—the trial coming up, his protest starting on Monday. But what was that, really? He and others like him hanging outside the courthouse in the cold, holding up signs, and none of it was going to bring his daughter back. He was doing it because it was something to do—they were motions to go through, motions that were putting off what he really wanted to do to himself while he lounged around inside his house wearing his pajamas for entire days at a time, stains forming on the sleeves where he'd spill tomato sauce or whiskey on them. Last night Stella came into his life. He bought the coffees and she shared the plan. It was a great plan. Good coffees, but a great plan.

The sheep truck turns off. The motorway carries on. For all the conversation they made last night, this morning it's different. He's ready to explode with excitement, but he's too afraid of saying the wrong thing, too afraid that Stella won't turn out to be as capable as he first thought. At the same time he doesn't want to disappoint her.

This is going to happen, he keeps telling himself. It's going to happen and Joe is going to die, and Raphael is going to be the one to pull the trigger. It won't bring Angela back, but it sure as hell beats protesting. It will bring peace to his life. Perhaps a destiny too. There are others who need his help. Others from the group. This feels like it could really be the beginning of something.

Of course he has to be careful not to get ahead of himself.

"We're nearly there," he tells her.

"When was the last time you were out here?" she asks.

Out here is thirty minutes north of the city.

"A long time," he says, only it wasn't a long time ago, it was last year. "My parents used to own a getaway nearby," he tells her, "but it burned down years ago. I used to bring my wife and Angela out here for picnics during the summers, but not in a long time now. Not in almost twenty years."

He takes a side road from the motorway, through farm country for another five minutes, and then another turnoff—this time onto a shingle road that after two hundred yards becomes compacted dirt as the scenery changes from open fields to forest. The road is bumpy, but the four-wheel drive manages it easily enough. He goes slow. There aren't many twists and turns, but the back wheels occasionally skid off large tree roots as they round the few corners there are. It's almost untouched New Zealand scenery. It's why people come here, film movies here, farm sheep, and raise children. Snowy mountains in the near distance, clear rivers, massive trees.

He pulls into a clearing. It's just like he told her. Nobody around for miles.

"It's scenic," Stella says.

"Easy to fall in love with," he says.

They climb out of the car. The air is completely still. And quiet. The only thing Raphael can hear is the engine pinging from the SUV, and Stella moving about. No birds, no signs of life—they could be the last two people in the world. He walks around to the back of the SUV and pulls out the gun case. Stella starts messing around with a rucksack, reorganizing the order of things inside it before throwing it over her shoulder. His wife used to do the same thing with her handbag. Their feet sink a little into the dirt as they move beyond the car, through the trees, and toward another clearing, toward where the getaway used to be until one day somebody thought it would be fun to set fire to it.

"I can't believe I've never fired a gun," he says, and he really can't believe it. What kind of guy gets to fifty-five years old without ever having fired one? "It's always something I wanted to do," he says, and he wishes he hadn't said it. All he's doing is confirming he might not be the right guy for this. And nothing could be further from the truth. Just ask the Red Rage.

Stella doesn't answer him. He knows she's fired one. It's one of the reasons she's come to him. She told him she's a terrible shot. She told him that if he is a terrible shot too, then this mission is over. Only she didn't call it a mission. He wonders if the police would call it a movement.

She opens the rucksack and starts taking out some tin cans. They're all empty. Baby-food tins, spaghetti tins, soup tins. She starts lining them up a few feet from each other. She leaves some in full view, others slightly hidden behind roots, others she pins in between branches at different heights. After a few minutes they have a shooting gallery and some very ugly tree decorations.

They move thirty yards into the clearing. They're now two hundred yards from the car with a belt of trees between them, trees that will stop any stray bullets from hitting the SUV. Another hundred yards away are the foundations of the cabin, but they're covered in long grass, as if the scorched earth made the ground more fertile. "This is a good distance," she says.

Raphael drops to his knees. Immediately moisture seeps out of the ground and into his pants. He rests the case on the ground and pops the lid. It's the first time he's seen the gun and he whistles quietly at it. It just happens instinctively—maybe the same way people whistle at nice-looking women or sports cars. There's no instruction booklet. "Wow," he says. And then again, "Wow. I hope you know how it goes together?"

"I was given a lesson," she says.

"From the gun store?" he asks, and he's fishing for information, and it's obvious he's fishing for information, and obvious he's not going to get it.

"Exactly," she says.

He picks up the barrel. It's black and solid and feels dangerous and is a little lighter than he thought it would have been. He puts it back into the case. He's itching to try slotting things together, but instead he waits. It's her show—and he doesn't want to risk breaking something. That'd be a real mood killer. It takes her a few minutes, the pieces snapping together with firm clicking sounds. He stands up to watch her doing it; kneeling down over the case was hurting his back a little. She pulls a box of ammunition out from her rucksack and loads it into the magazine. It takes twenty bullets, and there are twenty-four in the case. He can tell from the way she goes about it that she wasn't kidding when she said she's not good with guns.

"How many boxes?" he asks.

"Three," she says. "We can practice with them all. We just need to keep two rounds, plus our special round." She reaches back into the rucksack. "Here," she says, and she hands him a set of earmuffs. Then she starts looking back through the bag.

"Lost something?" he asks.

"No," she says. "I know they're . . . Oh, wait, I took them out back at the car."

"Took what out?"

"My earmuffs."

"I'll get them," Raphael says.

"It's okay," she says, "I'll go. Here, set this up," she says, and hands him a blanket from the rucksack before walking off in the direction of the car, taking the rucksack with her.

He spreads the blanket out. It's big enough for two people to lie on without feet or hands overlapping onto the grass. It's thick too, but it'll only be a matter of time before it starts soaking up the rain from the damp ground, especially once they lie on it. It reminds him of when he used to picnic here. Janice, his wife, and Angela, his little girl. Janice still lives in the city and Raphael talks with her, but not often—there is too much sadness there, it was a downward spiral neither of them could break. Best to focus on the good times. Like coming out here with a picnic blanket and a fishing rod. They'd hit the river half a mile away, but in all the years never did they catch a single fish, which was a relief, really, because he wouldn't have known what to do with it. Of course those were summer days. He has never been here in the winter.

Stella comes back. She's carrying her earmuffs. His are orange and hers are blue, but other than that they look identical. She holds them up and gives him an apologetic smile before putting them on. He smiles back, then puts his on too. The sounds both he and Stella are making are dulled dramatically. She lies down and takes hold of the gun. He stands a little behind her, watching the curves of her body, watching the gun, watching the targets up ahead. She stabilizes her elbows into the ground. She shrugs her shoulders around a little, twists her head back and forth, and finds a comfortable position. This time yesterday he was watching morning TV and eating toast that he'd been too lazy to put butter on. He'd been hanging out in his underwear with the heaters on full so he wouldn't have to get dressed. He'd been wondering what the hell to do that day before the counseling session, and had ended up continuing to do what he'd started doing that morning.

Stella reaches up and brushes her hair back over her ears to keep it away from the scope. She adjusts herself one more time, then reaches for the trigger. Her finger settles on it. Raphael holds his breath.

The gun kicks up as the bullet explodes from the barrel. It

sounds like a thunderclap. It's so loud for a moment he thinks the earmuffs are there just to hold the blood that's going to run from his ears. Only there is no blood. There would be, he's sure of it, if it weren't for the muffs. He can't tell which tin she was aiming at because none of them have moved.

"Wow," Raphael says, the word sounding like it's coming from deep underground.

She lines up the tin again. Takes her time. He watches her breathe in. Breathe out. He can't wait to have a turn. He can feel his heart racing. She pulls the trigger. The same explosion. This time he sees a divot appear in the ground about a foot from a tin. She wasn't kidding about being a bad shot.

"Third time's the charm," Raphael says, though he doesn't know if she can hear him. It turns out third time isn't the charm. Nor is the fourth. Nor fifth. She lays the gun down on the blanket and rolls off to the side and takes off her earmuffs. She gives him a small *I tried my best* shrug, and he gives her a small *Don't worry about it* smile.

"See what you think," she says.

Raphael nods. He feels like a kid at Christmas.

He squats down, his knees hurting a little, the left one popping, and he feels a little embarrassed, he feels old. Stella puts her earmuffs back into place. He lies in the same position she was in. The gun feels like a natural extension of his arms. It makes him feel powerful. He likes feeling that way. He puts his eye up to the scope. It's incredibly clear. So clear he doesn't see how anybody could miss with something like this. Of course people miss because the conditions change. Wind. Rain. Glare from the sun. Other people around. All sorts of stuff. Shooting a tin can is different from shooting a man. The cans are still. There is no sense of urgency, no sense of panic, no sense of hitting the wrong can and ruining the lives of other cans who loved it.

He squeezes the trigger. The tin can takes flight, landing and skidding to a stop five yards away, where it lies on its side, half dented with a hole going through one side and out the opposite.

He eyes up one of the tins half-hidden by a thick tree root. That one goes flying too. He's two for two. He's a natural.

He looks back through the scope. He thinks about his daughter. He knows how she died. He knows Joe broke into her house. He killed her cat before dragging her from her bathroom. He knows exactly what he did to her. The way he tied her to the bed, the way he pushed an egg into her mouth, the way he pushed himself into her. . . .

This third shot misses. Wild right. He pulls his face away from the scope. Stares at the ground beneath his chest.

"What's wrong?" Stella asks.

He looks up at her. "Nothing," he says. "Just . . . just nothing. Give me a second," he says, and he sucks in a few deep breaths and he wants to scream. He wants to drive to the prison right now and take this gun into the cells and shoot Joe where he stands, shoot the fucker in the knees, stomp on them, punch him in the face over and over. He wants to cut his eyelids off, rip his organs out, drown him, revive him, set fire to him. There isn't a single bad thing he doesn't want to do. The Red Rage wants to keep the fucker alive for as long as he can, and just keep cutting and stomping, cutting and hurting.

And Stella—sweet, sweet Stella is going to give him that chance.

He puts his eye back up to the scope. He takes another shot and misses by just as much as the last one. Damn it. He closes his eyes. This isn't working. Not when he's angry.

"Raphael?"

He gets onto his knee. "Give me a minute," he says, and gets to his feet, the other knee popping this time, only this time he's too angry to feel embarrassed. He stares out at the foundations of the cabin, and in those long blades of grass hidden from view are parts of the walls too. If he's missing now, he's going to miss when the shot presents itself.

Stella puts a hand on his shoulder. "It's going to be okay," she says. "You just need to focus."

"I am focusing," he says, but he's focusing on the wrong damn things. He has to stop thinking of his daughter, of her naked beneath Joe, of the fear racing in her head, of Joe being the last thing she would see and of her knowing that. He can't think about how there were many people who loved her and how none of them were there to help her. He has to think about Joe. Joe with a bullet in his head. Joe with his head in a cardboard box. Joe with a lot of bad shit happening to him.

None of it will bring Angela back.

He lies back down, his knee popping again. He looks through the scope. He stares at the tin can hanging from the tree. That tin can is Joe's head. That's what he thinks. He has to let go of the anger. Not for good, just for now, just when he's behind the barrel of the gun. Breathe in. Breathe out. Stay calm. Empty his mind. He's doing a good thing here. Focus on that. Stay calm and fantastic things are going to happen. Not closure, he can never have that, but he can have revenge. It's there waiting for him. He just has to take it.

He squeezes the trigger. The tin can doesn't disappear, but he does wing it. He takes another shot. This time it flies out of sight. He shoots another one. And another. His heart rate is slowing. He could probably shoot a thousand tins now if he wanted to.

He's calm now. Calm and this is easy. He uses up the rest of the clip. All the tin cans are gone. Stella shows him how to take the magazine out. He reloads it himself. He shoots more tins, shooting the ones now that have already been shot. He goes through the magazine once again.

Then he rolls onto his side and looks up at Stella. He thinks about the Red Rage. The Red Rage is happy. "We're really doing this," he says.

"We really are," she says, and he loads the magazine back up and carries on shooting.

CHAPTER TWENTY-SIX

Twelve months ago I couldn't even remember it had happened to me. Twelve months ago there were more important things on my mind, wonderful distractions—the kind of distractions that had an entire police force hunting me down. Since being locked away I've had time to think about things—in fact time is the only thing I have had. My past is a blend of memories so distant they feel like they belong to somebody else, or perhaps they're TV moments I've seen and somehow claimed as my own.

I was sixteen years old and I had never done a single illegal thing except for breaking into a few homes, shoplifting, and once burning down a barn that had goats inside that I didn't know were there. I used to sneak out of my room at night and walk around the streets, not looking for anything, but just walking, being one with my neighborhood and thinking of those that were in it. I could always hear the ocean only a few blocks away. Sometimes I'd walk down the beach and stare out at the water as the moon hung over it. On calm nights when the moon was full it'd reflect off the wet ripples in the sand that were formed by the leaving tide. I'd think about swimming, but then I'd think about how cold that water would be, about the things out there swimming beneath the surface. Hungry things.

I shift on my seat and look at Ali, at her soft skin, at her face. She's taking notes even though the recorder is capturing everything. I tell her all about it, my remaining testicle throbbing as the memory stirs up more than just some emotions.

I used to break into people's homes. It wasn't about money. I couldn't buy things without my parents noticing. I couldn't steal a TV and bring that home because back then TVs were almost as heavy as dishwashers. I broke in for a different reason. I used to pick out girls at school I liked, and during summer holidays when I knew their families were away I'd sneak into their bedrooms. When the house was empty like that, you could spend all day long in those rooms, lying on the bed and really getting to know somebody. You could really make yourself at home. The fridge and pantry would provide sustenance, the bed somewhere to relax, the underwear I'd find in the girl's drawers would provide texture to the fantasy. When school was back the girls would never know what I'd touched while they were away, and that gave me a feeling of superiority. They'd be walking around wearing panties that I'd spent time with. That's the truth, and it's a truth that I can't tell the woman opposite me.

When I broke into my auntie's house, it was purely about money. I wasn't breaking in to spend time eating her food and cuddling her underwear. I was being beaten at school by a pair of brothers—twins, actually, who told me the solution to making those beatings go away was for me to pay them. So in a way all of this started from those two. Simple, really. Two bullies who were older than me created a serial killer. I had no money. But I knew I had to get some. Up until my auntie's house I'd only broken into homes where I knew the people were away on holiday. Nobody holidayed during the school term.

"I needed the money," I tell my psychiatrist, and I tell her why. She doesn't look saddened by the tale, she doesn't frown and go

Poor Joe, you were even a victim back then, but she does perhaps jot it down since her pen doesn't stop moving. I wouldn't put it past her to be doodling a picture of her and me naked. "The only place I could think to get it was my auntie's house. Auntie Celeste. She was my mom's sister."

"Was?"

"She died about five years ago."

"How?" she asks, and her tone is suspicious.

"Cancer, I think," I say, but it could have been anything. A tumor. A heart condition. Whatever it is people tend to start getting when they're over sixty. It certainly wasn't me.

"So you broke into her house?"

The house was a single-story dwelling that was a little nicer than my parents', but not nice enough for me to break in and stay a while. It was a town house built on the edge of South Brighton heading toward New Brighton, not that there's really anything that new in either suburb. It was a ten-minute bike ride between the two houses. Auntie Celeste's house had a concrete tile roof and wooden siding, it had aluminum joinery and windows that my auntie cleaned the salt spray from every day. It had a pretty good lock on the back door that was stronger than the hinges on the door, so if you gave it a good kick the screws would rip away from the frame and the door would cave in. Or, you could take the alternative option—I used my mom's key. My mother and her sister had swapped keys after Celeste's husband had died from an unexpected heart attack. They felt safer knowing they could get into each other's house in an emergency.

This was an emergency.

I snuck out of my bedroom a little after midnight. It was pretty easy to do, it was just a matter of opening the window and having the athletic ability to drop a few feet. I rode my bike to within a block of my auntie's house where there was a park. You had to be careful with parks at night in Christchurch. I knew it back then and I've certainly had bad experiences in them since. I didn't see anybody about, so I hid my bike in a bunch of bushes. I didn't lock it. I walked the rest of the way. The street was pretty dead. People were in bed for work, or for school. It was a Sunday night. People are pretty much less alert on a Sunday night than any other night of the week. There were a few lights on, but not many, and certainly none inside my aunt's house. I could hear the ocean, the tide bringing in the waves. They crashed against the shore only a few hundred yards away, each one covering any sound I made.

It was dark around the back of the house. There were no gates or fences blocking access from the front to the back. There were fences on each side between properties, and one running along the back. All the fences in this part of the neighborhood were run-down, the sun and salt air having warped the planks enough to make archery bows out of them. The backyard was mostly brown patches of burned-off grass. There was an old vegetable garden that was overgrown with weeds and old potatoes—my uncle's pride and joy, but not my auntie's. She was letting nature take its course the same way it took its course with my uncle.

I reached the back door and used the key and made my way inside. I was as nervous as hell. So nervous I'd even thrown up back at the park where I parked my bike. I knew the layout of the house. My parents had dragged me here a thousand times over the years. The bedrooms were at the back, and only one of them was a bedroom, the other one was a sewing room that my auntie never really used for sewing, but my uncle used for drinking. The back door took me into the lounge and dining area. I didn't turn on any lights. I had a small flashlight and no knife because I didn't need a weapon. I was sixteen years old and had never had the desire to kill anybody—not for real, other than those who were bullying me at school, and maybe some of the neighbors, and the fantasies I had about the girls at school whose underwear and bedrooms I spent time with may have involved some nasty thoughts, but me stabbing them wasn't one of them. Not back then.

My auntie had a wad of cash inside a tea-bag container in the pantry. She'd always go to it if she was giving money to my mom if mom was going to the store, and could mom pick up a packet of cigarettes or some sugar or whatever else Auntie Celeste was short of. I opened the lid and pulled out the money, but didn't take the time to count it. There was no point. I wanted to get out of there. I was nervous, and the kitchen stank of cigarette smoke just how it always did, and I wanted to be gone. I closed the pantry and had halved the distance to the back door when the lights came on. My auntie was standing in the dining room. She was wearing a pink robe and her hair was in curlers and she had a crossbow in her hands. It was my auntie—but I didn't recognize her. She had a hard look on her face.

"A crossbow?" the psychiatrist asks when I get to this part of the story. "Your auntie had a crossbow?"

"I never knew she had one," I tell her. "If I'd known, I wouldn't have gone there."

"But a crossbow? Really?"

I understand her surprise. Aunties aren't the kind of people to own crossbows. Except for the ones who do. And my auntie was one of those. "I'm not lying," I tell her.

"No, I didn't think you were. Why do you think she had one? Did your uncle go hunting?"

"Not that I know of. I don't know why she had one, and I never asked her. I remember seeing it five years ago when she died. We had to go around to her house and go through her stuff. It still looked the same. I don't know if she ever fired it."

"Was your mum surprised to see it?"

"If she was, she didn't say."

"That night in her house, what did you do?"

"She told me to stand still, and that's exactly what I did. I thought I was going to throw up again. I was sure if I moved, even if I blinked, she was going to shoot me. I'd seen enough movies to know exactly how it was going to happen. She'd pull the trigger then there'd be a whistling sound that lasted half a second, then I'd clutch my stomach with my fingers around the end of an arrow. I even held my breath in case that was enough of an incentive for her to shoot me."

"What happened?"

"Nothing happened. Not right away. Neither of us said anything for about ten seconds or so, and then she said my name. I think it took her that long not to figure out it was me, but to figure out that it *really* could be me. I think she recognized me immediately, discarded it, went through a whole bunch of other possibilities looking for a better fit before coming back to me. When she got there she didn't lower the crossbow.

"She said she was going to call the police. I asked her not to. She said it would be for my own good. I begged her not to. She said she was disappointed in me. Extremely disappointed. I'd heard that before, but didn't tell her. She said it was going to crush my parents. I told her I was desperate for the money. Then I told her why, about the bullies and their threats and how paying them off was the only way I was going to be able to walk around school without having my pants pulled down around my ankles in front of everybody, or not getting pushed into walls and dog shit smudged into my hair. She nodded and seemed to understand, but kept the crossbow trained on me. She said everything I told her was awful, that school sounded tough, but no matter how tough it was that gave me no excuse for breaking into her house. I still had her money in my hand. It felt warm in there, it was crushed into a ball and my hand was sweating. Both hands were shaking a little, but hers were rock solid. It was like I was the fourth or fifth person she had caught that night."

I was nervous about being shot, but given the choice, I was starting to think I'd prefer getting shot than having my parents find out. There was no way my aunt wouldn't tell them. My mind was racing for ideas, for something I could bargain with. All I could think of was somehow getting my hands on that crossbow. My parents would know of my burglary attempt by morning. I didn't know what would happen then, but it wouldn't be good. I would be grounded, but that was no big deal. They would be disappointed in me, but that didn't mean much either. They might call the police. That's what I was afraid of. I'd rather have been shot than accept what the police would do to me. At sixteen years old, that's the way my mind worked. So I was thinking about how I could get hold of the crossbow and how I could leave the house and my dead auntie and have nobody figure out it had been me.

"You felt guilty," Ali-Ellen says.

"Yes."

"Are you sure?"

"Of course I'm sure. I felt bad, really bad."

"Hmm," she says, and notes something down, then looks back up at me. "Tell me, Joe, was it the fact you were stealing from your auntie that made you feel bad, or the fact you had been caught?"

It's a good question. I had been breaking into people's homes for the best part of a year and I thought I was above being caught. And caught by a woman more than three times my age. That meant even if I could get hold of the crossbow, I would probably get caught afterward.

"At both," I say.

"Uh huh. Okay, what happened next?"

"My aunt asked me what my parents would say if she told them," I say, and as the words come out I travel back in time again, back to that moment leading up to what I would later think of as the Big Bang. My aunt's exact words were *What would your parents say if I told them?* She didn't say *when I tell them*, but *if* I tell them.

They'll hate me for it, I told my aunt. *And maybe they'll want to kick me out*. I didn't think they would, but I wanted my aunt to feel sorry for me.

They probably would, she said, and yet she still didn't lower the crossbow. *Are you armed, Joe?* she asked.

No.

Have you ever been with a woman, Joe?

What?

A woman. Have you ever made love to a woman?

I'm only sixteen, I told her.

That doesn't mean anything, she told me. *Every TV show on these days has teenagers screwing. It's what soap operas are becoming about. They've gone from adult story lines to children story lines, giving the children adult lives. Forty years ago they were about differences between people, struggling to run pubs and businesses; these days it's all about fucking. Do you know how long your Uncle Neville has been dead?*

Have you forgotten? I asked.

No. No, of course I haven't forgotten. He's been gone six years now.

Then why did you ask me?

It doesn't matter, she said. *All that matters is I miss him. I miss having a man around the house. Things tend to be let go.* She lowered the crossbow. I wondered how far through the floor it'd go if she pulled the trigger. It was more relaxing than wondering how far it would have gone through me. *How much money have you got there, Joe?*

I don't know.

Count it.

I counted the money. I had to count it twice because I was nervous and messed up the first attempt. I had grabbed all the notes, but left all the coins. I had three hundred and ten dollars. It was a good amount. I figured I could get through most of the school year with that amount.

That means you owe me three hundred and ten dollars' worth of work. There's plenty of things around here that need taking care of. The house hasn't seen fresh paint in ten years. The vegetable garden out back is a jungle. You'll come here when I need you and you won't ever say no to me. Ever. Do you understand me, Joe? You help me, and I help you by not telling your parents I caught you here. Deal?

I have to work off three hundred and ten dollars, I said. *That's what? A few weeks' worth of work?*

No, Joe, it's worked off when I say it's worked off. I have to figure out an hourly rate. It might be five dollars an hour. It might be one dollar an hour. I'll let you know when everything is done that I want done. Of course it's up to you. We can run with the alternative and I can phone the police right now and see where that leads.

I couldn't see any other option. Mowing lawns and painting walls were going to make up my immediate future—and they did.

So would the Big Bang—only I didn't know it then. At least she didn't emasculate me by having a poodle I would need to walk and clean up after.

I suppose so, I answered.

You suppose so? You need to sound a little more enthusiastic than that.

It's a deal. I said, trying to put some heart into it.

Good. *Lock the door behind you on your way out, Joe, and I'll call you on the weekend.*

I didn't move. I understood everything she had said, but I still felt unsure about it. *I can go?*

You can go.

Umm . . . thank you, I said, unsure what else I could have said.

"And then I left," I tell my psychiatrist, having just relived the whole scene with my auntie for her.

Ali has a puzzled look on her face. "That's it?" she asks. "That's the traumatic experience you had when you were sixteen? Almost getting shot by your auntie?"

"That was only the start of it," I tell her.

"Then what?"

Before I can answer, there's a knock on the door, and a moment later a prison guard, one I haven't seen before, comes in.

"You've got a visitor," he says.

"I know," I answer, shaking my head at his stupidity. "She's sitting opposite me."

"No, not her, another visitor." Then he looks at Ali. "I'm sorry ma'am, but you're welcome to wait here—should only be fifteen minutes."

"That's fine," she says.

The guard uncuffs me from the chair and I behave just like any model citizen would behave. He escorts me down the hall. I've already figured out who I must be going to see, so when I'm put into another room and sit down opposite the former detective, I already know what it is I'm going to say.

CHAPTER TWENTY-SEVEN

He hates being here. In many ways, Schroder knows he's lucky, damn lucky, not to be an actual guest of the prison. The last case he worked got about as bad as it could have gotten. He and his partner, Tate, were forced to make a decision. A guy was starting to cut up a little girl. He gave them an option. Do his bidding, or the cutting would continue. He'd already cut that little girl's finger off, and there would be more. That's where the old lady that Schroder killed came into it. That was the guy's bidding.

The crime was covered up. If it hadn't been, he'd be in here, probably in the same damn cell group as Joe. He'd know a lot of people too. Others he'd arrested. Santa Suit Kenny is one of his. Edward Hunter. Caleb Cole. There are others too who would love the chance to see him every day in here. He would be joining them for fifteen years.

Only a few people know what Schroder really did. Theodore Tate. A few other cops. And Caleb Cole, because Cole is the person who made him shoot that woman. There are two things

Schroder is counting on. First, nobody would believe Cole if he told them what really happened. Second, Cole agreed to keep his mouth shut in order to stay out of general population. Cole had spent fifteen years in general population and it had not gone well for him. He would do anything to stop going back. Plus Cole has a somewhat fucked-up moral system, a real sense of what's right and wrong. Making Schroder kill that old woman was right. Talking about it was wrong. Cole had wanted that woman to pay, and Schroder had made that happen. So Cole was indebted to him. In some weird way.

Schroder stands while he waits. He's tired. His baby boy woke up every two hours, and his daughter crept down into their room around three a.m. for cuddles. Before he had kids, he never thought it possible to like them. Sometimes, like last night, he sees he was right in thinking that.

Joe is finally brought in. He doesn't look healthy. Not many people in jail do. He can still remember last year when the Carver investigation was wrapping up. He was also dealing with another case that involved Theodore Tate and a bunch of corpses found in a lake at the cemetery, and he was dealing with being a dad. When the pieces all fell together at the end in the Carver case, he simply couldn't believe it. He felt sick. Betrayed. For a few minutes he refused what the evidence was telling him. They all did. Joe Middleton wasn't a killer. He couldn't be. There was a mistake. Only there was no mistake. Not only could Joe Middleton be their guy, he *was* their guy.

Joe sits down in the chair and is handcuffed to it. Schroder doesn't see any point in pleasantries. He'll save small talk for the innocent.

"Okay, Joe. What's your answer? I have other places to be, so don't jerk me around."

Joe holds his hand up. "Slow down, cowboy," he says. "We're still waiting for my lawyer."

He wasn't expecting to hear the *L* word. "What?"

"If we're going to agree to anything, I want my lawyer to be here. I think you'd want that for me, to make sure my rights aren't being tackled over."

"It's *trampled* over."

"What is?"

"It doesn't matter," Schroder says. He had seen Joe's lawyer out in the waiting area. A guy by the name of Kevin Wellington. He had just assumed Wellington was waiting to speak to another of his clients—why he assumed that he doesn't know. Just bad detective work, he guesses. One more reason to suggest his firing wasn't such a bad thing. Well, at least he doesn't have rainwater dripping off his clothes today.

It takes another minute, but then Wellington walks into the room and sits in a spare chair next to Schroder. He's wearing a cologne that for a few seconds tickles the back of Schroder's nose. They don't shake hands.

"Why am I here, Joe?" Wellington asks, and it's not hard hearing the contempt in his voice. He wonders if it's that contempt which has kept Wellington alive. Joe's first two lawyers were full of bravado, they were keen to make names for themselves and it didn't end well for them. The body of the first lawyer still hasn't been found.

"Because Schroder has a deal for us, don't you Schroder?"

"What kind of deal?" the lawyer asks, sounding interested, but only barely. Schroder is starting to warm up to the guy.

"First of all, let me start out by saying I don't remember killing anybody," Joe says, and Schroder glances at the lawyer and the lawyer has the same look Schroder must have on his own face, and he bets Joe hates being the subject of that look. Is it possible that Joe, somehow, can really believe people are going to buy his story? If so, then perhaps he really is insane.

"Come on, Joe," Schroder says, "don't waste our time."

"What kind of deal are you offering?" the lawyer asks. "No, wait, are you still even a cop?"

"Not anymore," Joe says. "He was fired. Why don't you tell us why, Carl?"

"I'm not here in the interests of the prosecution," Schroder says. "I'm here with a private deal from Jonas Jones."

For the first time Wellington looks genuinely interested. He puts his elbows on the table and shifts his weight forward. "The psychic? I don't—" he says, but Joe interrupts him before he can add *see where this is going*.

"He wants me to help him find one of the bodies," Joe says.

"He what?"

"In return for fifty thousand dollars," Schroder says.

The lawyer tilts his head and frowns. Then his elbows come off the table and his weight shifts in the back of the chair. This is about to get difficult, Schroder is sure of it.

"I hope you haven't agreed to this," the lawyer says.

"Not yet."

The lawyer turns to Schroder. "I get it," he says. "You want my client to give you the location of one of the bodies for Jones to find—and you want this done quietly, for which my client will be rewarded—and Jonas wants to take credit for it. That's it, isn't it? Jones wants to show the world he's a true psychic."

Schroder is shocked at how quickly the lawyer figured that out. And perturbed. If the lawyer is that good, then that could be a problem. Nobody wants to see Joe be given a good defense. "Something like that," he says.

"Something? Or exactly like that?"

"Closer to exactly," Schroder admits.

The lawyer turns back to Joe. "If you know where this body is, Joe, this could go toward getting the prosecution to take the death penalty off the table. To sell this information for money you can't even use in here, well, that would be stupid. Let us use it to bargain with the prosecution."

"The death penalty won't be on the table," Joe adds. "I'm an innocent man. I can't remember hurting anybody, and it's just not in my nature to have done that. I'm going to be released, most likely into a hospital for treatment and medication, and when I'm released from there I'm going to need the money."

Wellington stares at Joe, and then he stares at Schroder, and Schroder knows in that moment that if he were ever to play poker, he'd want it to be against that lawyer because he can see exactly what the guy is thinking. Schroder certainly isn't going to argue with Joe—the psychopath can believe what he wants if it will help get this deal signed. He's disgusted at paying a single cent to the man, disgusted at Jonas Jones for using the situation for his own gain, disgusted at himself too for taking the bonus. There is a whole lot of disgust to go around, but there's also a silver lining—Detective Calhoun will be found. He deserves to be properly buried.

The lawyer starts tapping a finger on the table and he stares at it at the same time, deep in thought. He looks up at Schroder and says, "To confirm, you're not here in any capacity for the prosecution or the police force."

"That's right."

"Then what gets said in here is between client and lawyer, and right now you're privileged to that, which means right now you can't reveal any of our conversation."

Schroder nods. He isn't sure if that's true or not. He never really got lawyers. Nobody really does, except other lawyers, and even then he gets the idea half of them don't know what the other half are on about. He's happy to go along with it.

"Fine," he says.

"Can't we all just get along?" Joe asks, and Schroder wants to kick him. "I can't remember killing anybody, that's the truth, but I might remember where Detective Calhoun was buried."

"Where?" Schroder asks.

"Well, it's hard to say really. It's all so vague. Trying to remember it is like trying to remember a dream. Every time I get a handle on it, it's whipped away."

"But the money will make it clearer, right?" Schroder asks.

"Like your boss would say, I'm getting a vision that it would, yes."

Great. So there are going to be no straight answers. Joe is going to play with them for his money because it's the only thing in his life he can control right now, and Schroder is just going to have to accept that if he wants this deal to go ahead. Once again he wonders how the hell his life has gone so badly wrong over the last month. Once again he has to focus on the silver lining—on getting Detective Calhoun back.

"Who buried the body?" he asks. "You or Melissa?"

"Like I said, it's all so vague," Joe says. "I know I didn't kill him, and you know that too, because there's a video of it. I don't know who filmed the video."

"The video was in your flat," Schroder says. "It had your fingerprints all over it."

"All so vague," Joe says, and Schroder wants to punch him.

"And fifty thousand dollars will help you remember," Schroder says.

"That's the feeling I get," Joe says, and then he flashes that stupid smile of his that he used to flash back at the police station when he was walking around with a bucket and mop. Back then it was endearing, but now it's repulsive. "You know, Carl, you don't give people enough credit. You need to be more positive in life. These bad thoughts—they'll bring you down."

Weirdly, he would have to agree, which in itself is a pretty dark thought—one that brings him down.

"You have a contract already drawn up?" Wellington asks.

"We do," Schroder says, and slides a thin folder over to the lawyer, who doesn't pick it up, but stares at it, and Schroder wonders if the lawyer can see a future that he doesn't want to be a part of and if so, then good for him.

"I'm going to need ten minutes with my client," he finally says.

"No problem." Schroder stands up and knocks on the door. "Let me know when you're ready," he says, and one of the guards comes and gets him and leads him back out to the waiting area.

CHAPTER TWENTY-EIGHT

My lawyer is wearing the same outfit and has the same annoyed expression on his face. We sit in the same room and make the same kind of conversation.

"What's going on here, Joe?" he asks.

"It's simple. I tell them where I think the bodies are. If I'm right, I get fifty thousand dollars."

"No, Joe, what you do is risk your entire defense. For a guy who can't remember anything, this is a stupid ploy. You tell them where the body is, that proves you can remember things."

"Doesn't work that way," I tell him. "Jonas Jones is going to 'find' the body," I say, and I use air quotes around the word *find*, and when I do I realize I've never used air quotes before and never will again because they must make me look like a complete asshole. "That's what the contract is for. They can't afford for the public to find out what really happened. It's safe," I tell him.

"This is a dangerous game you're playing, Joe."

"This isn't a game," I answer, somewhat annoyed at him. "This is my life. The world is telling me I've done these terrible, terrible things, when I really haven't. Not me, not the person in front of you. A different Joe, maybe, but this Joe doesn't remember that Joe. When the jury realizes that, when I'm set free, I'm going to need money. It's that simple."

I can tell he doesn't believe a word I tell him. I can tell he's starting to think that I really must be insane. "Well, it's your decision," he says. "Things must be going really well with the psychiatrist for you to be this damn confident."

"Things are going okay," I tell him, confident that this isn't going to go to trial. I'm going to show Schroder where the body is. And Melissa is going to come and save me.

"Fifty thousand dollars isn't going to help you if you're executed. If you want to make a deal, then we'll make a deal. If you want to show them where the body is, then we use that as a bargaining chip. We can start by getting them to take the death penalty off the table."

"It's not even on the table."

"It will be," he says.

"The public won't vote for it."

He shakes his head. "You're wrong. They're going to vote for it."

"I need the money," I tell him.

"You need to listen to your lawyer."

"I am listening," I tell him, "but you're not the one facing life in jail, you're not the one being accused of these awful things. It's your job to tell me what you think, but I still get to make the decisions, right?"

He nods. "That's right," he says.

"Then let's do this," I tell him.

"Let me read this contract," he says, and he opens up the folder.

I watch him as he reads it. He's either a slow reader or a slow understander. Or it's written by a lawyer who's never used plain English in his life. The contract is three pages long. I could write it up in two paragraphs. When my lawyer has read it, he reads it again—this time making notes on a pad. I grow impatient. I don't interrupt him. I just keep staring at him, and after another few minutes I let my mind drift. I start to think about Melissa, and how we're going to spend our first night together. I have a pretty good idea of what we'll be doing. Then I drift further into the future—a week, a month, ten years. Then my lawyer brings me back.

"Are you sure you want to do this, Joe? There is every risk it will come back and bite you in the ass." His face is without any expression. He's like a man watching a football game who not only doesn't care who wins, but also doesn't understand the rules. Or perhaps this is the face of a lawyer who doesn't give a damn about his client.

"I want to do it," I say.

"Okay," he says. He gets up and bangs on the door. The guard opens it and they talk for a few seconds, then my lawyer sits back down and a few minutes later Schroder comes back in. He looks tired. And annoyed. There's a lot of that going around.

"Do we have a deal?" Schroder asks.

"We do," my lawyer says.

"Almost," I say.

Both men look at me. My lawyer sighs and breaks his *don't give a shit* expression. Schroder sighs too and maybe they'll leave here together and sigh each other to sleep tonight.

"The thing is, it's vague," I say. "I can't quite remember where he's buried."

"Yeah. You said that a thousand times already," Schroder says.

"Because you need to understand just how vague it is."

"We get the point, Joe," my lawyer says, "now how about you get to yours."

"Well, my sense of where Calhoun is is so vague it's impossible to give directions. I'd have to show you."

Both my visitors go quiet. Schroder starts shaking his head. Then my lawyer starts shaking his head too. It looks like they're having a competition. Then they look at each other. To their credit, neither man gives a *What are you going to do?* gesture.

"You're not showing us anything," Schroder says. "We're not

making any deal that lets you outside of here even if it's only for an hour."

"Then you'll never find Calhoun," I say.

"Yes we will. Dead people have a way of showing up eventually," he says.

"Not all the time," I answer. "And you know that. Let me show you. Maybe you'll find something there that will help you track down Melissa—that's what you want, right? More than anything? You get that, and your psychic sidekick gets what he wants."

"More than anything I'd like to see you hang for what you've done to this city," Schroder answers, and I think what he really means is he'd like to see me hang for what I did to him. I made him look like a fool. He starts to stand up. My lawyer reaches out and puts a hand on Schroder's arm, and if my mother were here she'd be convinced by now that outside of these walls these two men would start doing the kind of thing my mother would highly disapprove of.

"Wait," my lawyer says, and Schroder lowers himself back into the chair. My lawyer looks at me. "What exactly is it you want, Joe?" he asks. "What is it you're trying to gain by showing where Calhoun is buried? Do you think that by showing instead of just telling that somehow you'll manage to break free?"

"I don't need to break free," I tell them, and then I laugh just to prove how stupid their suggestion was. Even if it is accurate. "No jury in the world is going to convict a man who wasn't in control of his actions. But I can't tell you where the body is because I just can't," I tell them. "If I could, I would. Honestly, Carl, it's impossible. What am I supposed to do? Tell you to turn left at the third rock down a dirt path? It was a year ago. Come on, even you must know that's impossible. You're going to have to believe me," I tell them, "no matter what else you think, this is the truth," I say, but it's not the truth. Not even close. "The absolute truth."

"You don't deserve an hour out there, let alone a minute," Schroder says.

"Doesn't matter what you think," I say. "What matters is whether you want me to show you where Detective Calhoun is."

"What matters even more is you staying put," Schroder responds.

"Why? You think I'm going to escape? I can see how you'd think that—after all, you're the man who let the Christchurch Carver roam free for years. It's only natural you don't think you can stop me from escaping."

"Nice try, Joe, but you're not going to goad me into taking you out of here."

"Well, it's your choice, Carl. You take it or leave it. There's a lot riding on it. Your new boss is going to make a hell of a name for himself. And I need the money, so I want to make this work. And let me ask you, Carl, how much are you making on this? Huh? You wouldn't be doing this unless there was a little something in it for you," I say, holding up my hand rubbing my fingertips against my thumb in the *We're talking about money* gesture.

"Fuck you, Joe."

"And you want Calhoun back, don't you?"

"Gentlemen," my lawyer says, putting his hands out. "Can we stay on point here?"

"I'm not a cop anymore, Joe," Schroder says. "You know that. I can't organize a deal like that."

"You'll find a way," I say.

Schroder shakes his head. "You just don't get it," he says. "God," he says, throwing his head back and looking up at the ceiling. "How the fuck could somebody so stupid have gotten away with it for so long?" He looks back at me. "I must have been stupider than I thought for not arresting you sooner than I did."

"What are you going on about?" I ask.

"For me to make what you're asking happen would involve the police. If the police are involved, then there is no deal, because they're going to know you led us there. And if the police are involved, then that doesn't help Jonas Jones, does it?"

It takes a few seconds for what he's saying to sink in.

"He's right," my lawyer says, and fuck it, he is. They both are.

I shake my head. I could waive the deal, and just agree to show the cops. It just means no money. If I have to, then that's what I'll do. I have to do something to be outside tomorrow twilight. That's all that matters.

"You two need to figure out a way to make it happen," I tell them, "and it needs to happen before the trial starts."

"Joe—" my lawyer starts.

"We're done here," I tell them.

"You're so fucking stupid," Schroder says.

I stand up. The one thing I hate is being called stupid.

The one thing I hate even more is looking stupid. My wrist is still cuffed to the chair and I'm almost pulled back into it. "Guard," I shout out, and I bang on the table. "Guard!"

The guard opens the door. He gives me a really unimpressed look. I tell him I'm done here. He comes in and takes off the handcuff.

"Make it happen," I tell Schroder when I reach the door, and I'm escorted back to my psychiatrist.

CHAPTER TWENTY-NINE

"She called me the following day," I tell my psychiatrist, and I've switched from Joe Escape Artist back to Joe Victim, and that's fine, because Joe Victim gets a much prettier view. "I thought she was going to wait for the weekend, but she called me after school. First she spoke to my mother and told her she wanted me to help around her house, and in return she would pay me. My mother thought it was a great idea because it meant that was less time I would be spending around our house. So I went there and mowed her lawns. Then it turned out she wanted the garage painted, inside and out, including the roof. So that became the project for a few weeks. Only it wasn't the only project. She kept calling me day after day to go around there until . . . well, until she grew tired of me."

"Tired of you?"

"Tired of me."

"Grew tired of you doing the chores?"

"Not exactly," I say, and I look down at my cuffed wrist, at the arm of the chair, at my feet and at the floor. The view might be prettier for Joe Victim than it was staring at my lawyer ten minutes ago, but looking into the past is ugly. "She grew tired of me about two years later."

"Joe?"

I look up at her. "Do I have to spell it out for you?" I ask her.

Slowly she's shaking her head and she's trying to hide the disgust on her face, but she's not doing a great job. She pauses, taking a few breaths before continuing. "Are you trying to tell me your auntie kept your secret in exchange for sex?"

"I'm actually trying not to tell you about it," I say. "But yeah, that's what happened. Like she said, she was lonely. She hadn't had a man around the house for six years."

"She blackmailed you."

"What else could I do? If I didn't do what she wanted, she would go to the police. She would tell my parents. She said she would tell people I had raped her if I didn't go along with it. So I had to keep going back. I mean, the only thing I could think of was to kill her. And no matter what you think of me, I'm not a killer. At least I don't want to be one."

"Was it the first time you'd ever had sex?"

"Yes."

She keeps staring at me as if she's about to ask me how much I enjoyed it, and if it went anything like this, followed by her taking her clothes off and bending over the table. "Tell me about it," she says.

As much as I want her turned on, I don't really want to tell her about my auntie. "Why?"

"Because I asked you."

"About the sex itself?"

"Tell me about your auntie. About leading up to what happened."

I shrug. Like it's no big deal. Like being forced to have sex with one's auntie is as trivial as talking about the weather, although marginally more entertaining. But it is a big deal. One that for a long time had stayed bottled up inside of me. After my auntie died and we were going through her house, after I saw the crossbow, and after mom packed everything away, I felt sick. I actually went to the cemetery she was buried in that night, and I found her grave and I took a shit on it. For me it was a form of closure. It was a way of saying good-bye to a woman who made me feel bad about myself, good about myself, and then bad about myself all over.

"I had just finished painting the roof," I tell my psychiatrist. "It was a hot day. Back then summer was always hot days and blue skies—at least that's how it seemed. These days we're lucky to see blue sky twice a week," I say, and my earlier thought was right—auntie rape is as trivial as weather watch. "I got burned pretty bad up on that roof. I'd been working for my auntie for four days. The Big Bang happened on my fifth, which was our first Saturday together. I was up on the roof and—"

"You call what happened the Big Bang?"

"What would you have me call it?"

"Carry on," she says.

"So my auntie came outside and called me down. I went down there expecting her to tell me that suddenly the garden needed doing or a lightbulb needed changing, or that I wasn't painting the roof as well as she wanted, and when I got inside she reminded me why I was there," I say, and I can still remember it, can still remember the dress she was wearing, and she was wearing lots of makeup too. I can almost feel the sunburn and smell the aloe vera she would rub into my skin later that same day. She told me to sit down on the couch and I did and she handed me a drink of lemonade that she had made that tasted how I imagined cat piss would taste if you carbonated it and threw in a slice of lemon. Then she sat down next to me. She put a hand on my leg, then told me not to flinch when I flinched. Then she told me she had another job for me, and that if I said no, I'd be going to jail. She put one hand in my lap and one hand on the back of my neck and told me to kiss her. I didn't know what to do. She pushed her face into mine and I'd never kissed a girl before, and it tasted like cigarette smoke and was wet like coffee, and I still remember that my thought was to try and bite her nose off, but before I could think how, she was straddling me. I tried falling back further into the couch, I put my hands on her shoulders and pushed her away. She said if I pushed her away again she would tell my parents what I had done and that I had raped her."

I tell the psychiatrist this and I can feel my face going red, as if the sunburn and shame from then is finding a way back into my life.

"And in the bedroom," the psychiatrist says, "your auntie was in control?"

"I don't . . . I don't really want to talk about it," I say.

"Joe—"

"Please. Can't we just drop it?"

"What happened afterward? When you were finished in the bedroom?" she asks.

"She sent me back outside to work on the roof."

"Just like that? She didn't try talking to you first?"

"A little, I guess. Mostly about my uncle. She said that I reminded her of him in many ways. I didn't know what ways she meant and didn't know if she meant sexually. Things had been . . . you know, pretty quick. Then she made me go back outside."

"How did you feel?"

"Well it was hot out there and I burned some more."

"I mean how did you feel about what your aunt had done to you?"

"I'm . . . I'm not sure."

"Angry? Hurt?"

"I guess."

"Excited?"

"No," I say, but maybe just a little. Not that excited though. There's a reason my uncle died—looking at my auntie every day couldn't have helped his health. If my auntie had been hotter—well, that might have been quite conflicting. As it was I felt strange about the whole thing. "It happened again a few days later. Then it just kept on happening, and every time when I got home all I could smell was the cigarette smoke."

"And this lasted two years?"

"Almost, yeah."

"Did you try to stop it?"

"I didn't know how," I say.

"But you tried something, right?"

I nod. "I killed her cat," I say.

She doesn't look alarmed at my response. "You said earlier you hadn't killed any animals."

"I pretty much forgot about it," I say, and it's true. In this case, anyway. "There's a lot I had forgotten about that time until you wanted to talk about it."

"And the cat?"

I shake my head. "The cat didn't want to talk about it."

She doesn't laugh. "You killed the cat, Joe. Tell me why."

"I thought if I killed her cat it would give her something else to focus on and she wouldn't want to keep having sex with me," I say, "only the opposite turned out to be true. She needed me more at that point."

"How did you kill it?"

"I drowned it in the bath," I say, "and then I used a hair dryer to dry it out so my auntie never knew what happened. She just thought it died naturally."

"At what point during the sexual abuse was this?" she asks.

"What the hell? I didn't fuck the cat," I tell her. "I just drowned it. I had to do something."

"That's not what I mean, Joe. I mean the abuse between you and your auntie."

"I wasn't abusing her," I say. "Why are you thinking the worst? How am I going to have a fair trial if everybody keeps—"

She puts her hand up to stop me. "Listen to me, Joe. You're misunderstanding me. Your auntie was abusing you. You were an innocent kid and she took advantage of a bad decision you had made. What I want to know is how long had she been abusing you for before the cat died, and how much longer after that did the abuse continue."

"Oh," I say, and yes, that makes more sense. Only . . . the *abuse*? Is that what it was? "Oh," I repeat, relieved that she's on my side. Everybody is on my side once they get to know me a little. But really—once you start throwing that *abuse* term around, it makes me sound like a pussy. "It was halfway in, I suppose. A year into the . . . into the . . . abuse, then a year of abuse after the cat died."

"How did it stop?"

"She just said that she was done with me. I didn't understand it. Just like that. I should have seen it coming. I was going around there less and less near the end. I felt . . . I don't know. I felt something."

"Rejected?"

"No. Relief," I say, only she's right, I did feel rejected, then I realize that's just the kind of thing that might be worth sharing, the kind of thing that will make me look more fucked-up than the stable person I really am. "I mean, of course I felt rejected. I didn't want to be having sex with my auntie, but I didn't understand why it just stopped. Was I not good enough for her?"

"It's not about that," she says.

"Then what is it about?"

"You were the victim," she says. "It was about power. It was about finding somebody she could dominate. She probably found you were becoming too confident, too grown-up. What kind of relationship did you have after that?"

"We didn't. I actually never saw her again."

"Not at Christmas, or other family events?"

"My dad's funeral," I tell her. "I guess that's the only other time. We didn't speak to each other. I mean, I tried, but she didn't have time for me. She was hanging around with Gregory, who's one of my cousins, five years younger than me. It was weird. In some way, I missed her."

"That makes sense," she says.

"What does?"

"It doesn't matter," she says, and she's right, really. None of this matters. It's just filling in time in a room slightly more pleasant than my cell until Melissa rescues me. Killing time in a room with a very pretty lady. Life should have more of those killing moments.

"It wasn't your fault what she did to you, Joe."

"Yes it was. If I hadn't broken into her house—"

"She took advantage of you, Joe. She was an adult and you were a kid."

"I know that," I tell her. "But if I hadn't broken into her house, then none of it would have happened. Who knows where I'd be now?"

"What do you mean by that?" she asks, leaning forward, and I sense a red flag on the horizon.

"I don't know."

"Yes, you do."

"I mean, maybe that was the start of everything."

She taps her pen against her pad. "Everything? It sounds like you're self-analyzing, Joe."

"I don't mean it like that," I say. "I just mean, you know, maybe that path led to another, which led to another."

"Are you sure you never considered killing her?"

"No. No, of course not."

"Most people in that situation would think of it."

"Yeah, well, I didn't," I say, but the truth is I did. I wanted to wrap my hands around her throat every time I had to look down at her face when she was beneath me. Hell, I wanted to wrap my hands around my own throat and squeeze. And yet I missed her.

"When was the first time you killed somebody, Joe?"

"I don't know."

"You don't know?"

"I don't remember killing anybody, and if I did, well, I don't know when it began."

She reaches for the recorder and switches it off. "Okay, I think that's enough for today."

"What's wrong?"

"You've just started lying again. I'll tell you what. You think about what it is you're trying to achieve here, and I'll come back tomorrow and we'll talk again. Okay?"

"Wait."

"We still have time tomorrow," she says, and she stands up and knocks on the door.

"I just want to be helped," I tell her.

"Good."

The guard opens the door and leans in to get a good look at me. I smile back at him, the full Joe smile with all the teeth. My eyelid stretches a little and hurts. Then I show Ali the full smile too. She walks out. The guard closes the door and I stare at the walls and my eyelid sticks and I have to manually pull it down. I let the smile fall from my face and I hang my head and rest it on my arms, my face only an inch from the table, my breath forming a thin film of condensation on the surface. I haven't thought about my auntie in a long time, and Ali is the first person I've ever told. I always thought therapy was about unloading burdens and sharing pain, but all it's done is open up a lot of old wounds. I don't want anybody to know about it.

Suddenly it's more important than ever that Melissa gets me out of here. If this were to come out in court I don't know how I could face the world. Even though my mum wouldn't be there or watch the news, I think somehow she'd hear about all the things her sister did to me, and no doubt she wouldn't believe me.

Ali better not share any of this after I've escaped.

Suddenly I'm glad my mom won't be there.

I do what I've been doing the most of lately—I wait, and I try to be positive. I try not to think about my auntie and I try to focus on a positive future, but sometimes, in a place like this, thinking positive thoughts is just so, so hard to do.

CHAPTER THIRTY

"This is bullshit," Schroder says.

"I agree. This *is* bullshit," Wellington, says. "This deal you're bringing him, this is no good for my client."

"You don't even want to defend this case," Schroder says. "So why make this difficult?"

"You're right, I don't want to defend him, but I'm going to do the best I can for him because that's the job, you know that. If you killed somebody, Detective, I'd do my best to represent you too."

"What do you mean by that?" Schroder asks.

"What do I mean by what?"

"That if I killed somebody?"

"Just how it sounds. If you killed somebody and hired me, you'd want to know I'd do all I could. If I didn't, who would hire me again?"

"Okay," Schroder says.

"Anyway, I'm not the one making it difficult," Wellington says. "It's Joe."

Both men are still in the interview room at the prison. Schroder hates it in here. The room smells. And it's cold. And it's depressing. And Wellington has just made a good point.

"He's asking for something I can't help arrange," Schroder says.

"And if we do arrange it," Wellington says, "it goes against what's best for my client. There is no way we can have a police escort to the body, and then try to convince a jury Joe had no idea where it was."

Schroder agrees. "And there's no way we can have a police escort, then have Jones use his psychic abilities to find the body."

They're going around in circles. The deal isn't going to happen. Jonas won't get to show off his body-finding abilities. Schroder's not going to get his bonus. Joe won't get his money. And Detective Inspector Robert Calhoun isn't going to be going home. Schroder doesn't care about the first three things, but the fourth one is important to him. It's been important since Calhoun went missing. Important enough for him to still be in this room trying to figure out a way to make Joe's life easier.

"How does it feel?" Wellington asks. "Working for a guy like that?"

Schroder winces at the question. The way Wellington asks it makes it pretty obvious what Wellington's views are. It makes Schroder think everybody must be feeling the same way. Yet despite it all, Jonas is doing well for himself. Not everybody can hate him. "Probably about the same as it must feel defending Joe," Schroder says.

Wellington slowly nods. "That bad, huh?"

"Look," Schroder says, "I know you don't want him to take this deal, I see that, but Detective Calhoun deserves to be returned. That's what we have to focus on here. He was a cop, damn it, a good cop, and like any cop he deserves a proper burial, he deserves to be mourned and remembered as something other than the policeman who disappeared and never came back."

Wellington says nothing as he takes it all in, and Schroder is reminded of how quickly this guy thinks, of how far ahead he really is.

"There has to be a way," Schroder adds.

"There is no way," Wellington says. "As soon as we involve the police Jones doesn't get his deal."

Schroder gets up and starts pacing the room. Wellington watches him. He starts running different scenarios through his head. If he were still a cop, this would be a whole lot easier. But if he were a cop, he wouldn't be coming to Joe with a deal that gives a serial killer fifty thousand dollars. The cops aren't going to get Calhoun's location from Joe. They've tried. The prosecution has tried.

The only way to get that location is to pay him.

And the only way Joe will tell them is to show them.

And the only way Joe can show them is if it doesn't involve the police.

And that's just not going to happen.

"I'll try working on him," Wellington says. "See if he can just tell us the location. I mean, if he doesn't tell you, he doesn't get the money, and that's why he's doing this. I think he really believes he's going to be going free after the trial."

Schroder turns and leans against the wall. He stares at Wellington. An idea is coming to him. He just has to work at it for a few more moments. "And what do you think?"

Wellington shrugs, but then gives his view. "I think the very fact he thinks he's going free, and the fact he thinks everybody is believing what he's saying, may just prove he really is completely insane."

The idea is close now. Schroder can see it stretching out ahead of him. He just has to follow the path and shore up the crossroads. He pushes himself off from the wall and sits down opposite the lawyer. "What if," he says, then doesn't follow it up. He's staring at the wall, at the cinder block, but really he's on the path and checking that the angles all line up.

Wellington doesn't interrupt him.

"What if," Schroder says again, and yes, yes this might work. "What if we make two deals? We stick with our deal. The people

I work for pay Joe his money for the location of Detective Calhoun."

"Okay. And what's deal two?"

"We go to the prosecution and we ask for immunity for Joe on what happened to Detective Calhoun. We all know he didn't kill him. He buried him, sure, and he probably set up the circumstances and no doubt he would have killed him anyway, but we have Joe on all these other homicides. Pinning Calhoun on him isn't going to make a difference. Technically we don't need him on this one."

We. He hears himself saying the word. Once a cop, always a cop. At least according to those who are no longer cops. To everybody else he's just a pain in the ass.

"Technically," Wellington says, nodding. "I don't think too many people would be happy hearing that."

"I'm not even happy saying it," Schroder says.

"I think I can pretty much tell you the prosecution won't go for it."

Schroder gets up and starts pacing again. "We ask for immunity, and in exchange for it we offer to give them the location of Calhoun's body. They still have plenty to convict Joe with, so there's no reason for them to say no. They get Calhoun back. It's a win-win situation. Two deals. And Joe gets his one hour of freedom in which to show them the body."

Wellington sits still and Schroder can see him absorbing the information. He's churning it over in his four-hundred-dollar-an-hour head. "It might work."

"It will work," Schroder says.

"It might. The other problem is the police aren't going to be too keen about leaving the body where they find it for your boss to come along and take the credit."

"First of all, he's not my boss," Schroder says. "And second of all, they will go for it if it means bringing home one of their own."

Wellington almost laughs. "You're kidding, right?"

"No."

Wellington shakes his head. "There is no way they're going to go for that. This is real life, Carl, not one of your TV shows. The police aren't a tool for Jonas Jones and the TV network."

"I know that."

"Then why suggest otherwise?"

"Because it's the only way we're going to get Calhoun back," Schroder says.

"No," he says. "And you know what? I'm not even going to suggest it. I go in there with that idea, and I get laughed back out. Nobody will take me seriously again. There isn't one cop on the force who would want to help out Jonas Jones."

"They're not doing it for Jones," Schroder says. "They're doing it for Calhoun, and that's a big difference. A really big difference. They're doing it for Calhoun and his family. That's the selling point to all of this."

Wellington is still shaking his head. "And if it's a trap?"

"It can't be," Schroder says. "We only brought this deal to him yesterday. I bet if we check his visitor logs we'll find the only people he's seen or spoken to are you, me, his psychiatrists, and his mother. There's no way he could have set something up in that time."

"And if you're wrong?"

"I'm not wrong," Schroder says.

"Okay," Wellington says. "I agree. You're not wrong. But it's still not going to work. Even with a small team taking him out there, there's still a big problem you're overlooking."

"Yeah? And what's that?"

"These people need to keep their mouths shut."

"They're cops," Schroder says. "Keeping your mouth shut is part of the job. We just need four or five people who can be trusted to do their job."

Wellington is still shaking his head, but Schroder can see that slowly he's changing his mind. "We have to at least try," Schroder says.

"Okay. I'll go to the prosecution with it. I mean, it can't hurt."

"If Joe doesn't keep his mouth shut he'll blow it all to hell," Schroder says, and he feels like he's sold a part, just a little part, of himself to the devil. That's one part to Jonas Jones and one part to Joe Middleton. Soon he'll be out of parts.

"He'll keep it shut," Wellington says. "I point out the benefits to the prosecution, I point out it can't be a trap, and I point out the good faith on my client's part."

"Point out what you need to," Schroder says. "Let's just get this done before this whole thing turns into a circus."

Wellington taps his index finger on the surface of the table. "My daughter is a university student," he says, and Schroder knows there are two ways this can go. Wellington is either going to say a guy with a daughter doesn't want a guy like Joe out on the streets. Or he's going to say something worse. He's going to say something bad has happened to his daughter. Only he's wrong, because Wellington doesn't tell him either of those. Instead he says, "She phoned me an hour ago. My daughter studies law. She's into her third year. She loves it. Wants to be like me. Wants to defend innocent people."

"She's going to be in for a shock," Schroder says.

"Because there are no innocent people?"

"They're just rare, that's all."

"Maybe. Maybe not as rare as you think. But you want to have a guess as to what the Canterbury University students are going to be doing on Monday?"

It doesn't take much of a guess. "Protesting," Schroder says.

"Yeah? What do you think, for or against the death penalty?" Wellington asks.

Schroder shrugs. "I don't know. Half for it, half against it, I guess."

The lawyer smiles. "Neither," he says. "They're planning on going just for the show. My daughter says it's *the* talking point all over social media at the moment. Hundreds if not more students are going to treat the event as a party. There's even a competition where the student who can get the most airtime on camera wins a bottle of vodka. So for the chance of one bottle of vodka a bunch of these kids are going to be dressing up in costumes and trying to get into every camera angle they can to get on TV, but that's not *why* they're going—it's just an additional bonus. They're going because it's an excuse to drink and be loud and drink some more and throw up in the gutters. They're going because they think it's cool. Even my daughter is going. They don't care about Joe Middleton or the justice system because all they care about is drinking. That's their generation. It's my daughter's generation. Kind of makes you wonder why the hell we're doing all of this, why we're trying to make a safer world when that's who we're making it safer for."

"I'm not sure what you want me to say," Schroder says.

"Nothing you can say. It is what it is. But I just want to point out that if you think you can avoid this turning into a circus, then you're probably the only genuinely insane person I've truly ever met."

CHAPTER THIRTY-ONE

If Raphael had known he would be having guests, he would have tidied up more. He feels embarrassed and hopes Stella doesn't think he always lives like this. He *actually does* live like this pretty much all of the time these days. For a while there he used to care about how badly he lived, how badly he ate, then, thank God, he just stopped caring.

"Sorry about the mess," he tells her, but she doesn't seem to mind. He suspects her own house is in a similar state after she lost the baby and her husband left. She rubs her belly as if she were still pregnant. He remembers his wife doing that all the time when she was pregnant with Angela. He remembers lying in bed beside her at night with his hand on her stomach, feeling the baby kick, his wife smiling and amused, him being somewhat freaked out by it all. Back then he wasn't seeing too much difference between a kicking baby and what happened to that poor bastard over the dinner table in *Alien*.

"Can I get you a drink?" he asks.

"Just water."

He goes into the kitchen. The dishes from breakfast are still scattered over the counter, along with a week's worth of toast crumbs and splashes of water around the sink. He grabs two fresh glasses and fills them and gets out to the lounge. Stella is looking at the photographs on the wall.

"This is Angela?" she asks.

"Yeah."

"And these are your grandchildren?" she asks, looking at a photograph of the kids.

"Adelaide is six," he says. "She started school this year. She goes to school in England and keeps hoping her school is secretly like that school in Harry Potter. Hoghoofs, or whatever it's called. Vivian is four and wants to be a ballerina," he says, "and a pop singer too."

"Cute," she says.

"I don't get to see them," he says, and he's angry at his son-in-law for that, which is why there are no photos of him on the walls, but at the same time he can't blame him for moving away. Can't blame him at all. "I get to speak to them once a month if I'm lucky."

Stella hands him a plastic bag full of clothes that's been riding in the car with them all day. "Try it on," she says. He pulls out the light blue shirt and the dark blue pants. "Should be your size," she says.

"Where did you get it from?"

"It's a rental costume," she says. "Try not to damage it otherwise I won't get my deposit back."

He isn't sure if she's joking. He unfolds the police uniform and looks it over. "It seems real," he says.

"Of course it does. That's the entire point of costume-rental shops. Go ahead, try it on."

"You really think this part is necessary?"

"Hopefully not, but I imagine it will be. There's going to be a lot of confusion and a lot of people running around. Wearing this will stop you from being arrested."

He takes the uniform down to the bedroom. His bedroom, like the rest of the house, isn't a mess, but it isn't exactly tidy. The bed hasn't been made and there are clothes on the floor, but it's not like the carpet is stained with food or the windowsills with mold. He lays the uniform out on the bed and quickly changes. It's a little loose, but not bad.

"Well? What do you think?" he asks, walking back out into the lounge.

Stella smiles. It's the first time he's seen any positive emotion in her. Even her eyes are sparkling. It must be true, what they say about men in uniform. If he were twenty years younger, hadn't lost his daughter, wasn't still technically married, and if Stella weren't a rape victim seeking out revenge for the loss of her unborn baby, well, maybe things would happen while he was wearing that uniform.

"It fits pretty good," he says. "You must have a keen eye for sizes. I'm impressed it even comes with the belt," he says, and fiddles with the compartment holding the handcuffs. "And it even has a radio. All this stuff looks genuine."

"The radio doesn't work," she says. "But aside from that, you're right, it almost is genuine."

He moves over to a mirror in the lounge. He studies the way he looks. If he pauses to think about what's going on, he risks coming to a grinding halt. He has to keep moving with it. He's going to be killing Joe. He suspects the next few days are all going to be about momentum, and if he doesn't keep pushing forward then none of this is going to work. He's sure the Red Rage will help him.

"Are you sure we're going to be able to get away?" he asks, tugging at the uniform. In theory it's just as good a part of the plan as the rest, but it still gives him a bad feeling. He stares at her in the mirror and catches her eye.

"Would it matter if we didn't? she asks. "If somebody right now gave you the option of putting a bullet into Joe's head, and in return you had to spend ten years in jail, would you take it?"

"Yes," he says. He doesn't even have to think about it. And

it wouldn't be ten years. No judge would give him ten years for shooting the man that raped and killed his daughter. Although perhaps that's just hopeful thinking. Other judges have given people longer for doing just that. "You?" he asks.

"In a heartbeat," she says.

Knocking at the door. They both freeze.

"Are you expecting somebody?" she asks.

He shakes his head.

Stella moves over to the window and peeks out from behind the blind. "It's the same car from last night, the one with the cops."

"Shit," he says, and starts to unbutton the shirt. "They can't see me like this."

"Just don't answer the door."

"It might be important," he says, tugging the shirt over his head to speed things up, half the buttons still clasped. "Plus my car is in the driveway. They'll know I'm home." He kicks off the shoes and tugs off the trousers and is down to his underwear and socks when the knocking is repeated.

"Hang on a second," he calls out, and he looks left and right for something to put on, but there's nothing. "Shit," he says, then moves to the bathroom just off the hall and grabs a towel. He wraps it around his waist and heads to the door.

CHAPTER THIRTY-TWO

Schroder is on his way to the casino when he decides to drop in to see Raphael. The writers and producer of *The Cleaner* were annoyed at yesterday's absence. He has the bad feeling that later on today or early next week somebody at the studio will be sitting down with him and telling him that was strike one, and in a disposable world he's only going to be given one more strike and then he's gone.

Coming here might be his second and only other strike.

"Detective," Raphael says, and Raphael has a towel wrapped around his waist and nothing else on except a pair of socks, and Schroder hopes he can look as good as Raphael does when he's that age.

Schroder smiles. "It's just Carl these days," he reminds him. "Bad timing, huh?"

"Unless you're planning on jumping in the shower with me," Raphael says, laughing, and Schroder laughs at the joke too even if it was predictable.

"I just need a few minutes of your time," Schroder says. "Should we go inside or do you want to stand on your doorstep in the cold and put on a show for your neighbors?"

"Umm . . . well, the thing is, Carl, I'm kind of in a hurry. Can we maybe do this later?"

"It won't take long," Schroder says, and it reminds him of last night, of Raphael standing on the doorstep to the community hall and not inviting them in. It makes him suspicious. Of course all the years he was a cop means everything seems suspicious to him. He feels like adding the good ol' classic *unless you have something to hide*. He's used that line plenty of times over the years to people who do have something to hide. Sometimes it works, sometimes it doesn't.

"Umm, sure, I guess."

Raphael turns and heads down the hallway. Schroder follows him. He's been in this house before. This is where they came to tell Raphael and his wife that their daughter had been murdered. It was over a year ago, but being back here now makes it feel like it was only last week. Back then Raphael and his wife knew within seconds of opening the door that the news wasn't going to be good, not when Schroder and his partner back then, Detective Landry, held out their badges and asked if they could come inside. Police didn't show up to tell you good news—they didn't show up and say you've just won the lottery or a vacation. The wife broke down before they even made it into the lounge, and Raphael and Schroder had to help her onto a couch. Raphael sat next to her and held her hand and kept shaking his head as if he could dismiss the news, and he kept saying *But we saw her this morning* as if those words could ward off the evil that was entering their lives. Schroder and Landry spent an hour with them. It was a life-changing hour for Raphael and his wife, and it was just one of many hours for Schroder and Landry, who had knocked on other doors and given similar news. He's thought about Landry a lot lately, about Landry's own life-changing hour, about Landry's funeral almost a month ago. This house was tidier back then. Now the woman's touch has gone, along with the woman.

They get into the lounge. Raphael is looking around as if he's lost something.

"You've got guests?" Schroder asks.

"What? No, no guests."

"You normally have two glasses of water?"

Raphael shakes his head. "One's from last night," he says, glancing around the room. "I poured it and didn't finish it and, well, you know, just ended up being too lazy to clean up. I'm embarrassed to admit it, but if you look around the house you'll find plenty more. If you're offering to tidy up for me, I would appreciate the help."

Schroder sits down on the couch. He believes him. The place doesn't look like it's been cleaned in a while. There's a stack of unopened bills on the coffee table. The *TV Guide* next to them is from last year. It's been used as a coaster.

He reaches into his jacket pocket for the photograph that should have been in his car last night. He never did find where he lost it, but he did have another copy at home. There were a few things he'd copied twice. "Have you ever seen this woman before?" he asks, and he hands it over to Raphael, who is still standing, which Schroder is thankful for because if he sits it will be a view Schroder won't want to see.

Raphael takes it and stares at it for a few seconds. Then a few seconds more. There's no indication of recognition. No tilting of the head like last night when he was trying to remember if the names they gave him meant anything. There's no changing the angle of the picture to get a better look. Then slowly he's shaking his head. He hands it back.

"Should I?"

"Yes," Schroder says. "At the very least you should recognize her from the news."

"Why? Who is she?"

"Her real name is Natalie Flowers," Schroder says.

"Oh, of course," Raphael says. "Melissa. I didn't recognize her. I don't really watch a lot of news these days. It's too depressing."

"So you haven't ever seen her at one of your meetings?" Schroder asks, and he hands back the picture.

"At a meeting?" Raphael laughs, then shakes his head. "Why the hell would she come to a meeting? He takes the photo and holds it closer to his face. Then he starts angling the photograph. He starts tilting the head. "This is Melissa?" he asks.

"Yes."

"She doesn't look . . ."

When he doesn't finish, Schroder looks for the word. "Evil?"

Raphael doesn't respond. He keeps staring at the photograph.

"You recognize her, don't you," Schroder says.

Raphael shakes his head. "I guess I do, you know, like you were saying, from the news. But other than that I've never seen her. Certainly not at one of my meetings."

"Are you sure about this, Raphael?"

"Well, no, I can't be positive. She must be using disguises, right? That's why you've never found her. But as far as I know, no, she's never been. I can't imagine any reason why she would."

"She might come along to enjoy the pain she's caused," Schroder says.

Raphael nods. "I hadn't thought of that."

Schroder takes the photo back and tucks it into his jacket. It was worth a shot. He stands back up. He has a job to get to, and this isn't it.

"Call me if you think of anything," he says, knowing he'll never hear from Raphael, that if Raphael does think of anything it will be the police he calls, not Schroder. Well, he's done what he came here to do. He shakes Raphael's hand.

"Any time, Detective," Raphael says, and follows Schroder to the door.

CHAPTER THIRTY-THREE

"You weren't supposed to see any of that," Raphael says.

Melissa turns from the wall toward him. He's standing in the doorway, wearing the towel and the underwear beneath and nothing else. "What is this room?" she asks.

He takes a step toward her. "This used to be our daughter's bedroom when she used to live at home with us. When she moved out, we turned it into a study and all her childhood stuff was put into storage. When she died we set the room up how she used to have it as a kid."

"Not *exactly* how she had it," Melissa says, looking at the wall with newspaper articles pinned to it. This is quite fascinating. She can imagine Raphael sitting in here on the edge of the bed staring at this wall, plotting his revenge, the day turning to evening to dark to the middle of the night. Obsession mixed in with a little bit of alcohol.

"Like I said, you weren't supposed to be in here," he says, taking another step toward her. He reminds her of her own father when she was being naughty. He would grab her by the arm and lead her away. Raphael looks like he wants to do just that.

"I had to go somewhere," Melissa says, "otherwise that policeman would have seen me."

"Would it have been a big deal if he had?"

"No, no I suppose not," Melissa says, but yes, it would have been a very big deal. What she has found in his dead daughter's bedroom is good. Really good.

"I suppose you want an explanation," he says.

"I think with what we're planning on doing together, yes."

"Are you going to go to the police?"

"That depends on your explanation," she says, but no, of course not.

"Give me a minute to get dressed," he says. "And I don't want you waiting in here. This was Angela's room."

Melissa heads into the lounge and takes a seat. She had waited in here earlier, listening to Raphael and Schroder until it became obvious they were coming inside. From Angela's room she had been able to hear them clearly, and at the same time she had studied all the interesting stuff pinned to the walls that no teenage girl would ever find interesting.

Raphael comes in a minute later. He's wearing the clothes he was wearing when they were out shooting, minus the boots. He definitely looked better topless, and definitely looked a whole lot better when he was in uniform. The casual handsomeness he usually displays has disappeared, his face lined with strain. He sits down on the couch opposite her and picks his water up from the coffee table and drinks half of it and then gets back up and goes into the kitchen and comes back out with a bottle of bourbon. He finishes his water and fills the glass back up with the good stuff. He offers some to Melissa and she shakes her head. It could hurt her fake baby.

"At least now you know I'm going to pull the trigger," he says, then grunts a small laugh.

"Is that supposed to be funny?"

"No. Not really."

"You killed them? Both of them?" she asks.

He nods. "They were going to defend him," he says.

She already understands why he did it. Had done from the moment she saw the articles on the wall of the first two lawyers that were going to defend Joe. On those articles Raphael had drawn red Xs across their faces.

"I don't get lawyers even at the best of times," he says.

"And at the worst of times?" she asks.

"At the worst of times they're putting their hand up to defend people like Joe Middleton. These two bastards were using the tragedy of my daughter to make a name for themselves, to become famous, famous in lawyering circles so they could then represent other Joes out there and become more famous and earn more money. People who are capable of that are capable of anything."

Melissa says nothing. She knows what people are capable of. She also knows Raphael will carry on without prompting. She senses it will be good for him. Cathartic. This is something he's kept inside. She picks up the glass she hadn't touched earlier and takes a sip. The water has made it to room temperature.

"I went there," he says. "I made an appointment with the first lawyer and he saw me, and I begged him not to defend Joe. Really begged him. And you know what? He said he understood where I was coming from. He said he could imagine how I felt. Can you believe that? This son of a bitch tells me he knows how I must be feeling. Then he went on to say that everybody is due a defense, that's what the law says, and Joe was entitled to what the law says just as anybody was entitled, and that didn't make sense to me. I mean, you have a guy disregarding the law, disregarding humanity, then suddenly he has civil rights? Fuck that," he says, and it's the first Melissa has heard him swear.

"So you started sending him death threats," she says.

He shakes his head. "No. I read about that, how both lawyers got death threats in the mail, but none of that was me."

"You just killed them," she says.

"Yes. But not right away. That first guy, after talking to him, I gave it a month. I was sure if he thought about it more, he'd come around to my way of thinking. He'd have to, right? So a month later I thought it'd be better if I met up with him in a less formal location because I hoped that would make him less formal and more human. So I went back to his work in the evening and waited for him to finish, and I followed him to his car."

He holds up his hand to her. "I know what you're thinking," he says, but he's wrong. He has no idea what she's thinking. "I didn't follow him to hurt him, I just wanted to plead my case with him. I wanted to remind him of the pain he was going to cause."

"And he didn't listen to you?"

"No, he listened. That's the thing," Raphael says, becoming more animated now as he lifts his hands in the air. "He listened to everything I had to say, and even then he refused to stop defending Joe."

"And that made you mad."

"It would make anybody mad."

"So you killed him."

"It wasn't like that. It was an accident."

"How?"

He runs his fingers up over his forehead and through his hair, then slowly shakes his head a little. "I hit him," he says, then exhales deeply. "With a hammer."

"You normally carry a hammer in the car?"

"No."

"So you took one with you."

"I guess."

"And you spoke to him without him seeing the hammer, right? So you had it in your pocket, or tucked in the waistband of your pants. You took it with you because you knew if things went badly and he didn't take your side, you were going to kill him. You went there a month later because you knew the police would go through his appointment schedule, but would only be interested in people he'd seen recently."

"I know that's how it looks," he says, "but it really wasn't the way I thought it would play out."

"How did you think it would play out if he didn't agree with you?"

Raphael shrugs. "I don't know. Not that way, anyway."

Melissa is nodding. It's a great conversation. She wishes she was having it with Joe. They could talk about it and get naked. "Then what did you do?"

"I stuffed him into the trunk of his car, then I went and got my own car. I pulled up next to him and transferred him, then drove him out to . . . well, I buried the body."

"Out where we went shooting today," Melissa says. "That's where, isn't it?"

"Yeah."

"Did it make you feel any better?"

"It didn't bring Angela back, but I knew it wouldn't. But yeah, it did. It made me feel a little better. Within days another lawyer was putting his hand up to take on the case. I didn't bother going and seeing him because I knew the conversation would be the same. So I took care of him too. This time I left him for people to find. I thought it might make more of a message, you know, to other lawyers. And it did. Joe's third lawyer was court appointed. The third lawyer seems like a man who really doesn't want the job. So, you know, no reason to hurt him. At least not yet.

"And somebody else would have killed them anyway," he adds. "Somebody was sending those guys death threats."

"You killed two innocent people," she says, not that she could care less, but she thinks that Raphael should see her caring more.

"They weren't innocent," he says.

"I'm sure they'd disagree."

"So . . ." he says, "does this change things?"

She holds off on answering for a few seconds. Like she really has to think about it. Like weighing it up is a really tough decision. Only it's not. It's an easy decision. And it makes last night's decision to approach Raphael look even better.

"I just . . . I don't know, I've never known a killer before," she says. "I should be happy because it just confirms you'll take the shot on Monday, but, well, to be honest . . . it's a little weird. You killed two people."

"Two bad people," he says.

"Two bad people," she repeats. "Lawyers who were doing bad things."

"Exactly," he says. "So the question is the same—does this change things?"

"No," she says.

"Good," he says, and leans back into the chair.

"But we're only after Joe," she says. "Not any of the cops escorting him. No more lawyers. There's been too much blood spilled already. Just Joe."

"Of course," he says. "The cops are the ones trying to lock him away. They're on our side."

"And the cop who came to your door?" she asks. "What did he want?"

"Schroder? Well, he's not a policeman anymore," he says, sounding a little cautious. "He just wanted to ask if anybody else had come to mind."

"Come to mind about what?"

"About suspicious people at the group. I'm not sure who he's after."

"And what did you tell him?"

"I told him nobody came to mind."

She heard their conversation from Angela's room. She knows Schroder showed him a photograph of her. She knows they spoke about her, they even used her real name. It was probably a copy of the same photograph she found in the back of Schroder's car, the photograph taken the day Cindy got bookended by two guys at the beach she'd never met before. In that photo Melissa has dark brown hair. That was her natural hair color—well, still is, technically—though these days she dies it black and keeps it short. And of course she wears the wigs. Even long wigs. And for Raphael, her hair is long and black.

"That was it?" she asks.

"Yeah. It was pretty routine," he says, and she thinks back to last night when Raphael climbed into her car. In their time spent chatting before that, he'd been excellent at concealing the truth. He'd known then she wasn't who she said she was, and she's sure he knows it now. "So, how about we go over this plan a few more times? It's why we're here."

She takes another sip of her water and puts it down. "Okay," she says.

"It shouldn't change anything," he says. "At least you know I'll do it. I'll pull that trigger."

Raphael is wrong. It does change everything. Not the fact he killed two lawyers, but the fact he's lying about his conversation with Schroder. He knows who she is, and now it's her job to hide that she knows that. It also means she's going to have to adjust the plan because Raphael is going to adjust it too. It's a matter of staying ahead—and that's something she's always been good at. Only person who's beaten her since she stopped being Natalie and became Melissa is Joe.

Raphael is a killer, and that side of him is going to be on display on Monday morning, and not just with Joe, but with her too.

Bullet one will be going into Joe.

And bullet two, she is sure of it, will have her name on it.

CHAPTER THIRTY-FOUR

I end up missing lunch because of my busy schedule with my psychiatrist, with Schroder and my lawyer, and then my psychiatrist again. So by early afternoon my stomach is twisting in knots. Which is when prison guard Adam comes and sees me. He has a sandwich. I've missed meals before because of other appointments, and I faced the same problem back then that I'm facing now—you just don't know what's in the food that prison guards bring to you, and it's their job to make sure you get something.

"Bon appétit," Adam says, which I figure is Latin for *Fuck you*.

I unwrap the sandwich and peel back the bread. There's a bunch of pubic hairs between a slice of cheese and a slice of meat, enough of them to knit a jersey for a mouse—which is ironic because the last time Adam brought me a sandwich there actually was a dead mouse in it. I wrap it back up and hand it to Adam, who doesn't take it.

"It's either that, Middleton, or go hungry."

"I'll go hungry," I say, just like I went hungry with the Mickey sandwich.

"We'll see," he says, and he wanders off, leaving me alone in my cell.

I go back to staring at the walls. I think about Melissa and I think about my auntie and I think about the psychiatrist and I think about the death penalty, and all that thinking makes me hungrier, and I realize I have more doubts than I thought about my future. The public has built up a profile of me without even getting to know me. A jury pool will be drawn from people who have been reading and watching a whole lot of negative shit about me over the last twelve months. How is it I can be judged by a panel of my peers? Are there twelve men and women out there who have taken lives, banged a few lonely housewives, had part of their genitalia removed, and tried shooting themselves? No. I'm going to be judged by dentists and shoe salesmen and musicians.

The communal area between the cells is open. The same people are there doing the same things—playing cards, talking, wishing they were all outside doing the kinds of things that got them locked inside. Other than an hour a day exercising in a small pen outside, most of us haven't seen outside in a long time. Outside could be destroyed by aliens and it wouldn't make a difference to any of us.

Another hour goes by. My stomach is rumbling even louder. Adam comes back to see me. "You have a phone call," he says.

He leads me back through the cellblock. We head down a corridor and past a locked door to a phone that's been bolted to the wall, the same size and shape of a payphone. It's bolted pretty securely not because prison is full of thieves, but full of people who could beat somebody to death with a nice heavy object like that. The receiver is hanging from it, still swinging slightly from where it was dropped. Adam leans against the wall a few feet away and watches me.

I pick up the receiver.

"Hello?"

"Joe, it's Kevin Wellington," he says.

"Who?"

A sigh, and then, "Your lawyer," he says.

"You've got a deal?"

"It's your lucky day, Joe," he says, which is good because I need to string a lot more lucky days together and this could just be the one that gets the ball falling. "Between me and the prosecution, yes, we've struck a deal. You're getting immunity on Detective Calhoun if you show them where the body is. It can't be used against you in the trial. You just have to keep your mouth shut about everything else and just show them where the body is and nothing more. Do you get that?"

"Yeah, I get it."

"Repeat it to me."

I look up at Adam, who's still staring at me. I lower the phone. "It's my lawyer," I tell him, "doesn't that entail me to some privacy?"

"It's *entitle*, you idiot," he says, but I'm not so sure he's right. "I'm sure it does entitle you," he says, but doesn't make any effort to move.

I turn so my back is to him and talk into the phone.

"I get it," I tell my lawyer.

"No, Joe, tell me what it is you get."

"I'm to keep my mouth shut," I tell my lawyer.

"That's right. You don't answer their questions, you don't make conversation. And most importantly, you don't act like a cocky smart-ass because that's the exact attitude that's been making life difficult."

"What the hell are you talking about?"

"Your attitude, Joe. You think you're superior to everybody else, and you're not. Your belief that—"

"Uh huh, okay, cool," I say, interrupting him because he's making it sound like a bad thing to be superior to other people. It's that kind of attitude that turns small-minded people into losers. "Moving on," I say. "What happens with the money? How do we know they'll pay?"

"The money goes into escrow."

"Where the hell is that? Europe?"

"Are you for real, Joe?"

"What the hell are you on about?"

"It's not a *where*, Joe. It's a *what*. It's like a middleman for the money. It's like a referee looking after it. Once the body has been identified as Calhoun, you get paid."

"So I'll get it when, tomorrow?"

"That depends, Joe, on how easy he is to identify. What condition did you leave him in?"

"Shit," I tell him. "So this escrow guy, no matter what happens now, the money comes to me if the identity is confirmed, right?"

"That's right."

"No matter what."

A pause, and then, "No matter what," he confirms.

"Let's say a nuclear bomb goes off and half the country is killed, there are dead cops everywhere, nobody to run the prisons so we're all set free. I still get paid, right?"

"What are you getting at, Joe?"

"I just need to make sure. No matter what, I get paid. If I were to walk out of here a wanted man after I've shown them the body, then—"

"You get paid," my lawyer says. "The only condition it's subject to is Calhoun being identified. However, if you were to walk away somehow a wanted man, you'd find it very difficult to access your bank account."

"Oh," I tell him. "Can we get it in cash?"

"No, Joe, you can't. And what does it matter? Are you planning on walking away a wanted man?"

"No, no, of course not. But having a bank account is no use to me in here," I tell him. "It's not like there's an ATM in here. It's not like I can offer to write a check to somebody who wants to kill me."

"And it's not like you can store fifty thousand dollars under your mattress, Joe."

"Can you set up a separate account? Something under your name that I can access?" I ask.

"No. Listen, Joe—"

"Okay, then put it into my mother's account," I tell him.

"Why?"

"Because she needs the money," I tell him. "Because I want to look after her. And because she visits me every week and she can bring some of it with her each time."

"Do you have her account details?"

"She'll have them. You can contact her."

"Okay," he says. "I'll contact her tomorrow."

"What time am I showing them?"

"Ten a.m."

I shake my head. "Err . . . no. That doesn't work for me."

Another pause. "Are you serious?"

"Of course I am. Ten o'clock is too early."

"Come on, Joe, are you deliberately trying to make this difficult? This is a good deal for you. A great deal that a lot of us had to work hard to—"

"I'm telling you, it's too early," I say.

"Why?"

"I've got interviews with the psychiatrist all day tomorrow. That stuff is important. I'm not going to risk ruining it. You warned me about that."

"Well I'm sure she can work around it."

I start shaking my head as if he can see me. "Listen to me. David—"

"It's Kevin."

"Kevin. Morning isn't good for me."

"Because you have other appointments."

"Yes. This is my defense we're talking about here. My future. It's my life. I'm not going to mess around with that."

I can imagine him sitting at his desk. He's got one hand on his forehead and he's holding the phone away from himself and staring into it. Perhaps he's even thinking about hanging up. Or tying it around his neck and hanging himself.

"Joe, we've got the ball rolling here, and you're in danger of messing everything up. What's really going on here?"

"Nothing is going on, other than what I just told you. You're my lawyer. You convince them that if they want this deal to go ahead, it can't be in the morning."

"When then?"

"When I'm done with the interviews," I say. "Make it four o'clock," I say.

"Four o'clock," Kevin says. "Why four o'clock?"

"Why not four o'clock?"

"Jesus, Joe, you're really making this difficult," he tells me.

"Just make it happen," I tell him. "And by the way, it's *falling*, not *rolling*."

"What?"

"We've got the ball *falling* here. Not *rolling*."

He doesn't answer. I listen to his silence for a few seconds, then I hang up like they do in movies all the time without saying good-bye, when both parties seem to know the conversation has come to an end.

I turn toward Adam. "I need to make a phone call."

"You just made a phone call."

"No. I received a phone call. Now I need to make one."

He smiles at me. There is no warmth in that smile. "I don't give a fuck about what you need, Joe."

"Please. It's important."

"Seriously, Joe, which part of what I just said didn't compute? Take a look at me. Do I look like I care about what you need?"

I look at him. He actually looks like the kind of guy who cares about what I need and is willing to make sure I don't get it. If I tugged hard on the phone receiver and broke it free, I could use it as a club. I could entail the fuck out of him with it. Then the phone would be useless. Which makes it a paradox, since I need it. Or an irony. Or both.

"Please," I tell him. "Please."

"Tell you what, Joe," he says, pressing himself away from the wall while scratching at one of his bulging biceps. "Have you eaten the sandwich yet?"

"What sandwich?"

"The one I brought you earlier."

"No."

"Tell you what, Joe. Here's how it's going to play out. I'll let you make your call, and in return for me letting you do that, you eat that sandwich."

I say nothing.

He says nothing.

I think about the sandwich and what it would take to eat it. I think about tomorrow and getting out of here and never coming back.

"Well?" he says.

"Okay," I say, the word barely coming out.

"What was that, Joe?"

"I said *okay*."

"Good. And since I'm feeling in a good mood, I'm going to trust you. You go ahead and make that phone call first. I'll let you do that. But when we get back to your cell if you don't eat that sandwich then there will be no more phone calls for you in the future. In fact, your future will become all about misplacement. Your misplacement. We're not going to be keeping as good an eye on you as we should. Next thing you know, you're in general population by accident. You're showering with the big guys. And the thing about accidents is they happen all the time. We on the same page here, Joe?"

"I'll eat the sandwich," I tell him. Then after Melissa sets me free I'm going to find Adam and stuff him so full of pubic-hair sandwiches he's going to look like a mohair jersey.

I pick the receiver back up and dial my mom's number. It rings a few times and she doesn't answer.

"Deal still counts even if nobody is home," Adam says. "You're still making your call."

"It's not a call if nobody answers," I tell him.

"You're calling and nobody is home," he says. "Technically that's still a call."

Technically the pubic-hair sandwiches won't kill him. I'll make him eat as many as he can, though. But what will kill him will be a blade twisting slowly into his stomach.

Just then my mother answers the phone and, for the first time ever, speaking to my mom gives me a sense of relief.

"Hello?"

I can hear Walt in the background asking who it is.

"I don't know yet," she says to him. "Hello?" she repeats.

"Hi, Mom."

"There's nobody there," she says to Walt, because she's already pulled the phone away from her ear.

"Mom, it's me," I tell her.

"Hello?" Mom says.

"Perhaps let me try," Walt says.

"Damn it, Mom, I'm here. Can't you hear me?"

"Joe? Is that you?" she asks.

"Yes."

"Joe?"

"I'm here," I say, and I think about what the shrink was hinting at earlier, about surrogate victims, because this conversation has sent me back to the earlier thoughts of ripping the phone from its cable and beating Adam to death with it.

"Well why are you staying so quiet?" Mom asks.

"Is that Joe?" Walt asks.

"It's Joe," Mom says to Walt, her voice a little muffled as she pulls the phone away from her ear.

"Ask him how he is," Walt says, almost yelling at her.

"Good idea, honey," Mom says, and brings the phone back to her mouth. "How are you Joe?" she asks, almost yelling at me now because Walt is still talking to her in the background.

"Things are great," I tell her.

"He says things are great," she tells Walt, talking loudly to be heard over him.

"That's wonderful," Walt says. "Ask him if he's looking forward to the wedding."

"Of course he is," she says.

"Mom—"

"Ask him anyway," Walt says.

"Mom—"

"Joe, we want to know, are you looking forward to the wedding?"

"Yes. Of course," I say.

"That's fantastic," she says, then relays the news to Walt, who has the exact same reaction. "Thanks for calling and letting us know," she says.

"Wait, wait, Mom . . ."

But Mom hangs up.

I feel something tug at my eyes and hurt as I roll them too far upward.

"Phone call is over," Adam says.

"That's not fair," I tell him. "I got disconnected."

"You still technically made the call," he says.

"There has to be something else we can agree on," I tell him.

He gives it a few seconds of thought. "Okay," he says, and I realize I've just said something he was really hoping to hear. "Here's how things are going to play out," he says, which is what he said earlier. He must love that phrase. "You're going to get to dial her back, and the next sandwich I bring you you're going to eat without ever looking what's inside of it. Deal?"

"Deal," I tell him.

"Slow down there, big fella. I'm serious here. You try to renege, and I'll make you pay. You got no idea the things I can do to you."

"It's a deal," I tell him.

He smiles. A big, cold smile that doesn't reach his eyes. "When you came here, Joe, remember how they put you on suicide watch?"

I remember. They did the same thing to Caleb Cole, only I wasn't suicidal. I was angry and disappointed, but there's nothing you can do to rectify those things if you're dead.

"You asked me back then to put you into general population. You remember that?"

"I remember," I tell him, but it's not something I think about. Not only was I angry and disappointed, I was confused too.

"You thought if I put you in there, things would end for you quick. You thought it'd be like pulling off a Band-Aid—get it done fast—and I told you that was true, except it would be pulling off a Band-Aid while being raped in the showers while a filed-down toothbrush is pressing against your neck."

"I told you I remember," I tell him.

"You don't feel that way now, though, do you, Joe, because you've had time to calm down and now you've got the trial coming up and you think that somehow the jury is going to be made up of people so fucked in the head they're going to let you go. You want to live now, don't you, Joe?"

"Yes."

"So let me get this straight. If you don't eat the sandwich I bring you," he says, "all that stuff I told you about is going to happen. It's going to happen a lot. It's going to happen every day they bring you back from your trial. And if you find a way to complain about it, it will start happening twice a day. So let's be clear here, Joe, before you make that phone call."

I think about. If all goes well I'll be out of here tomorrow anyway. It could be days or weeks before Adam brings me that sandwich. Any number of things could have changed in that time. He could die. I could be free. The nuclear bomb I told my lawyer about might happen. All I know is that right now I have to make this phone call. Nothing else matters.

"I understand," I tell him. "But the phone call has to connect, and if I'm disconnected I get to ring back. What I'm talking about here is a phone conversation. If I ring and nobody answers, that's not the deal."

Adam slowly nods. "I'm a reasonable man," he says. "I can go along with that."

I turn my back to him. I phone my mom. It takes her a minute to answer. It's as if in the time I was gone she went for a walk into the lounge and got lost.

"Hello?" she says.

"Mom, it's me."

"Joe?"

"Yes. Of course. Listen, Mom, I need you to—"

"It's Joe," Mom says, calling out to Walt.

"Joe? Ask him how he's doing."

"Joe, how are you doing?"

"I'm doing great," I tell her. "Listen, Mom, I need you to do me a favor."

"Of course, Joe. Anything."

"He calling about the wedding?" Walt asks

"Are you, Joe? Calling to tell us how much you're looking forward to that?"

"I just called two minutes ago to tell you that."

"I know that, Joe. I'm not an idiot."

"So is he?" Walt asks.

"An idiot?" Mom says to Walt.

"No, is he calling about the wedding?"

"I don't know," she says to him. "He won't answer me."

I lower my voice. "I'm not calling about the wedding again," I tell her. "I need you to call my girlfriend."

"Your girlfriend? Why would I do that?"

"Do you have her number?"

"Yes, of course I do. I wouldn't be able to call her otherwise. Are you bringing her to the wedding? Oh, Joe, I'm so pleased! It's time you found a nice woman. I was getting worried, you know. And your girlfriend reminds me of how I was back then. She's very attractive, Joe. Of course I'll call her and invite her along! What a wonderful idea!"

"Okay, great, Mom, that's great, but I also need you to tell her I got her message."

"What message?"

"She'll know what I mean."

"Hang on, Joe, let me write this down," she says, and there's a clunk as she sits the receiver on the table and shuffles off. Nothing for about a minute and I become increasingly concerned she's either gotten lost or has fallen asleep or has got distracted by the TV. I twist my head and look at Adam who's grinning at me. He taps his watch and winds his finger around in the air. *Wrap it up.*

Scuffling as the phone is picked back up. Mom is back.

"Joe? Is that you?"

It's not Mom. It's Walt. "How are you doing, Walt?"

"I'm doing fine. Weather report says it's supposed to be fine all week now, but you know what weather reports are like—they're like fucking your sister in an elevator."

"What?"

"Wrong on many levels," he says, and he starts to laugh.

"I don't get it," I tell him.

"It's elevator humor," he says. "It suggests having sex with your sister is okay on some levels. That's what makes it great. I used to repair elevators. Didn't you know that, Joe? That's what I did for thirty years. Boy, we'd tell that joke all the time. Though it wasn't always your sister. It could be your brother, or your dog or your aunt."

"Why would you say that?"

"Just for a laugh. We didn't mean anything by it."

"No. I mean why would you say it about my aunt?"

"People always need elevators," he says, "aunts and uncles too." I wonder where the hell my mother is getting a pen from. The moon? "Buildings get bigger, elevator shafts get longer, more wear and tear. I wouldn't want to be doing it these days, mind you. Too complex. Too much technology. Back then it was all about cables and pulleys, now it's all about electronics. You gotta have an engineering degree in rocket science. There was this one time, ooh, let me think, twenty, maybe twenty-five years ago when Jesse, he was this neat kid who got his arm caught in one of the . . . Oh, wait, hang on," he says, then his voice is muffled as he holds his hand over the receiver, and then he comes back on the line. "Your mother is back," he says. "Don't tell her the joke," he says, then disappears with his joke and with his Jesse arm story.

"Joe? Are you still there? It's your mother," Mom says.

"I'm still here," I tell her.

"Now what's this number I'm ringing?"

"You have the number," I tell her. "For my girlfriend."

"Yes, of course, I know that. I just want you to repeat this message."

"I need you to tell her that I got the message."

"I. Got. The. Message," she says, writing each word down. "No, Joe, what's the message?"

"That is the message."

"You're saying the message is *I got the message?*" she asks.

"Yes."

"Does that mean *you* got the message or *I* got the message?"

"It means I got the message," I tell her.

"What kind of message is that?"

"I don't know, Mom, it just is what it is."

"It's a stupid message," she says.

"There's more. Tell her I got the message, and that it's happening tomorrow."

"It's. Happening. Tomorrow," she says, writing it down in that messy scrawl of hers. I know what's coming up before she even asks. "Wait, Joe, are you saying you got the message and the message is happening tomorrow? Or that you're not getting the message until tomorrow?"

Adam is still grinning at me. Something here is amusing him.

"Just say exactly what I told you," I tell Mom. "That I got the message and it's happening tomorrow."

"That doesn't make sense," she says.

"It will to my girlfriend."

"Okay, Joe, but you're really making this difficult," she says, and I imagine she and my lawyer are going to get on great when he calls her. "I'll talk to her first thing in the morning," she says.

"No. Call her now, Mom. And if she's not home and you call her tomorrow, then the message changes, okay? In fact, change the message. Tell her it's Saturday," I say, because if she rings tomorrow she'll say *tomorrow*, which will make it Sunday. "You get that? It's very important. You're telling her I got her message and it's happening on Saturday. This Saturday. Tomorrow Saturday."

"I'm not an idiot, Joe."

"I know that, Mom."

"Then why do you talk to me sometimes as if I am?"

"It's my fault," I tell her.

"I know it's your fault. Why would I think otherwise?"

"So you'll call her now then?"

"Okay, Joe."

"I love . . ." I start, but the phone is dead. "You," I finish.

I hang up the receiver. Adam smiles at me. He doesn't need to say how much he's about to enjoy this, because it's written all over his face. He walks me back to my cell. The sandwich is where I threw it, wrapped up, sitting on the floor opposite my bed. I was hoping somehow it would have disappeared.

"You remember the deal, don't you, Joe. You remember there are two sandwiches."

"I remember."

"See? That's good. Because lately all anybody hears from you is that you can't remember anything. Pick it up," he says, and points to the sandwich.

I pick the sandwich up and unwrap it. "Before you take a bite," he says, "why don't you go ahead and take another look at what's inside."

I take another look. Cheese. Some kind of meat that looks like it's come from a part of the animal nobody could identify, or perhaps the animal itself couldn't be identified. And in there the clump of pubic hair, tangled up and stuck to everything.

I put the sandwich back together. I think of Melissa and escaping jail, the books, the message. I think of better times from the past and think about the better times coming up.

"The deal," Adam says.

The deal. I hold my breath and take the first bite.

CHAPTER THIRTY-FIVE

Shooting *The Cleaner* at the casino fell through. The casino wasn't happy with the story line. They didn't like a TV show suggesting desperate people in desperate times would go into the casino with a Plan A and a Plan B. Plan A was to bet everything they owned on red or black. Plan B all depended on how plan A went. There were two plan Bs. The first was to take the winnings and pay off the mortgage. That was the Plan B everybody hoped for. A fifty percent chance of doubling your money to make your life much better. A paid mortgage, a new car, some cool toys. The problem was it also came with a fifty percent chance of losing your money and making it a lot worse. That's where the second plan B came into effect. That plan B involved heading into the toilets and taking a bunch of pills or slicing up your wrists or sticking a gun in your mouth.

The problem was the *other* Plan B happened more often than people would think. It wasn't something the casino wanted people made aware of. It's the sort of thing they would give low odds on if you could bet against it. They thought it wasn't good for business. They were probably right too. Having posters on the wall of guys in suits throwing money into the air at the roulette wheel while pretty women laughed and smiled weren't going to look good surrounded by posters of people dead in bathrooms with slogans saying *Come roll the dice*. So for the last month the casino has been saying yes and then last night they said no. The storyline is still going ahead. They have external shots of the casino. No problem there. And they have internal shots from a documentary shot five years earlier, and back then the casino signed a waiver to allow the footage to be used. Well, now it was going to get used in *The Cleaner*.

Instead of the bathroom at the casino, they are using the bathroom on the second floor at the TV studio. Some set dressing has been added. Nicer doors. Nicer furnishings. They'll fill in the background noise with some stock sounds of slot machines. It'll work.

"So what do you think?" the scriptwriter asks, and it's the same guy he dealt with yesterday, a guy by the name of Chuck Jones. Chuck is no relation to Jonas, and sometimes Schroder doubts that Chuck is related to anybody. "Blood look authentic enough?"

Schroder looks around the bathroom. Blood on the ceiling and high up on the wall. Blood from somebody putting a gun under their chin and pulling the trigger. Must be a powerful gun, going by all the fake blood. Must have made one hell of a make-believe sound. But he has seen it before, and this looks about right if only a little overdone.

"Looks fine," Schroder says.

"So in this story line the body and police are long gone," he says. "Suicide is three days earlier and the scene is clear."

"Scene would be cleared quicker than that," Schroder says. "Especially in a place like this."

"Okay, cool, but in this case it hasn't been. I don't know, maybe there were complications. We'll figure it out. Anyway the blood has dried. Dried pretty hard, and the guys are struggling to clean up. Jake, he climbs up on the toilet to try and reach up high and the toilet breaks away from the wall, and that's when they find the hidden casino chips because they come out of the toilet tank. Of course the guys decide to keep them."

"Sounds . . ." Schroder says, but doesn't finish. Sounds what? Charming? Stupid?

"It'll work," Chuck says. "Like all good drama you want to throw some comedy in there somewhere."

"The show is about cleaners scrubbing up after the dead," Schroder says. "Here you've got some poor bastard who came into the casino hoping for the best and preparing for the worst, and the worst is what he got. You really think that can be that funny?"

"Anything can be funny if you deliver it the right way," Chuck says. "Like I said, it'll work. So, the guys are struggling because the blood has dried really good. It's stuck between the tiles in the grouting."

"You seem to have everything under control," Schroder says.

"Good. Good, I just wanted to make sure."

Schroder doubts that. Everything he's pointed out so far since working on *The Cleaner* has been dismissed because it doesn't work in with the story line. It's like what Chuck said on day one—*sometimes reality can get in the way of a good story*. Schroder is learning that the other thing that gets in the way of a good story is bad writing.

More lighting is added to the bathroom and the fake toilet is finally bolted to a fake tile wall. The scene is still being staged when his cell phone goes off. It's Rebecca Kent. He's been both looking forward to and dreading this phone call.

"You heard the news?" she asks, and there is no hello, and he knows she's pissed at him.

"What news?"

"The prosecution just made a deal with Middleton. He's going to take us to Detective Calhoun's body."

"That's good news," Schroder says.

"They offered him immunity on Calhoun on account of the fact we know he didn't kill him."

"Really," Schroder says.

"Don't sound so surprised," Kent says. "There's more to the deal and you know it, since you're the one who put it together."

"Look, Rebecca—"

"This is a bullshit deal, Carl," she says, raising her voice loud enough for Chuck to turn and look at him. He steps out into the corridor to take the abuse so that the dialogue doesn't get added to a future episode. "And the worst part is fuck all people will ever know about it. You know how many people are taking Joe out there? Four. Four people. Including me, because they can't have many people knowing what's really going on. That's a risk, Carl. If it's a trap—"

"It's not a trap," Schroder says.

"That's what people keep saying. But I'll tell you this: if it's a trap, the first bullet any of us fire goes straight into Joe."

"I understand."

"Jesus, Carl, what were you thinking? First you make a deal with Jones, now with Joe? What the hell happened to you? Four weeks ago you were one of us. Now you've turned your back on us."

"I wanted Calhoun found," Schroder says, her words hurting. "He was a good man. He deserves to be buried. He doesn't deserve to be out in the woods or in a river or wherever it is that Joe put him."

"This isn't the right way to go about it. You're paying Joe a lot of money. This is wrong, Carl. You know it's wrong. You're rewarding a criminal. What do you think that will do if this ever gets out? Crime isn't only going to pay," she says, "but it'll be an investment that keeps on paying even after you've been arrested."

"Well somebody agrees with me," Carl says. "Otherwise the deal wouldn't be going ahead."

"That's a bullshit answer, Carl. If anything happens tomorrow it's on you," she says.

"I know," he says.

"And something is going to happen," she says. "We had a time all set for tomorrow morning. Then the defense lawyer rings the prosecutor back and says that time wasn't going to work. Says Joe is busy for the day with trial stuff. Says he can't make it till four o'clock."

"Shit," Schroder says.

"See? It's looking like Joe has a plan."

"It's not a trap," he says. "It can't be. Joe hasn't had time to make one."

"He's made two phone calls tonight—both to his mother, both after his lawyer spoke to him."

"Trust me, Joe wouldn't be using his mother to help him in any way. Whatever he planned with her would go the exact opposite way."

"There are going to be four of us and one of him," she says. "That's good odds if anybody is out there trying to free Joe. And that same somebody may be the reason two bodies were put into the morgue yesterday and we're dealing with missing explosives."

"I'm sorry," Schroder says.

"If it's a trap," she says, "then at least we're ready for it. And if we're dealing with Melissa, hopefully we'll be drawing her out into the open. Our people are trained for this," she says. "That's what the prosecution said. But we're not trained to be blown up," she says. "For all we know he's leading us right into a bomb."

Schroder closes his eyes and pinches the top of his nose. In the darkness he can see gunfire and explosions. He can see blood. Chuck would be pleased. It would look just how people imagined it would look. Very cinematic.

"Can I come with you?" he asks.

"I don't think that's a good idea, Carl."

"Please, Rebecca. I'd like to be there."

"If things go wrong you'd only get in the way, and honestly, Carl, I wish I could bring you along so if it is a trap that you've helped engineer, maybe we can use you as a shield. You fucked up working for Jonas Jones."

"I work for a TV station," he says. "Not Jones."

"Is that what you tell yourself? And the worst part is, once we find Calhoun, we have to leave him there for that slimy boss of yours to put on a show and make money. It gives bullshit hope to people out there who believe in these bullshit salesmen," she says. "You're giving a very large slimeball a lot of credibility here."

"I'm sorry," he says.

"So you keep saying. Good-bye, Carl."

"Wait," he says, and he's surprised a few seconds later to find she hasn't hung up. "Since you already hate me, there's something else."

"Oh, this ought to be good," she says, and she sounds the way he used to sound whenever Tate would call him. "You're not going to ask me for a favor, are you?"

"Look, I went and saw Raphael again today."

He can imagine her shaking her head. "Jesus, Carl? Why?"

"To show him a photograph of Melissa," he says, and he crouches down and leans against the wall.

"And?"

"And he's hiding something. I don't know what, exactly, but there's something off with him."

"*Off?*"

Schroder nods, then shrugs. "Off," he says. "I'm telling you, something isn't quite right with him."

"Something isn't quite right with him," she says.

"And you're repeating everything I'm saying," he says.

"Not repeating," she says, "but absorbing. Want to be a little more specific, Carl?"

"I got the feeling he recognized Melissa."

"Of course he would. Her photograph has been in the paper plenty of times."

"No. I don't mean that. I think he knew her from elsewhere."

"You think? Is that all you have?"

He pushes off from the wall and gets back to his feet. "He could know her from group. He could be lying to us."

"And why would he lie to us?"

"I don't know," he says, and no matter what angle he looks at it from, he can't come up with a reason. "I just don't think it would hurt to follow him."

"Yeah? You really think we have the man power to follow everybody who has ever given you a bad feeling?"

"I can follow him."

"Don't do that. You've got no reason to, other than a bad feeling. How many people in a day give you a bad feeling, huh? Ten? Twenty? Right now you're giving me a bad feeling. Does that mean I should follow you? Listen, I gotta go. I'll be in touch tomorrow once we've found Calhoun."

Before he can say anything else, she hangs up. He tucks the phone into his pocket and goes and finds Jonas Jones to update him on the deal.

CHAPTER THIRTY-SIX

"How'd you get that?" my psychiatrist asks, looking at my black eye.

I reach up and wince, unsure why in the hell I just put my finger against it. "I slipped and fell," I tell her.

"Who did that to you?"

"This is supposed to be an honest relationship," I tell her. "I want to be truthful with you, but I can't tell you who did this because it will only get worse if I do."

"No it won't, Joe. I can help you."

"You can't help Joe in here," I tell her. "You have no idea what it's like."

It's Saturday morning. It was a rough night sleeping, as the side of my face hurt like hell. Last night before we were all put back into our cells Caleb Cole came and saw me. He told me he'd decided that he'd rather kill me than take the money. He didn't see any reason in waiting. After all, prison was all about *waiting*, and all you had to break the tedium was *doing*, so doing was more entertaining than waiting. He came at me and his first punch got me in the stomach, and his next punch got me in the face. The problem is I'm a lover, not a fighter, and don't know how to defend myself. Before he could get a third shot in, Adam came in and Caleb stopped. When he asked Cole what was going on, Cole said he'd seen me fall and was just trying to help. He was shaking his hands afterward, the punches he gave hurting him just as much as me.

Is that what happened, Middleton? Adam had asked.

Things were a little blurry. I had nodded, said yes, that's exactly what it was, and Adam had been satisfied. He wasn't going to go home and be kept awake by any kind of guilt. I was just lucky he'd at least even put a stop to it. No doubt that's because he can't force-feed me whatever sandwich creation he's coming up with next if I'm dead.

"Joe, if somebody is threatening you, you need to tell me," Ali says.

"Why? Do you think the guards are going to care?"

"Joe—"

"Please, can we just talk about what we need to talk about for the trial? The rest will work itself out."

She doesn't answer.

"Please," I tell her.

"Okay, Joe, if that's what you want."

My psychiatrist—and I've decided to settle on Ali because it's a shorter name—has dressed a little more casually for the weekend. She's wearing tight jeans that give me bad thoughts. A buttoned shirt that also gives me bad thoughts. Maybe I'm just a bad-thoughts kind of guy.

"When did your auntie stop abusing you?"

"We're back to that, are we?"

"Just answer the question, Joe."

"I told you already," I say. "It was close to two years."

"I mean, when did she stop. What time of the year? Do you remember?"

I'm not sure why it matters. I close my eyes and picture it. Now

I'm a different kind of bad-thoughts kind of guy. School days were coming to an end, not just for the year, but for me they were ending forever. I had an unknown future, a world of unemployment was a strong possibility. I had never known what I wanted to do and, truth be told, I still don't know. Maybe open a pet store. It was a scary time. Throughout the previous six months of school, guidance counselors had been trying to help us all figure out what paths to take, and being a grade-A serial killer wasn't an option. Hell, back then I didn't even know that's what I wanted to be. Not really.

"It was near the end of my final year at school," I tell her. "About a month short—so around November I guess."

"You were eighteen?"

"Seventeen. My birthday is in December. The tenth, actually," I say, and I had to spend my thirty-second birthday in jail, but my thirty-third will be spent elsewhere. "You know what the tenth of December is?"

She shakes her head.

"It's Human Rights Day," I tell her, then smile. "Kind of ironic for a guy who the public's trying to kill."

"There are people who would see it as being ironic for other reasons," she says.

"Like what?" I ask.

"A serial killer being born on Human Rights Day, who believes nobody but himself is due any rights."

"It's not like that," I tell her. "I have no—"

"Memory," she finishes for me. "Therefore you can't remember what you were thinking in those moments. Yes, I get it. However, human rights are what this entire debate is all about. The people for the death penalty would say they want their rights heard, that it's the right of the victims to have their killers given the same sentences as they themselves were given. Have you thought about it from that point of view?"

I'm not sure if I have and, hearing what she's saying, I'm not so sure I want to give it any thought. Why should I care? "No."

"I think you should. I think you might find it insightful."

"Okay," I say, and sure, I'll get right on it.

"Tell me about the first time you killed somebody," she says.

At first I think I've misheard her. I'm not expecting the question, so it takes an extra couple of seconds to realize she hasn't said *Tell me about the first time you kissed anybody*, which would have been my auntie, and I hope the pause makes me look like I'm actually trying to remember. Which I can. But that's not what I tell her. "I don't . . . I don't remember."

"So you've been saying. So how about you tell me about the first time you *suspected* that you'd hurt somebody."

"Well, that would be when the police came and arrested me."

She slowly nods. Looks down at her hands. Makes a note. "So you're telling me you never woke up covered in blood? See, the problem we're facing here, Joe," she says, and I like the way she thinks *we're* facing the problem and not just me, it makes me feel like I'm part of a team, "is that if you don't remember any of it, why were you carrying a gun? Why did you try to end your life when the police surrounded you?"

"Well, that's tricky," I tell her, "and also a good point," I say, and I make out I haven't heard her ask this already. "I mean, I remember the police coming and getting me, and I know I got hurt pretty bad, but I don't remember trying to shoot myself, and I certainly don't remember ever owning a gun."

"The gun belonged to Detective Inspector Robert Calhoun."

"So I've been told. I just don't remember any of it."

"Okay, Joe," she says. "You want to stick with that story?"

It's the story I've been sticking with, and changing it now would make me look like an idiot. "Yes."

She nods. She accepts my story. Then she stands up. "We're done here, Joe," she says, and she knocks on the door and I know all I have to do is say the right thing and she'll stay.

"There was one time when—"

She puts her hands out to stop me. "I don't want to hear something you're making up on the spot, Joe. But I'll come back tomorrow. And that will be your final chance."

CHAPTER THIRTY-SEVEN

I've been back in my cell, lying down, staring at the door, waiting for Caleb Cole to show up, trying to decide what I'm going to do when he does. The timing of it all is pretty unlucky, but maybe that's just how I roll. I may be a bad-thoughts kind of guy, but also an unlucky kind of guy too—my surroundings are proof of that. All I have to do is make it through to this evening. That's all. Then I'm out of here. Caleb Cole, the prison guards, Santa Suit Kenny, they can all go to Hell.

I don't have anything to defend myself with. I'm not sure whether or not I'd be safer in the common area or whether that would just make it harder for the guards to get to me if I start screaming. Every time I hear footsteps I tense up.

"You missed shower time," Adam says, stepping into my cell. I relax when it's him and not Cole.

"I don't need a shower."

"Yeah, you do," he says. "You stink. And I hear you're going on some kind of field trip later on today, and the people you're going with don't want you stinking up their car."

He leads me out of my cell. My neighbors are sitting in groups or pairs shooting the breeze, only a few of them are alone. I can't see Cole and figure he must be in his cell, probably filing down a toothbrush. Adam leads me down to the showers. He opens the door and there's nobody else in there. The door closes behind me, then it's just him and me and a really bad feeling. I turn to face him.

"You heard the saying that life is a shit sandwich?" he asks me.

I don't answer him.

He nods toward a bench where there are towels folded and half-used cakes of soap. Sitting on the closest towel is a paper bag. "Pick it up," he says.

I back away from the bag. He reaches out and grabs my collar and pulls me forward so my face is only a few inches from his and I can smell onion on his breath.

"You owe me, Middleton," he says. "Remember? For the phone call. This was the deal."

"I'm not playing."

He lets go and pushes me back slightly. Then he reaches out with his left hand and points at the wall. I turn my head to see what he's looking at, then suddenly his other fist connects with my stomach. I double over, my breath knocked out of me, then he pushes me onto the floor where there are still a few footstep-sized puddles of water from the previous group who cleaned up here. I end up sitting on my ass and the water soaks into my jumpsuit and underwear.

"It's just you and me in here, Middleton," he says. "But tonight when you get back, you're not going to have time to have a shower with your normal group. So we'll have to arrange something else. You can be with some of the other inmates. It'll be just like I told you yesterday. A few of them will think you're their type. I've already had one guy offer me a thousand bucks if I could sneak him in here to bust your teeth out and fuck you in the mouth. Thing is, Middleton, there's a big-screen TV that I've been eyeing up and a thousand bucks would go a long way to getting me that. So I'm tempted. Now, what you need to realize is that the only thing between me and that TV, and between you and that inmate, is you eating that sandwich. You get me?"

I get my breath back. I get up onto my feet and pull the wet part of my jumpsuit away from my skin. Adam's muscles are tightly coiled. There's something glinting in his eyes, the same kind of something others may have seen in mine in their last moments. He's enjoying this.

"I'm not kidding," he says, and he shoves me against the wall and I don't fight back because I don't know how. "Eat the fucking sandwich," he says.

"No," I say, because I won't be here tonight. Melissa will be getting me out of here. Whatever plans Adam has for me won't be happening. Unless Melissa doesn't get me out of here. But Positive Joe doesn't think that way.

He punches me in the stomach again, this time much harder. Then he pushes me onto the floor, back into the footstep puddles. I look up at him. The veins in his arms are sticking out. He reaches down and pulls me up and shoves me against the wall. "I can keep doing this all day, Joe," he says. "And your shower buddies will keep doing you all night. Now eat the fucking sandwich," he says, and pushes the bag into my chest.

"No," I tell him again.

The shower door opens. Another guard comes in. "What the hell is going on here?" he asks, and it turns out to be Glen, Glen who has always given me such a hard time, but right now he's my salvation. He takes one look at Adam, then at me, then back at Adam, and closes the door behind him.

Adam doesn't answer.

"He's trying to—" I say.

"Shut up, Middleton," he says. "Adam, what the hell?"

"It's not how it looks," Adam says.

"Yeah? You sure about that?" he says, looking as mad as hell, so mad the veins in his arms are standing out more than the veins in Adam's arms. "It looks like you started without me."

"I haven't," Adam says. "Look, it's still here," he says, and holds up the paper bag to eye level. "He hasn't taken a bite yet."

I don't understand what's going on.

Glen takes the bag off him. He unfolds the top of it, and inside is a smaller plastic bag that's sealed, and inside that plastic bag is a sandwich. He peels the plastic bag open and the smell that comes out is potent.

"Okay," Glen says. "I didn't mean to overreact. I just don't want to miss this."

"I was just laying down some ground rules," Adam says.

I stare at the sandwich. Both men have turned their heads away from it. I turn my head away from it too. I stare over at the direction of the showers, where later tonight I'll have to deal with a bunch of assholes trying to invade mine. It reminds me of that saying about nine out of ten people enjoying gang rape.

"Come on, Middleton, eat the sandwich or we'll put you in a cell tonight where guys are going to knock your teeth out and make you eat a whole lot more," Glen says, giving me similar dialogue to his buddy. "You tell him we'll make him shower in general population?" he asks Adam, "Where he's going to have a lot of guys trying to populate his—"

"Enough," I say. "Okay? I get the point. Enough already."

Even if I wanted to eat the sandwich, there's no way I could. The smell alone is enough to make me gag. Adam pushes me into the wall again and Glen stands in front of me holding the sandwich. He punches me in the stomach, but I can't fall down because of Adam. Glen pushes the sandwich at my mouth. I have no choice. If I don't eat it, they're only going to make my life worse, and if Melissa isn't waiting for me this evening, then I'm not going to make it through to tomorrow. And what can I do? Go to the warden? Fill out a complaint form? Even if the warden did believe me, even if Adam and Glen lost their job, what then? What of the other prison guards who know and like them? Life already feels like an endless Monday. If I don't comply, it's going to be an endless Monday of shit sandwiches. The pieces of bread are almost flat against each other, so at least there are no lumpy bits. There is some lettuce hanging out the side. And I can see the edges of some salami that looks like it passed its use-by date around the time disco phased out. The whole thing smells exactly the way he described it earlier when he asked if I'd heard that phrase about life, so I know the compound holding it all together may look like peanut butter, may have flecks of peanut in it, but will taste nothing like peanut butter.

Glen pushes one hand against my forehead so the back of my head grinds hard against the tile wall. Then he digs his fingers into my cheeks to try and open my jaw. He punches me in the stomach again, and my mouth opens from the impact and his fingers dig my cheeks inward between my teeth so I can't close my mouth.

Adam brings the sandwich up to my face. It's a putrid smell, the kind of smell I used to have to deal with back when I was a janitor, back when some drunk asshole in the holding tanks at the police station would shit all over the floor and I'd have to clean it up. Only it's that smell times a hundred. It's like they've used shit to bury the smell of something that died, the same way hospitals use disinfectant.

Glen pinches my nose shut, and it helps, a little, and any help at this stage is a relief.

The sandwich touches my lips. I feel the lettuce dangling from the edge of it on my chin. I feel the bread—it's stale and firm and feels like it's been lightly toasted, but it hasn't been. Then that bread is on my tongue and scraping the roof of my mouth, and so far it's okay, it's okay because bread is all I can taste. The bread starts to get wet. Adam pushes more of it into my mouth, then Glen lets go of my cheeks and pushes my jaw upward and my teeth bite through the sandwich.

My taste buds all head for thc hills at the same time as flavors burst into my mouth, they run in the same direction, which pulls my tongue into the back of my throat and causes me to gag. Even with my nose pinched closed I can smell the sandwich again.

Something in the back of my throat starts clicking and still the sandwich is being pushed deeper. I can't breathe now. It's chew or suffocate. They're the two choices I have.

So I chew.

I picture my mom and her meat loaf and I try to imagine that's what I'm eating, but my imagination simply isn't good enough. What floods my mouth is dirty and foul and makes me wish I'd been quicker a year ago when I tried to shoot myself. I twist my head from side to side, but Glen keeps his hand pressed firmly on it, and as if to prove a point he punches me again in the stomach, only this time lightly.

I figure the best thing to do is chew the minimum amount of times and then swallow. So I do that, chewing even less than the required minimum, and when I try to swallow what happens is a giant wad of whatever the hell I'm eating gets lodged in my throat. I start to choke.

"You're not getting off that easy," Glen says, and he spins me around, digs his hands beneath my chest, and pulls upward. The ball of sandwich comes up and hits the wall. He spins me back around again. "Smaller bites are the key, Middleton," he says, and then we repeat the steps—the punching, the nose squeezing, the flooding of flavors—only this time I chew for longer and my second bite goes down, and then there's a third. I keep my tongue pressed down and I chew as best as I can without trying to taste anything, but it doesn't work. I look at the sandwich. Three bites gone.

Bite. Chew. Adam laughs.

Swallow. Repeat. Glen laughs.

The humiliation's worse than anything I've ever felt. Glen pulls out a camera and takes a photo. Then he films me taking a bite. If I can survive having my testicle crushed, I can survive this. It takes ten minutes and then the sandwich is gone. I keep expecting them to make me eat the bit I coughed up, but they don't. I can feel my face burning, the scar running up to my eye feels tight. My other eye is watering. My bad eye doesn't, something to do with a damaged tear duct.

"See, that wasn't so bad now, was it," Adam says, and lets me go.

I drop to my knees. I start to retch. I can taste bile in the back of my throat, but none of the sandwich wants to come back up, which is probably a good thing because these guys would make me eat it again.

It takes them a few minutes to calm themselves down. Glen has laughed so hard he's broken into a sweat. It takes me the same amount of time to know I can walk again without vomiting all over myself. They lead me back to my cell. They try to hurry me along, but I maintain a slow speed. They keep laughing at me, and when they leave me in my cell I can hear them laughing back along the corridor.

I look up at the door waiting for Caleb Cole to come in. If he does, there is nothing I can do. So with that in mind, there's no reason not to turn my back on the door and try to make things a little better. I hold my head under the tab in the basin and pour water into my mouth and rinse it out a dozen times. Then I swallow mouthful after mouthful until I can no longer bear it, and when my stomach seems to turn upside down, I crouch over the toilet. In a rush of surging water from my stomach parts of the sandwich finally appear, but nowhere near as many as I would have liked. It's turning into a bad day, and I know there are still plenty of ways it can get a whole lot worse.

CHAPTER THIRTY-EIGHT

Raphael should have trusted his initial gut instinct last night. It told him there was more to Stella than she presented, but he saw what he wanted to see. The lies were good. So good he imagined anybody would fall for them. And the change in looks. Boy, she could almost fool anybody. She fooled him. Even when Schroder gave him the photograph, he didn't pick it. Not at first. Not until he took a good look and then he started seeing. She looked different. Different makeup, different hairstyle—hell, a completely different hair color. Plus she's put on weight, not much, but a little around the neck and face.

He connected the dots.

Stella wasn't Stella. She wasn't a rape victim who'd lost her baby.

She was Melissa.

The realization was almost like a blow to the stomach. He felt his breath catch and it took all of his composure to stay calm, to not let on that he knew the woman in the picture. He stood there staring at it while his mind was racing. What he felt was a sense of betrayal. What he should have felt was a need to tell Schroder she was in his house—and yes, that was a consideration—but not what he settled on. Telling Schroder would be the first step in the process of he himself going to jail—after all, he did kill two lawyers.

Of course Schroder sensed something. How could he not? But he recovered from the pause—he told the ex-policeman that he recognized her from the news, and Schroder bought it. No reason not to. Will Melissa buy it too?

What he can't figure out is why she wants Joe dead. The trial must have something to do with it. That's what the timing suggests. She wants Joe dead, and he's okay with that. He wants Joe dead too. So their desires fall in line quite nicely.

Where things don't line up are their views on people who take innocent lives. Melissa has been doing a lot of that lately. Other cops. Security guards. Paramedics. People in uniform. The media even labeled her the Uniform Killer for a while there, though that name doesn't seem to have stuck much. The police uniform he has, it looks authentic because it is—it's come from somebody she's killed.

He knows the irony. He's a smart guy. Smart enough to know that he's a killer working with another killer to kill another killer. It's not complicated.

Law Abiding Raphael knows he should go to the police. Red Rage Raphael thinks he should just shoot both Joe and Melissa and let the chips fall where they may. Sensible Raphael knows he can't go to the police because Melissa saw the articles pinned to the wall in his daughter's bedroom. She made the connection. If he goes to the police then he'll be thrown in jail alongside her. Then Joe will get his trial. He'll have his chance to plead his insanity defense, and then you just never know what will happen. He'll be found guilty, has to be, but that doesn't sit well with Raphael. So Sensible Raphael agrees with the Red Rage. There are more than enough bullets to go around. The plan allows for that. In fact, the very nature of the plan allows for it perfectly.

And if he gets caught because he's taken that extra shot? Then so what. So. What.

So he covered with Schroder while these thoughts went through his mind, and then he covered with Melissa too while those same thoughts were there. If she suspected he knew who she was, she would kill him. He didn't know how. He wasn't arrogant enough to think that just because he was bigger and perhaps stronger that that gave him an advantage. There was a reason she had killed so many people. It was foolish to underestimate her.

But she didn't suspect. Had no reason to, not when he spoke about his anger toward Joe, and what Joe had done to him, his daughter, and to Stella. He spoke of his excitement to be the one to take Joe's life. They spoke about the plan. They went over and over the plan. It wasn't a simple plan. Not really. But he has a great way to streamline it.

Melissa rang him this morning. The next part of the plan was happening today. She said she would be by this afternoon to pick him up. Sometime around three thirty.

"It's important we're not late," she had told him.

And now it's three thirty and he's waiting by the door, and he only has to wait another minute before her car pulls up. He heads out and climbs in. She's still got black hair, but he wonders if it's a wig or if she's dyed it. He tosses the bag with the police uniform into the backseat.

"Then we're doing this," he says. "We're really going to shoot Joe."

"Gun's in the back," she says, and puts the car into gear and starts driving.

CHAPTER THIRTY-NINE

I end up lying down, hoping for my stomach to settle, which it doesn't seem to want to do. The sandwich has set about some motions that I don't know how to stop. There are cramps and there are sharp pains and there are occasional moments where the two combine, other rarer moments where there is no pain at all. I give up looking at the door every time I hear somebody coming near me. If Caleb Cole came in with his makeshift knife he'd be doing me a favor.

Eventually a set of footsteps slow down. They enter the cell. I'm too busy feeling sorry for myself to look up. It's more than one set of feet. Eight feet, four guards, one underlying current of anger. None of the guards are Adam or Greg. My hands are cuffed in front of me. There are ankle cuffs with a length of chain about a yard long between my feet. A length of chain runs up from that chain and connects to the handcuffs. It's the kind of thing Harry Houdini would wear to a fetish party.

I struggle to keep up with the guards, and when I do slow down too much I get pushed in the back. At the front of the prison is a police detective I haven't seen before. A woman. She's signing forms and talking to the warden. The woman is perhaps a couple of years older than me. Beautiful hair. Beautiful features. Great curves all wrapped up in some pretty sleek packaging. She glances up at me and barely gives me a second's worth of attention before carrying on her conversation with the warden. The warden is in his mid-fifties and is wearing the kind of suit telling the world there's just no point in mugging him.

Both the warden and the woman come over to me. I've got my stomach muscles clenched and my ass clenched because my organs are performing some weird kind of ballet, they're dancing around so fast they're turning into fluid.

"If you put one foot out of line," the warden says, "these people will shoot you."

"Which is the wrong one?" I ask him.

He doesn't answer.

"My name is Detective Kent," Detective So Hot I'd Rather Abduct You Than Kill You says, and my oh my, what fun we could have together. "And what the warden said here is absolutely one hundred percent correct," she says, and I could get lost listening to her voice, looking into her eyes, cutting her open. Even the warden seems to be mentally trading his wife in for her.

"Joe will behave," I tell her.

"Good," she says. "Because the general consensus is that Joe has something planned."

"Joe don't have a plan."

"Good. Because if anything happens, Joe's going to find himself with a bullet in the back of his head," she says.

"Joe just wants to do the right thing." Everybody is giving me the same kind of look they'd give a stand-up comedian misreading his audience. "Where is Detective Carl?" I ask.

"Detective Schroder won't be joining us," she says.

"I miss Carl," I tell her.

"I'm sure he misses you too," she says. "Now let's get this show on the road."

I'm escorted to the door. Outside are three heavily armed officers. The afternoon is chilly. Mostly gray skies, but some patches of blue in the distance. No sun. The day is cool, but my skin is feeling hot and my stomach is riddled with what feels like large worms on the loose. I'm led to the back of a white van. There is nothing special looking about it. The back doors are opened and I'm told to climb inside. There's a metal eyelet that's been welded into the floor. I step up and my legs buckle under me and somebody has to catch me.

"Stop fucking around," somebody says.

I suck in a deep breath and hold it. I can feel the world slipping a little.

"He's going to hurl," somebody says. "Get back!"

Everybody gets back. I drop to my knees heavily enough that I'll have bruises on both of them this time tomorrow. I open my mouth, but nothing happens. Sweat is dripping off my face. I widen my eyes and my mouth then exhale heavily. My stomach is struggling to hold on. The sandwich is threatening to fire out in all directions.

"Are you up for this?" Kent asks.

I nod. I appreciate her concern. When I come to her house when this is all over, I'll make things quick.

"Okay. Here are the rules," Kent says, standing over me. "You do what we say. You answer our questions. You make good on the deal. You don't do any of that and we bring you straight back. You try to escape, we shoot you in the spine. You have anything planned we shoot you in the spine. Hell, we may just shoot you in the spine anyway. You get what I'm saying?"

"I thought you were going to shoot me in the back of the head. Now it's the spine?"

"It will be both," she says. "And probably the balls too. Though we'll have to aim accurately since you only have one left."

"Funny," I tell her, and try to get back onto my feet.

"Is this some kind of gimmick?" she asks.

I shake my head. "I ate something bad, that's all."

"You going to toughen up and go through with it?" she asks, and she sounds like my mom used to sound when I was sick in the morning before school. Back then she would ask me if I was a girl or a boy or a man.

I find my balance and step into the back of the van, which answers her question. My handcuffs are connected to the eyelet by a chain that keeps me stooped over, which is fine because my stomach would be stooping me over anyway. There are no windows in the back. There's wire mesh between the back and the front, so I can see outside and I could jam knitting needles at the driver if I had them, but nothing more. The driver is armed and looks familiar, but I can't place him. Kent climbs in next to him. The other two heavily armed officers climb in the back with me. There's a shovel lying across the floor. Four people for Melissa to deal with and they've even brought along the supplies to hide the bodies.

The van starts rolling forward. This is the furthest I've been from my prison cell since I pled not guilty and was held over for trial. This is the view my mother and my lawyer see every time after they've come to see me.

"Which way?" Kent asks.

"Right," I tell her. "Can you open a window?"

"No."

We have to wait for a gap in traffic, then we're swinging out over the lanes and heading toward the city.

"Please? It's hot back here."

"It's not hot," Kent says.

"He doesn't look so good," Officer Nose says, and that's the name of the guy sitting opposite me, the guy with the nose that looks like it's been broken a few times. The guy next to him is wearing glasses and my name for him is Officer Dick.

"How far do we go?" Kent asks, winding down the window halfway.

"I don't know," I tell her. "I can barely see out the window."

"How about you just give me an address?"

"There is no address," I tell her. "That's why we're in this situation. We're looking for a paddock. I can't tell you where it is, but I can figure out the way."

"Great," the driver says.

"It is, isn't it?" I ask.

We get closer toward town. We pass the big *Christchurch* sign that somebody has added graffiti to, but I can't see what. We keep driving. More boring shit to the left. The same boring shit to the right. I don't know how people do it. I don't know why more people aren't shooting themselves.

"Go left toward the back of the airport," I tell them.

We slow and make the turn. I can see a plane overhead coming in to land. I've never been on a plane before. Never been out of the country, never even been up to the North Island, never really left Christchurch. I wonder where Melissa is planning on taking me. Australia? Europe? Mexico? I can't wait. It must be so cool, looking down on the world, seeing people scurrying around like ants. It *is* how I see them, most of the time anyway. I wonder how I'll see them from a few thousand feet in the air. Then I wonder why a cockpit is called a *cockpit*, who came up with the term, and what they were doing in the process.

"Keep going straight for a while," I tell them.

We do just that. We pass open fields and landing planes and runways in the near distance lined by lights and more fields. As we drive it's all coming back to me. The night with Calhoun. He was the detective who had killed Daniela Walker. I was the person who had figured it out. I'd have made a great cop. He had staged the scene so it would be pinned on me—the Christchurch Carver—and I wasn't pleased about it. At the same time Melissa was blackmailing me. So I tied Calhoun up and Melissa ended up stabbing him, and I filmed the whole thing without her knowing. It all worked out great. It got me and Melissa on the same page. I don't know how it works—she pulped my testicle with a pair of pliers, and yet I love her. Her sister was murdered by a cop, she herself was raped by a bad man, and yet she loves me. You can't deny the chemistry.

The sky is getting a little darker. I'm not sure of the difference between twilight and dusk. Is there one? Both are approaching. I guess one arrives first, and then the other. Twilight might be when there is still some light in the sky and dusk is when there isn't. Another hour and it won't matter because they'll both be gone. Perhaps that's part of Melissa's plan. When it's dark she'll start shooting. My stomach is feeling a little better, but not much.

"Take the next left," I tell the driver, and after that I tell him the next right. We go through a series of turns. Just when it feels like we're looping back in on ourselves, and right when they're starting to accuse me of messing them around, we reach the dirt road I found last year. There's a gate going across it.

"It's . . ." I say, then a bolt of cramp grips my stomach and I crouch further forward and grit my teeth until it passes. "Here," I finish saying, and the driver pulls over and comes to a stop. We all stay seated in the van. Kent is on the phone. Probably updating the address with somebody in case they all go missing. I no longer feel sweaty and hot. In fact it's the opposite.

"Take the road," I tell him.

"Not without a four-wheel drive," the driver says. "Track's too wet. How far in?"

"Not far," I tell him.

He looks at Kent. "This is private property," he says. "What do you want to do?"

She lowers the phone so she can chat to him. "Can't see any signs of life out there," she says. "Let's start walking."

Kent and the driver get out of the van. They come around to the back and open the doors. Officer Dick climbs out while the others point their guns at me, then Officer Nose unlocks the chain from the eyelet. He helps me out of the van and I try to straighten my back. It's sore from the twenty-minute drive. It'd help if I could push my palms into it and stretch it out. Kent has finished her phone call.

The view consists of rocks, trees, dirt, and mud. Mountains in the distance. A stream nearby. More trees and open paddocks and

I imagine it would be nice for a picnic if picnics are your thing. It would also be a nice place to string up the warden or Carl Schroder if stringing up assholes is your thing. What I don't see are any other cars. No sign of Melissa. But she's here. I can feel it. My ball is tingling. It feels it too.

Kent is wearing a bulletproof vest that she wasn't wearing back at the prison. She doesn't offer me one. That hurts. I give her my big Slow Joe smile and she looks mad at me, mad because it could be muddy where we're going and she doesn't want her hiking shoes getting dirty. The others are all wearing vests too.

"What happened to your face?" she asks.

"I walked into a door."

"Good," she says. "You should keep walking into doors. It looks good on you. Matches your scar," she says, and I try to reach up to touch my scar only my hands won't go that far because of the chain between them and my ankle bracelets. "How far away is the body?" she asks.

"Same as I told him," I say, nodding toward the driver.

"Well consider this your chance to tell me too."

"A few minutes' walk," I tell her. "And bring the shovel."

The driver reaches in and grabs it. I finally recognize him. It's Jack, the man in black who put the boot of his heel into my eyelid and squished it into the ground. He sees me staring at him and he figures out I've just figured out who he is.

He smiles at me.

"How's the eye?" he asks.

"Still good enough to see me fucking your wife when all this is over," I tell him.

He jumps forward at me, but two of his colleagues are quicker and they grab hold of him.

"Enough," Kent shouts, but it's not enough because Jack keeps struggling. "Damn it, guys, I said enough."

The message gets through. Jack stops struggling and the others let him go. Then we're all standing in a circle and I'm the odd one out.

"Now, Joe, stop jerking us around and lead us to Detective Calhoun," Kent says.

I head up to the gate. There's a chain and a padlock that took me only a few seconds last year to pick. The gate is just below chest height. A wire fence heads out from each direction and along the edge of the property.

"Cut the lock?" Jack asks. "Or climb it?"

"Nobody can know we were here," Kent says.

So we climb the fence, which is pretty awkward for a guy chained up. Two go over first, then they half drag me while the other two half push. When we're all on the other side we start walking. The road is in rougher condition than when I was last here, the winter months treating it the same way death treats a newcomer—parts of it black, parts of it lumpy in areas, parts of it dissolving. My prison shoes are not up to the task and a few steps further my right shoe is sucked off by mud. Tree roots and rocks are covered in moss. All these guns pointing at me. People all around me. I'm the center of attention. I crouch down to pull out my shoe, then I flick it to clear as much off it as I can and put it back on. We keep walking. More trees and no gunshot. I keep getting ready to duck. When somebody stands on a branch and it cracks loudly, I drop to the ground.

"Stop fucking around," Jack says, and drags me back to my feet, the cuffs digging painfully into my wrists.

A warm glow is starting to burn deep in the side of my stomach. We keep walking. A hundred yards. Two hundred. I can remember clearly driving out here last year. The weather was similar, though we'd just come off the back of a very long summer. The glow in my stomach is making its way into a sharp pain, an appendix-bursting pain if you had two appendixes. I bury my thumb into the area and it helps a little.

Another hundred yards.

Then I slow down. I start studying the trees. The open clearing ahead is full of dirt that a year ago was also full of dirt. It's all coming back, sure, but it's also all looking a little different. The leaves have fallen from the trees and formed a brown paste with the earth. There is moss on the stones and rocks. Last year the same trees were hanging onto life a little better.

"He's here," I say to nobody in particular. I point at one patch of dirt that looks like any other while keeping my other thumb buried into my side. "I think," I add. "If not here, then close to here."

"That's not too specific," Kent says.

"A lot better than what you had before, don't you think?"

The body is going to be a mess. These people hate me now, and what I did to Calhoun isn't going to win me any admirers. Unless people admire those who cut off fingertips and pull teeth. Maybe it's possible. If people can admire midget porn, they can admire anything. I dumped Calhoun's parts into a plastic bag along with his identification to dispose of later. As hard as I try, I can't remember what I did with that bag. It wasn't found on me when I was arrested. I must have dumped it somewhere. If I told that to Ali, she wouldn't believe me. But I was distracted that night. With blackmail and violence and love. Under the circumstances anybody could be forgiven for misplacing a bag of fingertips.

Jack begins to dig. Calhoun isn't deep, maybe only a few feet. It doesn't take Jack long to find evidence of it. The shovel hits a bone and Jack stops digging.

"We've got something," he says, then uses the tip of the shovel to carefully scoop away the dirt covering Calhoun, creating a funnel into which dirt starts to sprinkle back inside. "Remains," he says.

"Okay," Kent says. "Cover him back up. We're done here."

"You're kidding," Jack says.

"You knew the deal coming into this," Kent says. "You know we're leaving him here." Then she looks at all of them. "You all know the deal here. You're not expected to like it, but it's your job to shut up about it."

"This is fucked-up," Officer Dick says.

"No, this is the job," Kent says. "And it is what it is. Put the dirt into place and pat it down," she says, and she gets her cell phone out and starts playing with a GPS feature, marking the location of the grave.

Jack doesn't start covering the grave. He's leaning on the handle with both hands and he's deep in thought. Then that thought makes its way out into the open. "There's nothing to stop us from shooting him," he says, and if I remember rightly he brought that subject up during the drive from my apartment to the hospital on the day I was arrested. It's time to move on. "We shoot him and say he made a break for it. Then there's no deal left to be made, right? We shoot him and we bring Calhoun back home."

Kent lowers her phone. I start to raise my arms, but they don't get far because the chain makes a clanking sound and brings any movement to a halt. "That's not the deal," I say.

"But it's a good deal," Jack says. "I say we vote on it."

Nobody else says anything. They all look like they're thinking about it. Really, really thinking about it. The air is so still that any sound could travel a mile, but right now nobody within a mile is making any kind of noise. I look from one face to the next, there are some poker faces in there and some faces with thoughts written all over them.

"Can't we all just get along?" I ask.

Nobody answers. In fact only Jack is looking at me. The others are looking past me or through me. They're still playing various scenarios in their heads. They're playing out all the possibilities. Except Jack, who has played them out already. This is one of those moments that comes along in life that can change the direction of a man. A turning point. It's a Big Bang moment all over again.

"Everybody needs to take a deep breath," I say.

"The same kind of deep breath women would take when they found you in their homes?" Officer Nose asks.

Exactly! But I don't say it. I look at Kent. I get the sense if she agrees with the idea then in the next few seconds I'll be one part human and twelve parts bullet. Melissa is taking her sweet time about opening fire.

"I deserve a trial," I tell them, but I don't finish it up by saying I'm innocent. I think that would put them over the edge.

"We should take a vote," Jack says again.

"It needs to be unanimous," Officer Dick says.

"I agree," Officer Nose says.

Suddenly we're all looking at Kent. She is now the center of attention the way I was earlier. My life is in her hands. My heart is racing and my legs feel a little weak and I'm actually close to throwing up. A year ago I tried to shoot myself when the police found me, but that was impulsive and stupid. I don't want to die. Not here, not now. Not ever. Not at the hands of these assholes.

At least it would stop the stomach pains.

Then, slowly, Kent shakes her head. "This is ridiculous," she says, without any emotion, as if she's reading *The cow goes moo* off a cue card. Then she injects a little more conviction into it. But only a little. "I'm not going to risk my career for him," she adds.

"There's no risk," Jack says.

"Of course there is," she says. "You think we can say Joe ran so we had to shoot him? That we couldn't catch him?"

"Why not? You think people will care?" Jack asks, and suddenly it's looking like if Kent doesn't agree, I'm not going to be the only one having new holes made inside them. They can say I got hold of a gun and shot her before they shot me. Then they'll have an excuse for putting so many holes into me. Kent doesn't see it. If she did, she'd stop arguing.

"People will care," she says.

"Who?" Jack asks. "Come on, Rebecca, this is a freebie. This is why we became cops, right? To right some wrongs. To give justice. If we do this, then we can be honest about why we were out here. We don't have to fuck around with this psychic shit."

She doesn't answer right away. There's a pendulum swinging—or a wrecking ball—and she still hasn't decided to go with it or against it. "Family members of victims will care," she says.

"No they won't. They'll be thrilled," Officer Dick says.

"They deserve to face him in court," she says. "They deserve the right to confront him."

Everybody goes quiet. More thoughts and no Melissa, just tension mounting upon more tension, and more tension rising in my stomach. I push my thumb a little deeper. Something in there swirls around. Something in there doesn't want to be in there anymore.

"We can do this, Rebecca," Jack says. "We can do it and say whatever we want. You know that, right?"

She nods. A slow, purposeful nod. "I . . . I don't know," she says. "But . . ."

"You can't do this," I say.

"Shut up," Jack says. "Rebecca . . ."

"Can we live with it?" she asks.

"Don't—" I say.

"Shut the fuck up," Jack says.

"I can live with it," Officer Dick says.

My stomach does one final turn, then my legs turn to jelly and my ass muscles just can't hold on, and before anybody can add anything else a sound like a thunderclap tears itself free from my ass. It echoes through the trees and across the fields. The mess that follows is like a mudslide.

"Oh fuck," Jack says, and Officer Nose says something similar and so does Dick and Kent, so it's a chorus of *fucks*. They all jump back from me. I fall to my knees and into the mud. There are more thunderclaps, quickly followed by what sounds like a bucket of water being thrown at a mattress. I fall onto my side. Dick looks like he's going to throw up, and then Jack starts laughing. He throws his head back and he has to hold on to the shovel to stay balanced, and he laughs just as hard as Adam and Glen did earlier—harder, probably. He laughs like a man who is in danger of tearing his vocal chords. Kent starts to laugh too, just a grin at first that widens and makes her look even more beautiful. Jack's laugh becomes infectious, the harder he laughs the harder the others join in. Officers Dick and Nose are on the brink of losing control. My stomach lets go once more—not so much a thunderclap this time, but like somebody sticking a knife into a car tire. I can feel fluid running across my thighs. I try to get to my knees, but don't have the strength.

"Now we really should shoot him," Jack says, and he's laughing as he's saying it, but there's still some seriousness in there, some tension, but it's been broken. "Let him stink up the coroner's van instead of ours."

Kent is smiling and shaking her head. She is holding her nose with one hand and talking into her hand. "Let's just get him back," she says, "and let the prison clean him up."

Nobody objects. Nobody suggests they ought to shoot me again. Part of that may be to do with the technical details—I'm covered in shit, and shooting an unarmed man covered in shit is going to be a much harder sell.

"It's gonna smell," Dick says, and they're all still laughing only not as hard now. It's dying down.

"Let's just go," Kent says.

"Wait," I say. I'm still lying on my side with my face in the cold mud.

"What for?" she asks.

For Melissa to shoot you. All of you. For her to come and save me. It's getting darker, but the sun hasn't quite set yet. Isn't this twilight? Didn't Mom pass along my message?

"I want to pay my respects," I say.

"Let's go," Jack says, and he reaches down and pulls me to my feet. Officer Dick puts the dirt back into place and pats it down.

The trip out here is put into reverse order. Now the mountains in the distance are on my right. Same trees, same dirt, same rocks with mold. Same view all around except darker. A hundred yards. Two hundred. The seat of my prison jumpsuit is cold. It's sticking to my legs and ass and smells just like the sandwich. The walk is slow thanks to the chains around my ankles. The pain in my stomach has lessened, but I can already feel it starting to build again. Melissa is in the trees somewhere, but taking her time, just waiting for the perfect shot. Being covered in my own shit will be a mood killer for her, but I'll clean up good. I lose my shoe in the same place I lost it earlier, but don't have the strength to bend down and look for it. It's getting darker by the minute. My sock is soaked in mud and my foot is cold and it hurts when I step on a tree root or a stone or anything else that isn't flat. Then we're at the fence. We go over it the same way as before, two ahead of me to drag me, but the two behind me don't want to push. They don't want to touch me. So the two ahead have to do all the work because I don't have any strength to help them. When I'm over I break the fall with my arms and am given only a few seconds before being pulled back up. We approach the van. My feet are heavy with mud. My bank account is about to be heavy with cash. Cash I can't use unless Melissa starts shooting. Only she doesn't. Nobody does.

We all stand at the back of the van wondering how to make the next step less messy than it's going to get, but nothing comes to mind, there's nothing to lay across the seat first, so I head in and the reverse order continues. Hell, even Calhoun was found and then not found. The only thing that hasn't been taken back is me shitting myself—that one was for keeps. The chain between the eyelet and my handcuffs is fastened. I'm all hunched over. The two cops back here sit as far from me as they can. Jack opens his window. Kent opens hers the rest of the way. There's a moment where the van doesn't want to start, a good two-second turnover of the engine where I get to think Melissa has done something to it, but then it catches and Jack pumps the accelerator a few times then releases the hand brake and pulls a U-turn. More lefts and rights, but in the opposite order. Jack flicks on the headlights. A rabbit on the road twenty yards away is all lit up and seems happy with the idea of being hit by the van, and that happiness probably fades as he goes tumbling under the wheels. Moths are flying into the lights and splattering over the windshield. It's as though nature is trying to kill itself around me, that we are a van of death driving into town. Traffic is thin. My feet are wet and cold. Melissa didn't come.

She didn't come.

CHAPTER FORTY

The outer shell of the building is complete. Inside are offices in various stages of completion. The complex won't reach the finish line until hard economic times become good economic times. Nobody knows when that will be. Opposite the building are the Christchurch Criminal Courts that, until recently, were also under construction. Hard times or good times—it doesn't matter where the economy is at when it comes to prosecuting crime. The old courts are a few blocks away, but Christchurch was a growing city with bigger problems, and it needed bigger courts to reflect that and to feed bad people into the prison population at a faster rate.

The offices on the third floor of the complex where Melissa and Raphael are standing range from fairly complete to hardly started. The one they've chosen is mostly complete. All the walls are in place and there are light fittings and power fittings and no exposed wires. There are some tins of paint resting against a wall, some cleaning supplies, some loose tools, a couple of sawhorses, and a plank of wood that doubles as scaffolding. There's a whole lot of dust. Things have been sanded down, but nobody cleaned up. Everything looks settled, like it's been that way for some time and there's no reason to think that'll change.

Six months ago she killed a security guard who worked the building two blocks away, the one that overlooked the front of the courts that she was originally going to use. In an unfortunate twist of fate—at least for the guard—she wasn't trying to kill him. Just pickpocket his keys. He caught her doing it. She had no choice. She thought back then that that building was going to be part of the plan. She thought they'd be taking a shot from the roof. This building is easier. She didn't need to kill anybody. All she needed on Thursday when she picked this building was a minute with the lock of the entrance around the back. A child with a toothpick could have picked that thing. Once she opened the door, she used a screwdriver to remove the lock on the inside, leaving it so the door couldn't latch closed. She had to. If she locked up, then re-picked the lock in front of Raphael, she thought at the time that he'd ask too many questions. It's a miracle the offices in here aren't all like two-star hotel rooms for the homeless. She's surprised anything nailed down hasn't been stolen and sold.

Raphael opens up the case. He starts to assemble the gun. She could tell he loved shooting it. He loved being the man. All she could do was hit dirt. Or that's what she showed him. It cemented the dynamic in their relationship. He was the shooter. She wasn't the shooter. She was the collector. He wasn't the collector. It was a shooting and collecting relationship, hence it's a two-person plan. Nothing wrong with that.

Raphael doesn't put the scope on the gun. Instead he stands in front of the windows holding the scope in both hands. He's wearing a pair of latex gloves. They both are. There's no reason to leave their fingerprints everywhere. The police uniform is still in the bag.

"I can see everything," he says.

"What about the courthouse? How does it look?" she asks, but she knows how it looks. She's been here already. The office has a direct line of sight into the back entrance of the courthouse. A nice, clear view of the parking lot and the courthouse doors and the ten-yard strip of concrete between the parking lot and those doors. A lot can happen in a ten-yard strip of land. There are going to be thousands of people out in the street, but within the parking lot there's only going to be a couple of cops and Joe. Shouldn't be a problem. Crowd won't be in the way. All Raphael has to do is stay calm. Six months ago the view from the other building she chose was very different. Six months ago it looked like a mess from any angle. Cranes. Bulldozers. Work crews.

"Everything is so clear," he says.

"May I?"

He hands her the scope. It has higher-quality optics than the binoculars. She looks at the courthouse, then up and down the street where there is going to be lots of traffic. The courthouse is a single story. The elevated view from the third floor of the office complex means she can see over the top of the courthouse and further into town. The courthouse takes up an entire block, with the back entrance right in the middle. She can see roads leading in all directions, two main roads running parallel up and down the city—one road passing by the courts on the left, the other on the right. So many protesters will be here on Monday that some of these roads will be closed off. It's going to be perfect. Right now the roads are almost empty. Saturday evening in the middle of winter in a part of town where there are office buildings and a courthouse and nowhere serving beer—why would there be people down there?

"Here," she says, and hands the scope back to him.

He lies down and holds the scope. A nice elevation. Simple to look down on the parking lot without anything in the way. Not too high that they have to worry about wind swirling between the buildings. And not too high that they won't be able to escape quickly.

Biggest thing they have to worry about is weather. They don't need great weather, but bad weather won't work. It can't be pouring heavy with rain. Can't be gusts of wind. Problem with Christchurch weather is the way you forecast it is the same way you forecast who's going to win a horse race. You go with the favorite, but everything has a chance.

"I won't be able to lie down," he says. "It'd mean shooting through the window. Windows open waist high and above."

She looks at her watch. It's ten minutes from six o'clock. The transport is arriving at the back entrance of the court at six o'clock on the dot. She knows that because it was in the itinerary she stole from Schroder. She also knows the solution to Raphael's problem. She'd figured that out when she came here on Thursday.

"Help me with this," she says, and she moves over to the paints where a large, canvas drop cloth has been folded up into a neat square foot. They unfold it and carry it over to the window.

"What's the deal with this?"

"We hang it up," she says, and reaches into her bag for some duct tape.

Raphael seems to figure it out and together they start stripping off lengths of tape and a few minutes later they have a curtain that shields them from the street. The room, dark to begin with, now becomes pitch-black, and she uses a flashlight function on her cell phone to shed some light. She takes a knife and cuts a square of drop cloth away from in front of one of the opening windows, leaving a hole not much bigger than her head.

"I shoot through this?" Raphael asks.

"And you'll be lying down too," she says. "From out on the street nobody is going to see a thing."

"Lying down on what?" he asks, and she turns toward the sawhorses and the plank of wood and he doesn't have to ask anything else.

They drag the makeshift platform into place. He lies down on it and shuffles himself into position so he can see out through the drop cloth.

"Try it out," she says, and she attaches the scope to the gun and hands it over.

He shuffles himself a little further up the planks. He puts the scope against his eye. Tightens the gun into his shoulder.

"It's good," he says.

"So you'll be able to pull off the shot?"

He smiles up at her. "With the window open, yeah."

"Just don't open it when you're in the uniform," she says. "You open it before that."

"I know," he says.

She looks at her watch. "It's almost time," she says.

Raphael stays in position. Melissa moves to the edge of their makeshift curtain and kills the light on her phone before pulling the curtain aside. Street lights, building lights, tungsten and neon burning from every direction in the city, more than enough to see clearly. They don't make any further conversation. They just wait in silence. Somewhere in an adjoining office, or perhaps even the one below or above, an air-conditioning unit kicks into action, the low hum creating a background noise that makes the office complex feel less like a building in a ghost town. But not a lot less.

Right on time a series of headlights comes from the south. Three police cars leading a van, three police cars following it. They're driving slowly. None of the lights are flashing. They disappear from view, as the angle of the courthouse gets in the way as the cars get close to it, but she knows they're turning toward the front of the building.

On Monday their progress will be made slower by the traffic and by the crowds of people.

They're the decoy.

At the same time a van comes into view from the parallel street. It disappears from view as the courthouse blocks them, but then comes back into view as it comes around the back. It turns into the street between the office building and the back entrance. There's a chain-link fence stretching the perimeter of the court's parking lot. Somebody inside the compound pushes a button and part of the fence rolls open. The van drives in. The fence rolls closed.

The van parks up close to the door. The back of the van is facing the office window. Its doors swing open.

"I can see all of it," Raphael says.

"Focus," she says. "Don't miss the shot."

She can see it all too, but not in any great detail. Two men dressed in black step out of the back of the van. Then out shuffles a man in orange. She can't see the chains, but can tell by the way he's moving he must be wearing them around his ankles as well as his wrists. He steps down. People are pointing weapons at him. For two seconds nobody moves.

A lot can happen in two seconds.

The prisoner starts his thirty-foot walk.

"Do you have the shot?"

"I have it," Raphael says.

"How clear is it?"

"Clear enough."

The thirty feet get eaten up. The group stands around the back door.

"May I?" she asks, and she turns toward Raphael, but can't see him. She puts out a hand and takes a step toward him. The only light in the office is what's coming through the hole in the curtain. She feels nothing at first, then touches the side of the gun that's being held toward her. She grabs it and moves back into position. She looks at the four cops and the man in orange. Almost like a painted target. The man in orange is a police officer. She's seen him before. On TV or in real life she can't remember, and it doesn't rightly matter. Tonight he's playing the part of Joe. This small field trip's a rehearsal for Monday morning's big event.

Also a rehearsal for Raphael and her too.

The cops are chatting with a security guard at the entrance. One of them throws back his head and laughs and the others are grinning at him.

"Can't miss," Raphael says.

"There are going to be a lot of people down there," she says. "People will figure out the police may use the back entrance. The police may panic and have a couple of cars escort it. But no matter how many there are, there's still only going to be one van. One Joe. And he'll be covering the same ground his stand-in just covered."

Raphael gets onto his feet. He picks up the gun case and sits it on the plank he was lying on a moment earlier. Melissa uses duct tape to put the hole she cut in the curtain back into place. Then she switches her cell-phone light back on. Raphael starts taking apart the gun and putting it away. The magazine is empty. There is a mostly empty packet of bullets in the gun case—it's the last of their supply. There are only two bullets left inside it. Plus the bullet she had to order especially. That one she hands to Raphael.

"This one goes at the top of the magazine," she says.

He hefts it in his hand, checking the weight, as if it would make a difference.

"This is the armor-piercing bullet?" he asks.

"Don't miss with it. It's our only one."

"I won't," he says.

He puts the round into the case, jamming it downward into the foam to separate it from everything else.

"Try not to use the other two rounds," she says. "The longer you stay up here, the higher chance of getting caught. We need this done in one round. More rounds also means more people being put at risk."

"It'll get done in one."

Melissa climbs up onto the platform and gets to her feet.

"What are you doing?" Raphael asks.

She reaches up and pushes a ceiling panel aside.

"Safer for us if the gun stays here," she says.

"Why?"

"Because I don't think it'll look good on Monday morning if you have to carry it in here. We hide it up here, you use it, then you put it back up there. The police are going to figure out where the shot came from, but there's no reason for them to think the gun will still be here. And even if they do somehow get lucky, it's going to be clean."

"Makes sense," he says. "Here, let me get it."

They swap positions. He reaches up and puts the case into the ceiling. She hands him the bag with his police uniform in it. "We keep this here too," she says.

He slides the panel back into place then climbs down.

"So you won't be back here," he says.

She shakes her head. "No reason to," she says, because she's going to be down among all the action, among the cops and the protesters, right in the middle of the tension and the chanting and the screamed insults. Raphael is the shooter. She is the collector. No reason to pretend any different.

"We're not going to practice anymore?"

She shakes her head. She tucks aside the curtain and looks out the window at the van as it starts to pull away. The only difference in the layout between now and Monday is there will be an ambulance there too. There'll be a few of them scattered around the streets near the courthouse.

There'll need to be because the protesting is a powder keg ready to explode.

That's why she got her hand on a paramedic's uniform months ago. After all, she's the one who's playing the collector.

CHAPTER FORTY-ONE

The prison comes up on the left. We turn off. Having the windows down in the van has helped, but only marginally. Being cold was a sacrifice everybody seemed prepared to make, only the damp air that flooded in seemed to soak up the smell and then cause it to stick to every surface like a thin film of condensation. We pass the barrier gates and go to the same entrance I was taken out of earlier. The warden is there to greet me. He looks at me with disgust. Everybody does. Just because I'm used to that look doesn't mean I like it. In a fair and just world, I wouldn't be in chains and these people would all be drawing short straws.

"Get him cleaned up," the warden says to nobody in particular, and nobody in particular takes any notice because I end up standing there with people who don't want to look at me. I'm standing on a slight angle because of my missing shoe. The warden seems the most annoyed out of everybody, and if he'd joined our trip and been part of the vote I'm sure I'd still be out there now, surrounded by spotlights and crime-scene tape. There is more paperwork. I stand there watching it get filled out and signed.

Then the same four guards that escorted me out earlier escort me back in. They don't look pleased with the job. They don't want to touch me. I'm tossed the key for the cuffs and told to undo them myself then step away from the chain. I'm told to take my remaining shoe off first because it's muddy, and the opposite sock too. The concrete floor is cold. The pressure in my stomach has built back up. I'm taken directly to the showers. I'm given sixty seconds to clean myself up. I make use of every one of them. I don't think I've ever had a shower feel so good. When the water is shut off I'm thrown a towel and a fresh jumpsuit and socks and given another minute to get dressed. Then I'm taken back to my cellblock. There are others sitting around playing cards and watching TV and making idle chitchat, the kind of idle five-or-ten-or-twenty-year-passing chitchat that gets repetitive after day one. I don't partake in it, instead I head into my cell and I climb onto the toilet and I spend ten minutes feeling about as sorry as a guy can for himself, the toilet no doubt feeling even sorrier.

I keep waiting to feel better. I don't.

I try to figure out what happened with Melissa. I can't.

I should have been free by now. I'm not.

Optimistic Joe is struggling to live up to his name.

I'm off the toilet for barely a minute before the guards come in and lead us all away for dinner. I still have no shoes. There are no new people in our group. Nobody has left. It's the same mystery meat. Caleb Cole is sitting a few tables away. He's sitting by himself. Seeing him, my face starts to hurt. I look at the food and can't touch any of it.

"Looking forward to Monday?" Santa Suit Kenny asks me. He sits down on my left and starts in on the meat that could have easily started out the day as somebody's pet. Or as somebody.

I think about his question. I'm not sure. In some ways no, because there could be a travesty of justice and I'm found guilty. In other ways yes, because it'll be different from the rest of this bullshit. It gives me a chance to clear my name.

I sum all of this up by shrugging.

"Yeah, I know what you're saying," he says, which really goes to prove I should sum more things up by shrugging. I'll remember that for when I'm on the stand. Mr. *Middleton, did you kill those women? You're shrugging? I see . . . well, I think we all understand now.*

"Trials are tough," Santa Kenny says. "People don't see the real you. They judge on the potential of bad things you can do just because of the bad things they think you've done, and that potential grows with every cop show and serial-killer movie they've seen. To them, we're all Hannibal Lecter, but without the class."

I don't bother pointing out that to them Kenny is just a child rapist in a Santa Claus suit, and no amount of cop movies or Christmas movies is going to alter that.

"It's totally unfair," he adds.

I push my tray aside. At this stage any food entering my body would trigger a violent reaction. Santa Kenny stuffs in his mouth some mashed potatoes that, like the meat, probably started the day as something completely different. He chews quickly and swallows it with an audible gulp, then starts up the conversation again. No matter what anybody hears, prison can be full of really friendly folk.

"I've been thinking," he says, "of what I should do with my life if the band doesn't want to get back together."

For the first time I answer him. "It seems being an inmate is something you're good at," I tell him. "And you're experienced at it."

"I've always wanted to be an author."

I can't contain my surprise. "Really?"

"Yeah. A crime writer," he says. "You read romance books right? Well, people love crime books more than romance books," he says.

I have the urge to tell him to fuck off.

"I think I'd try and combine the two," Santa Kenny says.

"Yeah? How's that going to work out?"

"I don't know, that's the thing. I just need one really good idea."

"You probably need lots of really good ideas," I tell him, but I'm not looking at him, but over his shoulder at Caleb Cole a few tables away. Cole is looking at me too. He looks angry. If I were a betting man I'd bet that after dinner and before we're put back into our cell, he's going to come for me. My heart starts racing at the thought and my stomach starts to rumble, but not the hunger rumble—the rumble of things getting ready to let go. "Especially if you want to write more than one novel."

He starts nodding. "Yeah, that's true. Completely true," he says, almost as though he hadn't thought of this. "Between you and me," he says, but he doesn't lower his voice so it's between him and me and the guy to my left and the guy to his right, and the few guys sitting opposite us too, "I've tried a few times, you know. Back before I was arrested. I'd sit at the kitchen table with a computer and try to come up with something, but it never happened. I thought it'd be like writing lyrics, you know? But it's not."

"You need to write what you know," I tell him, which is something authors always tend to go on about.

"Yeah, I've read that before," he says. "And it makes sense. I need to write what I know," he says, his voice trailing off.

"The problem is I don't think people want to read books on how to molest children."

He frowns at me and tries to figure out if I'm joking or being mean or being helpful, and comes to the right conclusion. "You really can be an asshole, Joe," he says, then picks up his tray and walks off.

When dinner is over I ask one of the guards who isn't Adam or Glen if I can use the phone. He's a big guy made up of as much muscle as fast food, the kind of guy who looks like he could knock your head off in a single blow, but would double over after it from the exertion.

"This isn't a vacation you're on," the guard says. He's one of the night-shift guards. He starts at six o'clock and escorts us to and from dinner or showers then sits in a cubicle watching TV for seven hours while we're all stuck in our cells. I think his name is something like Satan, but not Satan—Stan or Simon.

"I have a right to use the phone," I tell him. "It's important and my trial starts in two days."

"You don't have any rights in here," he says, but at least he doesn't laugh.

"A hundred dollars," I tell him.

His eyes narrow as he stares down at me from the few inches of extra height he has. "What?"

I figure I have money to spare. "I'll give you a hundred dollars."

"Hand it over."

"I don't have it, but my lawyer can bring it in tomorrow."

"Two hundred," he tells me.

"Deal," I tell him.

"If there's no cash tomorrow your day around here is going to become a little more difficult," he says. "Don't fuck with me."

I think about how bad today was, and the sad thing is that he's right—it could have been worse. It's like what Santa Kenny said—it's all about the potential. The guard leads me down to the phone. He leans against the same patch of wall that Adam leaned against earlier, but he doesn't keep making the same threats.

"Two calls," I tell him.

"Just make it quick."

First call is to my lawyer. It's getting late and it's a Saturday, but I have his cell number. He picks it up after a few rings. I can hear conversation and music in the background.

"It's Joe," I tell him.

"I know," he says, and I figure he probably has the prison phone in his caller ID. I figure I'm lucky he even answered. Could be the ball is still falling when it comes to my luck—after all, I wasn't shot this afternoon. From here on out I'm going to be living the good life.

"Did the deal go ahead?"

"You've held up your end of the bargain," he says. "Of course it's going ahead. Once the body is identified the money will be transferred into your mother's account. I have the details. Your mother is . . . well, she's quite something," he says, which on one hand is exceptionally accurate, but on the other hand doesn't sum her up in the least.

"How long until they identify the body?" I ask him.

"You've got a break," he says. "Five years ago Calhoun was chasing a rapist in his car," he says, and I wonder if that's the way most rapists get caught. "There was an accident. So now Calhoun has a metal pin in his leg. Pin has a serial number on it. So if the body you led them to has that same pin, then the money will be cleared. Jones is going to have a vision in the morning. It's too late tonight and too dark and he wants a buildup. Autopsy will take place tomorrow afternoon. Funds will be transferred tomorrow night. Monday morning your mother will have them."

"What time are you coming in tomorrow?"

"It's my day off tomorrow," he says. "It's Sunday."

"But we need to talk about the trial. It's our last day," I say, more desperate now since Melissa hasn't set me free, so maybe the luck ball isn't falling that much at all.

"Well, we'll see what happens. If I can make it I'll make it."

"And I need you to spot me two hundred dollars," I tell him.

"Good night, Joe," he says, and hangs up.

The prison guard is still leaning against the wall. He's playing a game on his cell phone. I make the second of my two calls listening to the theme music and then to the explosions coming from the guard's direction. My mother answers after the first ring, as if she were expecting the call.

"Hello, Mom. It's me."

"Joe?" she asks, as if it could have been one of any amount of people ringing and calling her mom.

"It's me," I tell her.

"Why are you calling? It's Saturday night. Date night. We're about to head out for dinner."

"I wanted to—"

"You can't come along, Joe. It's date night. Why would you try to ruin date night?" she asks, sounding annoyed, and I can picture her on the end of the phone frowning at the wall. "It's our last one before the wedding."

"I'm not calling about date night," I tell her.

"Why? You're too embarrassed to be seen with your mother on a Saturday night?"

"It's not that."

"Then what?" she asks, no doubt the frown now being joined by, rather than replaced by, a look of confusion.

"I'm calling about something else."

"About the wedding?"

"No. Remember how I called you last night?"

"Yes. Of course. You called about your girlfriend," she says. "I'm so glad you have a good woman in your life, Joe. Every man deserves a good woman," she says, sounding happy again. "Do you think you'll get married? Is that why you're calling? Oh my, I'm so excited for you! Perhaps we can have weddings on the same day! Just think about it. It's so fantastic isn't it? Oh, oh, how about if Walt is your best man? By golly, that's a great thought!"

"I'm not so sure that's going to happen, Mom."

"Because you're embarrassed to be seen with me. You know, Joe, I didn't raise you to be this way."

We're getting off track—but of course my mom has been off track for at least thirty years. "Mom, did you call her?"

"What?"

"Did you call my girlfriend? Did you tell her that I'd gotten the message?"

"What message?"

"Did you call her?"

"Yes, of course I called her. That's what you asked me to do. She didn't know what I was talking about."

"The message," I tell her, "the message in the books."

"What books?"

"The books you brought in for me. The books she gave you to give me."

"Oh, oh *those* books," she says, and I hope the force of everything flooding back to her knocks her over. That way she'll break a hip and the wedding will have to be postponed. "Did you enjoy them?" she asks. "I thought they were okay. Not as good as TV, but nothing ever is. I can't count how many times I've read a book after seeing the movie on telly and been so disappointed. I just wish authors could get it right. Don't you think so, Joe?"

I don't answer her. I can't spare the energy, because I'm using all of my strength to have an out-of-body experience. I'm trying to figure a way to reach my arm down the phone line and put my fingers around her throat.

"Joe? Are you still there?" she asks, and then she taps the phone against her hand—I can hear it banging once and twice, then a third time, and then it's back and her lips are against it and I'm still trying to reach her with my hand. "Joe?"

"You read them?" I ask.

"Of course I did."

"But you're a slow reader."

"So?"

I face the concrete wall. I wonder how far I could bury my forehead into it. "So when exactly did my girlfriend give them to you to give to me?"

"When?" she asks, then she goes quiet as she's figuring it out. I can picture my mom standing in the kitchen on the phone, dishes behind her, cold meat loaf on the counter, using her fingers to count off the days. "Well, it wasn't last month," she says.

"So it was this month."

"Oh Lord no. No, it was, now let me see . . . it was before Christmas, no, no, wait—it was after. Yes, I think it was after. Probably around four months ago, I suppose."

I tighten my grip on the receiver. The other hand curls into a ball. I can't hear my mom choking. "Four months?"

"Maybe five."

I close my eyes and lean my forehead against the wall. It's painted-over cinder block, so it's cold and smooth and easy to wipe blood off.

"Five months," I say, and somehow my voice stays level.

"No more than six," she says.

"No more," I say. "Mom. Listen to me. Very carefully. Now, why the fuck didn't you bring those books to me straightaway?"

"Joe! How dare you speak to me like that! After all I've done for you? After raising you, looking after you, after squeezing you out of my vagina!" she shouts.

And sixteen years later I was being squeezed into my auntie's one. I figure between them both they owe me some Goddamn consideration.

"Six months!" I shout, and I don't even make the decision to do it, it just starts happening, my hand starts crashing the receiver against the wall. "Six months!" I scream back into it, only it's just shattered plastic holding a string of wires and components. I smash it against the wall again. All I have now is a disconnect signal and a blossoming headache. I don't get to speak into it again because then I'm being tackled. I'm on the ground and my arms are being pulled behind me. I'm being shouted at to stay calm. I shout *six months* again, and then the guard puts his knee in my back and I'm punched really hard in the kidneys, so hard that I almost throw up.

He rolls me onto my back. He's been joined by a second guard.

"Let's go," he says.

They drag me to my feet. It's Saturday night. Date night. I'm not taken back to my cell. Instead I'm taken in a different direction, through two more sets of doors that are buzzed open from a control booth somewhere. We're watched by cameras in the ceilings. I haven't been in this direction before, but I'm pretty sure I know where it heads. It's solitary confinement—and my first thought is it has to be better than what I've had so far, then my second thought is that this has actually worked out pretty well. Not the part where my mother fucked up, but the part where I fucked up and broke the phone. I'm going to be safe here. Caleb Cole can't get me here.

The cells are wider apart. All the doors are closed and there's no sound coming from within any of them. There is no communal area. Everything is darker. Even the cinder-block walls seem to be a different shade of gray. The two guards march me to the end of a corridor and then we wait as a cell door is buzzed open. None of us make conversation along the way. A piece of my soul is still back at the phone, trying to figure out a way to get to my mother. The second guard disappears.

"Sleep it off," the original guard says, and he shoves me into the cell. He takes the cuffs off. "Don't forget you owe me two hundred bucks," he says. Then the door is slammed behind me. There is no light. I have to walk slowly to find the edge of the bed. I lie on my side. My stomach is starting to make noises again. The darkness of the cell is going to make it all very awkward if that rumbling continues.

For the first time since being in jail I start crying. I let my face sink into the pillow and I wonder whether things would be better for me if I just buried my face into it and went to sleep and hoped the Suffocation Fairy will come and take me away.

I wonder what Melissa is doing right now, who she's doing it to, and—as the pressure in my stomach builds—I wonder if she even thinks of me anymore.

CHAPTER FORTY-TWO

It's cold but dry and Melissa is relieved that the weather seems like it's going to do its part. It's Sunday morning. People are sleeping in. Some going to church. Some hungover from the night before. Kids are climbing into bed with their parents, kids are sitting in front of TVs, kids are playing in backyards. Melissa remembers that life. She and her sister on Sunday mornings snuggled in bed with their parents. Her sister's name was actually Melissa. That's where she got it from. Her own name was Natalie. *Was* being the key word. Melissa and Natalie watching cartoons and eating cereal and, on occasion, trying to make breakfast for their parents. Once they set fire to the toaster. It was more her sister's doing, really—she was the one on toaster duty, whereas Natalie was on cereal and orange-juice duty. Her sister had put jam on the slices before toasting them. Something caught fire. After that their parents made them promise not to try making breakfast for them again, at least not for a few more years, and that's a promise they would keep.

She misses her sister. They used to call her sister Melly—

though Natalie would call her Smelly Melly whenever she was trying to annoy her. Which was reasonably often. Melly was younger. Blond hair in ponytails. Big blue eyes. A sweet smile that became sweeter as she started a journey through her teens she wouldn't finish. Everybody loved her. One day a stranger loved her. He loved her and killed her and then stuck a gun into his mouth and killed himself. The guy was a cop. They'd never seen him before. Don't know how his life and Melly's life shared the same orbit. But they did. For one brief painful afternoon they did. There was no meaning in it. It was—for no better summation—just one of those things.

She struggled with the loss. Eventually that loss killed her father. Life carried on. And life was strange. It was a policeman that had killed her sister, yet it was policemen she started to become fascinated by. Not obsessed—that would happen later—but in the early days it was just a fascination. Her psychiatrist at the time put it in terms she was too young to understand. She didn't understand how she could like the very thing that had hurt her so much. So her psychiatrist, a Dr. Stanton, had explained it more simply—he had said she wasn't becoming fascinated with the police because it was a cop that had hurt her sister, but because the police represented justice. She got his point. After all, it was the police she loved, not individuals who raped and murdered young girls.

It was only a handful of years between the events of losing her sister and it becoming her turn to share an orbit with a really bad guy. It felt like her family was cursed. This time the bad guy was a university professor. She was studying psychology. She wanted to know what made people tick. She wanted to be a criminologist. Then came the bad orbit and the curse, and she shared the first half of the same fate Melly had shared. The other half she would have shared too, she was sure of it, but that's when Melly came to help her. From the dead she could hear her sister's voice telling her to fight back. And she did. She did all the things Melly wasn't able to do. She fought back and she's been fighting ever since. So much in fact that she got to like it. Like it a lot. And it didn't make sense. She hadn't studied psychology enough to understand it, and she didn't think Dr. Stanton would be able to explain it either. Dr. Stanton was at least right about something—she didn't become fascinated with policemen because it was a cop who killed her sister, because if that had been true then she would have become fascinated with professors too. What did happen is after her own attack her fascination with the police became full-blown obsession. She would hang outside the police station. She would follow some home. She would sneak into their houses. She knew it was crazy. She knew it made her crazy, but there it was. She was fascinated by policemen and by the men they looked for.

She started calling herself Melissa back when she heard her sister's voice, but she doesn't hear it anymore. That's because Melly wouldn't approve of all that she's done. She knows that, because Melly told her. It was the last thing her sister told her from beyond the grave. It was in a dream. Melly said she didn't approve, and Melissa told her that men were bastards. All men. Melissa pointed out some are better at hiding it, but all deserve to be treated like the pigs they are. Melly didn't have a response for that—unless disappearing forever was a response, which Melissa suspects might just be.

She still misses her.

In the process of following the police, she began to learn good ones from bad ones, and there were a few bad ones around. And then she met Joe. She didn't follow him because he was a cop. In fact, she didn't follow him at all. He was a janitor. That much was obvious. Then a year ago she ran into him in a bar and they started chatting, and the rest is history.

She misses him.

Her obsession with the police ended that night, and her obsession with Joe started. Joe, a man she should hate—a man similar to the man that took away her sister, similar to the man that raped her—and she's obsessed with him. She's in love with him. There is something wrong inside of her, something terribly, terribly wrong. She knows it, she's felt it every day since the police came to her house and spoke to her parents, the day she hid at the end of the hallway where she could just make out snippets of conversation that included the words *dead*, *naked*, *policeman*, *suicide*. If she asked Dr. Stanton to put it into layman's terms, he would tell her she was fucked-up. But knowing you're fucked-up doesn't solve anything, not when you like how it feels, and Melissa likes how it feels. In fact she's come to like it a lot. It makes her feel alive. If the bad shit in her life hadn't happened, if Melly were still around, would things have turned out the same? Would she have found another way to become this person?

She has asked herself this question a thousand times, and she's no closer to answering it now than she was a year ago when she first met Joe.

There are a few cars parked out front of the hardware store, but for the most part the store feels deserted. She hasn't been into a hardware store since she was a kid and her dad came here a few times the way dads do when they're planning on fixing something around the house or building a deck. It's been a while, and while hammers and screwdrivers all look the same, the power tools all seem to be made of brighter colors than the last time she was here, some of them going as far as looking like they were made in the future. She's wearing the red wig, but not the pregnancy suit. She isn't real sure where to look, but a bald guy with moles littering his arms and neck helps her out, and a few hundred dollars later she has what she wants.

The next stop is town. She parks outside the office building, getting the same parking space as yesterday evening. She goes inside and takes the lift up to the third floor, feeling too lazy to use the stairs. The environment might not thank her, but her calves do. The office is just how she left it. Why wouldn't it be? The drop cloth is still playing curtain, but there's enough ambient light to see. The gun is exactly where it was left. She gets it down and rests it on the bench they made then goes to the window. She gets her hardware-store purchase out and quickly browses the instructions. The device uses a laser to measure distances. She points it over the road where Joe is going to be standing, but can't see the red dot of the laser pointer and can't tell where she's pointing. She gives it a minute and is about to give up in frustration when she suddenly spots it in the shade of the back door to the courthouse. She follows it to the spot where Joe will be standing tomorrow and locks in the distance. With the elevation, it's almost forty yards.

She takes the tool and the gun and heads back down in the elevator. She puts the gun into the trunk. Traffic doesn't increase over the next hour. It never does, no matter what the hour on a Sunday morning. The temperature doesn't increase much either. Maybe one degree, if that. She drives with the heater on and the radio on. She's listening to Bruce Springsteen. He's singing about a guy who went on a killing spree with his girlfriend in the fifties. Things were simpler back then.

Driving the car is easier when you're not eight or nine months pregnant, but she puts the suit on now. She pulls into the parking lot of the gun store and goes inside. The guy who helps her is in his forties, has thick glasses and eyebrows reaching across to shake hands with each other. His name is Arthur. Arthur seems a little in shock. He seems to think she's going to give birth to a redheaded baby right there in the store. He looks like a friendly guy that the world hasn't beaten up. She tells him what she needs. A box of ammunition. Plus a bullet puller for taking apart bullets and a bullet-seating die for reassembling them. She tells him they are for her husband. He nods thoughtfully, probably thinking the husband was planning on shooting himself rather than face what was balancing a fine line between staying in her womb and spilling out of it onto the floor. He gets the items for her and she pays in cash.

"Tell him," Arthur says, "if he has any questions to come in and see me. People messing around with this stuff, using pliers and vise grips instead of the right tools, can blow off their fingers."

She thanks him and gets back on the road.

When she gets to the forest she takes the same route as before and parks in the same place and takes a blanket and the gun, but forgoes any tins as those from last time are still here—not that she needs them. The ground is a little drier today. The air is still. It's going to be the same weather conditions tomorrow morning, but it's supposed to rain later on in the day. At least that's what the weather report is telling them. She uses the tool to measure out the same distance from a tree and lays down the blanket when she gets there. She gets out the gun. She loads the magazine. Puts the gun together. And points it at the tree.

She picks a spot. A big knot. She aims in on it, calms her breathing, and fires. The gunshot is muted through her earmuffs. The knot in the tree is splintered as the bullet crashes into it. She lines the knot back up. Takes another shot. Fires the second bullet within an inch of the first. Accurate enough. Way more accurate than she showed Raphael. A few hundred shots she could probably shoot the tree down.

As she shoots, she thinks about how the plan has changed for both of them. In some pretty big ways too. Instead of Melissa being the collector, she will be victim number two. And Joe, instead of being collected, will be victim number one. She's sure of it. The plan was never to shoot Joe in the head, but to wound him. Melissa, dressed in her paramedic's uniform, will pick him up. Then, thanks to the C-four, she'll evade the police. Raphael originally thought they were picking Joe up to torture and kill him. That was never the real plan. The first part, yes, but not the second part.

She looks through the sight at the bullet impact. It's four, maybe five inches below the knothole. She adjusts the sights again. Takes aim. Fires. This time the bullet hits the tree even lower. She sets the gun down and walks to the tree and gets out a tape measure. Puts it from the knothole to the last bullet hole. Eleven inches. Just about perfect. She walks back to the gun. Adjusts the sights again, this time slightly to the side. Takes aim at the knothole. Steadies the gun. Fires.

This time the bullet hits the tree eleven inches down from the knothole and a few inches to the left. She uses up most of the bullets.

It's perfect. A calculated risk, certainly, but perfect nonetheless.

And the truth of it is it's not her life on the line here, but Joe's. And that's an acceptable risk.

CHAPTER FORTY-THREE

Schroder hates working on Sundays. It seems he's busier now than he was when he was a cop. His wife sure thinks so. She was grumpy with him this morning over breakfast. The excuse that *This is his job* was no better today than it has been over the last twenty years. And the kids were being annoying. The baby last night was hard work. He'd sleep for half an hour and then whimper and be grizzly and then wake up. So Schroder would wake up too. So would his wife. They'd take turns at feeding him. At one point the baby shit himself so bad Schroder thought they were going to have to call in an exorcist to clean up the mess. It's been a night of broken sleep, following a week of broken sleep, following what has now felt like forever. He loves his kids more than anything, but every night as four a.m. rolls into five, he figures the difference between being a good dad and a bad dad is that a good dad doesn't put a pillow over the baby to make it go quiet. He knows from the job that there have been plenty of bad dads over the years. Bad mums too.

There are things to be pleased about this morning. Reasons to be calm. Joe led the police to a body yesterday evening. It hadn't been a trap. Melissa didn't reveal herself. There were no explosions, no splashes of blood. Schroder had been expecting bad news. When the call came he was almost too afraid to answer it. It wasn't Joe calling on the dead detective's cell phone, it was Kent herself reporting in.

The deal was going ahead. The body, as far as the rest of the world was concerned, was still missing. So Jonas Jones was going to become a hero. Or he is facing a huge embarrassment if the body belongs to somebody else. Though, knowing Jones, there'll be a way to spin that into a positive. He'll probably say Calhoun, even from the spirit world, is still first and foremost a cop.

Also, Kent had said, *have you heard about the university students?*

Yeah, I've heard.

I just don't understand young people, she said.

Nobody does, he said. *Not even young people.*

People have been killed, people are hurting, but it's just an excuse for a party for these kids. I just hope none of them dress as any of the victims. You think they'd do that?

Schroder didn't know, but hoped not, and told her so.

He stopped for coffee on the way to the TV station. He popped a couple of caffeine pills into his mouth and they disappeared with the first swallow of coffee, the extra hit helping him wake up, but the problem with those extra hits is they just don't last as long as they used to.

There aren't many people in the studio. Sunday isn't a popular day for making stuff happen. Even God thought that way. There's a small crew. Two camera operators, a man and a woman who Schroder is sure are involved with each other in some way. A sound guy with a German accent whose job is to hold up a boom microphone and stay out of the way. An intern holding the lights. And the director, a very butch-looking woman who looks like she could field strip a rabbit and turn it into stew. They're all on the set where they normally film. Schroder hates this part. He is the police presence to give the show more authenticity.

Schroder's used to talking into the camera. He's done it with cases in the past. It's not difficult. Not when you're speaking about a case. But it is when you're talking from a script. He is sitting opposite Jonas Jones, Psychic. They are at a table with a black cloth over it. There are flowers in the center, more flowers in the backdrop, some candles too. There are two product-placed bottles of McClintoch spring water on the table. The labels are facing the camera and the advertising department of McClintoch spring water are contributing funds to the making of the show.

Everyone's a winner.

Schroder feels sick.

He looks into the camera.

"Today we're investigating the disappearance of Detective Inspector Robert Calhoun," he says. Then he freezes. Suddenly he's thirsty. His voice is catching in his mouth.

"Take a drink," the director says, "and try again."

"Okay," he says, and he grabs himself a bottle of water and takes a few sips, then places it back, careful to keep the label pointing outward. "Ready?" he asks.

"Yeah. Just waiting for you," the director says.

He coughs into his hand even though he doesn't feel the need, then carries on. "Tonight we're investigating the disappearance of Detective Inspector Robert Calhoun," Schroder says, "who was killed twelve months ago by a woman by the name of Natalie Flowers, who has become better known as Melissa X. Attempts to find Detective Calhoun's body have all been in vain. Today Jonas Jones is going to change that. Today Jonas Jones will be offering his much-needed assistance to the police and to Detective Calhoun's wife and will lead us to his body."

"Cut," the director says.

"What was wrong with that?" Schroder asks.

"It was good. Just don't say *Today Jonas Jones is going to change that*. Say *Jonas Jones is going to* try *and change that*."

"Okay," Schroder says, and he starts at the beginning.

There is a camera pointing at Schroder and a camera pointed

at Jonas, and it will get cut and edited together later on today. Jonas is slowly nodding. Schroder can feel an itch growing at the base of his nose, but doesn't want to scratch it. No doubt during his speech the camera will cut to Jonas during the *much-needed assistance* part of his dialogue, as the words made his face scrunch up a little like he'd just bitten his tongue.

"Yes, yes," Jonas says. "It was a very horrific killing," he adds, leaning back and crossing his left leg over his right. He sits with his top two fingers pressing against each other, and his bottom two interlocked. He rests his hands on his lap. "Detective Robert Calhoun is not resting peacefully. He is a man who demands justice, and a man begging to be returned home. He has come to me for help, and he has a lot to say," Jonas says, then he pauses and slowly nods and lowers his voice as if letting the world in on a big secret, and at the same time his hands come up to his face so his top two fingers, which are shaped like a gun, touch his lips. "I've been loaned one of his uniforms," he says, and there's a uniform on the table that Jonas puts his hands on top of. He closes his eyes and bunches some of the material up into his hand as if having a stroke, then lets it go and smoothes it out. "I can get an extremely strong sense of Detective Calhoun," he says. "He was—or still is—a very strong-willed being."

Schroder feels his stomach turn. Last time he felt this sick was when his brother invited them over for a barbecue and undercooked the chicken. He should quit. None of this is worth it. In forty years when he's facing cancer and lung disease and whatever other sickness cocktail life throws at him, this is one of those weeks he's going to look back at and hate himself for. Unless the Alzheimer's has set in by then—and Alzheimer's would be just like his Wake-E pills, a godsend.

Jonas carries on. Schroder takes another drink of water, knowing it won't make the TV cut. Jonas tells the audience the pain that Calhoun is in. He pads it out. The candles are flickering. Jonas is deep in concentration as he makes a connection to the dead policeman. His legs are no longer crossed. Ever the professional, Jonas gets it right the first time. There is no need for a reshoot.

"He's buried," Jonas says, which is a nice generic beginning, but Schroder knows it's only going to get a whole lot more accurate. "Out of the city, but not far. Half an hour away perhaps. I sense . . . I sense water," he says, then slowly shakes his head, "no, not water. Darkness. Damp darkness. The ground is exposed. It's wet from the rain. I see . . . I see a shallow grave." He tilts his head, like Lassie listening for children stuck down wells, only Lassie had ethics. "North," he says. "North and . . . west a little."

Jonas Jones opens his eyes. He looks directly into the camera, just the right amount of happiness in his features because he's been able to help, just the right amount of sadness the occasion demands, all mixed in with a pinch of looking drained—being in touch with the spirit world is bound to take its toll. He doesn't blink. "I have a very real sense of what happened to Detective Robert Calhoun," he says. "I believe I can . . . yes, yes, I believe I can lead us to him. I . . ." he squeezes his eyes closed and tilts his head the other way, grimacing slightly as if in pain, proving once again the burden of being a gifted psychic, Schroder guesses. That and always knowing the lotto numbers. "I think I know where he is."

"Where?" Schroder asks, frowning slightly, looking serious, playing the part.

"It's hard to explain," Jonas says, but then goes about explaining it anyway. "He's calling to me. He wants to be found. He wants *me* to find him," he says, stressing the word *me* because after all it's Jonas that's having the vision, not any one of these four-dollar-a-minute psychics you find on the other end of a phone line at two o'clock in the morning helping you with your love life.

"That's good," the director says, and Schroder thinks they might cut that last line, otherwise it suggests that if Jonas can't find other murder victims they don't want to be found.

"I didn't go over the top?" Jonas asks.

"It was perfect," the director says. "Let's pack up and get this show on the road."

The show gets on the road a few minutes later, starting with the parking lot. In the hour and a half they've been inside the morning hasn't gotten any warmer. It's sunny, thank God, but it's still the kind of cold that makes you wonder just what temperature frostbite kicks in. He brings up the rear, the others ahead chatting contentedly among themselves, the way tight-knit groups do who have worked plenty of times together before. Jonas climbs into the driver's seat of a dark blue sedan, which is two years old at the most. One camera operator sits in the passenger seat, and the sound guy sits in the back. The director and the lighting intern take a separate car, the second camera operator sitting in the passenger seat so they can shoot footage of Jonas's car driving through the city. Schroder takes his own car, driving alone. It's creeping up toward noon and he's already tired. He needs to do something—he can't carry on like this. Can't be the whipping boy for a guy shooting what Schroder knows ought to be as appealing as late-night shopping shows. He just doesn't get it, never will, and hates that he's helping to make it more credible.

They head north. The view of the city changes as they pass through different suburbs, old houses next to new, new houses next to shops—the style of Christchurch evident at every turn. It's his city, a city many of the people here have a love/hate relationship with. He remembers reading that most people die within a few miles of where they were born. They either never leave the city, or they go out into the world and come back many years later. He wonders if it's true. It's something he's been thinking about a lot since last December when he almost died. Well, for a few minutes back in hot, sunny December he actually did die if you want to get all technical about it. He can't shake the memory of it. It's wedged down deep like a splinter buried beneath a fingernail that he can't tweezer out. His hands were cuffed behind him and his head was held down in a bathtub full of water. When he died, he saw no light at the end of a tunnel, felt no peace, and then he was brought back. Since then he's been seeing the world in a slightly different way. He doesn't like it. He doesn't like raising his kids in it. Doesn't like the memory he has of his lungs flooding with bathwater.

He turns on the radio and flicks through various stations looking for one where people aren't talking about Joe or the death penalty, then tries to find one where there is music and not ads, then gives up. The damn CD player doesn't work since his daughter dripped water into it a year ago hoping to, as she said, make the music clearer. He guesses he's lucky any of it works. Could be that's the balance the city has struck with him—it drowns him and fires him and takes his CD player away, but he can have all the AM and FM he could want.

Kent sent them the GPS location of the body. It was accurate enough to get him and Jones to the farm earlier this morning. They had shared a car ride out there just before nine. Schroder had driven. He didn't like the idea of Jonas being in control of the car in case he was suddenly struck down by a vision of Elvis. The problem is Jones decided to be in control of the conversation instead. It takes a brave man to say the things Jones was saying, and on the drive Schroder started to wonder where the line was between being committed for speaking to the dead and going on TV to help the public for a fee. What is insanity for some is showmanship for others, he guesses.

So Jonas Jones had rambled on for the twenty minutes they'd been together in the car. They had both worn thick jackets and hiking boots and the conversation dried up when they made the trek from the car to the grave. It wasn't difficult to find where Calhoun was buried. Turned-over dirt was one big clue, footsteps leading all the way from the road another. So he and Jonas spent thirty minutes doing what Schroder thought was a pretty good job of hiding the fact anybody had been there within the last twenty-four hours. It had been an eerie feeling out there, and one that was spent mostly in silence. Jonas had been happy. Schroder had been sad. He was at the grave of a former cop, a man who had fought the same war; they had been brothers in arms and now Calhoun was the prop in some cheap parlor trick and Schroder had made that happen. The sun had come through the trees, none of which had any leaves, and hit the ground, burning off some of the moisture so it looked like rising steam. It was a good location for a TV shoot. The cameras were going to love it. He knew that's what Jonas Jones, Psychic had been thinking. Whereas Schroder had been thinking about physics. About leverage and exertion and the effect an event can have on another. He was thinking about how hard it would be to dig Calhoun up and replace him with Jones. He was thinking about how that would make him happy, but Jonas sad. He was thinking about driving Calhoun to the morgue where he would be treated right. The dead man deserved more from both of them.

Of course he hadn't done that. Instead they had finished up, using branches to break up the footprints on their way out. Back at the car they threw their jackets into the backseat and used cold, soapy water and rags to wash down their hiking shoes because they needed them to be clean for the shoot. Then they had left. They hadn't spoken on the way back to the TV station. Jonas had been busy writing down notes in his journal. His mind had been racing. He'd been putting together his script.

Now they are heading out there again. They have to pull over a few times on the way for Jonas to clutch his head and tell the camera he was being drawn toward Calhoun. It was like he was dialing in the dead policeman on a receiver.

It's like I'm being pulled toward him, it's an actual physical feeling. He had seen Jonas write that line down, and no doubt he'll be using it now.

When they get to the paddock they park up on the road and get out and into position and then it's lights, camera, action. The cameraman shoots footage of them pulling hiking boots on, Jonas looking up into the camera at the time and saying, "I believe Detective Calhoun is around here somewhere."

For the most part, Jones does look somber, and Schroder knows that's a combination of practice and the fact that coming here has cost him a lot of money. The talent Schroder is most impressed by is how Jonas keeps the excitement out of his features.

The cameraman shoots footage of them dressing in warmer jackets before doing the same thing, then he hoists the camera back up and filming continues. Jonas tilts his head—another Lassie impression—then starts nodding, agreeing with the message Detective Calhoun is sending him.

"It's this way," he says.

The first obstacle is the fence, which Jonas climbs with ease. Then he leads them up a path made up of mud and stones and tree roots, the camera taking it all in. To his credit, Jonas doesn't pick up a forked branch and use it as a divining rod. The psychic moves forward. Goes left, pauses, goes right, carries on. They walk a hundred yards. Two hundred. Then they're there, the grave ahead of them, the director and camera crew having no idea that both Schroder and Jones were out here this morning, having no idea about the money Jonas paid for the information. To them, this is the real deal. There are a few footprints left from their earlier visit, and from Joe's visit yesterday, but either nobody notices them or they choose not to mention it. Certainly he and Jones did a better job hiding them around the grave than they did on the path.

"Here," Jonas says. "I believe Detective Inspector Calhoun is buried here," he says, "somewhere within a ten-yard diameter. Perhaps . . ." he says, then tilts his head a little more, "yes, yes, it's quite strong now. I can hear him. He wants to be found. Perhaps just over here," he says, and then he's standing next to the grave. "A lost soul crying out to be found. He's very sad, but relieved now," Jonas says. "We need a shovel. Quickly now," he says, then more urgently to the camera and to everybody else around, he says, "we must help him."

"Perhaps we should call the police," Schroder says, injecting no enthusiasm into the line.

"The police," Jonas scoffs. "If we just call them they won't come. They need a reason to. They need a body."

Schroder has been carrying the shovel. He points it at the ground. "Here?" he asks.

"A few feet to your left," Jonas says, and when this has gone through editing, when haunting music has been added, this is going to be a powerful moment. Hairs on necks all around the country will be bristling.

"Not too deep," Jonas says.

Schroder carefully puts the blade of the shovel into the earth. He scoops it away slowly and creates a low mountain of wet earth behind him. A minute later he steps back.

"We have something," he says, and the crew all move in. "It looks like human remains. Okay, look," he says, turning toward Jonas and the camera crew and sounding like the policeman he used to be, he says "I know what you just said, but we have to shut this down. There's enough here now to call the police. This is now officially a crime scene," he says, and he puts his hand up to cover the lens just like they spoke about. "Don't go wandering off," he says, "don't risk disturbing the area. And stop filming this."

They stop filming.

"This is incredibly good shit," the director says. "I gotta say, I had my doubts, but you're the real deal, man," she says, looking at Jonas.

Jonas smiles back at her, but Schroder can tell he's looking a little offended by the fact that the director may have suspected he wasn't on the level. "I'm just glad I can help," he says.

Schroder gets his cell phone out and calls Detective Kent.

CHAPTER FORTY-FOUR

I wake up with a queasy stomach and I'm a little unsure of where I am. For the first week in prison I woke up like that every morning. Somewhat sick, somewhat forgetful of where I was, only the sickness would hang about all morning and the forgetfulness would last two seconds at the most, maybe three, before the reality would come crashing back in. The second week was easier, and since then it's only happened a handful of times—certainly never as bad as that first morning. This morning my stomach is clenched tight, and the room is just a dark room and not a cell in solitary confinement until the memories start filling in the gaps left by the seconds ticking by and leaving. I climb off my cot and hover in front of the toilet for a few minutes thinking I'm going to throw up, but it doesn't happen, and then it almost does again, but still doesn't. The only moisture coming out of my body is in the form of sweat. It turns out the room isn't as dark as I first thought. I have no idea what the time is. I know I'm going to be taken out of here soon—I have to be. Still, there is that nagging sense of doubt, that small voice telling me that this is it, that these four walls and the cave-dwelling light are going to make up my future. No trial, no lawyer, no more guards—just this.

I move away from the toilet and lie back on my bed. My knees are sore and starting to bruise from when I fell on them in the van yesterday to start retching. In fact, I've fallen on them a lot over the last few days—when being force-fed a sandwich or when being punched by Caleb Cole. What I think is probably an hour goes by before there's a buzzing noise and the door unlocks and swings open, a prison guard I've never seen before standing on the other side of it.

"Let's go, Middleton," he says.

So we go. The guard has the height of a basketball player and the girth of a truck driver and leads me toward the breakfast hall, one big hand on my shoulder the entire way. All the guys I've come to know and love and wish were dead are already eating breakfast. I'm given my share and sip at the water and look at the food, but can't eat it. I sit uncomfortably, focusing on keeping what's inside me still inside me, focusing on winning the battle—which I'm managing to do. Then we're taken outside. I look at people exercising and don't join in. My stomach still feels like a meat grinder, which is better than it felt yesterday. It's looking like it's going to be a pretty nice day, though cold, but good following-women-home weather, though the reality is I'm kind of like the mailman in that regard—I deliver no matter what the season. After an hour we're led back inside. Nobody mentions the broken phone, but I know it's only a matter of time. Maybe the message will be delivered in the form of another shit sandwich.

When I'm back in my cell I divide my time between staring at the books and staring at the toilet, but my thoughts are divided between Melissa not saving me and Calhoun being found. I'm waiting for twelve o'clock to roll around. When it does we're allowed out into the common area. My stomach isn't feeling great, but it's certainly feeling better. Things down there are on the mend. I find a good position where I can see the TV. The news has already started. There's a special report. An exciting report.

A body has been found in Canterbury farmland. *Yes!* The reporter is live at the scene. She's attractive. *Yes!* Female reporters in their twenties often are. I wish she was reporting live from my cell. It would be an exclusive for her. *This just in*.

Over her shoulder are police cars and trees and a piece of land that is having its fifteen minutes of fame. The land belongs to a guy by the name of Mark Hampton. Hampton is a farmer. He grows wheat and paints barns and fucks cattle and is helping police with their inquiries. The identity of the body has not been confirmed. However, the circumstances in which the body were found strongly suggest it's Detective Inspector Robert Calhoun, who went missing a year ago.

"We can't confirm exactly how he did it," the reporter with her lush lips and beautiful eyes says, "but Jonas Jones led a film crew here shooting next week's episode of *Finding the Dead*, which revolves around the disappearance of the policeman. It's been well-known that the policeman was murdered last year by Melissa X, who so far has continued to evade police capture. According to the producers of the show, Jonas Jones was experiencing a psychic link with the deceased detective."

The story carries on. I wait for her to pitch the fact that *Finding the Dead* is on the same network as them, but she doesn't. At one point the camera focuses on Carl Schroder. He looks tired. The reporter confirms Schroder works for the TV station that produces Jonas Jones's show. It confirms Schroder was present when the body was found. Then it focuses on Jonas Jones, who is being spoken to by the same woman who escorted me out to the farm yesterday.

Watching it unfold, I feel buoyed by the entire situation. Not just because there is now a guaranteed payday, but because if there are people out there who believe in psychics, and there are people out there who watch their shows, then that means there are people out there who will believe anything.

That means there are people who will believe in my innocence.

CHAPTER FORTY-FIVE

Some warmth is finally starting to creep into the day. What isn't creeping into the day is any more traffic, for which Melissa is thankful. She hates getting caught in traffic. She always has a fear of somebody rear-ending her, some kind of confrontation, some weird shitty set of coincidences lining up in which she gets caught. It's happened in the past—not to her, but to others like her, other people who have taken lives have been caught by parking tickets and speeding tickets and flashed by red-light cameras. The sooner she is off the roads the better, and she wants to get this over with and back home because, after all, she still has a homelife that she's been neglecting. She needs to get things prepared for Joe.

She gets back to the office. Again she gets the same parking spot. The door is closed, but hasn't been repaired and swings open without any resistance. She carries the gun up to the office. She peeks behind the curtain and stares out at the back of the courthouse, and she visualizes the tree she just shot, she visualizes Joe standing there, and now she's even less confident this is going to work. She is sure Raphael will take the shot—but is he good enough? A hand shaking a fraction of an inch up here can result in a few feet down there. But there is no alternative. She spent months trying to think of other ways to get Joe out of jail—and this is it. It's not that this is the best of a bunch of bad ideas—the fact is this was always the only idea.

She has two bullets left, plus the armor-piercing round. She leaves the armor-piercing round as it is. The bullet puller she bought from the gun store is shaped like a hammer and uses kinetic energy to separate the bullet from the casing. It takes one bullet at a time. Arthur sold her the right-sized components, and the bullet slots easily into the end of the device. She crouches down and has to strike it against the floor, just like swinging a hammer, and after three hits the bullet comes apart. The second bullet takes four hits to come apart. She's good with tools. Joe could verify that. She can imagine people doing the same thing with pliers and vise grips and blowing their fingers off. Using the tool is easy. It separates the bullet from the cartridge. She removes the powder. Then she uses the second tool she bought from Arthur—a bullet-seating die, to reassemble them. The bullets look and feel like the real deal—and the weight difference without the gunpowder is negligible.

She puts the gun away just as it was left, all ready for Raphael to come along and use tomorrow morning. She has plans for the rest of the day, but she takes a moment to steal one more glance out over the back of the courthouse. Tomorrow is either going to go really well for Joe or really badly for Joe, but either way, by the end of the day Joe will no longer be a prisoner.

CHAPTER FORTY-SIX

When Ali arrives and I'm escorted through to see her, I'm nervous. Suddenly there's a lot more riding on me convincing her I'm an innocent man. I may have just earned myself fifty thousand dollars, but I'd gladly part with every one of them to have her believe me.

"Tell me about your mother," she asks, once we're seated and I'm cuffed to mine.

"My mother? Why?"

"Because I asked."

I shrug, the handcuff rattling against the chair. "Well, Mom is Mom," I say. "There's not much to say," I add, which is about as much as I feel like adding.

"You have a good relationship with her?"

"Of course. Why wouldn't I?"

"Most serial killers have very strained relationships with their mother," she says.

"Can you not use that term?" I ask her.

"*Serial killer?*"

"Yeah. It sounds so . . . I don't know. Something. I don't like the label," I say.

"You don't like the label."

"That's right," I say.

She stares at me as if she can't really believe I just said that. As if innocent until proven guilty isn't relevant in my case. "Whether you remember it or not," she says, "you still killed those people. The serial-killer label is accurate."

"Is that the label my lawyer will be using?"

She nods. "I get your point," she says. "But let's get back to my point, which is most people in your . . . situation . . . don't have great relationships with their mother."

"Joe isn't most people," I tell her, and truer words have never been spoken.

"How long did you live with her for?"

"I moved out of the house when Dad died," I tell her.

"Why?"

"My mother became unbearable. When Dad was alive it gave her somebody to talk to all day long, but when he died that only left me."

"She ever abuse you?"

"What?" I say, and the handcuff goes tight as I pull my arm up. "No. Never. Why would you ask something like that?"

"You sure?"

"Of course I'm fucking sure," I tell her. "My mom's a saint."

"Okay, Joe. Try to stay calm."

"I am calm."

"You don't sound it."

I take a deep breath. "I'm sorry," I say, which are words I'm not sure I've heard myself address to anyone before other than my mother. "I just don't like it when people think bad things about my mother," I say, but I'm not sure anybody has ever had good thoughts about her either. "Plus I miss my goldfish," I tell her.

"What?"

"My goldfish. There were two of them. Pickle and Jehovah. They were murdered."

"We were talking about your mother," she says.

"I thought we had moved on," I tell her.

She jots down something on her pad. Then the pen moves back and forth as she underlines something. I'd almost give my right—and only remaining nut—to see what that is.

"You killed your goldfish?" she asks.

I try to stay calm, but I can feel the anger building up inside of me. For her to ask that means she just doesn't get me. It seems to be a common problem. What is wrong with people? First she thinks my mom abused me, now she thinks I killed my fish. What is the world coming to? Now I'd almost certainly give my right and only remaining nut to get hold of the pen she's using and drive it into her neck.

"No. No I didn't," I say forcefully. "It was a cat."

"You look angry, Joe."

"I'm not angry. I just hate the fact people always think the worst of me."

"You killed a lot of people," she says.

"I don't remember any of them," I say, "and I sure as hell didn't hurt my fish."

She writes something else down. She underlines it, then she rings a couple of circles around it. I'm pretty sure she's doing it deliberately. I think she's trying to throw me off guard, and that's why her questions are all over the place. It's not going to work. I think good things about my mom and about my fish, good things about Melissa. I think about doing good things to Ali once I get out of here. I might be a bad-thoughts kind of guy, but I'm a good-things kind of person. I'm Optimistic Joe. It's how I roll.

"Tell me," she says, "does the name Ronald Springer mean anything to you?"

Ronald Springer. Now she really has thrown me off guard. "No," I say. "Should it?" I ask. The police asked me about Ronald a few months ago. Schroder did. They asked if I had known him. If I had any idea what had happened to him. I told them I never knew him, and they seemed disappointed, but had no reason not to believe me. No reason, sure, but they still spent a few hours questioning me about him.

"It means nothing?"

"It means something," I tell her, knowing I've already reacted to the name, knowing she'll have been told about my previous interviews. "Detective Carl came to see me a while ago to ask if I had known him. Ronald went to my school."

"Did you know him?"

"No. I knew who he was, but that was only after he was murdered. I could tell Schroder wasn't expecting any connection, he was just hoping to wrap up a cold case, only I had nothing to do with it."

"You're positive?"

"Of course I'm positive."

"So how is it you can be positive when you don't remember killing any of these other people?" she asks.

"Because killing isn't in my nature."

"That's a quick response," she says.

I shrug. I don't really know how to respond to it.

"Killing is in your nature," she says. "You just don't know you're doing it. Which means it's possible you did hurt Ronald and just don't remember it. Ronald went missing the same month your auntie stopped raping you."

"*Raping?*"

"That's what she was doing, Joe," she says, but I'm shaking my head.

"That's the wrong word," I tell her.

"What's the right word then? *Punishing* you?"

"No. She was *forgiving* me. Forgiving me for breaking into her house."

"Is that really how you see it, Joe?"

"Of course it is. Why wouldn't it be?"

"You say you only knew of him after he was murdered," she says.

"That's right."

"The police never said he was murdered. Ronald just disappeared. How would you know he was murdered?"

"It's just an assumption," I tell her, and I hate her for trying to fool me. "The police thought so. Everybody thought so. That's what normally happens when people go missing, right?"

"Sometimes," she says.

"Well if he wasn't murdered, what then?"

"Tell me about Ronald."

"There's nothing to tell. He was a kid that nobody knew until he was mur . . . until he went missing, then people were figuring out who he was, then suddenly he'd been everybody's best friend. People were going around school telling Ronald stories. There were rumors, right, that he had run away, that he had been abducted, that his parents had killed him. School was nearly over and the way people were talking, you'd think Ronald had been a hot topic since school started. It was weird. Knowing Ronald made you popular. I didn't understand it. Ronald would have hated all of those guys. Every one of them."

"You knew him, then?"

"No. I mean, I'd spoken to him a few times because we were in some of the same classes. But people gave him a hard time. They gave me a hard time too. We had that in common, I suppose."

"Sounds like you knew him a little."

"I mean we didn't hang out. Maybe a few times at school we'd eat lunch together because neither of us really had any other friends."

"Why did the other kids pick on him?"

"You know already," I tell her. "If you've read about him."

"Because he was gay," she says.

I shrug. "It didn't matter if he was gay or not, not for real," I say, "but once people start throwing around labels like *gay boy* or *serial killer*, they stick. People need to be more careful with that kind of thing—but at that age nobody is."

"How long had you known him?"

"For always. We started school together when we were five, so I've always known who he was."

"Did you kill him, Joe?"

I shake my head. "No."

"Or you did, but can't remember."

"I guess that's possible," I say. "Why are you so interested in Ronald anyway?"

"Because your lawyer asked me to ask you about him. It seems the people prosecuting you have been looking into the case. We don't know what their interest is, but they may introduce it at trial."

I shake my head. "I liked Ronald," I tell her. "I wouldn't have hurt him."

"How long were you friends?"

"We weren't friends. I just knew who he was, and I liked him because he was the guy people teased, and you need kids like that in school so the rest of us are safe."

"How long had you been having lunch with him?"

I shrug. I think about it. "A year. Maybe two. Not long. And it wasn't every day."

"Did you see him outside of school?"

"Never."

"Did you used to think that he was attracted to you?"

I almost laugh at that. "What? No. No way. I'm not gay," I tell her.

"That's not what I asked," she says. "I asked if you thought he liked you."

"I'm sure he probably did. I was the only guy who talked to him that wasn't giving him a hard time."

"I mean, Joe, do you think he liked you in a sexual nature?"

I shake my head. "I don't know where you're going with any of this," I say, "but I didn't kill him. I don't know what happened, and the prosecution can dig into it all they want because I had nothing to do with it. Can we move on?"

"No. Not yet. Tell me something else about Ronald. Tell me about the last time you saw him."

"Jesus, why the hell is everybody hung up on Ronald? I'm telling you, I don't know what happened to the guy."

She stares at me and says nothing and I realize I've been shouting. I shake my head and I think about Ronald, and I picture him the way I saw him last. School wasn't a whole lot of fun for either of us, and I imagine it's like that for most people. We weren't best friends, but he was a pretty good friend. He'd come around after school sometimes, we'd head down to the beach, sometimes mountain bike around the sand dunes, or climb trees in the park. We'd talk about the kind of stuff that sixteen-year-old boys talked about, except for women. We didn't talk about them. I knew he was gay. When we were fifteen, though, he was so deep in the closet I'm sure he could taste Turkish delight. I knew he liked me. I didn't mind—having a gay guy like you doesn't make you gay, it just makes you feel flattered. Then things changed. The Big Bang happened, followed by two years of smaller bangs, and my friendship with Ronald got pushed aside. I saw him around at school, but I hardly spoke to him. I saw him getting a hard time, but that just meant things were easier for me, and now that I was paying off my bullies, life was actually pretty good. Except for the auntie-loving rape, as Ali would put it.

When my relationship with Auntie Celeste stopped, I started hanging out with Ronald again. Only things were different—I think the most awkward thing between us was the fact he didn't want me hanging out with him anymore, but I'd still follow him around anyway. I knew he'd come around. After all, the guy had had a crush on me the previous year, and crushes like that don't disappear. It only made sense he'd want to be my friend again. Truth is, him ignoring me annoyed me just as much as my auntie ignoring me. I felt abandoned all over.

I wanted to punish my auntie. Not for what she had done, but for finally making me enjoy it, and then for cutting off the supply. So when Ronald started rejecting me too—well, I didn't just feel abandoned, but I felt angry too. The same anger I felt toward my auntie—only with Ronald I could do something about it.

"I can't really remember the last time I saw him," I tell her. "One day he was there, and the next day he wasn't, and that's how most people will always remember him."

"But not you," she says. "You remember him in a different way."

The way I remember him is indeed different. The way I remember him is with a hole in the side of his skull that a claw hammer would fit nicely into. "I didn't kill him," I say, only I did kill him. He rejected me and I hit him with a hammer. People say you always remember your first—and people don't get much right, but in this case it's spot on. Ronald was my first—I remember him—I just don't think about him.

"Are you sure?" she asks.

"Positive," I say.

"He didn't come on to you, and you rejected him by killing him?"

"Nothing like that happened at all," I say.

"That's a shame," she says. Again it takes a few seconds for her words to sink in. They only just have when she carries on. "If you had, then we could have linked everything back to the events with your auntie. We could have shown it all started back then, and that what has happened to you since were results of that. People aren't going to believe that you let twelve years slip by between the events of your auntie and killing your first person."

It feels like a test, like she is baiting me to suddenly say that I do remember killing him.

"Joe?"

"Yes?"

"I think I have what I need," she says.

"Already?"

"Yes," she says, and she stands up.

"And?"

"And what?" she asks.

"What are you going to tell the courts?" I ask.

"I'll spend the rest of the day going over my notes, Joe, and then I'll talk to your lawyer."

"So you believe me?"

She knocks on the door and turns toward me. "Like I said, Joe, I'll talk to your lawyer," she says, and then she is gone.

CHAPTER FORTY-SEVEN

It's a lazy Sunday. He used to have them with his wife most Sundays, really. Before they had Angela, while they were raising Angela, and they carried on the tradition after Angela moved out of the house. It'd always been their job as parents to prepare her for the world—to set her on a journey into the world—but for the last year he's thought that that was a mistake. If they'd kept her closer she'd still be alive. If they'd encouraged her to stay at home. If they'd put a lock on her door and protected her.

Ultimately, Raphael knows no matter how you look at it, he let his daughter down. He let his family down. You can attack the argument from any angle, he's heard it all before—but the proof is, as his mother used to say, in the pudding. Angela was dead. He had failed her. End of story.

The last two days have been good for him. Therapeutic. He's been thinking that killing Joe Middleton will start a healing process. He doesn't expect to be able to move on—how can you after what that maniac did to his daughter—but he can expect, perhaps, to start coping better. To live again. Maybe he can try to patch things up with his wife.

Most days since losing Angela have been lazy Sundays, and though he made some progress since Thursday night, he's reverted back to what has become his normal self. He spent a few hours this morning in Angela's room, staring at the newspaper articles pinned to the wall. Then he spent some time going through photo albums.

Lazy Sunday is progressing along nicely now. He's sitting in the lounge and the sun has been and gone and he's watching video footage of Angela's twenty-first. She had moved out of the house the year earlier and was renting in town with two of her friends. The party was held in this house. It feels like a hundred years ago. He certainly looks a hundred years younger. He was happy back then. He's not sure where the Red Rage is right now—buried somewhere, he guesses, beneath the alcohol and the depression, waiting for tomorrow to get on with the show.

He knows why he's watching the video today. He knows the reason for the sadness. This is his last lazy Sunday. There'll be no more flicking through photo albums and watching home movies. He knows the Red Rage will get the job done tomorrow. He has one bullet for Joe and one bullet for Melissa, and he has one bullet left over in case he misses—but he won't miss. He's on a mission—a movement—and he can't fail.

It's after the shooting where things get tricky. Even if he does manage to get away from the scene, he knows the police will come for him. Of course they will. They're not stupid. Stupid enough, maybe, to have let Joe Middleton kill for as long as he did—but not stupid enough to not figure out tomorrow's events.

Tomorrow may be therapeutic, but he's kidding himself when he thinks it's going to start a healing process. He's kidding himself in thinking he can get back together with his wife. By the end of tomorrow he's pretty sure he's going to be in a prison cell, but he's okay with that. He will have avenged his daughter and for that he'd be happy to go to jail for a thousand years.

CHAPTER FORTY-EIGHT

Melissa is tired and excited and nervous. It's not a good combination. It's been a long day, albeit a good day, and she did manage to get some nap time a few hours ago. She's been trying to relax since getting home after stashing the gun back in the office ceiling. Her house isn't in the middle of nowhere, but her nearest neighbors are a two-minute walk away and she's never seen them. It's nice and private and she prepaid her rent the same way she prepaid her gardener. When she stopped being Natalie and became Melissa, she cleaned out her bank accounts. She has cleaned out bank accounts of others since then too. It's how she survives.

The day has gone now, as has the heat, and what's left is a cold winter evening of the type nobody in their right mind could enjoy. Her shoulder is hurting too from all of that gun use this morning and she wanted to pop some painkillers and anti-inflammatories, but decided against it.

She left the van she hired earlier parked in the driveway rather than putting it into the adjoining garage. She paid for the van in cash and used a fake ID and took out insurance on it not because she needed it, but because that's what most people did, and she wanted to be considered part of the most-people culture.

The van is important.

She locks the house behind her and walks to the van, tightening her jacket around her. It takes two minutes for the van to warm up, by which point she's tightened her jacket so much it's almost strangling her. The windshield is frosted over. Everything is frosted over. It's a still evening. No wind. No clouds. Cold, but perfect shooting conditions.

She turns on the wipers and tries to use the jets to spray water onto the windshield, but the jets are blocked. The wipers don't help, they just swish back and forth over the thin ice. The heater warms up the windshield and then the wipers start tearing at the ice. A few minutes later she can see.

There are a few other cars around. Not many. She turns on the radio to break the monotony of the van engine. Like she knew there would be, a radio DJ is talking about the day's events, and those that will follow tomorrow, and perhaps later this year. A body—most likely to be that of Detective Inspector Robert Calhoun—has been found. Found by a psychic, of all people. She finds that hard to believe. Impossible to believe, and wonders what the real truth is and suspects Joe may have played a hand in giving up the location. If so, for what? Something to do with the trial, no doubt.

"And of course tomorrow is the big day, ladies and gentlemen," so the DJ tells her and anybody else who's listening. "Tomorrow the trial of Joe Middleton begins. The Christchurch Carver. The man for whom the death penalty is being voted on." She's expecting the DJ to open up the lines to callers from around the country to give their views on the death penalty, but he doesn't, not that that matters because she, like everybody else, has heard them all before. Everybody thinks that it's a dividing issue, that you're either strongly for it or strongly against it. She doesn't care one way or the other.

It takes her fifteen minutes to get to the house she wants,

the van warming up early in the drive. She rubs her hands together. Warms up her fingers and grabs her handgun. It's an okay neighborhood. Not great. Not cheap. Just okay. The kind of place people living by themselves tend to flock to. Two-bedroom dwellings, small yards, not old, not modern, but okay—heaven for people who are in love with all things bland. TVs are glowing from behind windows, lights are on in lounges and bedrooms, but otherwise there are no signs of life, other than a couple of cats sitting at opposite ends of a fence. Last time she was here was three months ago. It was warmer. A lot warmer. She made a mess. A big mess. There was blood and tearing flesh and crying. A lot of crying. Through it all she knew that she would be back here tonight.

She parks the van out on the street and locks the door and knows the entire plan will fall apart if somebody steals her ride. She walks up the path. The garden is neat and tidy. There are the legs of a garden gnome and no body, just jagged edges where the body used to be attached. Out there other gnomes are suffering the loss. There are lights on inside the house. She can see patterns of moving colors from a TV behind the curtain. She climbs up the step and holds her finger on the bell for half a second. She doesn't have to wait long before the footsteps come toward her.

Melissa holds the gun down by her side, just slightly out of view.

The door swings open.

The woman doing the swinging is dressed in winter pajamas and a robe that are a little too big for her, even though the woman is a little too big herself. Still, she's not as overweight as she was in the papers twelve months ago after she jumped on Joe during his arrest, or even as she was three months ago when Melissa came to see her. Her face is somewhat flushed. She looks like she is running late. She's wearing a crucifix around her neck. A little Jesus on a little cross. A little Jesus who doesn't seem happy to be hanging where he's hanging.

"I thought we had a deal," the woman says. "You promised you were going to leave me alone."

"And I have until now, Sally," Melissa says. "But I'm here to make another deal. You need to start by letting me in," she says, and she raises the gun and sticks it into Sally's chest, right where Jesus is doing his best not to look. "Or if you prefer I can shoot you in the stomach and leave you here to rot."

CHAPTER FORTY-NINE

Raphael wakes up expecting fate to intervene, that he'll have a sore throat or a bad stomach from something he ate, maybe a racing heart from too much bad food, or at the very least a hangover—even though he didn't really drink that much yesterday. Fate has never been one for the *Can't we all just get along* school of thought, there are too many sad stories in the city that prove that, so for he and Fate to be on the same page about Joe seems like a small miracle.

He holds his hands in front of his face in the six a.m. light and can barely make them out, but can see them enough to tell he doesn't have any signs of the shakes. For a guy who hardly slept last night, he's doing remarkably well. It's been a clock-watching night, where every passing hour his mind would do the math, telling him just how much sleep he wasn't getting. His mind was racing. In the beginning it was racing with positive thoughts. Then around one a.m., the first negative thought came along. Within thirty minutes the balance had shifted. The negative thoughts were chasing away all the good ones. By three a.m. there were no positive thoughts, just a bunch of frayed nerves he was struggling to keep under control. When he finally fell asleep at around four, he entered a dream world and somewhere in that world all the bad shit disappeared, and he's woken up feeling good.

He throws back the covers. Even though he sleeps alone these days, he still sleeps on the side of the bed he has slept on since being married. The other side barely has any wrinkles in it. He puts on his robe and slippers and walks through to the kitchen. The house is warm thanks to two heat pumps that have been running during the night. He has no appetite, but forces himself to eat anyway. A bowl of cereal and a glass of orange juice and his hands stay calm the entire time. *These are*, he thinks, *the hands of a killer*. He makes toast and burns it so he tosses it into the trash. He puts in four fresh slices and gets it right, but doesn't eat them, just leaves them in the toaster. It was the same way when he killed the lawyer. Same way when he killed the second one too. No appetite. No reason this morning should be any different.

It's cold outside. For some reason he's suddenly transported back to when he was a kid, when he'd have to bike to school in freezing-cold weather along with thousands of other kids across the city, icy roads and frosty air, breath forming clouds in front of his face. Only right now it's a bit darker than what it was when he used to leave for school. It's still only seven thirty. People are driving to work with the lights on and with coffee cups in their drink holders, driving to a job involving numbers or materials or words or physical labor—none of them, he imagines, with the idea in mind of killing somebody. It's too early for the protesters to be showing up. He turns on the radio. Not too early for the protesters to be calling in.

He parks on the street between the office building and the courts, thinks better of it, then moves his car just around the corner, adjacent to the building he'll be shooting from. Soon this whole area will fill up, and after the shooting he doesn't want to get caught in a traffic jam ten yards from the back entrance to the court.

It's a thirty-second walk back to the office building. He takes the stairs up to the third floor and unlocks the office door. The duct tape has held the drop cloth in place, so the office is dark. He paces the office for half a minute, then sits down and leans against the wall. He's brought a thermos with him full of coffee, and he pours himself one and slowly sips at it and watches the office as it slowly becomes lighter. He takes a photograph of Angela out from his pocket and rests it on his thigh.

What are you doing? she asks him.

"Today's the day," he tells her.

You're going to kill him?

"Yes," he tells her, but of course she isn't really here, he knows that, but boy, wouldn't it be great if somehow, somewhere, she really could hear him. "I know it doesn't bring you back," he tells her, "but I hope it makes you feel better."

You think killing him honors me? she asks. *You think taking a life in your daughter's name is something mom would want? Or I would want?*

"Yes," he says.

She doesn't answer him.

"Isn't it?"

Yes, she says.

"I wasn't there to protect you. This isn't going to make it right, but it's all I can do."

I'm sorry you weren't there to protect me either, she says. *You were meant to be there. That was your job.*

"I know," he says, and he's crying now. "I'm sorry."

Thank you for killing him for me, she says, *and I'm glad you're doing it in my name. Make him suffer, Daddy. Make him suffer and then he can rot in Hell. I just wish you could kill him ten times over. A hundred times over.*

"I miss you, baby," he says, and he puts the photograph back into his pocket and reaches up into the ceiling for the gun.

CHAPTER FIFTY

I wake up at seven o'clock. We all do. A loud buzzer goes off. It rips into our dreams and puts an end to any of the good stuff going on in there. Though in this case the good stuff was me remembering the blank look on Ronald's face when the hammer cracked open his skull. He just stood there staring at me for a few seconds. I think he knew he was dead, but his body was still catching up. I thought he would have dropped like a rock, but it took two or three seconds for him to fall. It was the strangest thing, a physics-defying thing. Killers like to say they don't remember what happened—that they just snapped, that it was a dream. But the exact opposite is true. Killing has a way of making you feel alive—who the hell would want to forget that?

I use the toilet and wait patiently in my cell for thirty minutes until my block is taken through for breakfast, which appears to be something a patient with the Ebola virus coughed up. My stomach is feeling good. Whatever was in that sandwich has done its best, it's gone through the motions, and I've come out on top. Adam comes and finds me. He looks me up and down. He doesn't look happy.

"You look better, Middleton."

"Fuck you," I tell him.

He laughs. "We showed those photos of you eating that sandwich to a lot of our buddies," he tells me. "Got a whole lot of laughs."

"I just need a list," I tell him.

"What?"

"A list. Because when I get out of here, I'm going to fucking kill every one of them, and I'm going to start with you."

He laughs at me again, even harder this time. "Christ, Joe, you really do make me laugh. This prison needs people like you, and thankfully for us you're going to be here for a very long time—unless they end up hanging you, which would be a shame, I guess, until the next funny bastard comes along and we forget all about you."

He takes me down to the showers. I get cleaned up and Adam tosses me some clothes. It's a suit. It's the same suit other prisoners have worn in the past who are my size. The same suit I wore when I was charged a few days after I was arrested. A gray suit with a dark blue shirt and black shoes. I look like a bank manager. Only one without shoelaces or a belt. Adam promises me I'll be given those before I leave. The shirt has stains in the armpits and smells like cabbage and I shake it out, hoping whatever head lice are asleep in there lands on the floor.

I'm taken back to my cell. I have to wait an hour. Most of it I spend sitting on the edge of my bed wondering about the trial. For the first time the reality of it is all kicking in. I always knew this day was coming, but part of me always believed it never would—part of me was sure I'd be out of here by now, that the police would have found a reason to let me go. The trial date just kept on rolling forward and now it's here, and suddenly the nerves of the trial kick in and I almost throw up. And then I do throw up. When I'm done I back away from the toilet and Caleb Cole is standing in my doorway.

"A farewell present," he says, and then he rushes me with something sharp.

I don't even get to my feet before he hits me, but I manage to lift my pillow so whatever he is trying to stab me with—it actually is a filed-down toothbrush—goes into the pillow, but doesn't come right through, stopping somewhere short of my hand. I use my other hand to punch him in the balls. He staggers back, but not as far as I'd have thought, and then I throw the pillow at him in what, to anybody else, would probably look quite comical.

He comes at me again, only this time I'm able to get to my feet. I don't know what I'm doing other than reacting. A survival instinct has kicked in. The room, other than our footsteps and muffled grunts, is silent. This is what a real fight sounds like. I get both my hands around his wrist with the toothbrush, and he uses his free hand this time to punch me in the balls. Or ball. I drop quickly to my knees, but don't let go of his wrist, knowing it's the only thing keeping me alive. I pull him forward at the same time. His breathing gets louder. So does mine. I topple back—my back on the bed, my shins on the floor, and feet pinned beneath them. He topples onto me, and for the moment neither of us are throwing punches. Instead both of us are focusing on the toothbrush. I'm guessing nine out of ten dentists wouldn't recommend having your stomach perforated by one. And the tenth dentist is either a prick or is the one doing the perforating.

"Die, you fucker," Cole says.

I say nothing. I just keep focusing on the toothbrush. It's angling at my chest and getting closer as he pushes his body weight into it.

"Die," Cole repeats, the word thrown at me with spittle and hate. I try pushing upward, but it's a losing battle.

So I do the only thing left to do. I scream like a girl.

Cole pulls back a little, as if the sound waves are too much for him to handle. The sound reminds me of a year ago when Melissa gripped me with a pair of pliers in a place pliers should never be gripped. I put more effort into the scream. Only it's not powerful enough, and a few seconds later as the scream fades the toothbrush comes back toward me.

The last thing going through my mind as the toothbrush also threatens to go through it is my mother, my mother and her stupid fucking wedding, she in some ugly dress and Walt saying *I do* and then them kissing in front of a priest and whoever is unlucky enough to be attending. Then suddenly Caleb Cole is being pulled aside, and there standing behind him is Santa Suit Kenny. Santa Suit Kenny throws him against the wall, then looks down at me.

"You okay?" he asks.

Before I can even answer, the toothbrush that had my name on it now has Kenny's name on in instead, and Caleb jabs it into him and twists it and turns it and there's the sickening sound of flesh being punctured and a strange smell too, and then a snap as the toothbrush breaks, half of it left inside Kenny, half of it in Cole's hand. Santa Suit Kenny staggers back and looks down at his side, where blood is blooming over his prison overalls, a look of disbelief on his face, like he can't believe this is where his journey of music and molestation is going to come to an end.

Caleb takes another run at me, and he swings the remaining half of the toothbrush at me and gets me hard in the stomach, only the handle doesn't penetrate me because it has no sharp point on it—it just slides back through his hand, which is wet with blood, but the impact is enough to fire the storm back up in my stomach. It fires up hard and fast and things in there turn over, they turn and turn and I can't hold on for much longer—scattered showers and a hurricane are on their way.

The guards come in and drag Caleb, the fight mostly out of him now, away from me. I rip my pants down and squat over the toilet and the relief is sudden and painful, but relief nonetheless. Santa Suit Kenny stares at me as his life slips away and I stare back at him, my stomach burning hot as the world fades a little.

"Queen," Santa Suit Kenny says. "Muff. Punch. Queen," he says, and I guess as far as dying words go, others have done better.

I lean my elbows on my knees and do my best to stop from passing out, and we stare at each other—me doing the shitting, Kenny doing the dying—and he never says another word and the storm rages on.

CHAPTER FIFTY-ONE

Schroder doesn't want to get out of bed. Ever again. He has somewhat of a headache. Or more accurately somewhat of a hangover. Brought on by somewhat too many drinks and the fact that yesterday was somewhat of a disaster. Jonas Jones loved every second of it. He was all over the news. He was the man the dead detective had come to in order to be found, and the camera loved him. The camera soaked up every second along with the public. Helping the living contact the dead was Jonas's calling in life. A gift. Proven over and over. People shouldn't doubt him, and less people doubted him after yesterday, and, if you wanted to know more about Jonas and his abilities, his books can be found at any good bookstore.

Of course the media didn't know if the body was going to be Calhoun's—nobody knew that, not for a fact, not until later last night when Kent had rung him and told him about the pin put into Calhoun's leg five years ago when he'd lost control of his car. No amount of pins would have helped the rapist he was chasing back then, because that guy was pinned between Calhoun's fender and the brick wall of a dairy, and now that event has a serial number and that number confirms the body they dug up belongs to the dead detective. That discovery put a transfer of funds into place. People making money on a dead man. Including himself. A dead man who had been tortured. Ten grand showed up in Schroder's account overnight. It's the easiest money he's ever earned and it's the sickest he's ever felt.

"This will be made public tomorrow," Kent told him, "and if you release that information before then I swear, Carl, I'll never—"

"I won't say anything," he said. "How are you getting on with your three dead bodies?"

"We're getting on," she answered, and then she hung up.

So last night he drank to numb the pain of what he had done, of who he had climbed into bed with. He drank because it helped, even though drinking wasn't helping his marriage, but it wasn't as though he was drinking every night. Jesus, the last time he even touched a drop was at Detective Inspector Landry's wake four weeks ago—he hasn't touched it since because that drink back then was the start of him losing his job. Things keep slipping away from him. A few months ago Kent was the new detective on the force, and now she was talking down to him, like he was worthless. A few months ago he was the one telling her what to do. How. The. fuck. Have things gotten to where they have?

Of course, he knows exactly how.

His daughter has helped wake him by jumping repeatedly on the end of the bed, each bounce like somebody squeezing his brain between their palms. He watches some cartoons with her for five minutes, then jumps in the shower.

The hot water helps wake him, it helps massage the hangover away a little. When he's done he puts on the same suit he wore yesterday when he was on TV, which is the same suit he wore when he was on the force, which is the only suit he has. His wife is making breakfast for the baby and his daughter. He smiles at her and she frowns at him and it's not looking like it's going to be a great day. It's almost eight thirty and he's feeling tired again. He shakes a couple of Wake-E pills out a packet from his pocket and takes them when his wife isn't looking, not needing her to nag him again about how many he's been taking.

They don't talk much over breakfast, which is common these days, and their lack of talking is becoming a habit and a problem and he wonders if he's losing his marriage and hopes like hell he's not. The baby is looking up and laughing at him, and smiles at her and she laughs some more.

When this is over, all this stuff with the Carver, then he'll tell Jonas to . . . to what? Shove his job? And then what? Have no money? He can spend more time with his family, as much time as he wants, then they can all starve in the cold, huddled beneath blankets and be together forever.

He finishes his breakfast and his wife wishes him good luck at the trial. Then she kisses him good-bye and he hugs her back and maybe he's just reading too much into things, maybe his wife is just as tired most of the time and there's nothing wrong with their marriage because the hug feels good and warm and makes him wish he wasn't going anywhere at all except back to bed with her. He kisses his baby good-bye and the baby smiles and giggles before a hiccup bubble appears between his lips, popped a moment later by a thick but short stream of undigested milk. He hugs his daughter and heads for the door.

The trial starts at ten o'clock. Joe will arrive at the courthouse at nine forty. That's thirty minutes away. He starts the drive into town. The airwaves are full of people expressing their opinions. There are reporters at the courthouse already, saying there is a large crowd with more people coming, many carrying signs, many chanting slogans. Then there is another growing group, one of teenagers in costumes—he can see Spider-Man, he can see a couple of Xena Warrior Princesses, he can see four Batmans, and at least half a dozen Waldos from Where's Waldo?, among dozens of other costumes from Manga characters to popular movie personalities. The reporter says it's going to be a tough day for everybody, which immediately restores Schroder's faith in reporters—when they want to, they really can get the facts right.

He turns off the radio. Right now there will be bomb-sniffing dogs going through the court building. If they'd found explosives he would have heard. So the trial is going ahead.

At his next red light, he uses his cell phone to look up the number for a florist and is given several options. At the next red light he calls the number, and is halfway through ordering flowers for his wife when the light turns green. He rolls through the intersection and pulls over and focuses on his order and comes up with a message for the card. He smiles at the thought of his wife getting them. It's not going to solve any problems—but it's a step in the right direction.

"Good choice," the woman tells him, and he's happy somebody at least thinks he's making a good decision. "She'll have them by lunchtime."

Schroder spots his first vampire a few blocks from the courthouse—she's arguing with another girl who's also dressed as a vampire, a guy standing in between them not doing a great job at moderating, but certainly doing a great job of looking uncomfortable. Schroder wonders if it's the classic cliché of wearing something unique only to find somebody else wearing it too. Neither vampire seems bothered by the sun.

Traffic gets thicker, drivers having to slow down as pedestrians start to spill into the street. A few blocks away from the courthouse it comes to a standstill. Hundreds of people are outside the courthouse already. There have been suggestions those numbers could get into the thousands. He turns the radio back on. Callers for the death penalty want people going down there to support their cause. People against the death penalty want people going down there to support their cause. Everybody wants somebody. The students just want to hang out and drink themselves stupid.

He makes his way to the back of the courthouse. He can see Jonas Jones, who is dressed as a smug psychic, and once again Schroder suspects somebody is leaking him information. The only thing here for the psychic is one more opportunity to get his face in front of a camera.

There are fifteen parking spaces back here, and four of them have been assigned to the police. One of those four has been given to Schroder, as he was the lead detective on the case and will be here every day. The other spaces are reserved for judges, some for lawyers. There's even a spot that's been reserved for an ambulance that will be here soon for the duration of the trial—thanks to all the death threats that have come Joe's way. Emotions will be running high, so the ambulance is there also for family members of Joe's victims—it's easy to imagine people getting upset and fainting or passing out, or having heart attacks brought on by the anger.

He gets out of the car. Magnum PI, Smurfette, and a couple of nuns are walking by, Magnum making eye contact with him for a split second before stroking his mustache and saying something to one of the male nuns before they all start laughing, and Schroder has the bad idea whatever it is it's about him. He makes his way to the entrance and shows his ID to the security guard, who looks at it, looks at Schroder, looks out at the street as a guy dressed in a suit with a top hat and rubber chickens hanging from his arms yells at somebody to wait up. The guard looks at the ID again and then writes something down on a clipboard. He shrugs one of those *The world is going to shit* shrugs, then hands Schroder a pass to clip onto his jacket. More people are on the street now, and he wonders if some of them are figuring out this is the entrance that will be used. He hopes not, because Joe just might not make it inside alive.

A few seconds later he changes his mind—he decides it wouldn't be such a bad thing if the crowd got hold of Joe, not really, not a bad thing at all.

CHAPTER FIFTY-TWO

Melissa has slept well. No dreams. No nerves. She's confident in her abilities. Not so confident in Raphael's, but definitely in her own. It's a cold morning. She uses Sally's shower to warm up. She dresses in Sally's clothes. She eats a good-sized breakfast in Sally's kitchen with Sally's food. She uses up the last of Sally's milk and puts the container into Sally's bin, the one labeled *Recycling*. She's all about the environment. Last night she slept on Sally's bed. It was too soft. It reminds her of a fairy tale.

Sally doesn't do much as Melissa goes about getting ready. There's not a lot for her to do, really. Last time Melissa was here things were quite different. She needed a nurse. Sally was a nurse. Melissa needed help and Sally gave it to her, and as a reward Melissa let her live. All she had to do was convince Sally not to go to the police, and she had a lot to convince her with. Plus she let Sally live because she knew that three months later—that today—she would be coming back. Of course Sally didn't know that.

So now she's back and Sally obviously isn't pleased, but there's not a lot she can do about it. Melissa finishes off her breakfast. It's not as healthy as she'd have liked, but a good meal. A filling meal. The kind of meal you want on the morning of the day your boyfriend might not make it back out of.

By now Raphael will be at the office building. He'll have assembled the gun and have changed into the police uniform. She can imagine him sitting down and trying to contain his nerves. Maybe he brought a photograph of his daughter along with him to keep him company. Melissa is worried about just how nervous he's going to be, and whether those nerves are going to send his bullet off target.

There were always cracks in her plan. But now they're becoming more obvious.

She's starting to worry.

The nerves that weren't there during the night have rolled into town, so much so that suddenly she doesn't see any way for the plan to work. She should cut her losses, cut Sally free, and move on.

Instead of doing any of that, she leaves Sally tied up on the bedroom floor and she drives into town. Traffic is thick, but she's allowed for it. There's roadworks and renovations going on in and around the hospital parking lot. She checked it out a few days ago and confirmed what she suspected—that there are no security cameras in the lot. That's the thing about Christchurch—the places there ought to be cameras there never are. Or perhaps that's the thing about hospitals—they figure a good old-fashioned beating isn't a big deal when the victims only have to drag themselves thirty yards for help. Or maybe they see it as being good for business. She drives there now, past a construction crew rolling out a new piece of pavement, who all pause what they're doing to stare at her. She's not wearing the fat suit. She smiles at them, then parks around the back and locks up the van. She drops some coins into the meter and takes the ticket that comes out and rests it on the dashboard before grabbing the rucksack and locking up. She walks toward the hospital. Jackhammering and engine noise and men talking loudly bounce off every surface all around her. She's wearing Sally's dark blue nurse's scrubs. It's not a great fit, but outside of porn movies and get-well singing telegrams, scrubs never are. That's not all she took from Sally. She uses Sally's swipe card to open a staff-only door. She steps into a corridor that's air-conditioned on a day where it really doesn't need to be. It's about sixty feet long with no natural light and dozens of fluorescent tubes in the ceiling. She walks its length and uses the swipe card to gain access to the emergency department. She keeps walking. She takes another corridor and follows the directions Sally was willing to give her. Well, perhaps *willing* isn't quite the word Sally would use. After all, Melissa had lifted Sally's pajama top and squeezed the muffin-top waist and threatened to cut it off.

It'd been worse for Sally three months ago. Back then Melissa had forced her to strip naked. She had taken photos of her in compromising positions. Sally had just received a fifty-thousand-dollar reward for her help in Joe's capture, and Melissa wanted what was left of that money. So she photographed Sally and that made up part of what she used to blackmail her. The other part is something she needs to discuss with Joe when the timing is right. Three months ago with Sally naked and tied to the bed, Melissa had considered paying somebody to come and rape her, to take photos of that too to make it even worse. She wasn't sure she had enough money to cover it, because whoever took on the job was going to ask for a lot. Ultimately it didn't get that far. A voice inside her—perhaps belonging to Smelly Melly, or perhaps belonging to her former self before she got this way—told her that with all the line crossing she'd been doing that was one thing that was just too far. She agreed and felt ashamed she had even thought of it, and Melissa hadn't felt shame in a long time.

She makes her way to the ambulance bay. It's situated near a staff room, where nurses and doctors are sitting around drinking coffee and reading magazines, while the other nurses and doctors are playing nurses and doctors in broom closets and bathrooms.

She waits by the ambulances and fiddles around on her cell phone because that's what people do in this day and age when they want to look like they're doing something other than stalking or looking alone. She knows what to look for—the ambulance crew that isn't in a hurry.

It takes five minutes. Then they step out of the staff room. A man and a woman, both wearing paramedic outfits that don't fit much better than her own. They're chatting and laughing. They're not on their way to a road crash or a shooting or a heart attack. They split up and each moves around to one side of the ambulance. The woman is driving. She fires up the engine. Melissa taps on the passenger-side window and the guy winds it down, a good-looking guy in his late twenties who has every chance of living through this if he just does the right thing.

"Hey," he says.

"Hey," Melissa says, and flashes him her door-opening smile. "You're the team going to the courthouse?"

"Yep," the woman, the driver, says, and she has to be in her midforties and has blond hair streaked with a few grays—it's pulled back tightly into a ponytail, one of those quickly formed ponytails women make when they're tired or lazy or don't give a shit about their appearance anymore. "We're on duty there all day."

"Good. I was wondering, can you guys give me a lift there?" Melissa asks.

"Would love to," the guy says, looking her up and down.

"Not if you're going there to protest," the woman asks. "Not dressed in your scrubs."

Melissa shakes her head. "No. It's completely unrelated to the Carver trial," she says, looking at the man who can't take his eyes off of her. She widens her smile a little more. The woman looks skeptical. The man nods.

"Climb in back," he says.

She moves around to the back of the ambulance and climbs in. They move forward. About forty yards away is the intersection where the hospital road merges with other traffic. Melissa moves up the ambulance so she's right behind the paramedics.

"Before we leave," Melissa says, "can we pull over for a second before we hit the intersection?"

"Sorry, we're on a tight schedule," the driver says, not glancing back.

"Does this help change your mind?" Melissa asks, and points a gun at her, then at the guy, then back at the woman. "Right now I want a reason to let you both live," she says. "But if you can't give me that reason, then I'll find another paramedic who can."

CHAPTER FIFTY-THREE

There is blood all over the floor, and there's some on the wall too. The wall blood is in the form of two handprints, each with lines of blood leading from the palm to the floor, each from a left hand even though I can't remember either Cole or Kenny touching it. I'm still sitting on the toilet. I don't want to be, but I have to be. The room smells of blood and shit and Kenny shit himself too and I guess it's one more thing he'll be remembered for. Santa Suit Kenny—singer of songs, lover of children, and savior of the Christchurch Carver. I wonder what they will say at his funeral. I wonder who the real Kenny was and I guess nobody will ever know.

Glen and Adam come in. Glen grabs Kenny by his feet and Adam grabs Kenny by his arms, and they don't even look at me. They just pick him up and he sags in the middle and for a brief moment I think they're about to fold him in half like a bedsheet, but they don't, they take him out of the cell. When the police come and ask what happened, they'll say they rushed him off for treatment. Only there was no rush. They've let him bleed out because a guy like Kenny wasn't worth saving. They just had to make it look like they did something.

Kenny saved my life. I wish I could thank him. Best I can do is imagine I would have bought one of his books if he'd ever written one. At the least I should buy one of his CDs.

I finish up on the toilet and flush it and get my clothes tided back up. I stare at the blood on the floor knowing how easily it could have been mine. There is blood on my shirt that isn't mine. I take it off. I lie down on my bed. I can still see the look on Kenny's face, the disbelief of being stabbed, the acceptance that he was in trouble, and the hope that he wasn't dying. I've seen that hope in others before, and I always enjoyed seeing that hope fade away, but not this time. This time was different and I don't want to think about it anymore, I want to move on—after all, I have a big day ahead of me. Kenny would want me to. He'd hate to think he'd died just for me to mope around my cell feeling sorry for myself.

I pick up the wedding invitation my mother sent me. There will be no support from her during the trial, and I don't know why that even surprises me. By the end of the day she will be married. I fold the card in half and tuck it into my pocket. My mom won't be with me today, but having the wedding invite with me goes some way to making me feel less abandoned. Maybe it will bring me some luck. I start to wonder whether I'll still have to go to trial today, or whether the events of the last few minutes will keep me here.

I have my answer less than a minute later when four guards come back into my cell. One of them throws me a fresh shirt—at least it's fresh compared to the one I'm wearing. None of them discuss what just happened as I change into it. It's almost as if the last five minutes just didn't happen—the only evidence of it is the blood on the floor and walls, which, I imagine, will be gone when I get back. Santa Kenny's cell will be filled with somebody new, a different kind of Kenny, but one equally bad.

They lead me down to the exit, the other prisoners quiet and staring at me out of the slots in their doors. I can't walk straight from the shock of what just happened—and I can't walk straight because of the cramping pains in my stomach. This is, without a doubt, what birth must be like—only worse.

I'm escorted to the front of the prison. It's just like Saturday. The warden is there and Kent is there and Jack is there and a bunch of other assholes are there and I feel like shit. The warden is wearing the same suit and tie and has the same disdain on his face. I'm given laces and a belt and everybody watches me as I thread them into my outfit. The warden looks annoyed at me. Then I'm chained up.

It's sunny outside but cold, though not frosty. There are six police cars out front, and in the middle of them is a van. In each car are two armed officers. There are a few in the van too. It looks like they're ready for a war. I take a step toward the van and somebody puts their hand on my shoulder and tells me to stop. So I stop. The officers get into the van and into the cars and half a minute later they're all heading away without me and without Jack and Kent and without the same two officers who were with us on Saturday.

"What's going on?" I ask. "Is the trial already over?"

Kent frowns at me. "I can see why people fell for your act, Joe."

"What does that mean?"

"Nothing. Just shut up, okay?"

The stream of cars is leaving and at the same time a van is arriving. It's similar to the other one, but that one was white and this one is red. It's dirty and looks a little beaten-up in places and has *Whett Paint Services* stenciled all over it, along with the name Lenard Whett and his mobile-phone number and a star that says *Money-back guarantee*. The money-back guarantee on the side of a tradesman van is a dead giveaway that it's a fake. It comes to a stop next to us.

"Come on, Joe, you know the routine."

I climb up into the van. I crouch over so they can handcuff me to the eyelet. Like I'm going somewhere. Then it's all the same as

Saturday only we don't turn off to go past the airport to go for a stroll through the edge of a farm to go body hunting and to take a vote on whether or not they should all open fire on me. Instead we carry straight on toward town. I haven't seen it in a year and didn't realize I'd missed it until now.

"Ah, for fuck sake," the officer opposite me yells as I vomit onto his shoes.

"I'm . . ." I say, but I can't add *sorry* because then I'm throwing up again, plus I'm not really sorry. My stomach is heaving. I didn't even feel it coming. I don't know what the hell is down there—a pancreas, liver, other meaty stuff that was weakened by Saturday's sandwich and then compressed violently by Caleb Cole's fist.

Jack starts to pull over.

"Don't," Kent says. "Just keep on driving."

"It stinks back here," the officer with the messy shoes says.

"What the hell is wrong with him?" Kent asks.

"He doesn't look too good," the other officer says. "Pretrial jitters, I guess."

Pretrial jitters mixed in with a bout of pretrial attempted murder, mixed in with a dash of shit sandwich.

"Joe? Hey, Joe, are you okay?" Kent asks and, for the first time in a long time, somebody sounds concerned about me. It's touching. So touching I start gagging and then something burns my throat on its way out, ruining my second shirt of the day.

"Joe?"

I look up at her. I nod. I'm fine. Super fucking perfect. I wipe my face in my hands and my palms come away wet and there's vomit on them. I wipe them on the shirt since it's ruined anyway. There are dark spots in some corners of the van and lights spots in others. Jack seems to be driving in extremely tight circles and quickly too, but when I look through the wire mesh I can see he's not, that we're still heading in a straight line. There is a steady stream of people flowing in the direction of the courthouse. There's something really wrong with me, because I see Jesus and the Easter Bunny and the Lone Ranger. I see men dressed as schoolgirls, girls dressed as fairy-tale characters, fairy-tale characters drinking beer.

I see the Grim Reaper walking alongside another Grim Reaper. I wonder if they are here for me. If it will take two of them.

I see a man wearing a Tampon of Lamb T-shirt with *The Queen and Cuntry Tour* stenciled across it, along with a set of dates that all passed by years ago. I close my eyes and I can see Santa Kenny looking up at me with his dying eyes, the sadness in his features. I can see him trying to cling on to a life that was spilling between his fingers.

The view darkens and changes. I think I'm going to pass out. I hold my breath and do my best to hold on as we get closer to the courthouse.

CHAPTER FIFTY-FOUR

Raphael opens the gun case on the floor. He takes out the box with the two bullets in it and places each of them into the magazine. He takes out the armor-piercing bullet and kisses it. For luck, he supposes, though he never thought about it and can't rightly say, it was something that just happened. It's cold. He slots it on top of the others. He assembles the gun. He's getting better at this. Next time he shoots a serial killer he could probably assemble the gun in the dark. He clicks the magazine into place. He stays in his own clothes for now.

He sits by the window with a corner of the cloth tucked aside and stares out at the courthouse. He thinks about the three bullets. One for Joe. One for Melissa. And one spare. Hopefully he won't need the spare. Traffic starts to build as eight o'clock arrives and builds even more the closer it gets to nine. Then a police car shows up and puts out road cones to block off the street. Good thing he got here early. Good thing he parked around the corner. Groups of people are walking from the direction of the bus station—he can see them from his viewpoint starting to fill the streets as they come his way. They're carrying placards and signs down by their sides. Soon they start coming from every direction. If he went to the office across the hall and looked north he'd see the same amount of people carrying the same kinds of signs coming in his direction. The protestors are wrapped in thick jackets and have scarves to keep their vocal chords warmed up for the yelling to come. Some he recognizes from group. They've brought friends and family. Media vans start to show up. They drive around looking for parking spaces, but can't find any, the drivers double-parking and reporters and camera operators jumping out. He sees brothers and sisters of people Joe has killed. He sees people carrying signs that say *Execution is murder* and *Only God decides who lives and dies*. He sees trouble brewing. He sees both signs as being wrong. He supposes that would make them *bad signs*. He sees Jonas Jones, the psychic who was on the news all day yesterday, arrive at the back gate and not go any further. Other people see that too, and a small squadron of them gather there, but mostly people are making their way to the front of the courthouse, where they are out of his view.

Around quarter past nine comes the chanting. "Two, four, six, eight, let us eradicate." Over and over it comes from the front of the courthouse, the words traveling easily on the cold, still air. The numbers start to grow. Soon people are arriving at the end of the block and can't go any further, the street right outside the courthouse is packed. They spill out onto the other roads. The intersection becomes jammed. Then Elvis appears. He's walking with Dracula and they're carrying a six-pack of beer. They are followed by four beer-drinking Teletubbies and a couple of thin girls dressed up as maids. There is a moment, a comical moment, where he wonders if he's having some kind of stroke, but no, what he is seeing is real. He doesn't understand why it's real, but it is. They disappear into the crowd.

At nine twenty a car waits for the gate to roll open, then enters the parking lot behind the court. Detective Carl Schroder—or just Carl these days—climbs out. The gates roll closed behind him.

Walking past the gates is Magnum PI and two nuns, Magnum saying something to make the two nuns laugh. With them is Smurfette. Raphael observes as Schroder watches the group walk past, then Schroder is slowly shaking his head before he disappears inside. Raphael pulls more of the drop cloth aside and reaches around the back and opens up the window. The air is chilling. The murmurs of street life kick up a few notches, he can hear people shouting and laughing and people arguing. He secures the curtain back into place.

He changes into the police uniform. He stuffs his clothes back into the bag along with the thermos, then he reaches up into the ceiling and throws it as far as he can. He knows he'll probably be in jail by the end of the day, but no reason to make it easy for the police.

At nine thirty Raphael lies down on the platform they made. He has the urge to unload the magazine and reload it, just to make sure everything is how it should be. The same urge makes him want to take apart the gun and put it back together. But ultimately there's no point. It wouldn't go any different to how he already has it—and he's satisfied it couldn't be any better. He looks at his hands for any sign of the shakes and doesn't see one. He positions the gun and he waits for Joe and Melissa to arrive.

CHAPTER FIFTY-FIVE

"Which one of you has children?" Melissa asks.

"What?" the woman asks.

"She does," the guy says, "but I don't."

"Then that makes this easy," she says, and she hands him a syringe.

"What is it?" he asks, without taking it.

"It's your chance to live," Melissa says. "You take that shot, and you get to fall asleep for the next hour. You don't take the shot and I shoot you in the face right now," she says, wiggling the gun a little. "Take your pick."

"Is it safe?" he asks.

"Safer than this," she says, wiggling the gun again.

"No," he says.

"If I wanted you dead, I'd shoot you," Melissa says. "The fact is I need you very much alive, but right now I need you very much out of the way. Now I know you're confused and scared, so I'm going to give you five more seconds to think about how you'd rather be unconscious than dead."

"And what are you going to do with her?" he asks.

"She'll get the same option when I'm done with her," Melissa says.

"I don't know."

"What's your name?" she asks.

"James," he says, "but you can call me Jimmy."

"This is a silencer, Jimmy," Melissa says, tapping the end of the gun. "I can shoot you both in the head and nobody would hear a thing. I can drive the ambulance myself."

Her words have an effect. You Can Call Me Jimmy takes the syringe. He rolls up his sleeve and uses his teeth to pull the cap off it, then holds the needle upright and taps the tube to get rid of any air bubbles. He looks like he wants to stab it into Melissa. Instead he puts the tip into his arm and keeps pushing until the needle disappears, then he pushes his finger down on the plunger.

"I don't feel so good," he says.

"Climb over into the back," Melissa says.

"I . . . I don't think I can."

"Yes you can. Come on."

He starts to climb over. He gets halfway then looks up at her. "I don't feel so good," he says again, and then proves just how un-good he's feeling by collapsing.

"What did you do to him?" the woman asks.

"He's only sleeping," Melissa says, then drags him all the way into the back.

"What are you going to do to us?"

"Give me your driver's license," Melissa says.

"Why?"

"Because I asked nicely," she says.

The driver lowers the sun visor. Her license is tucked into a pouch up there. She hands it over. Melissa looks at the photograph. It's five years old. She looks at the name and at the address. Trish Walker. Lives in Redwood.

"This address still current?"

"Yes."

"Okay, Trish," she says. "Rather than me explain everything to you, just listen in as we drive and you'll figure it out."

"Drive where?"

"You have a schedule, remember? Just stick to it."

Melissa gets out her cell phone. Trish starts driving. Melissa dials a number that doesn't exist and then talks to a person who isn't there. Trish sits at a red light, which ten seconds later becomes a green.

"It's me," Melissa says. "Here's the address," she says, and she reads out the address from the driver's license into the phone. "You got that? Now repeat it back to me," she says, and she listens to nothing as the address isn't repeated back. "No, I said sixteen, not fourteen. Repeat it back," she says, knowing the small detail makes it believable. "That's it," she says.

She hangs up.

Trish has gone pale. Very pale.

"Okay, Trish, by now you've figured out that you're in a very deep hole, and your children are in there with you. Think of it like this. Think of that hole slowly caving in, there's dirt all around you, and you have one chance to claw your way out of it along with your children. Are we on the same page here?"

"What are you going to do to them?"

"If you help me? Nothing. Absolutely nothing. You don't do what I say . . . well, then it gets interesting."

Trish nods. Melissa glances behind her at Jimmy. Not too many places to hide an unconscious body, but she can make do. First she just has to strip him out of his uniform. She's going to need it.

"I want you to tell me we're on the same page," Melissa says.

"We're on the same page," Trish says.

"Good," Melissa says, "because we've got a few things we need to discuss on our way. And you can start by giving me your cell phone—best you don't have it, because something like that in the wrong hands is only apt to see that hole of yours get a whole lot deeper."

CHAPTER FIFTY-SIX

The police escorting the empty van are nowhere to be seen. It's like a ghost being escorted into town. Except it's not. It's some kind of decoy van. There must be a crowd of people outside the courthouse. The police must be expecting trouble and are sneaking me through a different entrance. We reach the edge of town. Then we're closer to the center. We can hear people. Lots of people. We're on the one-way system heading toward the courts.

"Oh my God," Kent says.

I look up out the window. I've managed to not pass out, which I really think deserves a medal. Protestors are lining the street close to the courthouse. They're yelling and screaming at the police escort, which I can now see is further up ahead. The escort is swamped by a sea of people. Many of them are carrying placards, but I can't read what they say. In a way it's a relief to know all these people have come out here to support me. Nobody wants to see me punished. I'm too likeable. I wasn't in control of my actions. I'm an innocent man, driven by needs that I'm not even aware of, driven to do things that I can't even remember. I'm Joe

Victim. The justice system is going to save me. A six-foot monkey is waving at everybody going past, a can of beer in his hand with a drinking straw, a big monkey grin on his face. So maybe I have passed out or crossed over because I don't understand what the fuck is going on. But what I don't understand the giant panda does, because that's who I see next, and I guess it's friends with the monkey because it runs up behind him, throws his arms around him, and starts humping him before the monkey turns around and they touch beers and then both of them are drinking.

"This is going to be worse than I thought," Kent says.

"You think it'll end today?" Jack asks.

Kent shakes her head. Are we all seeing the same thing? "Either today or this week," she says. "University students like this can't commit to much more than drinking and smoking weed and fucking. I just think committing to dressing up as wildlife and movie characters for more than a week is too much for them."

I finally realize what's happening—they're university students in costumes, all of them have come along to support me. Young people get me, I suppose.

The van turns right. Beads of vomit run across the floor. We get to the end of the block and turn left. Beads of vomit run the other way. Now we're running parallel to the street we were just on. There are people, but not as many. They are carrying placards. It seems like the entire city has come out to let the world know of my innocence, to let the world know that the real crime is our justice system.

"Just keep driving," Kent says, even though Jack wasn't showing any sign of not driving. Just one of those dumb things people say. People are ignoring the van. I practice my big-boy, friendly-neighborhood-retard smile. I need it warmed up and ready for when we get to the courthouse.

Kent turns back and stares at me. "What the hell are you grinning at?" she asks.

"Nothing," I tell her.

"You're such a smug bastard, aren't you," she says. "You think it's all going your way. You think the money you earned by showing us where Calhoun was is going to help you, but it's not. Somehow it's going to bite you in the ass and people will find out."

"Detective Calhoun was a killer," I tell her.

"What are you talking about?" she asks.

"He's the one who killed Daniela Walker. He went to talk to her and he ended up killing her. Her husband used to beat her up, and instead of helping her, Calhoun took a shot at her too. Then he staged the scene so you would think it was me."

"You're full of shit," Jack says.

"It's true," I tell them. "Half the people at the station thought it was somebody else. Well, it was him."

"Shut up," Jack says.

"Hey, I don't care if you believe me or not. I got my money, so what do I care? But you people are worshipping the guy because he was killed in the line of duty, but you're worshipping a rapist and a killer. You know the difference between him and me?" I ask, and I'm ready for their answers, for the *You got caught and he didn't*, the *You're a sick fuck and he wasn't*, but none of them answer, and I realize they're all hanging on to every word I'm saying, they're praying for me to say something they can use against me, something one of them can get up on the stand and tell a courtroom full of people.

"The difference is he was a cop. I've only ever been the person I am," I tell them. "I've never pretended to be anything else. Calhoun pretended to be on the good side of good versus evil, he was supposed to be somebody above the law, he's the one everybody should be hating, not me."

"You're full of shit," Jack says.

"And you've said that already," I tell him, then I look at Kent. "I know you don't believe me, but give it time. By the end of the day you'll be thinking more and more about it, and by this time tomorrow you'll be working on proving it one way or the other. Let me know how it works out for you."

Jack has to swerve around somebody who walks out in front of him, the vomit on the floor starts moving in a new set of directions, and so does my stomach. Then we take a left, coming in behind the courthouse. I once stole a car from this street. I once kicked a homeless man in the nuts and threatened to set him on fire on this street—though of course I was only kidding. I'm not sure if he got the joke—that's the thing about people, they don't get irony.

"Are you enjoying this?" Kent asks.

"I'm just trying to do the best I can."

There are a few people behind the court—a few dozen at the most. Jack pulls up outside a gate and waits for a few seconds for it to roll open. There are office buildings opposite us and lots of parked cars and people walking to and from work. There are road cones in the intersection. I can see some of the signs now. They don't make sense. *An eye for an eye. Slow Joe must go. Kill the fucker.*

What the hell is going on? Kent sees my confusion and my smile disappears and now she's wearing one. "Did you think these people were here to support you? Oh, Joe," she says, "you truly are dumber than we all thought."

The gate opens and we drive through. The gate rolls closed behind us. My stomach suddenly constricts and I lurch forward a little. Jack brings the van to a stop. I'm still confused by the signs. *An eye for an eye* for who? *Kill* who? *Slow Joe must go*—well, that one makes sense, it means Slow Joe must be allowed out of jail. There are other cars, an ambulance, a security guard. I can tell I'm not the only one feeling sick now, the stench of vomit churning everybody else's stomach. Jack and Kent get out of the van and walk around to the back and open the doors. I stare at the ambulance, just wanting to climb into the back, just wanting somebody to take care of me. There's a sharp pain going across both sides of my stomach, but more so on the side where Cole punched me. I start retching, but all that comes out are a few flecks of vomit.

It takes me a minute, but eventually I get out of the van and onto my feet.

CHAPTER FIFTY-SEVEN

Melissa tenses up when she sees Joe. Her heart quickens. Last time she saw him for real was the Sunday morning he walked out of her apartment. They'd spent Friday night and all of Saturday and Saturday night in bed together. They had ordered pizza and watched romantic comedies on TV, and she hated romantic comedies, but with Joe they were funny. He liked them. He laughed. She laughed. Joe was a romantic guy. He was supposed to come back that afternoon. He was only going home to feed his cat. He even left his briefcase with her. It had some knives in it. He left and didn't come back and she was angry at him. She felt used. Angry. Angry enough to go looking for him and maybe take a knife to him. But she didn't. If Joe didn't want her, then fuck him. It was his loss. Only that's not what happened. She saw Joe again on TV that night. He'd been arrested.

Right now Joe is on his feet. He doesn't look good. He looks pale. What have the prison people been doing to him? Any second now the plan will either work or it won't. It all depends on how good a shot Raphael is under pressure.

Joe collapses.

He falls into a ball on the ground. Yet there wasn't a gunshot, was there?

The people who were in the van with Joe stand around him, then help him to his feet, and they're not panicking, so no, there's been no shot. They move Joe toward the courthouse, half carrying, half dragging him, and she knows from Raphael's viewpoint there is no way he can get an accurate aim on him.

Joe is whisked away into the courthouse. No screams and no blood.

"Why are we here?" the paramedic asks. "I mean, why did you want to come along?"

"Shut up," Melissa says. "I'm trying to think."

"Do you know him? The Carver? Listen, I understand if you're here to kill him, I do, and Jimmy, he'll understand too. Please just don't hurt my kids. I'll do what you ask."

Melissa stares at her. She's never killed a woman before, but she's starting to think it'd be worth it just for the life experience. It would be character building. "I said shut up."

"Please, please, you have to let us go."

Melissa turns and points the gun at her. "Listen, if you don't shut the fuck up I'm going to stick a hole in you. Okay?"

The woman nods.

Melissa pulls out her cell phone. Calls Raphael. He answers after one ring.

"There was no clear shot," he says, and he sounds panicky. "No shot."

"I know," she says. "Listen to me carefully," she says. "You need to stay calm. We still have time. In fact we have all day. They'll be bringing him back out. I'm not sure when, but it will happen later this afternoon. It has to. Just stay calm and stay put."

"You want me to wait around until then?" he asks, sounding incredulous. "Up here in my police uniform?"

"Yes," she says.

"What? Up here in the office?"

"Where else would you wait?"

"What if somebody comes in?" he asks.

"Nobody is going to. Listen to me, you need to stay calm. It's going to work out, I promise you."

"You promise? How the hell—"

She interrupts him. "I'll stay down here the entire time," she says. "Don't overthink it. Just stay calm and do what needs doing."

She hears him sigh. She can imagine him up there in his police uniform, running his hands through his hair, maybe covering his face with his hands.

"Raphael," she says.

"Suddenly all of this is seeming like a bad idea," he says.

"It's not a bad idea. It was just a small piece of bad luck. Or bad timing, really. There's something wrong with him. He's sick. For all we know they might bring him right back out. For all we know you'll get another chance in five minutes."

He doesn't respond. She can hear him breathing into the phone. Can hear him wondering if this may end up being true. Trish is staring at her. Within the last minute the crowd outside the back of the courthouse has swelled as people have figured out Joe came this way. The signs don't mess around—*Die fucker die* is a good litmus test for how the crowd is feeling. And what the hell is it with all these stupid outfits some of them are wearing?

"Are you still there?" she asks.

"I'm here," he says.

"We can do this. If not now then at the end of the day when Joe comes back out. It'll be just as good then. Maybe even better," she says, not really believing that last bit. *Better* would be if Raphael had taken a successful shot already.

"Okay," he says, "I'll wait and get him on the way back out. I promise," he says, and he hangs up and Melissa stares at the back door of the court building and tries to figure out how long is too long when it comes to waiting for a guy like Raphael, and hopes he can keep his nerve long enough to stay where he is.

CHAPTER FIFTY-EIGHT

They drag me toward the holding cells until somebody decides that it's a bathroom that I need dragging to, at which point they start me in a different direction. When I try to use my legs I find I just can't get them to grip the ground beneath me. The organs squashed earlier aren't bouncing back into shape. Instead they're getting tighter. I'm placed in front of a toilet and the view of a chunk of shit caked above the waterline is better at helping the purging process than jamming my fingers down my throat.

I have never in my life felt this sick. Sweat is dripping off me. I throw up again, then topple forward and somebody catches me before I lose my front teeth against the porcelain. They get me up and I don't see much of the journey except for some blurry walls and sometimes my own feet, but I'm taken into a first-aid station and I'm laid down on a cot, but none of the chains are removed. The room smells of ammonia and ointments and recently wiped-away vomit. It smells exactly how the first-aid station back in school used to smell, and for a moment, just one brief moment, I'm back there, I'm eight years old and I'm feeling sick and the nurse is soothing back my hair and telling me I'm going to be okay. That doesn't happen this time.

"Joe," somebody says. I open my eyes. It's a nurse. She's attractive and I try to smile at her, but can't manage it. She's looking down at me. "Tell me how you're feeling," she says.

"I feel sick."

"Can you be more specific?"

"Real sick," I tell her, being real specific. She hands me some water and tells me to drink and I manage a few sips, then roll onto my side and start gagging.

Hot Detective Kent, Jack, and the other two officers are in the room with us. The nurse is chatting to them, but I can't focus on what she's saying. Then Hot Detective is making a call somewhere. The nurse comes back, Hot Nurse, and I must be sick because as much as I try to imagine Hot Nurse making out with Hot Detective, my mind just won't go there. It wanders off to other things. I think about my mom's wedding. I think about Santa Suit Kenny. I think about my nights spent with Melissa.

"Joe, what have you eaten over the last few days?"

"Shit food," I tell her.

"Can you be more specific?"

"Real shit food," I tell her, being real specific again, wondering if this woman needs everything in life explained.

"Does this hurt?" she asks, then pushes her fingertips into the side of my stomach. I can hear fluid moving in there. We all can. It doesn't hurt and I don't tell her it doesn't hurt so therefore she doesn't ask me to be more specific. She pushes a little harder and I have to tighten my ass muscles to stop a huge mess from happening.

"Yes," I tell her, wanting to push something sharp into her stomach and ask her the same thing. "It's a sharp pain," I tell her.

"Where exactly?"

"Everywhere."

Kent comes over. She's shaking her head. "Nobody else at the prison is sick," she says.

"He's faking it," Jack says, but it sounds like even he doesn't believe it.

The nurse shakes her head. "I don't think so," she says. "I think we need to get him to a hospital."

"There's an ambulance out in the parking lot," Kent says, then turns toward the security guard. "Go get the paramedics," she says, "and let's hope we can get this sorted out so we don't have to delay the trial."

CHAPTER FIFTY-NINE

"Something went wrong," Trish says. "Didn't it. Please, just cut your losses and let us go."

"Not yet," Melissa says, tucking the phone back into her pocket. She can picture Raphael up in the office building staring through the gun scope at the ambulance. Maybe he's thinking he could use that armor-piercing round right now.

"How far along are you?" Trish asks.

"What?"

"You're pregnant," Trish says, and Melissa glances down at herself knowing she's not wearing the suit, but still checking just to make sure. "I can tell," Trish says. "You're trying to hide it, but I can tell. How far along are you?"

"I'm not pregnant," Melissa says.

"I can see it in the way you carry yourself, and you keep rubbing your belly. I've dealt with a lot of pregnant women. You don't need to lie about it."

Melissa says nothing. She didn't realize she was still rubbing her stomach. She can feel the girdle beneath her scrubs.

"I'm not pregnant," Melissa says.

"Then you were. And recently too. It doesn't show. You gave birth, didn't you?"

Melissa thinks of Sally, of the blood left all over Sally's bed when she drove to the nurse's house and forced her at gunpoint to help deliver Joe's baby. That was a long night. A hard night. One of the toughest of her life. "Three months ago," she says.

Back then she didn't know where else to go. She couldn't go to a hospital. She could change her appearance, but what she couldn't do was give herself a history of medical records. So she went to Sally. Sally helped her. When the baby was born, Melissa was exhausted, but not exhausted enough to not do what needed doing—and that was to force Sally to lie down on the bed at gunpoint and then handcuff her to it. That's when she took photographs of Sally naked. After that she forced Sally to go to the bank and draw out her reward money. Melissa wanted it in cash. And Sally had done that. She had done it because she wanted to save the embarrassment of naked pictures of her being put online. And she did it for the baby. Melissa told her that if she didn't do it, that if Sally went to the police, she would kill the baby. It was simple. All Sally had to do was weigh up her sense of justice against her sense of morality, and no matter what, Sally didn't want to be responsible for the baby's death. So she did what she was asked, she returned with the money, and Melissa let her live. Of course Melissa wouldn't hurt the baby. She loves it. She loved it before it was even born. A small girl named Abigail. And she let Sally live because she needed her for today. She needed her scrubs and her swipe card for the hospital and taking those things three months ago and killing Sally would only have resulted in the swipe card being deactivated. And she let Sally live because, really, Sally had saved Joe's life. She owed her.

"Are you strapping yourself up?" the nurse asks.

Melissa realizes she was zoning out. "Huh?"

"To hide the excess weight?"

"Yes," Melissa says.

"That's a really stupid thing to do."

"So is talking to me while I'm trying to think," Melissa says.

"The baby, it's his, isn't it," Trish says, nodding toward the courthouse.

Melissa knows she isn't referring to the security guard standing outside it. "Yes."

"He raped you, didn't he. All that stuff you said earlier, that phone call you made to somebody to hurt my family, that wasn't real, was it. You're not a killer, but you're here to kill him, aren't you."

Melissa nods again. Is there an opportunity here? Is this woman, this *Trish*, going to want to help her? Slowly she starts nodding.

"You're going about it the wrong way," the woman says. "It's not up to us to take a life. This whole death-penalty debate, it's a mistake. It's got people thinking stupid thoughts. It's causing rifts in the community. And it's wrong, just plain wrong. I understand you're angry, but every life is sacred. Everybody deserves the chance to be forgiven and to kneel in front of God and—"

Melissa hits her with the gun. She swings it hard into the side of Trish's head. Once. Twice. Then a third time. Trish isn't talking anymore, which is a good thing because Trish was really starting to piss her off. The woman slumps forward and Melissa pulls her back before she falls into the horn. The entire plan is turning to shit.

She reaches over and drags the either unconscious or dead woman back with her. She's heavy, and her limbs and clothes snag at the seat, but she gets her there.

This is getting out of hand.

The other paramedic is already underneath the gurney. She couldn't risk having a cop help her load Joe into the back and see him. So now she does her best to stuff Trish under there too. The blankets she had put over the guy she now puts over them both. Now it looks like two bodies stuffed under a gurney hidden by blankets. She needs to do better than that. Only she can't. It is what it is and she's too invested in this now to cut her losses and leave.

She climbs into the front and is settling in behind the steering wheel when she realizes somebody is standing next to the ambulance. It's a security guard, but not the same guy who'd been standing by the back door. He looks rushed. She winds the window down and keeps the gun out of sight, knowing that as bad as this day has been going, making it worse for this guy might just make her feel a little better.

"There's been a situation," he says, his voice low and quick, the kind of voice she thinks would be great for selling torture porn, "with the Christchurch Carver. We're going to need your help."

CHAPTER SIXTY

"Here's the paramedic," somebody says, but I can't open my eyes to look. I can't do much except lie on my back and pray things are going to get better. I'm scared as hell that this may be it for me, that whatever damage has been done inside my body is permanent, that I'll never be able to escape the tightness and the pain.

"I need a toilet," I tell them. "Right now."

There's a bathroom in the first-aid station. They lead me in there and then leave me alone with my exploding stomach, the sounds of it echoing out into many rooms beyond. I should care, I should feel embarrassed, but I don't. I'm all hunched over as I sit on the bowl, my wrists and ankles still connected by a chain, and I feel like I'm back in the van.

The relief is immediate and, for the first time since being attacked by Caleb Cole, my stomach remains relaxed. The tail end of the storm is passing. I clean up and walk out of the bathroom and nobody here is laughing. They all look concerned. I sit back down on the cot.

Then I see the paramedic. She looks familiar. And rape-worthy.

"What have we got?" the paramedic asks, and now it's not just the look of her that's familiar, but her voice too. My remaining testicle shrivels up, and for a moment I can feel grass on my back, I can see stars up above, and I'm back in that night a year ago where my favorite testicle said hello and then good-bye to Melissa's pliers.

I focus on her. I look at her eyes, only she's not looking at me. She's looking at the nurse.

"Looks like food poisoning," the nurse says, "but nobody else at the prison got it. He's vomiting and has bad diarrhea."

"You've taken his blood pressure and temperature?" the paramedic asks, then she looks at me. Melissa? No. It can't be. But those eyes . . . they're Melissa's eyes. I'm sure of it.

"Not yet," the nurse says.

"Then do it," Melissa says, and I can feel my heart rate rising. "Has he been given any fluids?"

"We tried giving him water, but he couldn't hold it down," the nurse says, who then starts to take my blood pressure.

"Take the chains off him," Melissa says.

"That's not a good idea," Jack says.

"There are four of you who are all armed, plus one security guard, and one very sick man. I think we can all handle the risk of his chains being removed."

"No," Jack says.

"We're going to remove them for his trial anyway," Kent says, "so may as well do it now."

Jack looks pissed off, and I can't tell what's annoyed him more, having to remove my chains or being overruled in front of everybody. He starts undoing the cuffs.

"Blood pressure is elevated," the nurse says, "but temperature is okay."

Melissa crouches over me. She starts pressing at the sides of my stomach. She's looking into my face. She's conveying a message. It comes through loud and clear. She touches my stomach. I double over in pain that I don't actually feel. My stomach is still feeling good.

"Don't touch me," I say.

"We should get him to the hospital," Melissa says.

I push her hand away. "It hurts," I tell her.

"We need to get him into the back of the ambulance. For all we know he's in the process of bursting his appendix, and if he is then he could die."

"It's a trick," Jack says.

I roll onto my side and start to gag. I try to throw up, but nothing happens, though the sound of me trying is enough to make Kent scrunch up her face.

"He said he ate bad food," the nurse says.

"And maybe that's the cause and maybe it isn't, but I didn't become a paramedic just so I could watch people suffer when instead they could be helped." Melissa puts her hands on her hips and stares at him. "If it's food poisoning, well, food poisoning kills approximately two hundred people in this country every year," she says, and I'm sure she must be making that figure up, but she delivers it extremely confidently. "Listen, people, I know what you have here. You have a serial killer about to face trial, but if you don't get him to a hospital you may just have a dead serial killer about to face trial."

"You say it like it's a bad thing," Jack asks, and I want to tell him that I get the point, that everybody does, that he should just get it printed on a T-shirt so then he can shut up.

"It's my job to save people," she says. "It's your job to save people too."

"Joe isn't people," Jack says, and I can feel another vote coming.

"Call it in," Kent says.

"What?" Jack asks.

"Call it in. Look at him, his trial is due to start in less than five minutes. Call it in. Let the others know we're taking him to the hospital and we want an escort. The faster we get him sorted, the faster we can get him in front of a judge."

Jack calls it in. He doesn't look happy. "Let's get him to the ambulance," Melissa says—or, at least, who I hope is Melissa.

The officers who helped me earlier help me again. I sway a little even though I'm still feeling much better. The officers get me out into the corridor, Kent and Jack behind me, the security guard and Melissa leading the way to the exit and back outside to the chanting crowds and placards and the occasional person dressed as Jesus.

CHAPTER SIXTY-ONE

Something is happening.

Five minutes ago Raphael watched the security guard come up to the ambulance, knock on the window, then Melissa followed him back inside. The second woman who was in the ambulance didn't get out. It didn't make sense. But then suddenly it did—Melissa has done something to her. She wouldn't have killed her. Since Melissa isn't really a paramedic, then she's going to need to keep the paramedic alive. Melissa wants to keep Joe alive. He's sure of it. So that explained the second paramedic, but it didn't explain what the security guard wanted. Something to do with Joe being sick? He sure as hell looked sick.

Raphael rests his finger on the trigger guard. His hands are still steady. There are no nerves now. That's a sign that he's doing the right thing. Like every fiber of his being is in on the decision, every cell is in harmony—they're all getting along and are going to make this happen. He's not going to shoot Joe in the shoulder like they talked about. Now he's going to shoot him in the head. It was meant to be about wounding him, not killing him. Raphael would do the wounding, and Melissa would pick Joe up in the ambulance.

Raphael was the shooter.

Melissa was the collector.

And together they were going to make Joe suffer.

Now Raphael is the shooter, and he's going to shoot to kill. Of course he's upset he can't torture Joe. But this will at least give him some satisfaction.

He watches the back of the courthouse. He keeps the sights on the door. Then the door opens. Melissa and the security guard step outside, followed by Joe with the same two officers who helped him earlier helping him now, followed by louder screams from the crowd, followed by Kent and the guy who drove the van earlier. Whatever was wrong with Joe before is still wrong with him now. His skin is pale. He looks to be in a lot of pain. Good.

Melissa looks up at Raphael. He can see her face in the scope. She slowly shakes her head and he slowly smiles, he can't help it. She doesn't want him to take the shot. There is no need to. Something happened and she's gotten Joe out of there, but not in the way they planned. Something to do with Joe being sick. Has to be. Joe's sick, and of course everybody down there thinks Melissa is a genuine paramedic.

He moves the scope back onto Joe.

Joe, the man who took away his daughter.

Joe, the man who took away his life.

He thinks about Vivian wanting to be a pop-singing ballerina. He thinks about Adelaide wanting to go to a Harry Potter school and learn magic. He thinks about how he never gets to see them, how much he misses his daughter, how Vivian and Adelaide will grow up without a mother.

Hello, Red Rage. Nice to have you back.

He holds his breath.

He puts the crosshairs over Joe's face.

He pulls the trigger.

The result is instant. Of course it is—yet somehow he was

expecting it to take a second, maybe a second and a half for the physics to catch up. The sound of the shot is muffled by the earmuffs, but it's louder than out at the forest, loud enough to make his ears ring. It echoes around the office and out into the street and as one everybody out there looks up in his direction.

Except Joe.

Because Joe is losing balance. The problem—and of course there were always going to be problems and he was a fool to think it could be otherwise—is that the shot has taken Joe in the chest, maybe in the shoulder, and certainly not in the head like he wanted. Maybe it was the dynamics of the bullet, or the nerves—he doesn't know. What he does know is that the Red Rage is screaming at him to take another shot, and of course he's going to. He still has time.

The two officers holding Joe up don't seem to feel any responsibility to him. They let him go and run for cover. Joe, without the aid of his human crutches, falls into a very similar pile to the one he started in when exiting the van earlier. Detective Kent hides behind Schroder's car. Everybody is hiding—all except Joe and Melissa.

Melissa. And why would she hide? He shot Joe in the shoulder just the way she always wanted him to. She starts dragging Joe toward the ambulance. The whole shooting and collecting part of the plan must still be going through her mind. He puts the crosshairs in the middle of her body. It may not be a kill shot, but at the very least the police will figure out who she is. The Red Rage is pleased by the idea.

He pulls the trigger.

This time the gun bucks in his hands and the gunshot is much quieter, almost only a fraction of the first, or at least it seems that way because his ears are still ringing from the first shot, and maybe it's quieter anyway because it's a different type of bullet. The barrel pulls up into the drop cloth and pulls it up off the ground. With the world reacting below him, he again spends a second determining what has gone wrong, and quickly decides nothing has, that he's lost balance because of the platform he's lying on.

He repositions the gun and sees Melissa hasn't been hit. He has one shot left. Her or Joe. Well, Joe's already been hit, and if luck is on Raphael's side and not on Joe's, then that fucker is going to bleed to death in the parking lot. So he chooses Melissa. He pulls the trigger in the exact same way he pulled the damn thing all those times out where he buried the lawyers and shot the shit out of defenseless tin cans, and this time the gun bucks so wildly it's wrenched from his hands. He hears his finger break. Feels it even more. He rolls off the bench and hits the floor, his shoulder taking the impact.

He doesn't understand . . .

And he's out of time now. And out of bullets.

He gets to his feet. He's already been here longer than he should have. A look out the gap in the drop cloth shows a cop helping Melissa and Joe toward the ambulance and Schroder bursting through the back door into the parking lot. He doesn't know how much time has gone. Fifteen seconds, maybe. Too long, definitely.

He doesn't bother putting the gun back into the ceiling. He peels the latex gloves off and it hurts his finger like crazy. He stuffs them into his pocket. He pulls off the earmuffs and tosses them onto the floor, then realizes that's stupid, that his fingerprints are going to be on them. Fuck. He's pulled his gloves off too early. Has he touched any of this stuff without gloves? Maybe. When he assembled the gun. When he fired it the other day. When he came here Saturday night. Was he wearing gloves then? He thinks he was, but suddenly he's not so sure.

He doesn't have time to wipe down the gun. He looks around. Looks at the paint. Looks at the gun. It'll work. He pulls his gloves back on, then twenty seconds later he's heading down the stairs.

CHAPTER SIXTY-TWO

All hell is breaking loose.

Joe Middleton is on the ground. There's blood over the front of him. His blood. He's writhing in agony. Kent has taken cover behind Schroder's car. Two of the armed officers have also taken cover behind different cars. They're hunkered down trying to figure out where they're being shot from and by how many people. One of them is talking quickly into a radio. A paramedic starts doing her best to drag Joe out of the line of fire and toward the ambulance. The security guard is staying low, making his way back toward the courthouse. People in the street are shouting and ducking down and covering their heads with their arms and placards, no more *two*, *four*, *six*, *eight* from anybody.

Schroder spends two seconds taking it all in. The way everybody is hiding tells him the direction the gunfire is coming from. There's an office building across the road. He looks up and sees an open window with a curtain behind it. He stays low and moves over to his car and squats down next to Kent.

"What the—" he says.

"One shot," she says, holding a pistol in her hands. "Office building over the road. I saw muzzle fire. Middleton is down."

"Why was he back out—"

"Doesn't matter right now," she says. "All that matters is some fucker is shooting at us."

"At us? Or at him?" he asks.

"Why don't you put your head up and find out?"

"If it's only the one shot then it suggests it's not us being shot at," he says, but even so, rather than putting his head up, he leans down and looks under the car. The paramedic is still dragging Joe toward the ambulance. She's the only one in the open. He can see her feet and legs and her arms and he has a view of the top of her head as she angles down to pull Joe along. He doesn't know why the hell she would risk her life for Joe, then decides she can't know who it is she's trying to save. Or perhaps she's running on instinct. It's her nature to save people. Either way, she's making a huge mistake.

"She's going to get herself killed," Schroder says.

"Who?" Kent asks. "The paramedic?"

"Yeah."

Kent lifts her head and looks through the windows of the car. "What the fuck is she doing?"

"I'll get her," Schroder says.

"The hell you will," Kent says, and grabs his tie and pulls him back down. "You're a sitting duck if you go out there. I'll go. At least I'm wearing a vest."

She starts to get up. Just then Jack runs across the parking lot. He puts his arm around the paramedic to pull her into cover, but she doesn't let go of Joe, and Jack ends up dragging them both toward the ambulance.

"We need to get into that building," Schroder says.

"No," Kent says. "You stay here. Backup is—" The ambulance starts up. The sirens come on. "That's one fearless paramedic," Kent says, without looking up. It speeds toward the gate, which is still closed, but doesn't slow down.

Schroder pokes his head up. Sees the paramedic through the side window. Sees her face. Sees the ambulance heading for the fence. Sees that the people on the street can see what's about to happen and are diving out of the way.

"Oh fuck," he says.

"What is it?"

He stands up, but nobody takes a shot at him. That's because the shooting has stopped.

"That was Melissa," he says. "The driver, it was Melissa. Come on," he says, climbing into his car, "let's go."

CHAPTER SIXTY-THREE

The ambulance crashes through the fence and the impact jars through my body. It's been a few days of hell, with vomiting and shitting and getting banged-up knees, and now I've been shot and now I'm in an ambulance that's probably going to tip over or crash into a truck.

I roll toward the left wall as Melissa turns right. The pain is the second worst pain I've ever felt. It feels like somebody has punched their fist into my chest and clutched their fingers around whatever they could find and yanked it out, then set fire to what was left. The ambulance is swerving all over the road. Stuff is falling off the shelves. I'm lying on the floor in blood and surrounded by all the things that can help me, but I don't know how to use any of them. There's a dead woman by my feet. She's half covered by a sheet, and the half exposed shows she's wearing the same uniform Melissa is wearing, and the dead woman is actually covering what appears to be another dead person—this one a man, and the man is mostly naked. The woman has one arm and one leg flopping against the floor.

The ambulance straightens and there are thuds as it bounces into people. There's lots of screaming and yelling and it feels like I'm slap-bang in the middle of an action movie. Melissa is talking to herself, telling people to get the hell out of the way, people who can't hear her, and she has to keep swerving and tapping her foot on the brake. She has the sirens on, but we're not traveling that fast.

When I try to sit up I can't. I know I've been shot, but it's a hard concept to grab hold of. Shot? I've never been shot before—but of course that's not true. I shot myself a year ago, though that wasn't really being shot—that was having my face plowed by a bullet. Shot? Not compared to this.

I give sitting up another go, and this attempt is better than the first, and I can see out the front window. I put my hand over the wound, then study the blood on the palm of my hand, then press it back to my shoulder. I want to say something to Melissa, but I don't know what. Plus she's focusing on driving. Focusing hard. Some people have dropped their signs and some of those signs she runs over, they crunch under the wheels like bones in a dog. A leprechaun bounces off the side of the ambulance, so do two zombies and one Marilyn Monroe. They fall into the distance, dazed and confused—all of them targets for whoever is going to follow us. I have no idea why people are dressed the way they are. I glance to our right as we go through the intersection, and I can see the front of the courthouse and the decoy cars from this morning. They're locked in by the swarming people, angry people rocking the cars and banging their fists on the windows because word hasn't gotten to them that I'm not in there. Only these people are dressed like normal people, they're in jeans and shirts and dresses and jackets—none of them with masks or Hollywood outfits, but many of them carrying signs. The armed officers can't move. They can't open fire. No doubt they want to climb onto the roofs of their cars and spray bullets into the air—or perhaps they're even angry enough to spray them into the crowd so they can part it like the Red Sea so they can follow us. In which case they ought to ask the guy dressed as Moses who is carrying two large old-model iPads made out of cardboard, each the size of a torso. On each tablet are the commandments, only they've been modified and I have time to read just *Thou shall rock out with thy cock out* before a guy dressed in a cowboy outfit complete with gorilla mask appears from the sea of people, jumps onto him, and they both disappear below the tide line.

I sink back down to the floor. I grab some padding and press it into my wound. Thank God my stomach is still feeling okay, but I'm concerned that it's not, that my body has other issues to deal with right now and is giving me a break on that one for a moment.

"My bag," Melissa shouts, and she glances over her shoulder at me.

"What?"

"My bag. Hand me my bag."

"What bag?"

She glances back over her shoulder, and this time her eyes move around the floor. "There," she says, "next to the woman's foot. The black bag."

There's a small black bag right where she said it'd be.

"Hand it to me," she says.

"What's in it?"

"Hurry up, Joe," she says. "Schroder is going to be right behind us."

I reach out and grab the bag. I hand it to her. She opens it up with one hand while keeping the other hand on the wheel. She pulls out a small box with a plastic top on it, and she lifts the top to reveal a trigger. It's a remote. She puts it between her legs so it doesn't fall on the floor, and then she puts both hands back onto the wheel. She keeps looking into her mirrors.

"It's all about timing," she says.

"I've missed you," I tell her.

"This confusion and chaos," she says, "it's just how I saw it. This is about to get easy for us, Joe, and about a hundred different types of messy for everybody else," she says, and she keeps watching her mirrors and then hovers one hand over the remote.

CHAPTER SIXTY-FOUR

Raphael thought he would have been caught. He thought he would have been cornered in the stairwell by cops armed if not with guns, then with batons and fists and pepper spray. He was prepared to give a description of the man he was chasing, something like *White uniform covered in paint, a hat on backward*.

None of that happens. On the street people are running in every direction. They bounce against Raphael and he lets himself get lost in them. They're running for their lives. None of them are hurt but many are acting as if they've just been shot. Suddenly he's not sure he's even going to be able to drive out of here. He can see the ambulance two blocks away. Its sirens are on, but the people around it keep it moving slower than Melissa would have liked. He reaches his car and at the same time Detective Schroder's car hits the street just ahead of him and turns the same way as the ambulance. It's all happening just ahead of him. He can hear other sirens far in the distance.

He begins to follow them. Did Melissa sabotage the gun? If so, then why give him a uniform? Why help him avoid arrest? He doesn't know. It's something to think about once he's gotten the hell out of here. There'll be a simple explanation, but he can't search for it right now.

Melissa keeps going south. Schroder follows, and Schroder is surrounded by the same crowd of people, though that crowd is starting to disperse. Raphael slows down. He'll go left. He'll start putting distance between him and the courthouse. The entire thing has been a disaster.

He hopes like hell both Joe and Melissa are gunned down in a hail of bullets. He hopes Joe is already dead. He extends those hopes and prays he won't be arrested, but only time will tell. He puts on his signal and waits for the people to get out of the way so he can turn into the intersection.

CHAPTER SIXTY-FIVE

Schroder is gripping the steering wheel so tight his knuckles have gone white. They are thirty yards behind the ambulance. There are people everywhere—many between them and Melissa, most though are on the sidewalks.

"There's no way she can get away," Kent says, looking around her, and Schroder can hear the message she isn't saying: *There's no way she can get away, so no reason for us to keep trying to close the distance, no reason we can't just stay hanging back so we don't kill anybody.*

"Maybe she has a plan," Schroder says, "or maybe she knows there's nowhere to go and doesn't care. That could be part of her plan too. But we're not hanging back. I'm not risking losing her."

"I agree she has a plan," Kent says, "but it doesn't make sense—how did she know she was going to be asked inside?"

"What are you talking about?"

"Middleton was sick, so we got one of the paramedics to come in. She was waiting for it."

"And you believed him?"

"He wasn't faking, and even if he was there's no way she could have known she'd be asked to come inside."

"I don't know then," he says, annoyed at this new information. If he'd still been a cop he'd have been involved, and he'd never have fallen for that crap. He has to brake slightly as a guy in a wheelchair starts to drift from the sidewalk out in front of him, and he wonders if the guy genuinely can't walk or if it's just a costume. He loses a few yards on the ambulance in his effort not to run him over and make the costume permanent.

"Well it had to be something," she says, "and it would have worked if somebody hadn't shot him. How's that for bad timing for Melissa, huh? Freeing her boyfriend and then another shooter trying to pick him off. I guess her plan was just to drive away without being chased."

Schroder claims back the few yards he lost, then a few more. "I saw her. A few days ago."

"What?"

"At the prison. When I went out to see Joe, I ran into her in the parking lot."

"Why didn't you—"

"Tell you? I had no idea it was her," he says. "But it was. Shit," he says. "My keys. When I came out of the prison I couldn't find my keys. Then I found them on the ground."

"She took your keys?"

"She was pretending to be pregnant. She had the bump and everything. I helped her out of her car. Oh my God she's good. I had no idea." He slowly shakes his head. "She must have swiped my keys then. She must have been in my car. . . . Oh shit, that's why I couldn't find the photograph of her."

"What?"

"When we were talking to Raphael. Remember I went back to grab a photograph of her?"

"Why the hell would she risk breaking into your car just to steal a photograph?"

A young man dressed as a teapot with two spouts extends a

hand to give Schroder the finger, probably annoyed at the speeding car without a siren that he almost stepped out in front of. This would be much easier if he had sirens. And a lot easier if people looked where they were going.

"I don't know," he says. "It doesn't make . . . Wait, what were you saying earlier?"

"About the photograph?"

"No. About the plan to escape."

"I don't know," she says. "I said something about how unlucky she was Joe was shot."

"You said it was her plan to drive away without being chased."

"Yeah. It must have been."

He shakes his head. "No. There has to be more. She was always going to be chased, not chased exactly, but there was always going to be an escort if Joe was sick in the back of the ambulance."

"Makes sense," she says.

"So how was she going to escape the escort?"

"Oh Jesus," she says, and he can tell she's coming to the same conclusion as him. "You think the explosives?"

"Has to—" he starts, but doesn't get to finish, because that's when the car blows up.

CHAPTER SIXTY-SIX

The explosion is almost ear shattering. There is no fire, just smoke and glass and twisted pieces of metal. The car is picked up like a child's toy, and just as casually dismissed like a child's toy—it's launched three feet high and a couple of feet to the left before landing back on its wheels. The shock wave blows all the windows out. Bits of flesh hit the interior like paintballs exploding across a wall. People start screaming. Some are running from the blast, others are caught in the shock wave and thrown outward, the explosion an epicenter. Cut faces and cut clothes and a few people aren't running at all, a few of them are lying on the road surrounded by, and impaled by, shrapnel. The side mirrors go flying, bits of tire, nuts and bolts and screws, and engine components are tossed in all directions, along with pieces of bone and tenderized body parts.

Schroder's shoulders climb up around his jaw in expectation of an impact. Kent twists in her seat and looks behind her. Schroder keeps driving, glancing into the mirror back at the explosion. It came from a car that was only twenty or thirty yards behind them.

A decoy explosion. Something to shut down the intersection and fill the streets with scared and panicked people.

"Oh my God," Kent says. "Somebody was driving that car."

"Oh fuck," Schroder says.

"I know, I know," she says.

"She was in my car," he says.

"What?"

"She was in my fucking car!" he shouts, and he slams on the brakes. "Get out, get out," he yells, taking off his seat belt.

"What—"

"Get the fuck out," he shouts, and he opens his door and so does Kent. People are running toward them. Away from them. In every direction. He slams the door closed behind him, hoping it will help contain the shock wave and blast that Melissa is going to use to help her escape.

"Get back," he screams. "Everybody get back."

"Carl—"

He looks back over the car. "Fire some shots in the air," he shouts. "Get—"

His car explodes right in front of him. He sees Kent ride the shock wave ten yards through the air, where she is thrown into a parked car, where she smashes the windshield and enters it. Only it looks like twenty yards because he's riding the shock wave in the opposite direction. A lot of people are. Twisted metal. Smoke. Flesh and blood.

Then darkness.

CHAPTER SIXTY-SEVEN

Two explosions and Melissa tosses the second remote onto the floor. The padding against my wound is soaked with blood so I replace it with some fresh stuff, which will no doubt soak up just as quickly. I realize there are two holes, one in front and one in the back, right through the right-hand side of my chest. I can't move that arm. I don't know what's been hit. I don't even know really what's in there. Bone and muscle and tendons, I guess, which means reconstructive surgery and physiotherapy or a future of having a gimpy limb. It seems too high and too far to the side to worry about lung damage, but I don't know—I'm not a doctor, and nor is Melissa—so I worry anyway.

I get onto my knees and clutch the wall and the back of the driver's seat and stare out the windshield as Melissa heads through the next intersection, then another, then turns right at the following one. Now we're heading back toward the courthouse, only one or two streets over. Then she pulls over.

"Nobody is following us," she says.

"Why are we stopping here?"

"Just wait a minute."

"Why?"

"You'll see."

"Melissa—"

"Trust me," she says. "I've gotten you this far, trust me to get you the rest of the way."

"Who shot me?"

"It's complicated," she says, "but it was a clean shot."

"How do you know that?"

"It was an armor-piercing bullet. It wouldn't have broken apart on impact. It went through cleanly. Anything else would have made a small hole going in and a much bigger hole coming out."

"Why are we waiting here?" I ask.

"We can't be the only ambulance heading away right now," she says, "because the police will be looking for us. We have to blend in."

"What?"

"Trust me, babe, just stay patient. We'll be out of here in a few moments," she says.

"If you know it was an armor-piercing bullet, then you know who shot me," I tell her.

"There was a plan," she says. "It was the only way to get you out of there in an ambulance."

"But you were getting me out because I was sick," I tell her. "Did you know about the sandwiches?"

"What sandwiches?"

"It doesn't matter," I say.

"I was waiting there for you to get shot, but then that security guard came out and asked for my help because you were sick."

I think about what she's saying, but it still doesn't make sense. "So you were working with somebody else, that same somebody who shot me. If you were getting me to the ambulance anyway, why did he still shoot me?"

"Like I said, babe, it's complicated, but I'll go through it all with you later."

"But you knew what you were doing," I tell her. "You said all that stuff to the nurse."

"It's the same stuff TV doctors say all the time. It was all showmanship."

"You could have gotten arrested."

A couple of ambulances speed through the intersection ahead of us, going left to right.

"It's time to go," she says.

She pulls away from the curb and we take another right and she pulls over again where the other ambulances are. We've circled our way around. There's one blown-up car behind us now and one blown-up car ahead. She climbs out of the ambulance and makes her way around the back and climbs back in. She drags the dead woman across the floor, then reaches down for the man. She shakes him. "Come on," she says, "what good are you to me asleep?"

He doesn't respond. She checks his pulse. Then she shakes her head. "No," she says, and I realize the guy has a good excuse for not responding. The best excuse, really. "He was going to help you," she says.

"You killed them both?"

"I didn't mean to. I guess I got the dosage wrong."

"Who's going to help me now?" I ask, pulling the padding away from my chest. It needs replacing again. "I'm going to die here," I say, my voice getting higher.

One of the Grim Reapers I saw earlier, or perhaps a different one, is out there lying on the road. He's not moving. His hood has been torn aside and half of his face looks gone, or it could be part of the makeup. I can't tell.

"We need to go," I tell her.

"Not yet," she says. There are other ambulances pulling over in style with sirens going and with doors popping open before they've even rolled to a stop. People jump out and within seconds they're working on people. Soon they're going to be loading victims up into the back and taking off as well.

"Here, let me take a look," Melissa says, and she crouches in front of me and puts one hand on my good shoulder and uses her other hand to start undoing my shirt. Despite everything I'm suddenly aroused and I put a hand around the back of her neck and pull her in for a kiss that she resists. "Not now, Joe."

"I've missed you," I tell her.

"I know. You've said already," she says.

She closes the ambulance doors and moves back into the cab. She starts the ambulance and turns on the sirens. The streets are still full of people, but they've dispersed somewhat—the big groups breaking up into smaller groups, the smaller groups breaking up into pairs.

We take the same route as before. We drive south. Then we turn right. I keep expecting a hundred police cars to cut us off—men with guns, that Sunday morning a year ago taking place all over, only this time me without a gun or a Fat Sally. It doesn't happen. We follow another ambulance. We stay in a straight line all the way to the hospital. Only we're not going to the hospital because that doesn't make sense. Except that's exactly what we *are* doing. Instead of taking the ambulance entrance, she takes the public one. She turns off the sirens. We drive around the back into the parking lot. It's full. She double-parks near a white van. I'm sick of vans. She kills the engine. She comes around and opens the back door and helps me outside. Sunlight floods us. Cars and trees and a machine to pay for parking, a picnic bench with a bucket full of sand next to it full of cigarette butts, a few empty coffee cups on the bench, but no people anywhere. Coffee break is over for everybody in the hospital thanks to Melissa.

Melissa fills up her rucksack with medical supplies. We start walking. Our target is the white van. I'm leaving a blood trail. She grabs keys out of her pocket and swings the back doors of the van open. She helps me climb inside.

"I'm sorry," she says. "You were supposed to have help."

"I don't want to die," I tell her.

"You're not going to," she says. "Just stay calm."

She gets into the front seat. She looks over her shoulders at me.

"I've missed you too," she says.

"I knew you'd come for me," I tell her.

"I was pregnant," she tells me. "From our weekend together. I had the baby. It's a girl. It's your girl. Our girl. Her name is Abigail. She's beautiful."

It's too much information to absorb. Me, a father? "Take me back to jail," I say, and finally I pass out.

CHAPTER SIXTY-EIGHT

Schroder can see the sky. It's blue in all directions, a few clouds, one of them looks like a palm tree. One looks like a face. There's a dark gray cloud forming close by. It's smoke. From the car. He tries to move his head, but can't. He can move his eyes. That's a start, but a frightening one.

He can remember every detail. It's strange. A thing like that has every chance of wiping a few seconds', a few minutes', even a few days' worth of memories. But not for him. For some reason he wonders if that's because last year he died for a few minutes and then came back, as if that experience means his mind is hard-wired a little differently now, immune to forgetting things, then he dismisses the idea for what it really is—a stupid one.

He's too frightened to try moving his arms and legs. He has to know they work, but what if they don't? What if he's never going to walk again? By not trying to move them, he can put that fate off for another time. His ears are ringing. He can feel the cold ground beneath him. He can feel one of his arms pinned under his back. His right. That makes him happy. If his back was broken he wouldn't be able to feel that, would he? His left arm, he can't feel. He can taste blood. He can feel more of it on his face. Over the ringing in his ears he can hear screaming.

He closes his eyes and he prays, he actually prays for the first time since he was a kid, back when he figured out that praying didn't get you anywhere in this world, that praying and misery went hand in hand just like peanut butter and jelly. But he prays now for his legs to move and they do, they move a little and without pain and he knows his prayer wasn't answered, that he's been lucky, that's all it is. He was lucky and others probably won't have been. Like Kent. He manages to tilt slightly onto his side, the blue sky disappearing, replaced with rooftops, then office windows and walls, then the street. His car has been lifted and has turned a quarter circle and come back down. There are no flames. It's all twisted to shit and there is glass everywhere. There are other people lying on the ground, some tilting onto their sides and viewing the world the same way as him, some not moving at all.

There is a death toll here. He prays it's a low one.

He prays God is listening to him.

He rests on his back. He doesn't want to, but he has no choice. He closes his eyes. His chest feels tight. Somebody puts a hand on his shoulder and he opens his eyes and Detective Wilson Hutton is crouching over him. People have stopped screaming and started sobbing instead.

"Hang on," Hutton says.

"Kent," Schroder says.

"It's . . . it's bad," Hutton says.

He can hear sirens. He can see ambulances. He didn't see them arrive.

"How long have I been out?"

"Three, maybe four minutes."

"Joe?" he asks.

Hutton shrugs, which sets off a chain reaction of rolling flesh down his chin and into his chest. "Gone," he says.

Schroder closes his eyes and for a few moments the chaos disappears, even the sobs and sirens. He opens them back up. "What about Kent?"

Hutton shakes his head. "She's not going to make it," he says.

"No," Schroder says. His neck is too sore to shake his head, but his eyes aren't too sore to tear up. He tries to get up. If he can just get up, then she'll be okay. Somehow. He's sure of it. "Help me up."

"That's not a good idea," Hutton says.

"Goddamn it, help me up."

"Listen to me. Carl. It's not a good idea. You're in bad shape. Okay?"

His breath catches in his throat. "How bad?"

"Multiple cuts. Your left arm is broken. Could be a broken leg. Could even be a broken neck."

"My neck is fine," Schroder says. He moves his head. Yep. Fine. He can move both feet so his legs are fine, but Hutton is right about the arm. He doesn't care. He wants to see Kent. If he'd pulled over a few seconds earlier, if he'd yelled at her to get away from the car louder, would she be okay?

It's none of that. The fuckup happened at the prison. When he didn't figure out he was talking to Melissa. Or for that matter, why not backtrack a year to when Melissa came into the station? Or go back even further to when Joe first started working for them. That's where they could have made a difference.

"Help me up," he says, then uses his good arm to start getting to his feet. Hutton shakes his head, then sighs, then helps him. When he's up he puts an arm around Hutton for support. His broken arm hangs by his side, all the pain flowing into it along with the blood, and it hurts, but he knows it's going to hurt even more soon because that pain is only getting warmed up. His legs feel fine. He can take his own weight. He's a little light-headed, but okay. He lifts his hand to his forehead and his fingers come away with blood on them. He focuses on them, then they fade as he focuses on what's behind them. On the view.

"Oh my God," he says. There are people lying in the street. A few near him, but most further down by the other blown-to-shit car. Some burns. Lots of blood coming from people who have friends and strangers trying to comfort them. There are five, six, no, maybe ten ambulances. Metal and plastic and glass have been shredded from the bombed car and thrown about like confetti, going further than he can see, the sun glinting off a thousand pieces of wreckage.

"Where's Kent?" he asks.

"This way," Hutton says.

Schroder is led past his car. It's still smoking. He's seen plenty of cars destroyed in accidents—he's seen cars with roofs missing as they've jammed themselves beneath trucks, he's seen cars cut in half by busses—but he's never seen one detonated by an explosive. It's charred and twisted metal, less of a car now than some weird modern-art exhibit. He carries his broken arm in his good arm.

Kent is lying on the other side of the exhibit and on the sidewalk. Nearby, Spider-Man is lying facedown in a gutter, a side mirror next to his head, a patch of blood on both of them from the impact. He doesn't know if Kent somehow bounced out of the car she was thrown into, or if the paramedics pulled her out.

Kent looks up at him. She smiles. "Hey," she says.

"Hey."

"I should have been quicker," she says.

"Yeah, you should have been," he says, trying to smile, and she tries to smile too. It breaks his heart. Breaking her heart is a piece of metal embedded in her chest. Her limbs are twisted. Her hands are burned. One side of her face is covered in blood, and beneath it he can see overlapping skin, like somebody has lifted a piece of wallpaper and set it back down slightly off-center. "You're going to be fine," he tells her, and then the paramedics get her up onto a gurney and start moving her toward the ambulance.

"Joe," Kent says.

"We'll get him," he says.

She reaches out and grabs his hand. The paramedics tell her to let go and she doesn't. "Joe said Calhoun was a bad guy," she says. "You always," she says, then coughs up a little blood, "you always said—"

"Just rest," he tells her.

"That somebody else killed Daniela Walker. Joe said it was Calhoun."

"Joe's a liar and a madman."

"I believed him," she says, and her eyes flicker closed and she lets go. The gurney starts moving again and he hobbles to stay with it. Her eyes open back up. She smiles. A sweet, bloody smile, what he thinks may be her last. "Should have been quicker," she says again.

He says nothing.

"Do me a favor, Carl," she says, and she reaches down and unclips the latch to her pistol. And then her arm falls away. "Promise me something," she says, struggling with her remaining breaths, and she nods down toward her firearm.

He already knows what it's going to be. He looks up. Hutton is looking back at the wreckage. He's not watching. "I'll get him," he says, and he reaches down and takes her gun. Neither of the paramedics seem to mind. "I'll get them both. I promise."

CHAPTER SIXTY-NINE

The roads aren't as congested out past the hospital. Melissa is calm. No reason not to be. Joe has passed out in the back. She hopes it's from the blood loss and the pain, and not from the news that he's become a father. He's still losing blood. She's sure it's a shoulder wound. She's sure the bullet hasn't hit his lung. If she starts freaking out he's going to die. She needs to start helping him, but first she needs to put more distance between them and the hospital and the courthouse.

The plan may have started unraveling, but she saved it. The explosions were perfect. When she left her earmuffs in Raphael's car on Saturday, that was no accident. When she went back she had placed C-four in the same place in his car that she did in Schroder's. Raphael will have been blown into a dozen pieces. Probably more. He probably rained down over five city blocks in bite-sized pieces. She knows Schroder got out of his car. But not by much. She saw him flying through the air. As for the by-standers, well, she didn't want them hurt, but there wasn't much she could do about that except hope for the best. People had to take responsibility for their actions—and in this case all those victims were accountable for being at the courthouse when they should have been at work or at home or studying, and they were accountable for not getting out of the way in time.

She drives for two more minutes. Then she pulls over. She gets into the back of the van. She opens up her bag and pours the supplies out on the floor. She lays Joe out flat. The whole point of the van was so she could have a mobile operating space. There were supposed to be two paramedics back here—or at least one. She unbuttons his shirt, then uses a pair of scissors to cut away the part of his shirt and jacket getting in the way. Like she hoped, it looks like a clean wound. She doesn't know what to do. She has the idea of getting the van cigarette lighter from the dashboard and using it to cauterize the wounds, but she doesn't know if that really works. She wads up some gauze and stuffs it into the hole. She rolls him onto his side and stuffs more into the back of the wound too. Then she puts padding on both sides and uses bandaging to apply pressure. It's the best she can do. For now. Until she gets help. And she knows where to get it.

She gets back behind the wheel. She turns on the radio and listens to unconfirmed reports that there are dozens dead and hundreds wounded and she knows it can't be that many. She keeps driving. The unconfirmed reports stay unconfirmed, and the estimates drop a little, and the only thing they get right are the amount of explosions. And the stampede—people are fleeing the area. There are unconfirmed gunshots and no mention of Joe.

Fifteen minutes later she pulls into the same street she was in earlier this morning and pulls into the same driveway of the same house. She gets out and uses Sally's keys to open Sally's front door, and Sally is hog-tied and gagged just where she left her, still dressed in her pajamas and robe. The fatty looks sad. She also looks like she's wet herself.

"Scream and I kill you. You understand?" Melissa asks.

Sally nods. Melissa takes off her gag.

"You help us, and you get to live. You understand?"

"Who's *us*?" Sally asks.

"I have a patient out in a van. I need you to help me bring him inside. It's Joe."

"Joe? I . . . I don't understand."

"He's been hurt, you Jesus-loving heffalump," Melissa says, quickly losing patience. "I want you to help him. If you don't, so help me, I'll shoot those flappy breasts of yours and leave you for dead."

"I—"

Melissa slaps her in the face. "Here's how it's going to work," she says. "You're going to help Joe and if he dies then you die and if he lives then you get to live. It really is that simple. You get it, right? You see how it works?"

"What's wrong with him?"

"He's been shot."

"I thought—"

"You people, you Jesus freaks, you're all about the forgiveness, right? It's your job to forgive what he's done," Melissa says. "And now you're a nurse so it's your job to help people. You get to combine your love of God with your love of helping people. Think of this as the perfect storm."

"I don't have any supplies."

"I have a bag full of them," Melissa says, then she pulls out a knife and cuts the plastic binds around Sally's arms and the binds from around her feet. Sally sits up and starts massaging her wrists. Melissa shows her the gun.

"One wrong move," she says, "and it's over."

They head outside. To her credit Sally doesn't try to run and to Melissa's credit she doesn't have any reason to shoot her in the back. They help Joe out and get him inside and the kitchen table is too small so they carry him down a very short corridor into the very small bedroom where Melissa slept last night. There are stuffed toys on the floor, thrown there last night when Melissa laid on the bed, and now those toys get stood on and stepped over. They get Joe laid down on the bed, then Melissa tips up the bag of medical supplies on the end of the bed near his feet.

"We need to cut away his clothes," Sally says.

"Then cut," Melissa says.

Sally runs the blade of the scissors all the way from Joe's waist to his collar, then cuts the shoulder of the jacket, cutting the bandaging Melissa had put there earlier. She peels back the clothes and the padding and pulls out the gauze, exposing the wound, a hole big enough to poke a finger into, but no bigger. The whole time Melissa stays a few yards back, the gun lowered to her side.

Sally shakes her head as she stares at the wound. "He needs a hospital."

"Think of this as a hospital," Melissa says. "Think of yourself as a doctor and me as your assistant. Think of this as the test run you've always wanted. You keep the patient alive and you fix him up and you get a gold star. You get promoted from a victim to a survivor."

Sally shakes her head. She's being stubborn. Melissa doesn't like stubborn people. "He needs a hospital," she says again.

"And you need to start doing your job," Melissa says.

"You're not understanding me," Sally says. "He's already lost a lot of—"

"Sally?" Joe says, opening his eyes and looking up at her. "Sweet, sweet Sally," he says, and Melissa instantly feels a pang of jealousy, until he follows it up with, "Sally with the wobbly belly." Then he grins, laughs for a couple of seconds, and closes his eyes again.

Melissa smiles. Good ol' Joe. "Fix him," she says.

"Even if I can, this isn't a sterile environment. He's going to be prone to infection, and we don't have—"

"Sally," Melissa says, saying the name in an abrupt voice that makes Sally turn from Joe and toward her. "Just do the best you can. I'm sure you'll be fine."

"And if it's not fine?"

"Then I'm going to shoot you in the fucking head."

CHAPTER SEVENTY

Schroder refuses the ambulance ride. He sees no point. A broken arm—so what? But he does accept the bandaging applied to the top of his forehead and the bandaging to his leg. The cuts aren't deep. They'll need stitches, but he doesn't care. At least the bleeding has stopped. Hell, for a few minutes last year he was dead—the broken bones and torn flesh life throws his way aren't a big deal.

"Can I have something for the arm?" he asks.

The paramedic is a guy in his sixties who looks like he spent his twenties and thirties as a professional wrestler. Big and with a disfigured nose, his voice is deep and gravelly, one of those *Don't mess with me* voices. "You can have the break set and a cast applied," he says.

"And I will," Schroder says. "Later today. But I need something for the pain right now."

"That pain is only going to get worse," the paramedic says. "I can put it in a sling and I can give you some painkillers, the kind of thing you'd buy at the pharmacy, but nothing stronger, and they're not going to do a hell of a lot. You want something stronger, then climb in the back of the ambulance and let me take you back to the hospital."

"I'll take what you can give me," Schroder says.

Both camps of protesters, along with the students, have broken up, and the crowd mostly dispersed so Schroder isn't banging into anybody as he walks back toward the courthouse. His arm is in the sling and already feels a whole lot better than having it hanging by his side. Hutton is carrying a police radio. There are reports of witness sightings of the ambulance leaving the scene, but there were and are lots of ambulances, and pulling them over is putting lives at risk, and as of the moment nobody can rightly say which one they should be looking for. Joe is out there in the back of one of them, though he doubts that's the case anymore. He wonders if the serial killer is dead and hopes that he is.

"So far there's two confirmed deaths," Hutton says. "Jack Mitchel," he says. "He was a good man."

"He was . . . ah, shit," Schroder says. "He was trying to help the paramedic. He didn't know it was Melissa."

"She shot him," Hutton says.

"Christ, I didn't even see him there. Who's the second?"

"The second is the driver of the first car that exploded. We were able to run the license plate. Car belonged to Raphael Moore."

Hutton is puffing a little, struggling to keep up. Schroder is walking like a man on a mission who was just half blown up, which is exactly what he is. The painkillers aren't helping yet, and he's not sure they even will. He pauses and turns toward the detective. The courthouse is fifty yards away. "Raphael Moore?"

"Yeah. I know you knew him."

"I just spoke to him," Schroder says, and he thinks back to Saturday and the conversation they had, and to the one on Thursday night too. He thinks of the bad feeling Raphael gave him. Now he knows why. Soon he will revisit those feelings and question what he could have done differently. He should have made more of an effort to convince Kent there was something wrong. Or he should have just followed him.

He reaches into his pocket with his good arm for his caffeine pills, but they're not there—they must have fallen out either while being propelled through the air or on impact. "Melissa must have known him," he says, searching his pocket.

"Could just be a coincidence," Hutton says. "She just planted a bomb in a car she saw in the area. Could be—" he starts, and then his cell phone starts ringing.

Hutton takes the call, leaving Schroder to think of what Hutton's *could be* was going to be, adding a lot of his own *could be*s to it. The two men start walking again. Mostly what Hutton says are a lot of *Uh huh*s and a few *Okay*s. Schroder is thankful it's not going to be his job to talk to the woman who was in the process of becoming Raphael's ex-wife, a woman who is now technically a widow. He thinks of Raphael's grandchildren and wonders how much they'll feel the loss, and wonders if the loss of their mother was so strong that losing a grandfather won't make much of an impact. Then he thinks of Jack Mitchel, and he thinks back to the day they arrested Joe Middleton and how much Jack was itching to put a bullet into the serial killer. That's not a *could be*, but a *could have been*. That *could have been* would have given today an entirely different outcome. His imagination takes another trip down the path not taken. No Joe, no trial, no protests, no gunshots and bombs. Tonight when the adrenaline has worn off, there's going to be a whole lot of guilt waiting for him.

They pass Raphael's car. The scene has started to clear of people and the police presence has grown. The small remaining crowds have been pushed back a block, but they are gathering back there with police officers trying to keep the scene contained. They're not doing as good a job as they'd like, because there are still a few people within the cordon, those who aren't cops or victims or paramedics are mostly media. No longer are the decoy cars surrounded. They walk through the intersection and turn left at the end of the block and head around to the back of the courthouse, where there are four patrol cars all with sirens off, but lights flashing.

"That was an interesting call," Hutton says. "Witnesses have said the man getting into Raphael's car was a police officer."

Schroder pauses again and turns his back to the courthouse and looks at Hutton, who is framed by the image of Raphael's smoldering car. "What?"

"That's not all," Hutton says. A couple of reporters start arguing a few yards away from them with a pair of officers trying to push them back. Schroder and Hutton carry on walking. "We got a report that it was the same person in the car that came out of there," he says, pointing over at the office building where currently a steady stream of forensic technicians is pouring into.

"Can never reply on witness reports," Schroder says.

"I know that, but the person who saw him getting into the car is one of us."

"So . . . so what are we saying here?"

Hutton shrugs. Schroder wonders how much time has passed. It feels like five minutes, but it's longer because he spent time unconscious and time watching over Rebecca as the paramedics worked at saving her. He looks at his watch, but it didn't survive the blast. For this amount of cops to be here and the crime-scene tape already up, it has to have been at least fifteen minutes. It could even be half an hour. He needs to phone his wife. Needs to tell her he's okay.

"What time is it?" he asks Hutton.

"Ten forty."

So it's been just over forty minutes since the first gunshot rang out. They reach the back of the courthouse. Jack Mitchel is lying on his back. Schroder stares at the dead man thinking of another *could be*, in this case it's a *could have been*, as in what could have been if Melissa had decided to detonate Raphael's car second. An hour ago none of this was a possibility, and now it simply doesn't feel like a reality.

"So," Schroder says, "we've got a police officer climbing into

Raphael Moore's car outside the scene of a shooting, and not long—"

"No," Hutton says, shaking his head and interrupting.

"You just said—"

"What we have is somebody dressed as a police officer getting into Raphael's car. That doesn't mean it's a cop."

Schroder takes a few seconds to think about it. It's a good point. He should have thought of that. Instead of the pain in his arm starting to disappear, it's getting stronger. The paramedic gave him only four pills, two to take now and two to take in another few hours. He takes the second two now, working up enough saliva in his mouth then dropping them in one at a time and swallowing. "Okay, so let's play this out. If it's Raphael and he's dressed as a cop and he's coming out of the building Joe was shot from, then it stands to reason Raphael is the guy who did the shooting. Right?"

"That's the going theory," Hutton says. "We think he dressed as a cop knowing officers would be on their way and he could blend in in case they got to the building before he got out of it. He got into his car and then *boom*."

Schroder looks up at the office building, his eyes fixing on the open window with a curtain behind it. For a moment he remembers a case last December where a guy with suction cups strapped to his hands and knees was found at the base of a similar-looking building, his body looking exactly the way you'd expect it to look after falling ten stories and hitting the pavement. With that thought he realizes his mind keeps drifting. He needs to focus on the case. This case, and only this case, but it's difficult. "Let's go take a look," he says.

"Listen, Carl, I know with all that's going on you've forgotten you're no longer a cop. It's one thing letting you this far, but you can't go up there."

Schroder wants to argue, but he knows Hutton is right. But he argues anyway. "Come on, Wilson, I know the Carver case better than anybody. You need my eyes on this."

Hutton nods. "Look, don't take this personally, okay, because we're all at fault here, but your eyes were on this case for a couple of years while Joe was running free and they've been on the Melissa X case for twelve months, so your eyes aren't really needed right now."

The comment comes as a blow, and he takes a moment trying to figure out how to respond and can't think of anything other than *Fuck you, Hutton*, but the sad truth is Hutton is right. Of course he's right. If he wasn't right then there wouldn't be so much blood on the roads.

"Listen, like I said, we're all at fault," Hutton says. "We all missed what we should have seen. You've been gone a month and none of us are any closer to finding Melissa, and I know you're the guy who got the break with finding her real name," he says, and Schroder knows even that's not entirely true—it was Theodore Tate who got that. "What I'm saying is we're all responsible."

"What you're saying is you don't think I can help," Schroder says.

"I'm not saying that," Hutton says, only he is and both men know it. "I'm just saying it's not your job anymore."

Hutton stares at him waiting for a response, and it takes Schroder a little over five seconds to come up with it. "I need this," he says.

"Carl—"

"I need this, Wilson. I'm the one who came up with the idea of a decoy route to the courthouse. I'm the one Melissa stole it from."

"She—"

Schroder holds his hand up. "She broke into my car when I was visiting Joe in prison. I spent a few minutes talking to her beforehand and had no idea who she was."

"Jesus, Carl, what the fuck?"

"I'm the one whose car she put the bomb in. What happened to Kent, that's on me too. If Joe kills anybody, if Melissa kills anybody else, that's on me. You see that, right?" He looks at Jack lying dead on the ground. "That's on me too," he says, and Hutton can see where he's looking. "Don't do this, don't send me away, please, Wilson, I'm begging you as a friend, don't do this."

Now it's Hutton's turn to say nothing for five seconds. He looks around to see who else is nearby and he must think *what the hell*, because then he shrugs, he shakes his head first in a *I can't believe I'm about to do this* gesture, and then starts nodding.

"Okay, but don't touch anything."

"I won't."

"Fuck it," Hutton says. "If the roles were reversed, would you let me in?"

No, Schroder thinks, and then nods. The roles have been reversed in the past, not with him and Hutton, but with him and Tate, and in those cases Tate always heard *no* as a *yes*. "Of course I would."

"Yeah, right. If anybody asks you're here as a witness, that's all, and if you end up getting me fired over this, you're going to wake up in bathtub full of ice and I'm going to have sold your organs because I'm going to need the money. I'll break your other arm too. Come on, let's go, before I change my mind."

CHAPTER SEVENTY-ONE

My daughter's name is Abby. She's twenty years old and has her mother's looks, the kind of looks I'd like to see on any twenty-year-old girl that I shared a deserted alleyway with. Abby isn't short for Abigail, but short for *Accidental Baby*, and me and Melissa are planning on telling that story at her twenty-first birthday party, which is tomorrow. Abby has a great sense of humor and she'll get the joke. I love her. Abby has changed my life, just as Melissa has. She's our only child. Abby was four months old when I had a vasectomy, choosing to have it done professionally rather than taking the shortcut of having Melissa take care of it. One child was enough.

My mom will be at tomorrow's party. So will her new husband, Henry. Walt died a few years ago. He was hit by a car. I've always suspected it was a lifestyle choice rather than an accident. My mother is in her eighties now.

One of the best things about having a twenty-one-year-old daughter was her twenty-one-year-old friends. Every weekend some of them would be around at the house and every weekend

I kept my hands and knives to myself in fear of going back to jail.

Of course jail is in the past. Melissa saved me. We'll tell that story too at Abby's twenty-first. Maybe show some photos of her as a baby, the first time she rolled over, the first time she walked, the first time she killed a pet. After I was shot and saved and healed, the justice system realized I'd been punished enough, they came around to my way of thinking. I was set free. Counseling was part of the deal. I would see Benson Barlow twice a week for ten years and we actually became pretty good friends. Not good enough to socialize, but good enough to chat about the weather if I ran into him on the street.

People say your life flashes in front of your eyes when you're about to die. I can't really be sure why my life is flashing at me now, mostly it's the events of the last few days that are replaying themselves—the trip out to the woods with Kent and her team, the money I earned, the . . .

Last few days?

No. That's not right. It was those few days twenty years and change ago.

It's a warm morning and the sun is on my face and I'm lying in bed, and from somewhere I can hear Melissa's voice. I can smell bacon and eggs. I feel happy. I'm content. I'm the man I never thought I would be. There's a white picket fence outside and later today I'm going to mow the lawns, I'm going to make idle chitchat with the neighbor and help him shift his old fridge from his kitchen into his garage. I can hear Sally's voice too, and it's something I haven't heard in years.

Months.

But there it is now, she's in conversation with Melissa because Sally is coming tomorrow too. So is Carl Schroder. Schroder turned out to be a pretty good guy, in the end, probably because he ended up spending ten years in jail having the cop raped out of him.

And I feel sleepy and the voices fade a little. Dreams within dreams. My past flashing at me. I open my eyes into a world that is full of Sally. She is leaning over me. Are we sleeping together? I try to get back to the white picket fence where bacon is being cooked in the kitchen, but something is keeping me here, it's something so strong that I can even feel the pain in my shoulder that I felt back then. I can smell antiseptic. The air tastes stale. The bed doesn't feel like mine. I'm lying in a stranger's bed and bad things are happening and I just close my eyes and let it happen, just like I did with my auntie all those years ago. I open my eyes. Melissa is standing by the wall. Sally is hovering over me. The Sally. I close my eyes. It's time to wake up. It's time to be with my family.

I don't wake up.

Things come and go. One moment The Sally is over me, then there is nobody, then she is back. She's working on the bullet wound. It reminds me of another time, back twenty years ago.

No it wasn't.

Long in the past, memories that should be dead and buried.

"Where's Abby?" I ask.

"She's safe," Melissa says. "You'll get to see her soon. She misses you," she says, which I figure is such a mom thing to say even though my mom has never said it. It also means that the Melissa I knew a year ago isn't the same as the Melissa in front of me.

A year ago?

The Sally looks jealous—and I realize the crush she has on me hasn't faded, her love still burns strong and Melissa better not turn her back on her because nothing sums up crazy as much as a fat woman in love.

"It's her birthday," I say.

"What's wrong with him?" Melissa asks.

"She's twenty-one," I say.

"It's the medication," The Sally says. "It's messing with his mind, that's all. It's nothing to worry about."

"Do you remember our wedding?" I ask Melissa.

She smiles at me and it's a stupid question—of course she remembers it. Why wouldn't she? It was an amazing day, made more amazing by the fact that my mother got the dates confused and missed it.

"I love you," I tell her.

"You're going to be okay, Joe," she tells me.

I'm naked from the waist up. My clothes are in a bloody pile at the foot of the bed. It's no loss—it's just the cheap jail suit the warden will replace with one of his own, or with thirty bucks from the petty cash drawer. I'm becoming increasingly concerned about how real the dream is feeling. I try to focus on Abby, which kind of works and kind of doesn't, because when I try to think about her features, I can't find them. What color are her eyes? What shape is her nose? Her cheeks? Her hair? Then I try to remember Mom's new husband. I try to remember my sessions with Benson Barlow. I try to remember Walt's funeral, but maybe I didn't go. The neighbor with the fridge, what's his name? And what did Schroder do to get himself locked up?

It's a bad dream. That's all. Just like the bad dream I had following the removal of my testicle.

So I go with it. I stick with the dream and see where it leads. My biggest red flag, if I'm looking for one—which I'm not—is that out of all the people I could dream about, why would The Sally be one of them?

It wouldn't.

I would never dream about somebody like Sally.

The Sally.

Never.

And that, more than anything, tells me that this is real.

"You need to go to a hospital, Joe," The Sally says.

I look around the room. Sally's bedroom. This must be a dream come true for her. There's a poster on one wall of a vase of flowers, but no vase of flowers anywhere. Why not put up a picture of a window and keep the curtains closed? There's a mirror above a chest of drawers and poked into the side of the mirror are what must be family photographs. They take up a lot of real estate and I guess that's so there's less reflective space and less of a chance for Sally to keep seeing herself.

"It hurts," I tell her, which is perhaps the most honest thing I've ever told her.

"The bullet went right through," The Sally says. "You've got muscle and ligament damage. I've stopped the bleeding, and you're okay for now, and I've cleaned it, but it's going to get infected, and you're probably never going to be able to use your shoulder properly."

I shake my head at the thought of that, of my shoulder locking up and going into spasm right when I'm in the middle of cut-cut-cutting. "Fix it," I tell her.

"You need surgery. It's not going to heal by itself," she says.

"Then operate."

"I can't."

"Find somebody who can."

Melissa steps away from the window. She looks down at me and she looks concerned. "I think what Sally is saying," she says, "is that she's done all she can. Isn't that right?" she asks, looking over at The Sally.

The Sally nods. "You should still take him to a hospital. If you don't want it infected and if there's any chance of him using it a hundred percent again, then you have to take him."

Melissa nods. "It's funny," she says, "because you're talking and all I hear you saying is that we have no more use for you," she says, and she raises her hand and there's a gun in it and she points it at The Sally, and in the moment I realize that Melissa hasn't changed at all, that she's still the same woman I fell in love with, that I'm so lucky to have found her.

CHAPTER SEVENTY-TWO

The office has no dividing walls. Just four walls and a door, and a window that's currently being covered by a painter's drop cloth. Duct tape is holding it up. Schroder doesn't need to pull it aside to know what it overlooks, but he does anyway—him on the left, Hutton on the right—and they stare down into the back of the courthouse. At the edges of the cordons police officers are restraining the last few university students who are trying to push their way into the scene to get photographs of themselves drinking, probably to post online, but for the most part the students are still hanging back. They're down there hugging each other—there are a lot of tears, a lot of people sitting down with their knees pulled into their chests. The majority of people are walking away from the scene, just wanting to get home. Some have blood on their faces.

"An easy shot to make," Hutton says.

For a moment Schroder thinks Hutton is talking about the students and their cameras, but of course he isn't—he's talking about the shot the shooter made. Schroder looks back into the courthouse, he looks at the spot where his car was parked, and he knows the shooter must have been up here for some time, and that getting a parking space nearby means he was here before this morning's cordons were set up. That means when Schroder showed up his face was in the sights of the same gun that's lying behind him. He shudders at the thought, and then agrees with Hutton that yes, it would have been an easy shot to make. There are three casings on the floor, they'll be checked for prints—maybe they'll get lucky.

The gun that would have focused on Schroder as he stepped out of his car earlier is beyond them lying on the floor. There won't be any prints on it, because it's been covered in white paint from one of the tins that's laying on its side, surrounded by more white paint that's soaked into the concrete floor. The top of a paint tin is open, and there's a set of earmuffs in there, one edge of them sticking out. The rule of renovating, Schroder knows, is work your way down. Ceiling, walls, then carpets. This office still had some work to do. There's a guy leaning over the gun, a forensic tech whose name Schroder on normal days can never pronounce correctly, but after today's explosion he's completely forgotten. The gun will yield ballistic results, and they'll know if it's been used before, but it was likely taken from Derek Rivers, and Derek hasn't been in a real talkative mood since either Melissa or somebody else put two in his chest.

The forensic tech is taking a photograph of three shell casings.

"You said there was only the one shot," Schroder says.

"There was."

"There are three casings," Schroder says. "And if Joe was shot, and Jack was shot, then that's two shots."

"I can explain that," the tech says, and he stands up to face them. He's a guy in his late twenties with a hairline Schroder wishes he had, and though he can't remember what his name is he suddenly remembers that the guy is a pub-quiz master who spends two or three weeknights every week winning bar tabs.

"Okay, so we have three casings because there were three shots, but you only heard one, right?"

"Right," Hutton says. "Everybody only heard the one shot."

"Okay," the tech says, nodding. "The barrel is clogged."

"Clogged?" Schroder says.

"With a bullet. And if you all only heard one shot, then it's probably clogged with two bullets. Bullet one was fired, bullet two got jammed, and bullet three got lodged right behind it."

"That's still three gunshots," Hutton says. "Wouldn't we have heard that?"

"My guess is the bullets were modified. I'm guessing the gunpowder was removed. Bullets are made up of four main parts, right? The bullet itself, the casing, the gunpowder, and the primer. The primer ignites the gunpowder and—"

"And we know how bullets work," Schroder says.

"Okay, okay, well, if the gunpowder was removed, you've still got the primer that's going to ignite, right? It's going to go *bang*, but it's not going to go *boom*. You're going to hear it in the office here, but you're not going to hear it out in the street. So the shooter, he fires the first bullet, then the second and third don't sound or react the same. And those bullets are going to travel into the barrel but aren't going to come out. I need to get it back to the lab to run some tests, but for now that's my guess. Also, the magazine is empty, so whoever was up here only ever planned on firing three shots."

"What about Jack?" Schroder asks. "He was shot."

"But probably not by this. Could be the same gun that killed Derek Rivers and Tristan Walker. I'll know more later."

He goes about bagging up the gun and Hutton and Schroder go about thinking what all this means.

"If Raphael and Melissa were working together," Hutton says, "then she really screwed him. But if she was planning on blowing him up anyway, why sabotage two of the three bullets?"

"There were two water glasses," Schroder says.

"What?"

"Nothing," Schroder says, and he should have trusted his bad feeling about Raphael. When he was at his house showing him the photographs, was Melissa there too? Is that what happened? Did Raphael think she was somebody else? Somebody who wanted Joe dead as much as he did? Yes—yes, it's possible. It's possible she heard his conversation with Raphael, possible she suspected he recognized her from the photograph. "They found an arm," Hutton says. "An arm with two fingers attached and not a lot more, and those two fingers were badly burned. We've got people heading to his house now to get prints. If it was Raphael we'll know it soon."

Schroder is sure the prints will match. He looks back out the window at the city. At his city. He wonders if he put this in motion the day he arrested Joe. He guesses he did. All that destruction down there, and yet in other parts of the city life is going on as normal, people going about their day-to-day business, carrying briefcases and handbags, eating lunch on the go, bike messengers weaving in and out of traffic.

"Fuck," Schroder says.

Hutton says nothing.

"Let's go," Schroder says.

"Where to? Raphael's house?"

"The hospital."

"Good idea."

They head back downstairs. Unbelievably, Schroder feels like crying. He doesn't know why—he's seen bad shit before, has lost people he worked with, but this is just . . . just too much. Rebecca Kent . . .

"We'll find them," Hutton says.

"Just like we found Melissa," Schroder says.

Hutton doesn't answer him.

The sling is still helping, but Schroder's arm is really starting to hurt now. They walk to Hutton's car. Journalists throw questions at them. People are standing around with blank looks on their faces. Paramedics are still working on people, though there doesn't appear to be anybody seriously wounded lying on the street—they've been rushed to the hospital already. He doesn't see any bodies either. Was nobody killed? Or have they been moved already?

"It all seems unreal," Hutton says.

"I know."

"Honestly, Carl, doesn't this make you thankful you gave up the job?" Hutton asks, but Schroder didn't give it up, it was taken from him, though he gets the point.

"I . . . I don't know," he says. "I really don't."

They get into the car. Schroder uses the side mirror to get a look at himself. He's a mess. The bandage around his forehead is pushing his hair upward. There's blood on it, but there's dried blood on other bits of his face. On his neck too. It only takes them ten minutes to reach the hospital, Hutton putting the sirens on at intersections. There are no free spaces out front. They're full of cars, and other cars are all double-parked around them.

"Just drop me off here," Schroder says, nodding toward the side of the road opposite the hospital. "I'll be okay from here. You should try to do something useful."

"I'm coming in," Hutton says. "Rebecca is in there."

"And she'd want you to be out here finding Joe and Melissa."

Hutton nods. "Listen, Carl, I know what you promised her."

"And?"

"And I think that means I ought to stick with you for a bit. You go in ahead of me and get your arm looked at, I'll park around back and meet you inside."

Schroder gets out of the car. He cuts between traffic. Hutton can't be too worried about the promise he made, otherwise he wouldn't have left him so quickly. He gets across the road and steps through the main doors into a crowd of people who are in shock, many with cuts and broken bones, pain etched into so many people's features. From what he heard on the drive here most of the injuries have come from the rushing crowds, from people falling and being trampled. There's a queue of people lined up behind a window all waiting to talk to the admitting nurse. He doesn't want to wait in line. He steps back outside and moves further around the building and into the ambulance bay where an ambulance is pulling in. He steps out of the way as ER doctors move into position. The back of the ambulance opens and a gurney is brought out, a man dressed as the Grim Reaper who is missing part of his face. He's conscious, his fists balled up tight. Schroder follows them through the doors until a doctor holds a hand up in front of him.

"Wrong entrance," a doctor with the wrong choice in combovers says to him. He has bloodshot eyes and smells like coffee and has a badge on his chest that says *Dr. Ben Hearse*, and Schroder figures it's a bad omen for his patients, but still one step removed from Dr. You're Gonna Die.

"I'm a cop," he says. "Detective Inspector Carl Schroder. Listen, I need to get in there. My partner is in there. She was brought in a few minutes ago."

Dr. Hearse nods. "They're working on her."

"Is she going to make it?"

"They're working on her," he repeats, a little more sympathetically. "Let me take a look at your arm," he says, then Schroder winces as soon as it's touched. "Okay, follow me," he says.

"Can't you just give me a shot or something?"

"A shot?"

"For the pain. It hurts like a bitch."

"No, I can't just give you a shot, but what I can do is set your arm and put it in a cast."

"I just need a shot. We can do the cast thing later."

"Let's do the cast thing now," Hearse says.

Schroder follows him into the emergency department. The doctors who aren't helping people are rushing around getting ready to help those still on their way. They keep going until they're past all the operating rooms and into a doctor's office.

"Wait here," Hearse tells him. "We'll get you x-rayed and figure out what's going on."

"I want an update on Detective Kent," Schroder says, and he feels impatient, like he needs to be doing something to find Joe, but he doesn't know what.

The doctor gives a brief nod. "Wait here," he says again, "I'll see what I can do."

Schroder has only been alone for a minute when his cell phone rings. He reaches into his pocket. The display was broken in the blast so he can't tell who it is. He realizes he still hasn't phoned his wife yet. She'll have heard the news and be worried about him.

"Detective Schroder," he says, the title out of his mouth too quickly to avoid. Right in this moment he still feels like a cop.

"Carl, it's Hutton," Hutton says, either letting the detective comment go or not picking up on it. "Listen, I got something here."

"Where?"

"Meet me out back in the parking lot, and make it quick."

CHAPTER SEVENTY-THREE

The Sally gasps inward when she sees the gun.

"Joe," Melissa says, "I was keeping her alive for you to kill, kind of like a present."

"Like a housewarming present," I say, and I'm not real sure why I say it because as great a housewarming gift as it'd be, it's not like me and Melissa are moving in here. Unless we are. "Are we moving in here?" I ask.

"No," Melissa says.

The Sally has backed up against the wall. Her palms are facing outward and they're in line with her shoulders. She's wearing a wristwatch that's spun around upside down, so the face covers the underside of her wrist. I can see the time. I can also see an alarm clock on the bedside drawer, and the alarm clock is two minutes ahead of her wristwatch, and suddenly I know why everything seems so fucked-up—I'm two minutes in the future and it's messing with my equilibrium. Which means whatever The Sally's fate is, it's already happened and I'm just watching now to see how it unfolded.

"So how do you want to do it?" Melissa asks me, her question crossing the time barrier.

"I don't know," I answer.

"Please don't, please don't hurt me," The Sally says and, for all that she's done, I don't really see any need to.

Of course not seeing a need isn't the same as deciding to let her go.

"Just shoot her," I say, because I want to get out of this place with its fractured time zones and, gun to my head, I'd have to confess I don't really want to do it.

"Please, Joe," Sally says. "I don't want die. I've always been good to you. I know I never came to see you in jail, but how could I, after what you'd done?"

"I'm sorry, Sally," I say, and the truth is I am sorry.

"I brought you books," she says.

"What?" I say, and point my palm to Melissa in a stopping gesture in case she's about to pull the trigger.

"I didn't bring them to you, but I gave them to your mother to give you. Romance novels. I remembered how much you loved them. So I gave them to her. I've been good to you, Joe, even after all the bad things you've done. Please don't hurt me."

Melissa looks at me for guidance, and I realize this is all playing right out in front of me—there's no dream, no difference in time. The Sally gave my mother those books, not Melissa.

"That was *your* message?" I ask. "You were the one trying to help me escape?"

Melissa looks confused, which is exactly how The Sally looks too. "Escape?" Melissa asks, then she looks back at The Sally. "You were trying to help him escape?"

The Sally doesn't answer, so I answer for her. "There was a message in the books," I say. "She wanted me to show the cops where Detective Calhoun was buried, and she was going to help me escape, only my mom didn't give me the books in time and . . . and . . . and I thought they were from you. Why are you looking at me like that?" I ask Melissa.

"You were given medication," she says. "You're not thinking straight."

"I am!" I say, louder than I wanted to. I grit my teeth and inhale deeply, and I notice there is no pain in my shoulder. Whatever drugs they gave me I want to keep taking. "They were romance novels. She picked specific titles, but my mom messed it up."

"Your mother?" Melissa asks.

"Please," Sally says to Melissa, "all I've ever done is help Joe. I helped him last year when you crushed his testicle, I saved his life when he was arrested, and now . . ."

And now I'm no longer listening. I'm thinking of my trip into the woods. It was The Sally who was planning my escape. Me and The Sally, running through the forest and leaving behind a pile of dead cops, me and The Sally sitting in a tree, *K-I-L-L-I-N-G*, we're running toward our future, only a future with Sally is about as appealing as . . . well, as having my testicle crushed, as being locked away in jail, as being given the death penalty, as being a father.

"Joe," Melissa shouts, and I realize she's said my name a few times now. "You're still thinking about those books, I can tell. She wasn't trying to help you escape."

"I . . . I don't understand."

"Did you give him the books he's talking about?" Melissa asks.

Sally nods. "He likes romance novels," she says, looking at me and talking to Melissa as if I weren't in the room.

"There was a message," I say, and my words don't even convince me.

"Yeah? Then ask her what the message is," Melissa says.

"Please," Sally says, shaking her head, and she's looking at me and talking to me, and I remember the conversations we used to have at work, I remember her making me a sandwich every day, good ol' reliable Sally, kindhearted Sally, Simple Sally. The Sally. Sandwiches that wouldn't make me sick, Sally.

"We have no use for her," Melissa says.

"No, I don't suppose we do," I say.

"Joe," Sally says.

"Sssh," I say, and I put my finger to my lips. "It's going to be okay," I tell her.

"Joe," she says, her voice higher now. "Joe . . ."

"I kept her alive for you, Joe," Melissa says. "I kept her for you to kill."

Sally. Poor Sally. Overweight Sally. Always trying to help. Sally always plodding her way around the police station and ignored by everybody, the same way I used to plod and be ignored, only I'd be plodding with forty pounds less than her. I shake my head. It's time to show people that I'm a human being, and what better time to start than here and now.

"I'm not going to shoot her," I tell Melissa.

The Sally looks happy. Melissa looks sad.

"You do it," I tell Melissa. "But make it quick," I tell her. I don't want The Sally to suffer. That is my humanity.

CHAPTER SEVENTY-FOUR

This part of the hospital is a maze. Schroder has been in it before, visiting people. He's waited outside operating rooms as victims inside have died. He's been in here as friends have fought for their lives—some making it, some not.

Dr. Hearse sees him and comes over. He has the same disapproving look on his face his dentist has when he sees Schroder hasn't been regularly flossing. "I know you're impatient, but they're still working on her."

"I need the quickest way out into the back parking lot."

"The hell you do. You need medical attention."

"Just give me something for the pain."

"What the hell is it with cops? You want us to perform miracles when your life is on the line, but when it comes to injuries you just don't seem to care."

"It's one of life's ironies," he says. "Look, it's important. Please, can you give me something or not?"

"No. You need to come back and—"

"Later," Schroder says. "Look, at least show me the way to the parking lot."

The way consists of a few more turns and a pissed-off doctor who rolls his eyes whenever Schroder looks at him. Then they're in a corridor that's about twenty yards long with doors at each end and no windows. Hearse has to walk with him to use his security card to get the doors to open. They both step outside into the sun. There are sirens wailing in the not-too-far distance.

"I don't understand," Hearse says, looking out at the parking lot and seeing the same thing that Schroder is seeing—an ambulance surrounded by sedans and SUVs and a few motorbikes. Dirt and dust from nearby construction floats above all of it like a blanket. The weather hasn't changed any—the sun has climbed a little higher and made the shadows shorter, but that's about it. Hutton has parked ten yards from the ambulance. He's standing behind his car.

"That ambulance shouldn't be there," Dr. Hearse says. "What is—" he starts, then stops when he notices Hutton is holding a gun.

"Stay here," Schroder says to the doctor, then skirts around the cars and, staying low, makes his way over to Hutton. "What's the situation?"

"Not sure. But it has to be the one, right? I've called it in. AOS is ten minutes away."

Schroder doesn't think they need to wait. The Armed Offenders Squad is going to arrive only to find an empty ambulance. Still, they need to be cautious. "We can't wait that long."

"I know," Hutton says. "That's why I called you. I'm going to go in."

Schroder nods. "And if somebody comes out? What do you want me to do? Shoot them with my fingers?"

"Why don't you use Kent's gun? I saw you take it."

Schroder nods. Fair point.

They approach the ambulance. It's clear there's nobody in the front. Hutton stands at the back and gives Schroder the go signal, then Schroder rests Kent's gun in his sling, uses his good arm to pull the door open, and at the same time he jumps back and grabs Kent's gun. Hutton points his gun inside and a moment later lowers it. Schroder puts Kent's back into his pocket then calls out to Dr. Hearse, who comes running over. He looks inside the ambulance.

"Jesus," he says. "That's Trish. And where . . . Oh, shit, Jimmy," he says, looking at the second body, then climbing in.

The back of the ambulance is a mess. There are supplies littered over the floor. Blood. A nurse's outfit. The man has been stripped down to his underwear. Hearse checks Trish for a pulse, then quickly turns toward Schroder.

"She's alive," he says. "Get some people out here," he says, and pulls off his security tag and hands it to Hutton. "Quickly," he adds, and Hutton runs toward the doors.

Schroder looks at the clothes. Melissa showed up in nurse scrubs, then changed into the clothes the naked victim was wearing. Hearse checks for a pulse on the second victim, then puts the side of his face against the man's chest, then checks for a pulse again. "It's weak," he says. "What the hell happened here?"

"This was used in the escape," Schroder says. Dressed in the nurse scrubs, Melissa would have found it easy to be given a ride. Then she probably pulled a gun on them. She could have ordered the scrubs from any work-uniform shop online. Or she got them from a nurse. If she got them from a nurse, then she might have gotten ID cards to open the doors to the hospital too.

"Help me with the gurney," Hearse says, and between them they get it onto the ground, Schroder using his only good arm. Then they get the woman loaded onto it. There is blood around her face and her hair is matted in it. Blunt force trauma to the head. Schroder has seen enough of it to diagnose the condition and knows if she survives there can be some serious ongoing problems. The second paramedic has no signs of violence at all. He looks like he's just fallen asleep. Hearse starts pushing the woman toward the door they came out of. He's almost there when it's thrown open and four doctors come running into the parking lot. Two of them take the gurney with Trish, and the other two come back to the ambulance with Hearse and another gurney. The second victim is loaded onto it, then for a moment it's just Hearse and Schroder.

"You're looking for the person who did this, aren't you," Hearse says.

"Yes."

Hearse nods. "I can't do this for you, but you see that plastic drawer up there?" he asks, nodding toward a whole stack of small drawers along the inside of the ambulance. "The one with the green handle?"

"I see it."

"You'll find something for your arm in there. It'll give you a few hours. You won't feel much, but you won't feel any pain either."

He chases after his colleagues and Schroder climbs into the ambulance and opens the drawer with the green handle. There are half a dozen syringes in there—all identical, and all loaded with some type of clear fluid. He uses his teeth to pull off the protective lid, then plunges the needle into his arm. He doesn't know what's inside it, but by the time he puts the cap back on the needle and tosses the empty syringe onto the floor, the pain starts to fade. He takes a second syringe and drops it into his pocket. He figures what the hell, and takes a third too. He steps out of the back just as Hutton arrives.

"I've canceled the call to AOS," he says, "but forensics are on their way."

"Look at that," Schroder says, pointing to a blood patch on the wall.

"It's not from the paramedic," Hutton says. "Doesn't fit in with the other blood patterns."

"It's from Joe. He sat down here and leaned against the wall. There are plenty of blood drops leaving the ambulance, and here too," he says, pointing at the ground. "Melissa switched vehicles."

"She probably had one here ready rather than stealing one," Hutton says.

"Exactly. Quicker and easier," Schroder says. He looks up around the parking lot. "No cameras," he says.

Hutton shakes his head. "That's where you're wrong," he says. "It's part of the upgrade. Cameras are getting installed in all the entranceways, and soon in the parking lot too."

"Soon doesn't help us."

"No, it doesn't, but the camera at the entrance there might," Hutton says, and points toward the public entrance. "It's designed to see people coming and going, but it does point toward the parking lot. Maybe if we're lucky . . ."

Lucky. He wonders how that word is defined. Joe was lucky because he escaped. Schroder was lucky he got out of the car before it exploded. So that means there has to be a balance. For each piece of good luck there has to be bad luck. That's the thing about Christchurch. Good luck for Joe and Melissa, bad luck for Rebecca and Jack and for Raphael too.

"Let's check it out."

"Listen, Carl—" Hutton starts.

"Hey, look, this is a hospital, and this is a broken arm," he says, "which means I'm going back in there anyway. You're going in there too—no reason we can't both go the same way."

"Carl—"

"You've let me come this far, Wilson. No reason to stop now. All I'm asking is to look at the security footage. That's all. Even that may lead to nothing. Then I'll get my arm fixed, and then I'll come into the station and maybe I can help."

A patrol car pulls into the parking lot. It comes to a stop next to them. Hutton goes over and talks to them about securing the ambulance, then the two of them head back into the hospital, circling their way around to the front and going into the main entrance. Hutton shows his badge to a woman behind a reception counter and tells her they need to talk to somebody about the security cameras. The woman looks excited. She's putting two and two together and coming up with an answer that suggests all the commotion on the other side of the hospital is linked to something these two cops are looking for. She nods, tells them it'll be just a minute, then makes a phone call. They say nothing to each other as they watch her, as if their focus can make her speed things along. It works because it takes only half the predicted time. She tells them somebody is on their way.

That somebody is Bevan Middleton—no relation to Joe Middleton—so he tells them as he shakes Hutton's hand and then stares at Schroder's broken arm. As he leads them to the security office he tells them he wanted to apply for the police force, but because he's color-blind he wasn't allowed. "I thought it was all about the thin blue line," he tells them. "I thought police work was going to be about shades of gray, but it's the reds and greens that fucked me."

The security office is on the ground floor not far from the toilets, so the room smells of urinal cakes and disinfectant. There's a bank of monitors on one wall, several different viewpoints across the hospital. There are a few computers on various counters, and one on the desk ahead of them, along with a flat-screen monitor that is almost as big as Schroder's TV. Half the stuff in here is brand new, some ten years old, except for the decor, which is twenty years out of date. Schroder's arm is good now. The shot he took has his arm humming along quite nicely, thank you very much. It has his mind humming nicely too.

"It's all getting upgraded," Bevan says. "So it's the rear parking lot you want, huh?"

"Exactly," Hutton says.

The guard starts playing around with a computer keyboard. A moment later the rear entrance shows up on the big monitor ahead of them. Its focus is on the five yards leading up to the doorway. Everybody leans forward a little, straining to see what's in the not-so-sharp distance.

"That's the ambulance," Schroder says.

"Only just," Hutton says.

"But it's enough," Schroder says.

"Can we enhance the image?" Hutton asks.

The guard shakes his head. "Not really."

Schroder knew he was going to say that. On *The Cleaner* they would have enhanced the image and cleaned it up and it would have been perfect. They would have enhanced a reflection off a nearby windshield to have gotten a perfect look from a different angle, to have a cell phone number scrawled across the back of somebody's hand. He wonders what Sherlock Holmes would have made of TV technology.

"Not even a little?" Hutton asks.

"It is what it is," the guard says, and he enlarges the image and the quality drops off. They can see the ambulance and the two policemen guarding it, but no detail.

"Okay. Wind it back," Schroder says. "Let's see when it arrives."

The guard starts winding it back. Other cars come and go. The shadows get fractionally longer. The day looks as though it gets colder. People are walking around backward. Twenty-five minutes earlier a car drives backward and parks near the ambulance, two people get out and walk backward and climb into the ambulance and then the ambulance backs away. The guard lets the footage play forward at normal speed without the need for anybody to tell him. The ambulance comes in. Blurry Melissa helps Fuzzy Joe out of the back. The sight of them both—even though the detail is poor—makes his skin crawl. They get into the dark blue van. They drive away. Then nothing, just a parked ambulance and other cars and life carrying on as normal. They can't get a plate from the van.

"None of it helps," Hutton says, "but we'll put a call out. A dark blue van—hard to tell what make. I mean, it could be nothing, they may have changed cars again, but I'll still put out the call. We might get lucky."

Lucky. There's that word again.

"Start going back," Schroder tells the guard. "I want to see when that van first arrived."

The guard nods enthusiastically as if it's the best idea in the world. He starts running the footage backward. He jumps it in five-minute intervals. An hour before the ambulance showed up the van is suddenly there. The guard jumps forward five minutes again, then starts winding it back second by second until they see Melissa walking backward and then climbing into it. He presses play.

"Where is she going?" Schroder asks.

"Hard to tell. She could be getting ready to circle around the entire building, and there are some more parking spaces out back for staff, but it could also be she's heading toward the staff entrance."

"You got a camera over that door?" Hutton asks.

"Sure we have, it's been there about two years."

"Line it up with this footage," Schroder says, tapping the monitor.

The guard plays around with the controls and gets the footage in sync with the other camera. It's the same entrance Schroder and the doctor came out earlier. They watch Melissa enter the corridor. It's a different camera and she's much closer so the quality is much better. The guard keeps switching cameras and they follow her through the emergency department and around to the ambulance bay. Schroder can't believe the confidence she has, how casually she behaves as though she is meant to be there. She pauses for a few minutes and does something with her phone, though Schroder thinks she may just be pausing for time and watching her environment. Then she chats to the two paramedics he saw unconscious earlier and climbs into the back of their ambulance.

Schroder can feel a pulse throbbing in his forehead. He can feel adrenaline starting to pump. He feels that if he had to, he could lift a car and flip it over, even with his broken arm.

"Whose swipe card is she using?" Schroder asks, pointing at the monitor, and the moment he asks the question, he knows—he knows for sure what the answer is going to be. He should have figured it out when he was in the parking lot.

"That's a really good question," the guard says, because the guard doesn't know Sally, the guard doesn't know she worked with Joe, was one of the reasons he was caught, that she returned to studying nursing last year and now her training is at the hospital. The guard's fingers fly across the keyboard for a few seconds. A moment later a photograph and an ID come up on the monitor, and Schroder looks at the picture of Sally, and Hutton looks at the picture of Sally, and then Schroder and Hutton look at each other.

"Shit," Hutton says.

"I know," Schroder says.

"Let's go," Hutton says, and the two men race out the door and back into the parking lot.

CHAPTER SEVENTY-FIVE

Joe stays mostly quiet as she gets him dressed into a new shirt. She had forgotten how his skin smelled. Forgotten how he felt. The last year without him was tough. Not the first few months. Back then she was annoyed he'd been arrested, but life goes on. Then she found out she was pregnant. Then a whole bunch of hormones flooded her body. Things would make her cry, random things, but mostly stories in the newspapers that involved animals or children. Bad stories. And there were always bad stories. She developed a craving for weird food. She would eat raw potatoes. Couldn't get enough of them. And chocolate. For a month there she was sure she was single-handedly keeping the chocolate labor force of New Zealand in work. Then those cravings left and new ones came—suddenly it was all about fruit, all about chicken and Thai food, and through it all her feelings for Joe intensified. Three months into her pregnancy she started figuring out how to help him escape. She wanted her baby to have a father—and most of all she wanted her baby. She's always wanted one.

"Where are we going to go?" he finally asks.

Melissa is also getting changed. She brought clothes with her last night for this. And a new wig. She's going shoulder-length light brown. "We're heading home," she says. "We lay low for a bit. The police look for people who run. They're easy to find. But we hide out and—"

"Do we really have a daughter?" he asks, "Or did I just imagine that?"

They are still in Sally's house. She hates it here. She can't imagine this being much better than where Joe spent his last twelve months, and she has a good imagination. The rooms feel damp. It doesn't get a lot of sun. And she's pissed off at Sally for not having kept the refrigerator nicely stocked. She's hungry and there's nothing here to eat.

"Yes," she says. "She's beautiful. She has your eyes." She knew it was going to be a shock for Joe. She knew he would need time to adjust to it. Hell, she had nine months to get her head around it and even then it didn't feel real until she was lying on Sally's bed with a baby turning her vagina into something that resembled a gutted rabbit. So she knows he needs to come around a bit—she was just hoping he'd be a little happier along the way. "Her name is—"

"Abigail," Joe finishes, adjusting the hat a little that she gave him so nobody will be able to clearly see his face once they leave.

"Did you mean before what you said that you'd rather go back to jail?"

"No. Of course not," he says. "Where are we hiding out?"

"My place," she says.

"You still live in the same place?"

"No," she says. "I moved."

"Before you started killing other people?" he asks.

"Something like that. Are you sure you don't really mean what you said earlier about going back to jail?"

"Of course I'm sure. Did you have sex with those men you killed?" he asks.

"Of course not," she says. And it's true. But she's not annoyed that he asked.

"Are you sure?"

"Of course I'm sure. Did you fuck anybody in jail?"

"No. Of course not."

"Did somebody fuck you?"

"It wasn't like that. I wasn't in general population, otherwise that would have happened. There's been nobody since you," he tells her.

She believes him. A guy like Joe—she imagines he'd rather kill himself than become somebody's pet. "How's the shoulder?"

"It hurts," he says. "A lot. But I'll make it."

She helps him to his feet. They make their way out of the bedroom.

"We have to go and see my mother," Joe says.

She throws him a *Why the hell would we do that* glance, then follows it up. "Why would we go and do that?"

So he tells her why and she keeps him propped up by the door and listens to him as he talks. At first she thinks he's still delusional from the medication. It's quite the story. Fifty thousand dollars. Detective Calhoun. Jonas Jones the asshole psychic she's seen on TV. A trip into the woods. Joe's confidence in what he is saying becomes infectious. Then she remembers the files she saw in Schroder's car from the TV station. It all makes sense. And fifty thousand dollars is a lot of money. She's done well with the forty she got from Sally three months ago, and another fifty would certainly help get their new lives under way.

They should just head back to her house. Relieve the babysitter. And stay inside for the next few months. Grow Joe's hair out. Dye it. Get him to put on some weight. Get him to look about as different as she can with what she has to work with. Get him to bond with Abigail. Then work at getting some false identities and leave the country. Difficult, yes, but not impossible. Just wait for the manhunt to die down.

"So the money was transferred into your mother's account," Melissa says.

"Yes."

"That means your mother will have to go into a bank and draw it out. We can't risk her saying the wrong thing. Too problematic."

Joe shakes his head. "You don't know my mother," he says. "She doesn't trust banks. She has a bank account purely because you can't really get by without one, but she hates them, hates them so much she goes in there every Monday morning and draws out her benefit in cash and takes it home and hides it under her mattress. She has done for years."

"You think she'll have gone there this morning and drawn out the fifty thousand dollars?" she asks, and she tries to imagine it, and for some reason she pictures an old lady with a sack slung over her back with big dollar signs on it. But of course that's not the reality. Fifty thousand dollars in one hundred dollar bills is five hundred of them. That amount would fit into a handbag.

"Without a doubt," Joe says. "It'll be at her house under her bed just waiting for us to go and get it."

"And you're sure."

"Yes," he says.

Fifty thousand dollars—is it worth the risk?

She decides that it is.

CHAPTER SEVENTY-SIX

Schroder and Hutton are leading the chase. He knows they are because when Hutton calls in the new information he's told backup is ten minutes away. While Hutton is on the phone organizing that, Schroder is once again searching his pockets for his Wake-E pills. Nope. Definitely gone. He has a headache coming on.

"A team has just reached Raphael's house," Hutton says.

"And?"

"And the results are interesting. Nothing there to suggest he was working with Melissa. But plenty to suggest Raphael wasn't exactly a Good Samaritan."

"Yeah? What'd he do?"

"Joe's lawyers," Hutton says. "It looks like Raphael's the guy who killed them."

"Shit," Schroder says.

"We've sent people to Joe's mother's house, hoping he'll turn up there, or hoping she may offer something, but there's no sign of her."

They both revert to their own thoughts. Schroder starts thinking back to the last time he saw Sally. When was that? It was last year, not long after Joe was arrested. Within days of being given the reward money she quit her job. She went back to studying. She never stayed in touch with anybody from work, and why would she? The night they figured out who Joe was, they treated her like hell. They arrested her and put her in an interrogation room because they'd found her prints on a piece of evidence. She ended up being the reason they caught Joe. Not police work, not detective skills, but pure luck because Sally had picked up something she shouldn't have.

"You should give me Kent's gun," Hutton says.

"You're probably right."

"I know I'm right. Come on, Carl. We're almost there. If you end up shooting somebody we'll probably both go to jail."

"They're armed," Schroder says. "It's only fair that I'm armed too."

"You think she's still alive?" Hutton asks. "Sally?"

"No."

"Nothing I can say to get that gun back from you?"

"Nothing."

"Just don't fuck up. Promise me that, okay?"

"You have my word."

"And don't tell anybody I knew you had it."

Town races by. The neighborhoods race by. Schroder doesn't take any of it in. Six minutes later they're pulling into her street. They watch the numbers on the letterboxes, but then stop watching when they see the blue van up a driveway six houses ahead, exactly where the numbers were going to line up. The houses are all pretty small and look like they've spent thirty years being blasted by bad weather and no love. Hutton does a U-turn and drives back to the start of the block. He takes out his cell phone and reports in. Backup is still four minutes away. He tells Schroder this when he hangs up.

"A lot can happen in four minutes," Schroder says.

"And a lot can happen for the worse if we go in there."

"We opened the ambulance before, right?" Schroder asks. This isn't any different from that."

"It's a lot different," Hutton says, and Schroder knows it. "We knew that thing was going to be empty. Whereas this time we know they're in there. If only we had Jonas Jones along with us. He'd be able to tell us what's going on inside."

"Funny. Look, they wouldn't have come here if Sally was dead," Schroder says. "They've come here for her help. Most likely for her medical skills. I say we go in. We have to. We owe it to Sally."

"We owe it to Sally to give her the best chance we can, and her best chance is if we wait for backup, and nobody from backup is going to have a busted arm. Three minutes, that's all," Hutton says, and Schroder knows he's right, and in Hutton's position he'd be making the same decision. So then why does the right thing to do feel so very, very wrong?

He opens the car door and steps outside.

"Jesus, Carl," Hutton says, and he does the same. Schroder starts walking. "Have you forgotten you're not even a cop anymore?"

"We have to do something, Wilson."

"Don't make me arrest you."

"And what? Cause a scene?"

"You're going to get me fired."

"And you're thinking of your job over saving Sally's life."

"That's a really shitty thing to say, Carl," Hutton says.

"I know. You're right, and I'm sorry. But we can't just stand by and wait."

"Two minutes," Hutton says. "Just two minutes now."

"Then that's less time for us to fuck up."

Schroder keeps walking to the house. He can do this. He can save Sally and Hutton can arrest Joe and Melissa. It's what they're trained for. Only it's not. They're trained to investigate. And they're trained to stand back and send in the AOS team in these situations. Melissa is armed. She's already killed one policeman today. No reason to make it easy for her to kill a second. He stops walking.

"Okay," he says.

So they wait twenty more seconds and then Schroder decides twenty seconds is long enough. The thing is, a lot can happen in two minutes. People can die. Joe and Melissa can hear the police arrive and cut their losses and kill whoever they have in there with them. So he takes a few steps toward the house. There's a throbbing in his head, a pound-pound-pounding, and he realizes it's the sound of his footsteps on the pavement as he runs toward the house.

"Goddamn it," Hutton says, but Hutton is overweight and hasn't seen the inside of a gym in years, and all that extra eating holds him back. Even with a broken arm Schroder outruns him.

He reaches the house. The van has been reversed into the driveway and it's easy to see the front is empty. Kent's gun is back in his hand. The back doors of the van are open and he comes around the side of it and peers in and it's empty too, except for some blood on the wall. Hutton is only a house away now, but he's stopped running. Not because of the strain on his body, but because to catch Schroder now would be to create a confrontation. Still there are no sounds of sirens in the distance. Either they're late, caught in traffic, or are running silent.

The house is a single-story dwelling with weatherboard walls and a concrete tile roof. The garden is tidy and looked after but uninspiring. There's a headless garden gnome by the step to the front door. The front door is closed. Schroder peers through the window and can see into the lounge. There's nobody in there. He ducks down and listens for any sound, but there's nothing. He moves to the side of the house and looks through another window into the same room and gets the same view, but from a different angle. Next window looks into the kitchen. Small but tidy. He tries the back door. It rattles, but it's locked. He puts the side of his face against it and listens. Nothing. No movement inside. No sirens approaching from the street. No sign of Hutton. Further around the house and now he's looking into the bedroom window. There's a body on the floor. It's Sally. She's face down. He can't tell whether she's dead or alive, but knows what he'd put his money on. The bed has blood on it. There are medical supplies scattered around the room. Some bloody clothes. A paramedic uniform. Joe and Melissa are gone, probably in Sally's car.

He moves to the front door. He tries it. It's unlocked. He pushes it open and moves into the bedroom, the gun pointing ahead. He crouches down next to Sally and has to put the gun on the floor so he can put two fingers on her neck. He looks for a pulse and finds one, steady and strong. He rolls her onto her back. There's a big bruise on the side of her forehead and some blood.

"Sally," he says, shaking her a little with his good arm. He wonders why they let her live. He wonders how Melissa and Joe go about putting a value on human life. "Sally?"

Sally doesn't stir. So he slaps her slightly on the side of the face, and then a little harder. "Come on, Sally, it's important."

Sally doesn't seem to think so. He moves into the kitchen. He finds a bucket beneath the sink. He fills it up with cold water. He thinks about the gun and knows what's going to happen within the next few minutes. He takes it out and wraps it in a tea towel and sets it on the counter near the sink. He carries the water back into the bedroom. His arm is starting to wake up.

"I'm sorry," he tells her, and then he pours it over her face. She wakes up a quarter of the way into it, starts sputtering, and by the end she's rolled onto her side and is coughing.

"Sally," he says, and he crouches down next to her.

"Detective Inspector Schroder?" she says.

"You're safe now," he tells her.

"Where are they?" she asks. "Have you arrested them?"

"No," he says. "Please, Sally, tell me what happened. Did they say where they are going? Do you still have your car? Did they take it?"

"The woman, Melissa, she came here last night," she says. "She threatened to shoot me. She tied me up and used my uniform and took my ID card. Then she left this morning and came back with Joe. He'd been shot. They made me help him. I thought . . . I thought they were going to shoot me."

"You're safe now," he tells her again. "What did they say? Do you know where they're going?"

She shakes her head, then quickly puts one hand on the side of it and closes her eyes, the movement enough to bring her close to passing out. He helps her up so she can sit on the bed. Okay, his arm is really starting to hurt now. He pulls out the second of his three syringes.

"What are you doing?" Sally asks.

"Don't worry, it's not for you," he says, and plunges the needle into his arm.

"You shouldn't be doing that," she says.

"Tell me what happened here," he says, and puts the cap on the syringe and dumps it on the floor. The numbness in his arm begins to return.

"They had a baby," Sally says.

"What?"

"Not with them," she says. "But . . . but Melissa made me help."

"Wait. She had the baby last night?"

Sally shakes her head. "Three months ago. She came here and—"

"And you didn't tell us?"

"I couldn't," Sally says, looking down.

"Why the hell not?"

She starts to cry. And she tells him why. He should be more sympathetic than he is, but all he can feel is the anger and frustration. People have died. Cops have died. She should have come to them. They could have done something with that information. They could have caught Melissa and the baby would have been safe.

"Tell me about today," he says. "How bad was the wound?"

"He was shot in the shoulder. The bullet went right through."

"And you're sure neither of them said anything that might help?"

"Nothing."

Before he can say anything more half a dozen men storm into the room, all of them dressed in black, one of them shouting at him to *Get down, get down*. A knee is put in the middle of his back and his face pressed into the floor, and then he screams into the carpet as his broken arm is pulled out of the sling and behind him, the numbness leaving in an instant as the handcuffs go on.

CHAPTER SEVENTY-SEVEN

It's been over a year since I drove out to my mother's house, but the same feelings I had back then I'm having again now. The dread. The shivers. The only good thing about being in jail was not having to come out here for meat loaf every week.

We're about five minutes away when Melissa slows down and pulls over. The pain in my shoulder is dull, it feels like a warm ball bearing has been sewn into it. Melissa's pulling over because the building tension is reaching its peak. If we don't get each other's clothes off within the next few seconds we're going to explode. Only there's a problem—if we get each other's clothes off in the car people are apt to see. Some even apt enough to go about calling the police.

"The police will be visiting your mother," Melissa says, turning toward me.

"Huh?"

"They'll be waiting for us there."

I'm not following her train of thought. Hopefully our relationship isn't going to be based on her not making sense and me trying to figure her out. "Why? They'll know I was shot. My mother would be the last place they'd think I'd go."

"I'm not so sure. I think it'll be one of the first places, not because the police think you'll go there, but because they have to start sending people somewhere rather than nowhere. They have more manpower than they do ideas, so they can afford to send them all on wild-goose chases. They'll send people there just for the act of something to do."

I shake my head. "Normally I'd agree, but today is different. Mom isn't home. That's what makes breaking in there and getting the money so much easier for us."

"Where is she?"

"She's getting married today."

"Do the police know that?"

"No," I say. "Shit, but of course the police don't know that, so they have no reason not to go to her house. Maybe they've been already and found out she wasn't home."

Melissa shakes her head. "Or maybe they've been and left people there. We can't go there, Joe. We can't take the risk."

She's right. I know she's right. But fifty thousand dollars is too much money to just not think about. There has to be another way.

"Plus we don't even know that she drew the money out," she adds.

"She will have," I say. Over the years I've dipped into my mom's savings hidden under her bed. If I had done that when I was a teenager instead of going to my aunt's house, I wonder how different life would have turned out. Only I didn't know it back then.

"We should just head back home."

"Home," I say, thinking about what home is now. It's not jail. It's not my mother's. It's not my apartment. It's Melissa's house. Home is with her and a baby.

"Unless you've got somewhere better to be?" she asks, and she says it in an accusing way that makes me think of my mother.

"Of course not," I tell her, and then because I think she needs to hear it, I say, "I love you."

She smiles. "I would hope so," she says. "After what I've gone through to get you here."

She turns the car around. We start heading back the way we came. I divide my time between staring out the window, and staring at her. She looks different from that weekend we spent together. Part of it is the wig. She looks puffier in the face and neck and her eyes are a different color too, meaning she's either wearing contacts or she was wearing contacts when I met her last year.

"What?" she asks, looking at me.

"Just remembering how beautiful you are," I tell her.

She smiles. "You know what I'm thinking about?"

I nod. I know. But like I thought earlier people are apt to start making phone calls.

"I'm thinking about that money," she says. "There has to be a way to get to it."

"You're right, though. We can't risk going to my mother's. Not now anyway."

"You're sure the police don't know about your mother's wedding plans?"

I think about it. My mother wanted me to be at the wedding. She wanted me to get the warden to let me out for the day. Will she have followed that up? Will she have gone to the police to try and talk them into releasing me just for that?

"If there's a wedding," she says, "often there's a honeymoon. If the police know she's gone away, they'll stop watching the house, which means . . . Joe, hey, are you okay?"

I'm not okay. I'm thinking about the honeymoon. I had forgotten about that. I don't know where they'll be going. Somewhere awful. I'm thinking about the fifty thousand dollars my mother will have drawn out in cash.

"Joe?"

I'm thinking that money may not be at the house at all, but with her, that their honeymoon starts right after the wedding and the trip will consist of her and Walt and all that cash. She doesn't think I'm ever getting out of jail. She doesn't see any reason not to spend it.

"Joe? What's wrong?"

"We need to go to the wedding. We need to find my mother now."

"Why?"

Because I know my mother. I tell Melissa this and she keeps on driving, her hands tightening on the wheel.

"We should just let it go," she says.

"It's not in my nature to let things go," I tell her.

"It's not in mine either. Do you know where the wedding is?"

"I can't . . . Oh, wait," I say, and I lean sideways and reach into my pants and find the invitation I'd folded in half this morning, the invitation I was hoping would bring me some luck. It seems it's done just that. I hand it to her. She glances at it then back at the road.

"We should let it go," she says. "We can see her in a few months and if there's anything left—"

"I went through a lot to earn that money," I tell her.

"And I went through a lot to get us to this point."

"The police have no reason to go there," I say.

She seems to agree, because we stop talking about it and we start driving in the direction of my mother's big day.

CHAPTER SEVENTY-EIGHT

Schroder is sitting down at the kitchen table. There's nobody else in the room. His hands are still cuffed behind him and he's doing his best to stay as still as possible because any movement brings him close to passing out. His mind is still buzzing. The sling is still hanging from his neck. The third syringe he took from the ambulance is sitting on the table in front of him, and the second shot he took earlier isn't helping in this position. A minute ago Hutton came in to check on him, and then to abuse him too—by the end of the day there was a good chance Hutton would be losing his job. Or at the very least he would be suspended. Perhaps demoted. It was a world of possibility.

"Where's the gun?" Hutton asks, keeping his voice low.

"I lost it."

"They patted you down. Where'd you hide it?"

"I can't remember," Schroder says, and he knows Hutton can't mention it to anybody else. Not only is Hutton in a world of trouble for letting Schroder come here, but if they found out he came here armed, then getting suspended or fired would be the least of his problems.

"Goddamn it, Carl, you promised me."

"Nobody knows I have it," he says, "and I promise I'll never say you knew I had it."

"You don't make great promises," Hutton says.

"I intend to keep the one I made Kent."

Hutton walks out. Superintendent Dominic Stevens walks in. Stevens is the man who covered Schroder's crime four weeks ago. He's the man that fired him.

"What the fuck is wrong with you?" Stevens asks. "Don't you see what you've become? What you're becoming? I could have you arrested for this. You could have cost people their lives."

"Kent—"

"I don't give a fuck about any of your excuses," Stevens says, "or your reasons. You're more trouble than you're worth. You used to be a great cop, and now . . . now I don't know." He sighs, then leans against the kitchen counter. He takes a few seconds to calm down. "Listen, Carl, I know how much you're hurting these days, and I know you're probably blaming yourself for some of what's happened, but you can't be here. You just can't. And the man I used to know would have known that."

Schroder doesn't have an answer.

"Do I need to carry on?"

"No," Schroder says.

"I'm tempted to leave you in cuffs for the next twenty-four hours. What's wrong with your arm? Is it broken?"

"From the explosion."

"You're lucky to be alive," he says.

"And Kent?" Schroder asks.

"They're still working on her," he says, "but we've been told she'll pull through."

Schroder feels his body flood with relief. It's a warm sensation. "Thank God."

"So here's what's going to happen. There's an ambulance

outside treating Sally. She's going to stay to help us, but you're going to climb into the back and they're going to take you to the hospital."

"I can still help," Schroder says.

"Go home, Carl."

"I know Joe better than anybody here."

"If you knew him that well he'd still be in custody."

"Let me help. I don't have to be on the team chasing him, but let me help figure out where he's going to go. Sally said they had a baby. We can start—"

"Listen, Carl, this is me staying calm, okay? This is me acknowledging it's been a tough day for you. But I swear to God if the next word out of your mouth isn't *good-bye* as you leave for the hospital then I will have you arrested."

"But—"

Stevens winces as if he's just been hurt. "That wasn't a good-bye," he says.

"Please—"

"Don't test me on this, Carl. Like I said, this is me calm. In about five seconds I won't be."

"Joe will—"

"Fucking hell, you don't get it, do you? Okay, we'll do it your way." He calls out into the hall for two men to come in. "Take him down to the station," he says. "Sit him in an interrogation room and leave him there until—"

"Good-bye," Schroder says.

Stevens stops talking. He looks at Schroder. His face is expressionless. He's working away at a decision and Schroder stays still and silent as the superintendent makes it. He looks down for a few seconds. Then he looks back up. Stevens nods.

"Belay that," he says to the two men, and tells them to go back into the hall. "Not one more word," he says, then crouches behind Schroder and undoes the cuffs. Now it's Schroder's turn to wince as he brings his broken arm back in front of his body. He says nothing. He nods at Stevens, who nods back.

Schroder knows he needs to take the risk. He can't imagine Stevens arresting him for his next request. But you never know.

"Can I have the syringe back?"

"No."

"Can I at least get a glass of water?"

"Make it quick."

He moves to the sink. Pours a glass of water and gulps it down. He keeps his back to Stevens the entire time. He grabs the tea towel with the gun inside and makes a show of drying off his hand, his back still to Stevens. He slips the gun into the sling and tucks it between his arm and chest. If Stevens sees it he knows he'll go straight into a holding cell. But Stevens doesn't see it. Then he makes his way down the hall and outside. Sally is being treated by a couple of paramedics. Hutton is talking to another detective. He throws Schroder an angry glance. Schroder gives him an apologetic smile, which doesn't work.

The paramedic looking Sally over finishes up with her, and she's escorted back into the house. "Let's take a look at the arm," the paramedic says. Schroder gives him a look. "Okay, climb in back and we'll get you sorted."

So Schroder climbs into the back. The ambulance doors are shut. He stares out the window at Sally's house. But he's not seeing the house. Instead he's seeing Joe and Melissa and he's thinking about what Sally said, about the reward money, and that makes him think of the fifty thousand dollars Joe earned from Jonas Jones.

The ambulance doesn't start. The paramedic is outside chatting to somebody.

Schroder reaches into his pocket. He finds the business card for Kevin Wellington. He drags out his cell phone and dials the number.

Wellington answers.

"It's Carl Schroder," he says. "I need your help."

"I've seen the news," Wellington says. "So whatever you're going to ask is covered by client-lawyer confidentially," he says.

"Goddamn—"

"Hear me out," he says. "Middleton is on the run and I didn't become a lawyer to help bad people, I became one to stop bad things from happening. So I'll answer anything you have to ask and in return you don't tell anybody where you got your information from. I think that's a pretty amazing deal under the circumstances. Agree?"

"Completely," Schroder says. "Do you know where he might go? Anything like that?"

"No."

"The fifty thousand dollars, has it been transferred?"

"Last night."

"Which bank does Joe use?"

"The money didn't go to him. It went into his mother's account."

"His mother's?"

"Yeah. She's a strange one, I'm telling you."

Schroder has met her and he agrees. You can't get much stranger. So Joe's mother has the money. That means Joe will go to her to get it. Hutton said before the police were at her house and there was no sign of her. Joe might have contacted her already. She might be at the bank.

"What bank does she use? Which branch?" he asks, and the front door of the ambulance opens and closes and there's a transference of weight and then the engine starts.

"She's already drawn it out," Wellington says. "She said on the phone that the money was a wedding present, and she was going to go in first thing this morning and draw it out in cash."

"She just got married?" Schroder asks, and the ambulance is moving now. Sally's house disappears, the cop cars appear, then some media vans and onlookers and then they break through. Hutton's car appears. It's parked where they left it with the doors still open. It must be Miracle Monday because it hasn't been stolen.

"Getting married," he says. "In fact it's happening today."

"Today?"

"Yeah. Early this afternoon."

"You got a location?"

"Ha," he says, and gives a small laugh. "Actually I do. She rang me back and left a message on my phone. She invited me along. Hang on a second and let me get it for you."

Schroder hangs on and he looks out the back window as Hutton's car get smaller, and then he thinks that Miracle Monday has come to an end for that car not being stolen, and he tells the ambulance driver to pull over.

CHAPTER SEVENTY-NINE

I'm not one for churches. They have their purpose, I guess, but their purpose could be to burn and keep the homeless warm and I'd be equally as fine with that reason as I would be for the real use they have. My parents were married in a church before I was born. My dad's funeral was in a church and then he was taken away and cremated. That was the only day I've ever been in one.

Rain clouds are looming on the horizon out toward the sea, but I can't tell which direction they're moving. We get out of the car and the temperature has dropped a few degrees and the wind has picked up a little and I don't like the look of where things are heading. Christchurch has a way of starting out sunny and ending very differently. The parking lot out front has five cars, ours becoming the sixth.

The church is made up of stone blocks and looks like it's about a hundred years old, and looks like it's going to be cold inside. The cemetery behind it rolls into the distance, fresh gravestones and old gravestones mixing up the view.

Melissa has the gun in her pocket. She's taken the silencer off so it fits. We climb the stairs up to the church doors and push the right one open. At first sight it's easy to think the church is empty, but it's not, it's just a very small crowd confined to the first two pews. My mom is standing at the front with Walt. Walt is wearing a brown suit with a wide brown tie that looks like something some insurance salesman would have been buried in forty years ago. My mom is wearing a flowing white dress that is made from satin or silk and hugs her body in all the places Walt has been hugging her body lately, but in this case these places only make her look fat. They are facing each other. Standing behind them is a priest, and he's the only one to notice me and Melissa walking into the room. He doesn't pause, but carries on with the ceremony and the audience of—I count them—eight people.

We sit down in the back. We have to, because if we go too close and my mom or Walt sees us, they'll talk to me, then the priest will figure out who we are, and then Melissa will have to shoot him to stop him from calling the police, and though we haven't talked about it I get the idea that Melissa is on the same wavelength when it comes to shooting priests—it just seems like an unlucky thing to do. Though, a year ago the priest who used to run this church had his skull beaten in with a hammer. That's kind of an unlucky thing to do too—more so for him.

The priest carries on, and even though it hasn't felt like a risk coming here, suddenly it does. Being stationary seems dangerous. Being on the move felt safe. I'm guessing Melissa feels that too because she keeps jiggling her legs.

"How long is this going to take?" she whispers to me, and we're too far away for anybody to hear us.

"I don't know," I tell her. "I've never been to a wedding."

"I don't like this," she says. "I think coming here was the wrong thing to do."

"Let's give it five more minutes," I say.

"Three," she says, and I don't renegotiate.

My mother looks happy. Walt looks happy. I feel tense. The priest asks if anybody here has a reason why these two shouldn't get married. I have a bunch of reasons. My mom and Walt look out into the church, but their eyes only go as far as the front two rows. Nobody says anything. Then the priest asks my mother a bunch of questions about taking Walt as her husband. The three minutes go by. We agree to stay three more. Then Walt gets the same kind of questions.

Then they kiss.

My stomach turns over and this morning's storm is coming back. The priest and Walt shake hands. Then everybody gets up and people are hugging, and then my mother and Walt move over to a table and sign something. One of the crowd steps forward and starts snapping off photographs. Then the happy couple walk down the aisle toward the church doors, and they walk right past us without even noticing. The priest opens the doors for them, the people that came along for the wedding follow them out, and suddenly we're alone with the priest.

I get up. Melissa gets up too.

"You're her son, aren't you," the priest says.

"No," I tell him.

"I don't know what you're thinking," he says, "but there's no sanctuary in a church. The police will arrest you in here just as they will arrest you anywhere."

"I'm not here for sanctuary."

"Then why are you here?"

I don't answer him. I walk past him and Melissa points the gun at him and he doesn't say anything, and then she smiles at him and hits him on the head about the same place she hit The Sally on her head. He goes down about the same way, and makes the same kind of pile on the floor, only his pile doesn't take up as much room as Sally's pile.

Then my mom comes back into the church before we can go out after her. The door closes behind her. She sees the priest on the floor first, and she says "Oh my," before she sees Melissa and then me. "Joe," she says, and she steps over the priest and embraces me. "I'm so glad you came! But you're late," she says, and she pulls back from me and gives me a slap on the face, nothing too hard, but enough to show her disappointment. "And who is this?" she asks.

"This is my girlfriend."

"No, no," she says, "this isn't your girlfriend. I've met your girlfriend. What's going on here, Joe?"

"Joe's here to get the money given to him last night," Melissa says, and her voice is cold, her voice has a *Don't fuck with me* quality that my mom doesn't seem to hear.

My mom gives a small laugh, and a small nod. "That was so wonderful," she says, "and I can't believe you did that for us."

"Did what?" I ask, but I'm afraid I already know.

"The money," she says. "It's a wonderful wedding present. I never, ever thought I'd fly first class anywhere. I could never have afforded it. And I never thought I'd go to Paris! Paris!" she says, then shakes her head. "All because of you. It's going to be a wonderful trip," she says, but I don't see how it can be, not with her in a body bag and Walt in a body bag too, because that's how they're going to be making their next trip.

"You spent it all?" I ask.

"No, no, of course not," she says. "Don't be so stupid. What's wrong with him?" she asks, looking down at the priest.

"He's tired," Melissa says.

"He looks it," Mom says. "No, no, we still have a few thousand dollars left for spending money."

"So you spent most of it," I say.

"Most of it, yes. It was so generous of you. Will you come to the airport to see us off? Or do you have to go back to jail now?"

"So you spent most of it," I say, and I realize I've just said it, but then I say it again. "So you spent most of it."

"What's wrong with you, Joe? You're like a broken record. I already told you we have some left."

"We need to go," Melissa says.

"Who are you again?" my mom asks. "Have we met?"

"Come on, Joe," Melissa says, and she tugs at my sleeve. "We should never have come here."

We step around the unconscious priest and my mom stares at us with an angry look on her face, as if spending all of my money has really annoyed her. "Good-bye, Mom," I say, knowing this will be the last time I will ever see her. I should feel relieved by that, but strangely I don't. No matter what, I'm going to miss her.

We step outside. Walt is out there talking to a couple the same age as him, and then he spots me and starts to come in my direction, but whatever he has to say I don't really want to hear. We're halfway down the stairs when Detective Inspector Schroder pulls into the parking lot.

CHAPTER EIGHTY

Driving is a bitch, but thankfully the car is an automatic, which makes it possible. Hutton isn't taking his calls. When Schroder calls him, it rings a few times and then switches over to voicemail. He's not sure whether the detective is busy, or whether he's deliberately dodging him. He has a pretty good idea which it is.

He knows Hutton's number from memory, but not any of the others, and because the screen on his cell phone is busted he can't look anybody else up. He could call the police emergency number and ask to be put through to Stevens, but he knows Stevens would yell at him and hang up without hearing what he has to say. He drives to the church, not expecting to find Joe there, but ready to call the emergency number if he does. If it leads nowhere, then he'll drive to the hospital.

He's not expecting to see Joe standing on the steps of the church when he pulls into the parking lot. In fact he has to do a double take, and even then he's not sure because Joe is wearing a hat, but the woman behind him is definitely the same woman from the prison, the same woman who shot Jack, the same woman who blew up Raphael and tried to blow him up too.

So there's no point in messing around. He stops the car and leaves the engine running and reaches into the sling for the gun, then has to put the gun down so he can open the door. He gets it open and the gun back into his hand and he doesn't bother yelling out, he just draws a bead on Joe, but doesn't pull the trigger because some old guy wanders up to Joe and blocks the view.

A second later Melissa steps out from behind Joe to the right of that same old guy and fires a shot at Schroder. Schroder ducks down behind the door onto the ground as bullets come thumping through the car door. Something tugs at his broken arm, and he looks down to see a dime-sized spot of blood that starts to rapidly grow on the front of the sling.

Melissa stops firing. People are running in all sorts of directions.

He peers around the edge of the door and back up at the church just in time to see Joe and Melissa disappear inside. The old man who was trying to talk to Joe is still standing on the stairs. He looks unsure of what to do. Schroder knows the feeling.

He tucks the gun under his arm and reaches for his cell phone. He dials one-one-one. "This is Carl Schroder," he says. "I'm currently under fire from two suspects—Joe Middleton and Melissa X. Send backup," he says, then gives the name of the church and hangs up.

He drops the phone back into his pocket. He still hasn't called his wife. Why the hell did he keep putting that off? If this were an episode of *The Cleaner,* then that'd mean he's about to get shot. That's how TV works—you start talking about a cop who has a family, and two minutes later that guy's starfished on the ground with blood running out of him. He points the gun ahead and makes his way out from behind his car. He has a promise that he has to keep.

CHAPTER EIGHTY-ONE

She knew this was a mistake. Should never have come here. Hell, for that matter she should never have helped Joe escape. She could have gone anywhere, just her and Abigail. Only now she's backed into a church and no doubt the police will be on their way. She has about twelve bullets left and nothing else.

"Let's go back out the front," she says.

"He'll shoot us," Joe says.

"No. He'll just *try* to shoot us."

"What's going on?" Joe's mother asks, and Melissa thinks she could spare a bullet on her. If it came down to it, she could probably spare two or three—one into the head, then two more into the head just for the hell of it.

"He'll do more than try," Joe says.

"Others will be on the way. We have to do this fast. We have to go back out there and we have to shoot him and then we have to leave. We can drive a few blocks and ditch the car and steal another, Or take one of the others that's already here. Damn it, we could have been home by now. This was a waste of time because your stupid fucking mother spent—"

"How dare you," Joe's mother says, and Melissa points the gun at her.

"Don't," Joe says.

"Why?" Melissa asks.

He opens his mouth to answer and comes up with nothing. "We can use her as a shield," he says.

Melissa pulls him toward her and kisses him hard but briefly on the lips, then pushes him away. "You're going to make a great father," she says.

She grabs Joe's mother, who resists for a few seconds, and then Joe grabs her too. They push her ahead of them toward the church doors. Melissa holds a gun to the woman's head and Joe opens the door and then they step back outside.

Schroder has made his way to the bottom of the steps. He's wearing a sling because his arm is broken or wounded or something. He points the gun up at them, but he has no clear shot. It's Joe's mom, then Melissa, then Joe—all in a straight line.

"Let her go," Schroder says.

"Put your gun down or—" she says, and that's when Joe's mom stumbles, trips, then suddenly she's rolling down the stairs toward Schroder. Joe moves to the side to try and reach her, but is too late.

For a moment both of them are exposed to Schroder.

And then two things happen at the same time. Walt steps in between them to try and reach Joe's mom. And Schroder and Melissa open fire.

CHAPTER EIGHTY-TWO

"What's—" is all Walt can manage because a moment later Melissa's bullet is rattling around in his wrong-on-so-many-levels skull. He stays standing as if being shot in the head is a momentary distraction, an annoyance, and then he's waltzing down the steps taking the same path my mom took.

The shot Schroder took has gone high and wide, but he points his gun at me to take his second shot. Before he can, I pull Melissa in front of me, which ruins the shot she's about to take, and ruins Schroder's shot too. Instead of him shooting me, he shoots her. I can feel the impact of it.

I back into the church as Schroder takes his third shot. Another impact into Melissa and I get back through the church doors, dragging her with me. The door closes behind me. I lay Melissa on the floor next to the priest.

"You fucker," she says.

"I'm sorry," I say, and I truly am. "It just . . . just happened that way."

There are twin pools of blood forming on her chest. She raises her gun toward me and I reach out and take it out of her hands before she can fire it. "I can make it quick," I tell her.

She shakes her head. Then she laughs. "I can't believe you did this to me."

"I didn't mean to," I tell her again, and it's true.

"Abigail," she says.

"I'll look after her," I tell her. "I'll do everything right by her," I tell her. "Where is she?"

"She's safe," she says.

"Don't let her grow up without either of her parents," I tell her, and I tell her this because I really need to know where Abigail is being hidden. I really need the safe place.

"Bullshit. You just want somewhere to hide out."

"I promise you that's not the case," I tell her.

She laughs again. "I'll tell you," she says, "because I have no choice," she says, and she hands me a key.

I don't know what she means by that, but she gives me the address.

"Leave me the gun," she says.

"No."

"I'll take care of Schroder," she says. "Go out the back. Go through the cemetery. Make your way out onto a different street and steal a car, but do it now. Go now!"

I'm about to lean down and kiss her when she coughs up a small amount of blood.

"I love you," I tell her.

"You have a funny way of showing it."

I leave her the gun. I don't know why I trust her, but I do. I run to the back of the church and turn to face her, but she's not looking at me, instead she's looking at the doors, pointing the gun toward them, and she's talking to somebody, but I don't know who. She laughs, and the only words I can make out are *Smelly Melly*. I have never in my life felt this guilty about a person. Or even guilt.

I go through a doorway into a corridor. I reach a back entrance and then I hear two gunshots that sound different from each other and then nothing. I go out the door and there's a car parked there. It probably belongs to the priest. I climb into it. I don't have the keys, but not having keys has never been a problem for me. I get it started and I drive around to the front of the church and there are no police cars, just people from mom's wedding hiding behind other cars. I get out onto the street.

I keep driving.

After a few blocks I can hear sirens approaching.

I turn off so we don't share the same road.

For the first few minutes my heart is racing so hard it feels like it's going to pop right out of my chest. Then it starts to calm. Ten minutes into it I'm feeling pretty good. Good enough to look back over the last few hours and think that it all went really well.

I already miss Melissa.

It takes me another twenty minutes to get to the address she gave me. It's a secluded house where the closest neighbors aren't in looking distance. It's a long shingle driveway and there's a lot of land here. It's not a modern place, but it's not old either, and it looks comfortable. This place is going to be my home for the next few months until I can figure out where to go next.

I park around the back. I unlock the back door. I can hear a baby crying. My baby. My heart starts to speed up again. I make my way toward the sound. It's a bedroom. I open the door. Inside is a woman. She looks to be in her twenties. Her hair is a mess. She's wearing no makeup. She's wearing clothes that look like they haven't been washed in weeks. And there's a metal chain going from her ankle to the metal pipe of a radiator. She's trying to calm the baby, trying to feed it. This is what Melissa said when she said she had no choice but to tell me where the baby was. The woman looks up at me.

"Oh my God, oh thank God," she says, and she drops the bottle of formula that the baby is refusing. The baby, Abigail, has a blank look on her face and she's trying to clutch at something that isn't there. She looks over at me and doesn't smile or look away and I don't know whether or not she can see me. She's cute. As far as babies go. Very cute.

"What's happening here?" I ask. "Who are you?"

"This crazy woman kidnapped us," she says.

"Us? You and the baby?"

"No, me and my sister," she says. "The baby belongs to the crazy lady. She said if anything happens to the baby she's going to kill both of us, so I have to do everything she says. Please, please, you have to help us."

"Is your sister younger or older than you?"

"A little older. Why? Why does it matter?"

"Just so I know what I'm in for."

"What do you mean?" she asks.

"I mean it really just isn't your lucky day," I tell her, and I close the door behind me and tell her about my day, then explain to her how she and her sister are my reward for getting through it.

EPILOGUE

I pull the car into the driveway. Sit back. Try to relax.

I have the car stereo going. Over the last three months since my escape, I've listened to the news a lot. It's always nice to know what's going on in the world. In the beginning, the news was all about me. Some of it was good news—like Walt being killed at the church. Some of it was heartbreaking—like Melissa being killed at the church. I miss her a lot.

I twist the keys in the ignition, grab my briefcase, and climb out of the car. I fumble with the lock to the front door of the house and make my way inside.

I can hear the shower going from down the hall. I make my way into the kitchen and open the fridge and help myself to the first beer I've had in over fifteen months. I carry it with me down to the bedroom and sit on the bed a few feet from the bathroom door, from which steam is steadily creeping under. I pop open the briefcase and sit it on the bed and pull out the newspaper. The front page is about Carl Schroder. Three months ago he was shot in the head, but survived. He was put into a coma. The paper makes a big deal out of it because he shared a hospital room with a guy he used to work with who was also in a coma. They were called the Coma Cops. The media really played it up. The other guy, Tate somebody, woke up two weeks ago. And yesterday Carl Schroder woke up.

Today is the first day I've been out of my house since the escape. I'm already missing my daughter. Right now she's being looked after by my housemate. My housemate's name is Elizabeth, and her sister's name is Kate, but Kate isn't at the house. She never was. Kate exists, but it's obvious Melissa only ever told Elizabeth she was there in order to manipulate her. I use the same tactic, and it works.

Mail comes to the house. Power bills, mostly. They all say they are being taken care of by direct payment to a credit card, but whose, or how Melissa set that up, I don't know. I found a notebook. It was a budget. Melissa prepaid the rent for one year. She prepaid some guy to come mow the lawn every few weeks too.

As well as leaving cupboards full of baby food, baby clothes, and baby supplies, Melissa also left a bag full of cash. I use it for groceries. The same credit card used for the bills also gets used to order groceries online from a nearby supermarket. So once every week or two I shop with a computer and the groceries are left at my door. There is a lot of money here. Almost thirty thousand dollars. It will come in handy when we leave. It's a nice house, but it does feel a little like prison since I never get to go anywhere. Feels like a prison too for Elizabeth, I imagine.

I'm growing my hair long. It looks awful, but I'm getting used to it. I've dyed it too. Blond. It was the color Melissa had chosen for me. There were a few boxes of dye left for me.

Abigail is getting bigger. I don't know her birthday, but I guess I can pick any day really. She smiles at me a lot now. And sometimes she laughs uncontrollably. I've figured out that the best sound in the world is a baby laughing. The worst sound in the world is pretty much any other sound a baby can possibly make. She smiles at Elizabeth too, and the two seem to like each other. Elizabeth is starting to like me too. Maybe there's something there. It does happen. Or maybe she's just wanting me to let her go.

But, like I say, the house feels like a prison, and it's nice to finally be out. I have needs that Elizabeth can't meet. Urges that keep me awake at night just as much as Abigail does. I've been a good boy. I've kept my hands off the babysitter. I like the idea of a more hands-on approach, but I don't like the idea of accidently killing the only person who can get Abigail to go to sleep.

Good things are going to happen.

The shower is switched off. I hear footsteps and a towel being pulled from a rack, then general bathroom noises of drawers being opened and closed. An extractor fan is turned on. I fold the newspaper up and put it back into my briefcase.

I take out the biggest knife I have and rest it on the bed. Then I take out the gun I found at my new house.

Then I take out the sandwich I brought along with me.

Adam the prison guard steps out of the bathroom and into the bedroom.

"Who the fuck are you?" he asks, because he doesn't recognize me. It's the hair—plus I've put on some weight.

I hold up the gun and I hold up the sandwich. "I'm Joe Optimist."

ACKNOWLEDGMENTS

Joe Victim is the result of a process that's taken more than ten years, starting with a vague idea for a sequel way back when I wrote *The Cleaner* in 1999 / 2000. During that process, and before the five or six years of rewriting that would follow it, I used to think – a sequel would be cool.

The sequel didn't progress beyond the idea of *I'd like to write a sequel, and for now I'll call it* The Cleaner *II*, for many years. Back in 2008, two years after *The Cleaner* was published, I wrote the first 20,000 words of The Cleaner II, then no more. Of course it was never far from my mind. I kept people updated on what Joe was up to in the other books – he was in jail. He'd show up, he'd get mentioned – Joe wasn't going to be forgotten. Then the end of 2011 and, after four or five years of emails from fans asking when I would write a sequel, it suddenly felt like it was time. The sequel went from something I'd been thinking about and had attempted and would probably never write, to something I had to do. That summer I spent inside writing, binging on junk food and ignoring my Xbox.

The book took shape. It had a direction. It even had a title. *Joe Victim*.

Like the six books before it, *Joe Victim* has had many helping hands. There would be no UK edition if it weren't for the wonderful team at Hodder & Stoughton, and especially Ruth Tross, who has given my books a home here, as well as Kerry Hood and Cicely Aspinall. Then there's Kevin Chapman at Upstart Press in NZ, a great publisher and a great guy who doesn't realise that gin-and-tonics have at least some tonic in them.

Of course I need to widen the scope a little here and thank my editor at Atria Books in New York, the wonderful Sarah Branham, who always makes me think in different directions. She helps shape the novels and makes me be a better writer, and makes me want to be a better writer – Sarah and the rest of the Simon & Schuster team are wonderful.

And since I'm widening the scope, let's go back in time too – and thank Harriet Allan who, back in 2005, gave Joe and *The Cleaner* life by publishing me in New Zealand, and Nerrilee Weir who went about getting me published in lots of other countries – Harriet and Nerrilee (and Joe too, you could say) changed my life.

Let me sign off once again by thanking you, the reader. Thanks again for the support, the emails, and the Facebook messages. Thanks for coming along to book signings and festivals to say hi. You're who I write for, you're the reason I like to make bad things happen . . . and – actually, you're the reason Joe has come back with another story.

Till next time!

Paul Cleave
August 2017
Christchurch, New Zealand.

Discover the brand new novel from Paul Cleave

TRUST NO ONE

His novels tell of brutal murders and bad people.

Was it just his imagination?

Jerry Grey is better known as crime writer Henry Cutter – whose twelve books kept readers gripped for over a decade. Now he's been diagnosed with early onset Alzheimer's, and his writing life has ended.

But the stories haven't. As his control loosens, Jerry confesses his worst secret: the books are real. He remembers committing the crimes.

His friends, family and carers say it's all his head. He's just confused.

If that's true, then why are so many bad things happening? Why are people dying?

Out now in paperback and ebook

Discover more edge-of-your-seat thrillers from Paul Cleave

The Cleaner

Joe is a janitor for the police department, and then there's his "night work". He isn't bothered by the daily news reports of the Christchurch Carver, who, they say, has murdered seven women. Joe knows, though, that the Carver killed only six. He knows that for a fact . . .

The Killing Hour

Imagine waking up covered in blood – but it's not your blood, and you can't remember a thing about last night. Welcome to Charlie's world.

Blood Men

Edward Hunter has it all – a beautiful wife and daughter, a great job, a bright future . . . and a very dark past.

Collecting Cooper

A former mental patient is holding people prisoner as part of his growing collection of serial killer souvenirs. Now he has acquired the ultimate collector's item – an actual killer.

The Laughterhouse

Theodore Tate never forgot his first crime scene – ten-year-old Jessica found dead in "the Laughterhouse", an old abandoned slaughterhouse with the S painted over. The killer was found and arrested. Justice was served. Or was it?

Joe Victim

Joe Middleton's story is this: He doesn't remember killing anyone, so there's no way a jury can convict him.

But others know Joe as the infamous Christchurch Carver and they want him dead.

Five Minutes Alone

The body of a convicted rapist is found, but no one knows if it's murder or suicide. Then two more rapists go missing . . .